Summer of Love

Also by Katie Fforde

Living Dangerously
The Rose Revived
Wild Designs
Stately Pursuits
Life Skills
Thyme Out
Artistic Licence
Highland Fling
Paradise Fields
Restoring Grace
Flora's Lot
Practically Perfect
Going Dutch
Wedding Season
Love Letters
A Perfect Proposal

KATIE FFORDE

Summer of Love

CENTURY · LONDON

Published by Century in 2011

2 4 6 8 10 9 7 5 3 1

Copyright © Katie Fforde Ltd 2011

Katie Fforde has asserted her right under the Copyright, Designs
and Patents Act 1988 to be identified as the author of this work

First published in Great Britain in 2011 by
Century
Random House, 20 Vauxhall Bridge Road
London SW1V 2SA

www.rbooks.co.uk

Addresses for companies within The Random House Group Limited can be
found at: www.randomhouse.co.uk/offices.htm

The Random House Group Limited Reg. No. 954009

A CIP catalogue record for this book is available from the British Library

ISBN 9781846056505

The Random House Group Limited supports The Forest Stewardship
Council (FSC), the leading international forest certification organisation.
All our titles that are printed on Greenpeace approved FSC certified paper
carry the FSC logo. Our paper procurement policy can be found at
www.rbooks.co.uk/environment

Mixed Sources
Product group from well-managed
forests and other controlled sources
www.fsc.org Cert no. TT-COC-2139
© 1996 Forest Stewardship Council
FSC

Typeset by Palimpsest Book Production Limited, Falkirk, Stirlingshire

Printed and bound in Great Britain by
Clays Ltd, St Ives plc

My darling husband, with love.

Acknowledgements

Research is always important to me but when I told my family and friends that I was going on a bushcraft course with Ray Mears's company they really thought I'd gone too far this time. It was one of the best weekends of my life. Thank you to everyone concerned – the brilliant staff who didn't laugh when I couldn't find my tent in the middle of the night, the wonderful people on the course with me who protected me from every little discomfort and for the organisation by all concerned. Can't recommend it highly enough.

To mysinglefriend.com who were so helpful and taught me all about internet dating in a safe way. Not that I tried it myself, of course!

To my wonderful agents at A. M. Heath who all do so much for me. In particular Bill Hamilton and Sarah Molloy.

Also my amazing publishers, Cornerstone, Random House. Editors, Kate Elton and Georgina Hawtrey-Woore who are endlessly tolerant and patient as well as being truly inspiring.

Charlotte Bush and Amelia Harvell who are not only brilliant at their jobs but tireless as well.

To the amazing sales and marketing team who just do better and better each year. They include Clare Round, Sarah Page, Rob Waddington and Jen Wilson.

As always to Richenda Todd who is the best copy editor ever, and so say all those who are lucky enough to have her saving their blushes.

Honestly, writing the book is the easy part!

Chapter One

❧

'Er, hello!'

Sian put down her fork and looked over the garden wall. A woman was smiling at her, holding a bottle of wine in one hand and a jam jar full of flowers in the other.

'Hello!' said Sian.

'I hope you don't think I'm appallingly nosy but I noticed the furniture van drive away yesterday and thought I'd pop round and welcome you to the village. I'm Fiona Matcham. I live in the house up the end.' She swung the wine bottle vaguely in the direction of the lane.

'Oh,' said Sian. 'Would you like to come in?' She suspected that her visitor meant the Big House, a beautiful building that her mother had raved about when she'd come down to help Sian move in.

'I don't want to stop you working, but I could come and watch you.'

Sian laughed and wiped her hands on her shorts. She'd managed to get all the strawberry plants in that her mother had given her. 'No, no, I'm quite happy to stop. I'm Sian Bishop.'

'Hello again, Sian.' Fiona waved the jam jar at her. 'Here, take these.' Fiona Matcham handed Sian the bottle and the flowers over the wall and then walked up to the gate and let herself in. 'Oh! You've got a boy! How lovely! I love boys!'

Rory, who was digging with his little spade in the soil

his mother had loosened for him first, looked up and stared quizzically at Fiona from under his blond fringe.

'You're doing good work there, aren't you? Are you going to grow something?' Fiona Matcham addressed Rory while producing a jar of jam from the pocket of her loose linen jacket.

'Yes,' said Rory seriously.

'We're hoping to grow our own vegetables now we're in the country,' said Sian. 'Rory's got that patch, and I'm going to have a bigger patch in the back garden. We've planted strawberries. Salad we'll do later. Rory, would you like to stop for a drink now? Or carry on while I make tea?'

'Carry on while you make tea,' said Rory, turning back to his digging and ignoring them both.

Sian knew her son felt shy and would probably join them when he realised the tin of chocolate biscuits his grand-mother had left had been produced. 'You would like a cup of tea?' Sian asked her guest. 'I've kind of assumed . . .'

'Oh yes, tea would be lovely. If you don't mind.'

Sian had already decided that this woman, who seemed to be in her mid-fifties, wasn't the sort who would be critical of a house not in perfect order, or why had she brought the wine? The flowers, too, were artistic and original – and no doubt from her own garden, not a conventional bouquet. Sian was inclined to like her already.

Sian led the way into the cottage. It seemed dark after the bright June sunshine outside and smelt of damp. But, as her mother had pointed out, it was very cheap to rent, had a big garden and the landlady, who lived in France, had expressed herself happy for Sian to make necessary improvements provided they weren't extravagant. She found space for the flowers on the table and instantly everything looked better.

'Excuse the mess,' said Sian, removing a half-unpacked

box of crockery off a chair. 'I couldn't bear to be inside when the weather is so lovely. Do sit down. And thank you for the flowers. They make the place look so much more homely, somehow.'

Her guest popped the jar of jam on the side with a 'For you', pulled out an unoccupied chair and sat at the table. 'Well, as this might be our entire summer it would be a shame to waste the sunshine unpacking.' She paused. 'I brought the flowers in a jar so you wouldn't need to hunt round for something to put them in. Nothing is more irritating when people turn up for dinner with flowers that mean you have to abandon your guests, the dinner and the drinks to find a vase. I no longer have a husband,' she added. 'Single-handed entertaining.'

'I'm a single parent, so ditto.' It wasn't really a test but Sian had discovered, in the four years since she'd had Rory, that people who were unlikely to become friends would flinch a bit when she said this.

'I've been that, too. The boys' father died when they were quite young. It's tough.'

Sian smiled at Fiona across the half-light of the gloomy hallway-cum-dining room. She had a feeling she'd made a new friend already.

'I'll put the kettle on. What kind of tea would you like?'

'I can't believe you're so organised as to have a choice already,' Fiona replied, perched on the chair as if ready to leap up and help at a moment's notice.

Sian smiled. 'My mother stayed with me for a few days. I drink builder's, she drinks Earl Grey. Those are the choices unless you want herbal tea.'

'Builder's is fine.'

'I've got some biscuits. My mother brought a huge tin of them. I'll be back in a moment,' Sian said as she disappeared off to the kitchen.

3

'I do think Luella ought to take that wall down and make this room into a big kitchen diner!' called Fiona. 'Why don't you suggest it?'

'Do you mean Mrs Halpern? She's been very co-operative and said as long as I don't go mad I can make changes. But I think she might consider taking down a supporting wall as going mad,' Sian called back.

She was no longer alone in the galley kitchen. Her guest, apparently not one to sit around and be waited on, had joined her.

'Look at the damp on the floor!' exclaimed Fiona. 'It's appalling. Mind you, it might only be the gutter that needs clearing. Would you like me to send someone round to look at it?'

'If it's only the gutter I can probably manage it myself,' said Sian. 'If I can't, I'd be grateful for the name of someone reliable.' Sian liked to be as self-sufficient as possible but she knew there would be things she couldn't deal with. Since she'd moved her dad was no longer round the corner to do those things for her.

'Well, just say. I've lived here so long – since Noah and Mrs Noah were courting – I know more or less everyone. Oh, hello, Rory,' she said as he appeared in the doorway.

'Can you take the biscuits?' Sian handed her son the tin. 'Why don't you take them out into the back garden?' She turned to Fiona. 'There's a table and chairs there. I'll make the tea.'

'Good idea. Rory and I can go and get settled and have a chat. My name is Fiona,' she said to the boy.

'Wouldn't you rather be Mrs Matcham?' asked Sian.

'Oh no,' she said firmly. 'Fiona is much better.' She smiled, possibly to offset the firmness.

'Would you mind taking the milk out?' asked Sian.

'Oh, just put it in the mugs in here, why don't you?

Then when you and Rory come over to visit me, I can be my usual slutty self.'

Sian smiled and put tea bags in mugs. She could just imagine her mother's delighted reaction when she told her about Fiona. She would see her as a wise older friend and a potential babysitter, not to mention someone who lived in a lovely house and so might perhaps be a customer for her daughter as well. Richard would be pleased too. Although it was because of him that she had moved to this particular village, and he had taken her and Rory under his wing, he'd be glad that the neighbours were being friendly.

Fiona Matcham and Rory were up the far end of the garden when Sian brought out the mugs of tea. Sian sat down on one of the chairs and sipped hers, watching them together. She was pleased that Rory had forgotten to be shy and was making friends. She had been a bit worried about taking him away from everything he knew in a busy city out into the country, although, as Richard had pointed out, it was in a village, not a remote location miles from anywhere. There was a school, a pub, a church and two shops, one of which was also a post office. 'Which makes it a heaving metropolis,' Sian's father had said dryly. He was less sanguine than his wife about his daughter moving away with his only grandchild, although both her parents accepted she was moving for very good reasons. 'Tea's up!' she called. 'And biscuits!'

Rory turned and ran back down what would be a lawn one day – if Sian was able to stay that long of course, she thought wistfully, and her landlady didn't object – followed by Fiona.

'I don't suppose you could spare me some of that wonderful cow parsley?' Fiona said as she reached the table. 'I've got to do church flowers tomorrow and a huge display of just that could look stunning!'

'Oh yes, of course. Take anything you want.'

'Thank you. You could come and help me do them if you want. My opposite number is away so I'll be on my own. Rory can help.' She paused. 'Although not if you're busy, or morally opposed to church flowers.'

Sian laughed. 'No, I'd like to help. I don't actually go to church . . .'

'That's all right, just help me do the flowers.' Fiona picked up her mug and sipped. 'Your reward will be an introduction to the Yummy Mummies. There are at least three I know moderately well. Will Rory be going to the school later?'

Sian nodded. 'In September. He actually started last year in London but it was a disaster. Having a summer birthday he was only just four and it was such a big school. His teacher wasn't very nice either.'

'How awful! I can't imagine anything worse. Poor Rory. Poor you.'

Sian smiled. 'I'm glad you don't think I'm a dreadfully over-protective mother. One of the reasons I wanted us to move away from London was the schools. I home-educated him when I finally gave up trying to get him to go to school, but we're going to start again here.'

'Our local school is brilliant. I was a governor for years. I'm sure he'll be fine there.'

'I am too. And when you get to the secondary stage, London schools are even more frightening.'

Fiona nodded. 'And you probably didn't want to send him away to school. Don't. I did – it was expected – and it broke my heart, nearly.' She frowned. 'Although maybe I wouldn't have minded so much if my first husband hadn't just died.' She drank some more of her tea. 'So what were the other reasons for moving?'

Sian made a gesture. Usually she was quite a private

person but something about Fiona made her feel comfortable about elaborating. 'There are lots. The country life, wanting to grow vegetables, be more self-sufficient. A friend suggested we came down here and found me this house. His sister – whom Rory knows well and loves – is starting up a nursery and play scheme here which means I can work through the summer holidays, which I really need to be able to do.' She paused. 'And I couldn't go on more or less living right next door to my parents for ever, even though they did do quite a lot of childcare.'

'No?' Fiona looked thoughtful. 'One of my sons is going to be living with me quite soon.'

'Oh no, it'll be fine!' Sian hurried to reassure her, although she had no idea what sort of relationship Fiona had with her son. 'What I meant was, if London was the wrong place to be living in every other way, I couldn't go on doing it just because my parents were so close. It wasn't fair on them in a way, me expecting them to drop everything if I had a lot of work. They have their own lives.'

'And how did they take the news you wanted to move away?'

'Obviously they were a bit unhappy but once Richard – he's the friend – found me this place they were fine.' Sian counted her new home's advantages off on her fingers. 'It's in a village so I won't be too isolated. There's a lovely school within easy walking distance. It's only just under an hour to London by train and the station's not too far away. It has a huge garden so I can grow vegetables and the rent is extremely reasonable.'

'Because the kitchen is cramped and damp,' said Fiona.

Sian laughed too. 'I can put up with that, or even change it.'

Fiona laughed too. 'Luella probably isn't the most attentive landlady, but she's very nice.'

7

'She sounded nice on the phone and while we were arranging things.'

'She doesn't really need the money for renting this place and she'll probably sell it eventually, but she thought she'd like to keep a foothold in England while she's in France.'

'I've got a three-month lease that will probably be extended,' said Sian, suddenly chilled by the thought that she might have to leave her cottage if it was going to be sold. It might be damp but it was perfect for her and Rory.

'And I'm sure you can stay much longer than that if you want to,' said Fiona, suddenly realising she'd worried Sian. 'Last time we emailed she said she had no intention of coming back to the land where you drink tea instead of wine. I missed her when she went to France. She was my best friend locally.' She took a chocolate finger. 'I love chocolate fingers. There's something about them, isn't there? Nothing else tastes quite the same.'

Sian agreed. 'Would you like another one? Otherwise I think I should take the tin inside to stop them all melting. Rory? One more?'

Rory helped himself to another biscuit and then leant against Sian's chair, playing distractedly with a toy truck he'd retrieved from under the table, whilst his mother went off with the tin.

'So tell me your plans?' said Fiona once Sian had returned with a damp flannel for Rory's face and everyone's fingers. 'Or haven't you got any yet?'

'Oh no, I have plans. For one thing I want to get going on the garden. I've never grown vegetables before but I'm longing to try. It'll be quick-growing plants to start with, spuds and things later. Then I need somewhere to carry out my business in. I'm hoping to rent something.' She didn't mention the possibility of settling down with

8

Richard. She was by no means sure she would, although sometimes the idea seemed tempting. He was a dear friend and definitely a 'catch', as her father would have said.

'What sort of business? I mean, do you need an aircraft hanger or a garret?'

'Something in between, but more hanger than garret. I paint furniture, customise it.'

'Oh?'

'If you're really interested I'll show you some pictures.'

'Oh do! I'd be thrilled. Rory, would you like to take me up the other end of the garden again while your mother gets the pictures? There seems to be a little house.'

'All right,' said Rory after a moment's thought. He clambered to his feet and they set off.

Sian found her albums easily and turned the pages on her own while she waited for Fiona and Rory to come back – they were engrossed in what looked like the remains of a summer house at the bottom of the garden. Sian hadn't had time to investigate it yet herself. She was pleased to have met someone so soon – she'd been a bit worried about her and Rory becoming too dependent on each other and Richard if they had no one else to talk to. She might meet some mums at the play scheme Rory was booked into, but she might not. And Fiona seemed so good with Rory, friendly without being patronising. She sighed. Richard was a bit of a worry to her. She liked him very much but she wasn't in love with him, not in the way he so obviously was with her, and while he knew this and accepted it, he clearly hoped she would come to love him as more than just a friend. Sian hoped that too, in a way. He was perfect in so many respects. But she couldn't marry a man she didn't love, not even for the financial security she longed for.

Rory dashed back when he saw his mother, Fiona

following more sedately behind. 'That's my one!' he said, pointing to a picture of a chest of drawers covered with dragons, castles and seascapes.

Fiona inspected it. 'It's wonderful! What beautiful painting! How did you get the idea?'

'Well, Rory was obsessed with dragons at the time – still is, to some extent. My mother had bought this chest of drawers for half nothing at an auction – she's addicted to auctions – and as it needed something doing to it I decided to do more than just sand it down and put on a coat of white gloss.' She chuckled. 'I went to art college. I wanted to earn my living doing something that was actually connected to my degree but I could do from home. This is perfect – or it will be, when the business has built up a bit.'

Fiona turned the pages. 'But not all these are yours – your furniture, I mean?'

'Oh no. But when my friends saw the chest of drawers they started getting me to paint things for them. Now I have a website and stuff, but I need somewhere where I can paint bigger items. I've done one or two adult pieces, too.'

'So what sort of premises do you need?'

'Do you think you might know of somewhere? I need a barn or something. Some of the paint is a bit toxic so I need plenty of air around if possible.'

'I might indeed know of somewhere – my own barn in fact, just by my house – but it's absolutely full of stuff.'

'Well, if you did think you wanted to rent it out, I could help you clear it first.'

'That would be worth it, even without the rent. I've been meaning to do it for years and have never been able to face it.'

'I think that sort of thing is fun.'

'I suppose I'd think it was fun if I didn't have to make decisions about everything, but if you can help me with that, well, I'd be thrilled.'

Fiona seemed a little tentative. Sian didn't want her to change her mind about the barn and so nodded enthusiastically. 'I'd love it. Apart from it being fun I might be able to buy some things from you that I could paint. It seems a waste to buy new when there's so much perfectly good furniture around that just happens to be hideous – before I get my hands on it, of course!'

'Personally I don't think if furniture is hideous it can be described as "perfectly good",' Fiona said dryly, handing back the album to Sian.

Sian laughed. 'That's just the sort of thing my mother would say.'

'I hope you mean that in a good way!'

'Oh yes, definitely. My mother and I have a lot of fun together.'

'Well, that's a relief.' Fiona put her hand on Sian's briefly and got up. 'I should go. Now, were you serious about being willing to help with the flowers?'

'Oh yes.'

'Then I'll pop by at about two tomorrow and we can pick the cow parsley and then arrange it. Will that fit in with nap times and things?'

'I don't have a nap now,' said Rory. 'I'm too old.'

'I have naps all the time and I'm much older than you,' declared Fiona. 'But we won't argue about it. Until tomorrow then?'

When Sian had seen her guest out and renewed her thanks for the house-warming presents, she rang her mother. She would be thrilled that Sian had a new friend already. Sian was thrilled herself.

*

'It's Fona,' said Rory the following afternoon, looking through one of the small front windows at the person on the front doorstep.

'Oh good.' Sian went and opened the door. 'Hello! Come on through to the garden, we'll get picking.'

Fiona was carrying a bucket in which there were a pair of secateurs and what looked like an old curtain. 'Good afternoon. Hello, Rory! Are you going to help us put flowers in the church? There are toys there if you get bored.'

The two women cut swathes of cow parsley, filling Fiona's bucket and another one they found in a shed, and then set off for the church.

'Can I carry the bucket?' asked Rory, anxious to be involved. He'd been a little put out that he hadn't been able to help with collecting the cow parsley but Fiona had said the secateurs were too dangerous and only to be used by adults and his mother hadn't felt his pulling at the plants was achieving the desired effect. He'd had to watch them both and had got bored.

Sian thought about it. The bucket was heavy but she didn't want to start a row in front of Fiona. Rory was an easy child on the whole but he could get terribly offended if anyone suggested he was too young or too small for a particular task, and he'd already sulked a bit when they wouldn't allow him to help pick the flowers. 'OK,' she said casually, hoping he'd abandon the idea quite quickly.

'Actually, I could do with a hand with mine,' said Fiona. 'Your mum could carry that one but I'm not sure I can manage this one on my own. If you'd be a kind chap and carry it with me, I'd be very grateful.'

Flattered by this request for help, Rory took hold of the handle.

'It's quite hard to carry with all this cow parsley, isn't it?' went on Fiona.

'It's not heavy,' said Rory.

'Not for you, perhaps!' said Fiona. 'But you're a strong boy.'

Sian let herself lag behind her son and her new friend. It was nice that they got on so well. Fiona was very good with him. She thought Rory might miss her parents, being used to the company of adults. She locked the house and put the key in the pocket of her jeans. Fiona and Rory began to sing as the three of them lumbered up the lane towards the churchyard.

The church was cool and dark and Rory was a bit over-awed until Fiona put on some lights, chatting away as if she was somewhere familiar and friendly. It took Sian a few moments to feel it was OK to talk above a whisper but by the time Rory had been shown the toys, which included a train set, she was soon helping Fiona pull out the faded flowers from the stand of oasis and fielding the dead leaves that missed the curtain Fiona had spread out to catch them.

A little later she was taking the lower leaves off the cow parsley and handing the sprays to Fiona as if she'd always done it. There was something satisfying about flower-arranging, especially in the calm interior of an ancient building. 'It only has to look good from the back of the church. That's where most people sit,' said Fiona, stepping away and looking at the display with a critical eye.

'It looks good from here!'

'Thank you! I do hope you'll come back to tea after-wards,' said Fiona. 'I've made a cake and Jody and Annabelle are coming. Annabelle's about Rory's age and you'll like Jody.'

'That's so kind. We'd love to meet them and we love cake. Especially homemade.'

'Me too. I've trained myself to believe that shop cake

isn't worth getting fat for, but I'm not sure I believe it.'

'You really needn't have made a cake just for us. We're not proud about shop cake!'

Fiona laughed. 'Actually, I've got a bit of a favour to ask you. I thought I'd soften you up first.'

Sian laughed too, hoping she wasn't about to let herself in for something she wouldn't be happy about. 'Well, anything you think we can do.'

'You don't really have to do much but it's not something I can ask Jody, for example.' Fiona bit her lip, frowning a little as she adjusted her arrangement. 'It is a bit mad and I don't want to ask anyone I know well.' Fiona stepped back from the pyramid of frothy white and green, which to Sian looked like a patch of starlight. 'Do you think that looks all right? People always say my arrangements are "unusual" and I'm never sure whether to take that as a compliment or not. No one's ever done anything like that as far as I know but I always remember my mother telling me about Constance Spry having a big jug of cow parsley in the window of her shop, in London, just after the war. I've always wanted to do it.'

'I think it looks stunning. Really simple and pure. And if it is unusual, it's lovely.'

'As long as it looks OK from the back of the church,' repeated Fiona, walking in that direction.

Once Fiona was happy with the arrangement and they'd cleared up and put the train set away, they headed back to Fiona's house. As they approached, Sian said, 'I don't suppose you could tell me your mad thing now? I'm dying of curiosity.'

'Well, we can't have you dying, although really I'd prefer to tell you with a paper bag over my head. And not a word to Jody.' Fiona plunged on. 'It's all your landlady's fault. She put me up to it.'

'But what is it?'

'Internet dating,' said Fiona. 'There, I've said it. And look, there's Jody.'

Chapter Two

An orange people carrier drew up and parked. The door opened and a young woman wearing shorts and a stripy top jumped out. She was tanned, freckled and looked very fit. She reminded Sian of a tennis player.

'Hi, Fiona! So kind of you to ask us. I'll just release Annabelle.' She slid open the side door and began fiddling with straps. By the time Fiona, Sian and Rory had reached them there was a small girl on the ground, scowling at them from under dark black brows.

She had bare feet, long curly black hair that tumbled down her back, pink pedal-pushers and a matching T-shirt. Sian thought she looked like a gypsy queen and quite magnificent.

Jody held out her hand to Sian. 'You must be Sian. Jody. And this little princess is Annabelle.' Jody looked at Rory and said, 'Don't worry, she's better with boys than girls. She's got two older brothers and apart from liking pink, thinks girly things are silly.'

Rory looked up at Jody and smiled, responding to her warmth and relaxed attitude.

'Fiona's got a train,' said Annabelle, proud of her greater knowledge.

'Why don't you two go and find it?' suggested Fiona. 'The gate's open, you can go in.'

Bustling importantly, Annabelle led the way, with a willing Rory following.

'She's a heartbreaker in the making,' said Fiona as the adults followed more slowly.

'Don't say that!' said Jody. 'She gives me enough trouble when the boys have sleepovers. She harasses their friends in a most embarrassing way.' Jody looked at Sian apologetically. 'You must tell me if she's too much for Rory. And you must come over soon. We live in a mess but it's a massive house so we seem to be sleepover central.'

Sian smiled, feeling immensely grateful to Fiona, first for knowing someone who seemed so much fun and secondly for introducing them. 'It sounds like heaven. We live in a fairly small house but we're still up for the odd sleepover.'

As she followed Fiona and Jody through the big gate into the yard, which gave on to an open-sided barn, now being invaded by Rory and the Gypsy Queen, Sian couldn't help wondering about what Fiona had confided.

Fiona was obviously a pillar of the local community. She was probably chairman of the WI and certainly did church flowers. The idea of her internet dating seemed bonkers! But fun. Sian acknowledged, going into the house of her mother's dreams, that the thought was definitely fun.

The kitchen was huge, with some sort of range cooker up one end and a table up the other. An island unit and various cupboards, a dresser and a desk took up the rest of the space. A long shelf above the window that looked out on to a charming garden held huge majolica plates and jugs. It was either designed by an expert or was a wonderful accident, but the result was delightful.

'This is lovely!' said Sian. 'What a perfect room!'

'Oh, do you like it? I sometimes think it's a bit of a shambles but the thought of sorting it out just makes me feel weak. Now, you two go and sit down and I'll make tea.'

Jody and Sian were seated at the table when Annabelle and Rory came in. Annabelle was obviously about to ask for a drink when she caught her mother's eye and didn't.

Fiona, apparently fluent in small-child-speak, said, 'Would you two like a drink? Apple juice? Annabelle, can you show Rory how to work the ice machine?'

'What an amazing fridge,' said Sian, watching Annabelle and Rory fill two glasses with ice.

'It's ridiculous really when it's just me most of the time. My sons gave it to me one Christmas so I would always have enough ice for my gin and tonics. Not that I drink that many of them, but I do like a lot of ice.'

'I think that's a lovely present. Far better than a new iron or something,' said Jody, when Fiona had added apple juice and straws to the ice.

'Yes, they're good boys. One of them has been away for ages and is coming back here to write a book. The other one lives in Canada.' She opened a cupboard and took out a tin. 'At least, that's the plan for Angus. Not sure I can see him doing it, he's always been a man of action, not to mention a bit dyslexic.'

'So why the book?' Jody asked.

Fiona shrugged as she took a plate from the drainer and opened the tin. 'I don't think he knows what else to do, really. Not that it's easy writing a book, of course – think of all those tortured souls. And it'll be very odd sharing the house with someone again, even though it's huge. One of the reasons I want to clear out the barn is I'd like to be able to convert it for him to live in, if he finds he can't live with his mother now he's grown up. I'm not the most organised person.'

'Nor me,' said Jody.

'I'm not all that organised but I love clearing other

people's clutter,' said Sian. 'It's so much easier than doing your own.'

The cake now on a plate and on the table, Fiona turned to the children, who were making loud sucking noises with their straws. 'Do you want cake now or later? More juice? Or the train?'

Annabelle looked at Rory. 'Can we take cake to the train?'

'Oh, I should think so. Mums? What do you think?'

'Definitely less messy if they have it outside,' said Jody.

'And you don't mind them having cake?' Fiona looked at Sian, apparently knowing Jody's feelings.

'Cake is fine in moderation,' said Sian, 'and I think taking it outside is a brilliant idea.'

Annabelle and Rory ran off happily, clutching chocolate cake in bits of paper towel.

'Oh the peace!' said Jody, flopping back into a chair.

'I'll make the tea,' said Fiona.

'That cake is delicious!' said Sian, picking at the crumbs the children had created in their excitement.

'Oh, have a proper slice, do!' Fiona handed Sian a knife and three plates. 'I don't want it in the house for long.'

'We'll do our best to help,' said Jody with a smile.

Two cups of tea and a slice of cake later, Jody got up to go. 'My boys' swimming lesson will be over by now. I'd better pick them up, I suppose, if I can tear Annabelle away.' She looked at Sian. 'She and Rory obviously get on. No one's come in crying or moaning about being bored. That's brilliant!'

'It is. Lovely for Rory to have found a friend so soon,' said Sian with a real sense of relief.

'You must come over . . .'

The party moved out into the yard where the children were playing with a wooden train set large enough to sit on. Eventually Jody extracted Annabelle with the promise of chips on the way home from picking up the boys. 'They're always so starving after swimming and if their blood-sugar level drops they become like animals – more like animals . . .'

Sian looked at Rory, wondering if they should go too when Fiona said, 'While you're here, Sian, come and look at the barn and see what you think.'

The barn was full of furniture – Fiona hadn't been exaggerating – and as Sian followed her between wardrobes, tables, cupboards and upturned chairs she realised it would make an ideal space to work in – without quite so much in it, of course.

'Who does all this belong to?' she asked Fiona.

'Various people. A lot of it can be just got rid of, but there are some family pieces the boys should have a look at, to see if they want them. Some of it's my ex's – my second husband's. That can all go. I do need this space cleared,' Fiona said with a frown. 'I shouldn't be hanging on to all this stuff.'

'You need a life-laundry person to come and counsel you over every oversized chest of drawers and convince you that you've moved on from it.'

Fiona smiled but Sian sensed she'd stumbled on a germ of truth.

'I could help you,' Sian went on. She didn't want to sound mercenary but the barn would be a perfect workspace. 'Pure self-interest, of course. I might like the furniture to paint and I'd definitely like the barn to work in.'

'Although,' said Fiona cautiously, 'as I said before, if Angus discovers he can't live in the same house with me, he might want me to convert it into living space.'

Sian brushed away an unexpected flicker of resentment for the absent Angus. He was Fiona's son: of course he should have first dibs on the barn. 'Well, that would be OK. I'll still help,' she said magnanimously.

'Would you?'

'Of course.'

'I've done a lot of clearing in the house. I've sorted out loads and loads of books; a whole library, in fact. Though I haven't gone near the attic.' Fiona sighed. 'It's not that I want to move, I don't, at all, but it's a huge house, I'm only one person, I'm rather rattling around in it and, much as I do like my space, I can't help feeling the boys might like to have a bit of capital now, rather than waiting for me to pop my clogs. Although Russell's well set up in Montreal.'

'Oh.' Fiona seemed as far away from popping her clogs as Sian herself did.

'I've found a shop that might take a lot of the books. Second-hand – or rather "antiquarian" – books are mostly sold on the internet these days. This man sells them. I'm going to take a selection over soon.'

Sian had spotted something. 'Oh, a nest of tables.'

'I hate nests of tables,' Fiona exclaimed. 'I know they're useful but I just hate them.'

'Why don't I paint them for you, all with different flowers or something, and you could put them in different rooms?'

Fiona laughed. 'OK. My ex-husband would be livid at the thought of his dead aunt's nest being painted with flowers. However, as he left them here and has shown absolutely no interest in reclaiming them, what he thinks is of little consequence to us!'

Sian's imagination was already fired up. 'Not too many flowers, of course, and I'd put some sort of glaze on before I started. What about a sort of pale clay colour? That would set off the flowers beautifully.'

Fiona was amused at the younger woman's enthusiasm over a nest of tables. 'Just you do what you think best. If I hate them I could give them to my friend to sell. She's got a shop in Fairsham. You know the kind: it sells things you don't really need but can't resist buying.' Her brow wrinkled. 'Sorry, I didn't mean it to sound like that. I've even bought stuff from there myself. She'd be a really good contact for you. I must get you together. Her name's Margaret Tomlin. Her shop is called something like Eclectica. You should have a look if you ever get the chance.' Fiona paused but before Sian could reply she continued, 'Hey, I've had an idea. I've been meaning to have a dinner party. I can invite Margaret and introduce you both. I've been wanting to welcome you properly into the village. This is the perfect way. I'll get on to it straightaway.'

'A retail outlet would be good,' said Sian cautiously, less certain about the dinner party. She wasn't sure she was ready to be launched into village life yet, although she had enjoyed meeting Jody. She much preferred more informal occasions. She climbed over a chair and headed for a corner. 'Look at that cupboard – perfect for a child's bedroom. I can just see it with delicate trails of ivy climbing up it and a tiny row of antique baby equipment along the top.'

'That sounds nice,' said Fiona, looking at the cupboard with renewed interest. 'Maybe I'd rather have that. It was my aunt's.'

'How did you come to be left with so much furniture?' Sian asked.

'Easy,' said Fiona. 'Whenever anyone died or people didn't know what to do with anything they said, "Fiona lives in that huge house, she'll store it for us." But no one ever took anything away again.'

'Abso-bloody-lutely!' Sian replied, looking out across a sea of assorted bits and pieces that lined the barn from ceiling to floor. There really was a daunting amount of stuff. 'Now, please, put me out of my misery and tell me about the internet-dating thing!'

'It's Luella's fault!' said Fiona. 'She put me on a site where you recommend your friends. She did ask my permission, but only after she'd done it.' Fiona shook her head slightly. 'I think what really clinched it was that she had a very flattering photograph of me, taken when I was staying with her. I was laughing and playing with her dog. A good look for the more mature woman. When I saw it I thought, why not?'

Sian hesitated. 'I wouldn't describe you as more mature. I mean – That's not to say I think you're immature, what I mean is you're like my mother, you wear jeans and funky jewellery and you're fun. More mature sounds, well, old.'

'Ridiculous as it sounds, I only feel about eighteen a lot of the time.' Fiona frowned. 'And goodness knows what Angus would say about me internet dating.'

'But surely, anything that made you happy . . . ?'

'Yes, but my boys don't trust my taste in men. We all had an awful time when I married my second husband.'

'But you're not going to marry anyone,' Sian pointed out, 'just have a good time.'

'That's exactly what Luella said,' Fiona replied with a smile as she led Sian out of the barn to a bench in the courtyard. Rory played happily with the trains as they watched.

'So, you need me to do you a favour?' said Sian. 'To do with the internet dating?'

Fiona laughed. 'To be honest, you're doing me a favour not dying of shock.'

'Well, everyone seems to be doing it these days,' Sian said in a reassuring tone (not that she could think of a single person she knew who had). 'But there's more to it?'

Fiona nodded. 'Just a bit. It's a safety thing. I've got a date and I need someone to know where I'm going and who I'm with and when I should be back, that sort of thing.'

Although she'd only met her the day before, Sian secretly felt that Fiona could handle any situation, however precarious, but didn't voice her thoughts. She would be very happy to help someone who had been so welcoming in any way she could. 'No problem. So where are you going?'

'We're going to an antiques fair. I mentioned that I liked them and he said there was one on and why didn't we go together? As it's not too far, I said yes.' Fiona paused. 'I can't remember the last time I've been out with a man like that.'

'That sounds a perfect first date.' Sian smiled enthusiastically. It must be nerve-racking, but exciting too. Just for a second she wondered if her life was rather lacking in excitement. It was full and productive but not exactly spine-tingling. And here was a woman her mother's age who wasn't afraid to get out there and try something different. Fiona put her to shame.

'I hope so. And you don't mind texting me during the date so I can alert you if I need rescuing? Which I won't, of course. I can just walk out and go home if I'm unhappy. But they do say it's better to be safe . . .'

'Of course. How much chance will you have to get to know each other at an antiques fair, though?' Sian asked.

'Enough, I should think. But there is one thing . . .'

'Go on.' Whatever it was seemed to be bothering Fiona.

'Well, on the dating site and in all the emails and phone calls we've exchanged, there's one thing they won't tell you and doesn't show on photographs . . .'

'What, chemistry?' Sian understood this. To her it seemed that good sexual chemistry was possibly a once-in-a-lifetime thing.

'No, although of course you're right about that. What I'm worried about is much more mundane.' She paused. 'Bad breath. Have you ever noticed how many older men seem to have it?'

'I hadn't, actually.' Once again Sian marvelled at the way Fiona's mind worked. She was wonderfully honest.

'You probably don't need to get near to many of them but I promise you, it's a problem. And unless there's some way you can drop "mouth wash" or "dental floss" into an email or chat on the phone without looking completely barking I'm not going to know until I'm committed to an afternoon of browsing antiques.' She gave a rueful smile. 'Shall we have another cup of tea?'

Chapter Three

Rory walked along next to Sian, his hand in hers, singing to himself. They were both tired and dusty but had had a lovely time with Fiona. She had invited them to supper but Sian felt she should get Rory to bed.

'We'll just have scrambled eggs on toast and then get you into the bath,' she said now, wondering if she had the energy to work after he was asleep. She needed to finish a piece of furniture but what with meeting Fiona, the flower-arranging, being introduced to Jody and Annabelle and checking out the barn she'd hardly had a moment.

'Will you read to me?' Rory asked.

'OK, darling.' Reading to Rory in the bath had started as a time-saving exercise but they had both come to enjoy it. Having first done the tooth-brushing, Sian would sit on the floor, leaning up against the bath, while Rory splashed around, getting more and more drowsy. When Sian judged the moment was right, she whisked him out with a big towel and popped him into bed. He quite often begged another story once he was in bed but was usually asleep before she'd finished.

Tonight he was full of chatter about Fiona, Annabelle and the train set in Fiona's barn. He was also thinking about going to the play scheme tomorrow.

'Emily will be there, won't she?' he asked, squeezing a sponge full of bubbles.

'Yes, and she'll have helpers, because she'll have more children. It won't be just you.' Sian wiped his face with a flannel. Relaxing bathtimes sometimes meant the washing part got overlooked.

'And will they be girls?'

'Who, the children or the helpers?'

'The helpers. Helpers are always girls.'

'They may not be. Emily might have got some young men to help now she's down here.'

Rory sighed. 'I don't think so. I don't think boys look after children. I like boys.'

'So do I.' She paused. 'Are you ready to come out now, darling? I've got a bit of work to finish and I'd like to get you tucked up.'

'OK, Mummy,' said Rory, resigned to there being no male carers and to going to bed. He did it with relatively good grace.

Sian had been working with all the doors open to minimise the smell of paint and had just wrapped her paintbrush in clingfilm when her phone went. It was Richard. She remembered he was due back from a business trip.

'Hey!' she said. 'Are you at home?'

'No, but I'll be back tomorrow. I just wondered how you were getting on?'

'Fine! We're nearly all unpacked. Mum helped quite a bit when she was here. And we've met a really nice woman. Fiona Matcham. Do you know her? She lives in the big house at the end of the lane. She seems lovely!'

'Oh yes, she is lovely. I was at boarding school with her boys, but I haven't seen her in a while. I'm not surprised she's taken you under her wing. That's just the sort of person she is.' He paused. 'And how's Rory? Looking forward to tomorrow?'

'Oh yes. He hopes there are boy helpers there.' Then she wished she hadn't said that. Richard felt that Rory needed an adult male role model and that he should be it. While Sian agreed on some levels, she wasn't sure marrying Richard so he could be a role model was the answer. She sighed and said more brightly, 'He's met a little girl called Annabelle, who goes there. And he's looking forward to seeing Emily again. Has she got lots of young helpers, do you know?'

They chatted on gently about Emily's project and ended with a plan for Richard to come over the following evening and have supper. He was driving down from London that afternoon for a flying visit home before his next trip. Sian went to bed feeling fond of him. He might never set the world on fire but he was nice, and niceness had a lot going for it. She hadn't always thought like that, of course. Once she'd followed her heart – and her hormones – and had a mad, brief affair that had resulted in Rory. But now, nearly six years on, she felt she'd grown up a bit and no longer looked for heart-stopping passion but for something more comfortable and secure. Her head was definitely sure this was what she needed and wanted, she just wished she could convince her stubborn heart of this. However, she had to be practical. It was no good thinking she was a heroine in one of those books she'd devoured as a teenager. Real life wasn't like that, and as she was never going to see Rory's father again she just had to get on with it. And the love one felt for a friend could grow into a deeper love, couldn't it? All the articles said that a relationship based on friendship was an enduring one and she knew that arranged marriages often lasted longer than those where the couple had married 'for love'. She was sure if she decided on a life with Richard, as he wished, she and Rory would have a very contented, safe, one.

Brushing aside the nagging little voice inside her heart that said, 'Contentment, is that what you really want?' she turned over and drifted off to sleep.

The next morning, Sian managed to persuade Rory to eat Marmite soldiers. At first he'd been too excited for breakfast but Sian had been firm. He couldn't go to the play scheme on an empty stomach. She had only been able to sip a cup of tea; she seemed much more nervous than her son.

As they walked up the lane, Rory chatted excitedly, swinging her arm and striding purposefully, his little backpack perched on his back. This was a very good sign, thought Sian. He liked Emily, who had helped tutor him when Sian had taken him out of school, but the last time he'd been around a group of children he'd hated it. But that was at a big ugly institution in London, Sian reminded herself. As he asked her about the other children – he knew Annabelle now, of course – she also realised with a pang of guilt just how much he must have been missing the company of children his age.

They had walked to the nursery the day before so that Rory had an idea where he'd be going and how far it was from the cottage – and his mother. Although the building itself was somewhat utilitarian it was in a lovely setting, a safe distance from the main road and with plenty of space for the children to run around in.

Much to Rory's pleasure and surprise, there was a young man helping out with the older children. Rory was delighted to see Emily and after saying hello to her and throwing a cursory glance at his mother, he rushed to join the other children. Emily raised an eyebrow at Sian as if to say, 'What did I tell you, there was nothing to worry about,' and Sian smiled. This was all a great relief to her.

She needed reliable childcare where Rory was really happy so she could work. She would only get paid for the few commissions she had outstanding when she could deliver them. She loved the fact that she had her own business and was making money from doing something she loved, but it could be precarious. When she wasn't doing the painting, she had to drum up more work. She hoped Fiona's friend with the shop would turn out to be a good contact. And at least Rory looked as if he was going to be happy. She said goodbye to Emily and waved at Rory, who was by now busily playing trains with another little boy, while Annabelle directed proceedings.

It was a slightly paint-spattered Sian who went to collect Rory some five hours later. She had had a very productive day. She'd even worked through lunch, so absorbed had she been in a particularly intricate design on a child's bedroom chair.

She was welcomed by Emily who said that most of the children were outside.

'It's so lovely doing this where there's space for them to play outside,' she said, leading Sian out into the garden. 'I'm hoping to get some more equipment for them to clamber over but this is good to start with.' There was a small paddling pool, a sandpit and a climbing frame.

'It's the room to run around that's the most important thing,' said Sian. 'And you've got plenty of that.' Much as Rory enjoyed the garden at the cottage, which was more outside space than he'd been used to in London, she knew this would be heaven for him. It would almost certainly tire him out too. She loved it when he was able to run around and burn off some of his boyish energy.

'True,' said Emily, 'and today we've had the weather to enjoy it.'

All the children – and there seemed to be plenty of them – were wearing baseball caps with flaps at the back to keep their necks protected from the sun. The boy helper was playing French cricket with the older children. 'That's Philip,' said Emily. 'He's a student. The children love him. I'm trying to persuade him to go into teaching.'

Rory spotted his mother and came flying up to give her a hug and then rushed back into the game.

'No need to ask if he's been OK then?' said Sian, resigning herself to watching the children a little longer.

'No, he's been amazing. He's a sweetie. He adores Philip.'

'He does like boys, as he calls them. He and my dad get on brilliantly, but older men are different.'

Emily laughed. 'Maybe you should marry my brother then, and give him a permanent "boy" to look up to.' She laughed. 'Only joking.'

Sian gave a rueful smile. She knew Emily was only half joking. Emily would like nothing better than for Richard and Sian to get together properly. She really liked Emily but that wasn't a good enough reason for her to marry her brother. 'Well, who knows?'

Sian and Rory were just walking up to the cottage when they saw a car parked outside it.

'I wonder who that can be?' said Sian, hoping it wasn't a visitor. She was wearing her painting clothes and Rory was worn out; he was dragging his feet already, and his manners weren't reliable when he was tired.

As they reached the front door, the owner of the car spotted them. A vision of Boden loveliness wearing a summer dress and designer sunglasses emerged from the neat little soft-top. She looked leisured and relaxed and had perfectly tanned legs and pretty sandals. 'I'm Melissa

Lewis-Jones,' she said, putting out a hand which Sian duly shook. 'Fiona Matcham told me someone had moved in. I thought I'd call, be neighbourly.'

Sian hoped her smile didn't show how unkeen she was for an elegant visitor. She felt grubbier than ever but she didn't want to alienate a potential new friend. Sian glanced at Rory, who had gone in through the gate and was waiting at the door to be let in, impatient to get back to his own toy trains.

'Of course,' said Sian, unlocking the door and letting Rory in first. 'You must excuse the mess though. I've been painting, as you see.' Sian didn't spend precious Rory-free time doing housework as she could do that with him there. She couldn't remember if the remains of breakfast and lunch were still on the table or had graduated to the kitchen drainer. 'I'm Sian, by the way. Do come in.'

The Boden-vision didn't hesitate and came through into Sian's front room. 'My God! It's a bit of a cave, isn't it? And smells frightfully damp! I've always wanted to have a look inside. I didn't realise it was in such a bad state.'

Sian, who had come to love the room despite the gloom, discovered it was fine for Fiona to say that the house was damp but not for Melissa Double-Barrelled. 'We're very comfortable here,' she said defensively.

'In summer! But what will it be like in winter? A fridge, that's what. I gather Luella Halpern was just too mean to get anything done about the house. She could have done it up and sold it for a fortune.'

'Then I'm glad she didn't,' said Sian. Realising her visitor was in no hurry to leave, she decided she'd better play the polite hostess. 'Would you like something to drink? Glass of water? Juice? It's dreadfully hot. The cool in here is actually very welcome.'

'I'll have some sparkling water if you've got some.'

Melissa followed her into the kitchen. 'This could be wonderful if you took that wall out and made it open plan. Properties like this are still selling – so handy for London.'

'It's not on the market.' Sian put the glass of water down on the table and then poured some juice for Rory before running the tap for her own water. 'Do sit down.'

'What's your name?' asked Melissa, smiling the smile that indicated someone who didn't really like children.

'Rory,' Rory said matter-of-factly.

'Well, Rory, do you think you might like to go and play in the garden? I want to talk about boring stuff with your mother.' She looked at Sian. 'If that's all right with Mummy, of course.'

Sian instantly wanted to say that Rory had to stay and have a snack but she also wanted to protect him from boredom and this slightly scary woman. 'Do you want something to eat, darling? You could take it out if you want?'

'Babybel please,' said Rory, looking dubiously at their visitor. He obviously hadn't warmed to Melissa much either. He was a good little judge of character, thought Sian, and then chided herself. She ought to give Melissa a chance.

Sian found two Babybels and handed them to him. 'And do you need a drink?'

'No. I had one at play scheme.' He snatched the cheeses and ran off into the garden, all signs of his earlier tiredness now gone.

'It's much easier to chat without little ears wagging.' Melissa pulled out a chair and smiled at Sian.

'Have you got children?' Sian asked, her thirst slaked but her mood not much improved.

'Good God no! I'm not saying I wouldn't have them, but not yet. And not without major support. I want to enjoy myself while I'm young and lovely.' She laughed, as if to indicate irony, but it didn't quite work.

Fair enough, thought Sian, taking another chair. She is young and lovely. Although Sian was sure they must be the same age, there was something extra youthful about Melissa. Perhaps it was because she didn't seem to have many responsibilities in life.

'So what brings you to these parts?' asked Melissa, breaking into her thoughts.

Sian had already ticked off most of her reasons for moving here with Fiona and she wasn't going to repeat them again – not to this particular visitor anyway. Something told her she should be slightly on her guard with Melissa. She decided to stick to what was common knowledge. 'Well, it's a lovely part of the world and it's fairly near London.' She didn't add the fact that the rent was cheap.

'So why do you want to be near London? Do you work there?'

Sian sipped her water, preparing for the interrogation she knew was coming. Much as she'd like Melissa to go she knew she couldn't be rude. The quicker she answered her questions the quicker the visit would be over. 'No. I work from home, but my parents live there so I didn't want to move too far away.'

'And your partner?'

Sian shook her head. 'Single parent. No ex-partner, either.'

Melissa's mascara flashed in amazement. 'So you just wanted to have a baby? How brave! And how on earth did you select the father? Did you choose brains or looks?'

Sian thought back briefly to the night that, nine months

34

later, had produced Rory and smiled, her sense of humour emerging from behind her resentment at Melissa's bluntness. 'I didn't get pregnant on purpose, but when I found I was, I was quite happy. Once I'd got over the shock.'

'That is so brave. No way would I have a baby on my own! Think of the work. Let alone the stigma.' Melissa could obviously think of nothing worse. Sian knew that not everyone would take Sian's current situation in their stride but even so Melissa's reaction seemed a little extreme. Perhaps Fiona had been right, people were much more set in their ways in the country.

'I lived very near my parents and they were very supportive,' said Sian quietly but firmly. 'There wasn't any stigma.'

'Oh. I didn't mean to imply anything.' Melissa had the decency to blush. 'It's just that some people are rather old-fashioned. Round here, I mean.'

Like you, you mean, thought Sian. 'I've found people very friendly,' she said.

'Oh, Fiona's OK. A rather eccentric old stick but kindly.'

'Yes.' Sian found herself deeply offended on Fiona's behalf. Being in your mid-fifties – Sian's mother's age – did not qualify you as being an 'old stick' in her eyes.

'Some of the others may be a bit off about it though, you being an unmarried mother. Maybe you'd better pretend to be a widow. What happened to the baby's father? Did he support you?'

As Sian hadn't told Rory's father she was pregnant and she had no idea what had happened to him, she sipped some more water to gain time. 'He disappeared on a trip. I had no way of getting in touch with him so I didn't tell him. There didn't seem any point. We hadn't known each other long.'

She looked directly at her uninvited guest, daring her

to comment on the fact that Sian must have gone to bed with him very early on. She had. At the time she hadn't been able to help herself, but it had been completely out of character for her. If it hadn't been for Rory, proof that it had happened, she might have thought she'd dreamt the whole incident. A very good dream though.

'Well, I think you should make the bastard pay!' Melissa exclaimed.

Slightly taken aback by Melissa's vehemence, Sian said, 'Why? I'm very happy to be a mother. I don't have any hard feelings towards Rory's dad.'

Melissa shrugged. 'Oh well. So do you live off the State then?'

There was bluntness and there was rudeness. This was rude. 'As I said, I work from home. I have a business, painting furniture.' She didn't add that she took anything the State offered in the way of support and was glad to have it. It was none of this woman's business. 'So what about you?' Sian said, feeling it was her turn to play the Spanish Inquisition. 'What do you do?'

'Oh, bits and pieces of PR, events management, things like that.'

'You're not married?'

'Not yet.' Melissa gave a little smile, hinting at secrets.

'Engaged then? Are you planning a big wedding?'

'I certainly am! But actually I'm single at the moment. I've just finished a long-term relationship. He was lovely but far too controlling.'

'Right.' Sian deliberately didn't say anything, not wanting to prolong the conversation. While this girl was amusing as a stereotype, she wasn't really likeable. Sian couldn't see them becoming friends any time soon. She thought of Jody and how different the other young woman was. Perhaps a village was like a city in miniature after all, the same mix of people and opinions, it's just you noticed those you disagreed with much more obviously and it was harder to avoid them in a smaller space. She'd caught enough snatches of *The Archers* whilst her mother was listening to it to see how like being under a micro-scope living in a village could be. Fiona was the good side, Melissa the bad.

Melissa sat there for a while, possibly waiting for Sian to get the conversation going again. Eventually she got up. 'I suppose I'd better go. Nice to meet you.' She paused. 'I don't suppose you'd give me a little tour of the house, would you? I'm thinking of buying locally and this might do me very well.'

'But it's rented. I live here.' Sian's hackles rose once more.

'I'm sure Luella would listen to a sensible offer from a cash buyer. After all, she lives in Spain now, doesn't she?'

'France, actually. And I'm afraid I can't give you a tour.' Sian found herself being unusually firm. 'I'm not fully unpacked yet. The place isn't fit for visitors and it's nearly time to feed Rory – he can be very cranky when he's hungry.' Sian felt mean using her son as an excuse, but it was nearly his teatime, and she'd do anything to get Melissa out of her hair.

'Oh.' Melissa seemed a bit surprised to find herself refused. 'Another time perhaps?'

Sian smiled and shrugged, hoping there wouldn't be another time and wondering how she could stop Melissa buying what she now considered her home. She couldn't imagine that Melissa had been denied many things in her life. She wondered if she should call Fiona and ask if she thought Luella might be tempted by a sensible offer from a cash buyer. But she thought better of it. Fiona's date was tomorrow and she didn't want to distract her.

After Sian had seen Melissa off the premises, she went to join Rory in the garden, suddenly wondering if they'd be there to see their strawberries ripen and their plants mature. She gave a wistful sigh and, putting her hand out for Rory to take, she said, 'Come on, Rory, we'll just water the strawberries and then it'll be time for supper.' And they went inside.

Once she'd fed Rory, Sian had a quick shower and got into a summer dress. It was old and faded but one of her favourites. With some jewellery and make-up and out of her gardening clothes she scrubbed up quite well. She wanted to cook something nice for Richard. He said he got fed up with hotel fare and liked more homely meals, there-fore she set about making a shepherd's pie while Rory watched television. As she peeled onions and chopped celery and carrots she thought about Richard. She was looking forward to seeing him again – he'd been away on business for nearly three weeks now. That was another thing about Richard that she liked, he was away a lot, which meant she was able to get on with her life and look forward to the times when she did see him. Neither of them got under each other's feet and had plenty to talk about when they did meet up. He would want to hear about all her doings as she would want to hear about his. He could be very funny about the people he met on his travels.

She decided not to mention Melissa saying she wanted to buy the cottage. Richard would want to sort it out for her and she wanted to cope with the problem herself. Sian was not at all reluctant to accept help but Richard had already done a lot for her. She knew he wanted to ease her path through life – he would quite happily whisk her into his own house if she said the word. But she didn't want to exploit his good nature or do anything she didn't feel comfortable with, just for an easy life.

Suddenly she remembered him saying that every now and again he craved the butterscotch tart they had at school. She didn't have a recipe but a quick trawl through her larder made her think she could make it up without too much difficulty. Rory would love the leftovers the following day.

'Hello, Richard!' Sian let him put his arms around her and give her a big hug. She liked his hugs. They were solid and dependable, like he was, and afterwards you knew you'd been hugged. She hugged him back, just as firmly.

'Sian, girl,' he said. 'You look as gorgeous as ever. No one would think you'd moved house since I last saw you.' He put the bottle of wine he had brought down on the table.

'The cottage looks as if I only moved in a few hours ago. I still haven't sorted everything out. Come in. Do you want to sit in the kitchen and watch me make a salad, or sit in state in the sitting room?'

'You know the answer to that,' he said, looking at her with a warmth in his eyes that made her feel guilty.

'I'll just run up and tuck Rory in.'

'I'll do that. I'd like to know how the little chap is getting on with my sis.'

'First day today but he loved it! There's a "boy" helping out and as you know he loves boys. Go up and see.'

Richard came back down a little while later. 'Although I'm a boy, obviously, he wants you to tuck him in. I did read a story but I don't think I did the voices in quite the right way.'

More guilt. He was so kind, why didn't Rory want to be tucked in by him? She ran up the stairs, having made sure Richard had a glass of wine.

When she came down she found he had finished making the salad and had tidied up the kitchen and set the table.

'You're such a star, Richard,' she said, smiling at him over her wine.

'Does that mean you'll change your mind and marry me?' He smiled. 'Don't look so distressed. You've given me your answer. I just hope one day you'll change your mind.'

Sian raised her glass to him. I sort of hope that myself, she thought, but didn't say it aloud.

Chapter Four

❧

'You only have one chance to make a first impression,' Luella had helpfully reminded Fiona by email that morning. Fiona, dressed in carefully casual loose linen trousers, a non-matching longish jacket (to cover the tricky thigh area)and chunky jewellery, felt if not at her best, at least OK. Sian, who had sympathised with her nerves and come round to help her with her outfit after a panicked phone call, had eventually said, 'I think I'm jealous! It's all so exciting.'

'Too exciting,' said Fiona wryly, but as she drove off, having got Sian's promise to send the pre-planned text for the hundredth time, she realised she relished the feeling. Her life as a 'good woman' was fine but latterly she had felt there was part of her that was un-addressed. She well remembered the stage Sian was at, but much as she had enjoyed it, it was good to be free of all that, even if she did still worry about her 'boys'. Maybe it was time she kicked over the traces a bit. She found herself a spot in the main town car park and checked the bookshop address in her hand. Making herself do some-thing useful on the way to her assignation at the antiques fair was a good way to make herself feel less guilty about the whole thing. Although there was no reason in the world why she shouldn't arrange to meet a man she'd met on a dating site she couldn't help feeling it was somehow wrong. Now, she picked up the box of books she'd sorted the night before and set off, hoping the shop wasn't too far away.

The bookshop sign caught her eye immediately she hit the main shopping street. I just hope the man wants some of these books and I don't have to drag them all back again, she thought as she opened the door with her hip and reversed into the shop.

'Can I help you with that?'

A man's voice, low and pleasant, came from the darkness and Fiona found the box being taken gently from her arms. She looked up and saw a slightly built man with thick greying hair and kind eyes.

'Oh, thank you. They were getting heavy. Are you Mr Langley?'

'Yes, James Langley. And you must be Mrs Matcham. Do come on through and we'll have a look.'

Fiona followed the man into the back of the shop, taking in the smell and the atmosphere and realising she liked it.

'There's something about bookshops, isn't there?' she said as they reached what was obviously the office. 'You feel something magical might come out from between the covers of one of the books at any moment.'

The man paused in the task of finding room for the box of books on the already crowded desk and looked at Fiona. 'You think so? How nice! That's how I always feel too. One doesn't expect non-book people to feel the same.'

'Oh, I am a book person!' Fiona hurried to reassure him. 'I just have far, far too many to read in my lifetime.'

'Well, let's have a look. Would you like something to drink? Tea? Coffee? Water?'

'A glass of water would be wonderful.'

'I'm afraid I haven't anything to put in it to make it more interesting.'

'Water is quite interesting enough, I assure you.'

'Do make yourself at home. I won't be a moment.'

Fiona sat down and looked about her. The room was small and full of bookshelves. An old wooden card index system commanded quite a lot of space but the rest of it was taken up with boxes of books very like the one she had brought with her. He obviously couldn't say no when asked to look at books, just in case there was a hidden jewel. She sympathised with this presumed sentiment but she accepted it probably wasn't a brilliant business model. She hoped there was at least one 'jewel' in her own box.

He came back with two glasses of water and found space for hers on the back of a view of a floral clock on a postcard. Taking a quick look at the card before it was obscured by the glass, Fiona guessed it dated from the 1950s and had probably been used as a bookmark, which was why it was now on James Langley's desk.

'Now, Mrs Matcham, let's have a look,' he said, putting his hand into the box and bringing out a book. 'Ah!' he said. 'Very nice.' He put the book to one side and put his hand in again. 'This is like a lucky dip where all the prizes are good ones,' he said. 'Where do they come from?'

'They're a selection from my husband's library. Deceased first husband, I should say, rather than divorced second husband.' Fiona suddenly realised she was giving far more information than was strictly necessary and explained, in a hurry, 'I wouldn't like you to think I was selling off my husband's books if he still wanted them.'

'So are there many more?'

Fiona nodded. 'A whole room. And bookcases and book-cases full. He inherited most of the library but he was also a compulsive book-buyer. The house is coming down with books, and I need to clear it really. If I had to sell the house it would take me years.'

James Langley had been going through the books as Fiona explained, grunting with pleasure at intervals. 'There are some good books here I'd be interested in buying, but I'm worrying about the rest of the library. What are you planning to do?'

'Well, if the books are worth anything, I'd like to sell them. Neither of my sons is interested in any of those that are left. They've had all the ones they do want already.'

'Had you planned how to do that?'

'Not really. I have no idea which ones, if any, are valuable. I just thought I'd put them into boxes, shelf by shelf, and find people like you.' She smiled and decided James Langley was rather nice. Appropriately for a bookseller, he wasn't smartly dressed but his clothes had once been of good quality. They could possibly have been handed down from his father, Fiona decided, but he looked right in them.

'Would you like me to come and have a look? It would save you having to bring box after box in here.' He smiled. He had a lovely smile: it lit up his whole face. It was a nice face too. Part of her wondered why she was checking him out and decided it was because soon she'd be off on her first date, when, inevitably, a great deal of checking out would be going on.

'Can you be bothered? Would it be worth your while? Obviously I'd want you to sell them for me. Or buy them from me – however it works. But still, there're an awful lot of books.'

'Going on the quality of these you've brought in I'm sure it would be worth my while.'

'Well, I would be extremely grateful. Although I do love books those ones have been a dreadful responsibility. I couldn't just chuck them out if they might be valuable and add to my sons' inheritance. And leaving them *in situ* isn't really an option. As I said, I'm thinking I may have to move.'

'It would be my pleasure to come and tell you which ones are valuable and how to dispose of the others.'

'Really?'

'Absolutely. Here, let me give you a card. Why don't you ring me and we'll find a good time?'

'Do you email?'

'Of course. Couldn't manage without the internet these days. Apparently some people even find their partners through it.'

The way he twinkled at her was a bit unsettling. He couldn't possibly know what she was up to, could he? 'Really?' she said again, hoping she sounded sufficiently incredulous. 'Well, whatever, I'd better get on. Do you want me to leave the books?'

'If you don't mind? I can value them individually and those I want to buy, I'll buy. Those I don't want but have a value, I'll track down someone who would want them. Is that all right? You trust me with them?'

Fiona smiled into his eyes, which still seemed a bit twinkly, and decided she did trust him. 'Yes, I do,' she said firmly, knowing everyone who knew her thought she was on the naïve side. But she trusted her instincts and had only once gone horribly wrong.

Feeling lighthearted and optimistic, Fiona made her way to the antiques fair. Having hit the jackpot with her box of books had to be a sign that the rest of the day would go well too. The fact that she found somewhere to park that wasn't in a muddy field was positive too.

However, once she got to the entrance to the stately home that was the venue for the fair she started to feel anxious. They'd agreed to meet 'at the fair' but now she was at the door she realised how unhelpful the word 'at' was in these circumstances. It should have been 'inside' or 'outside', 'by the lion at the gate' or 'the third pillar on the left'.

But as she approached the entrance, which had a queue of people filing their way in, she saw a pleasant-looking man who did look like the picture on the website.

Luella had warned her to expect people to be quite a bit older than their photograph suggested. Her own photo was a couple of years old, but this man seemed spot on.

Perhaps it wasn't him though. Perhaps it was someone else 'about six feet tall, greying at the edges, I'll be wearing a cream linen suit'.

Then she got a grip. What sort of parallel universe did she live in whereby someone who looked like their photograph seemed like an uncanny coincidence instead of exactly what you'd expect? It must be him.

Just as she reached him he turned and smiled.

'You must be Fiona. Robert.' He leant down and kissed her cheek. 'How delightful to meet you at last.'

Fiona returned the kiss, liking the feeling of his cheek against hers, his cologne and the brief contact with his crisp, striped shirt. He was better close to than he had been from a distance, but not gorgeous. However, he was pleasant enough and she hadn't really been looking for 'gorgeous', more someone she could do things with.

'Your photograph doesn't do you justice,' he said and Fiona felt instantly reassured. 'Shall we go in? And the tickets are on me, by the way. Can I take your arm? I'm very old-fashioned in some ways.'

'Is there anything you'd particularly like to see?' said Fiona. There were times when being old-fashioned was reassuring.

'I'm rather partial to cruet-stands,' said Robert.

The little spark of hope that she might have found

someone who could be more than a friend died with these words. There was something very depressing about the words 'cruet-stands' that made Fiona think of 1950s seaside boarding houses. Still, she mustn't judge too hastily. 'Shall we see if we can find any?' she said brightly.

'Unless there's something you'd rather look at?'

'Well,' said Fiona, 'we're bound to pass something jolly on the way to the cruet-stands.'

Fiona started to enjoy herself. As they wandered through the halls passing stand upon stand of antiques of all shapes and sizes her eyes were drawn to a silver frame here and a carriage clock there but Robert was determined to look at the cruet-stands first and Fiona was happy to be led.

Rather to her surprise, next to the cruet-stands (which were rather more beautiful in real life than she had expected) were some little place-name holders. She fell on them delightedly. 'Look at these! Like little pheasants. Just what I need for my dinner party.'

'You're having a dinner party?'

Was it her imagination or was there something a little wistful in the way he said this? 'Yes,' and before she could stop herself she added, 'You must come. It'll be fun.'

'Oh, dear lady, how kind of you! But I couldn't possibly intrude.'

'You wouldn't be intruding,' said Fiona, wishing her kind heart would talk to her head sometimes and perhaps get her mouth to stay shut. His protestations had clearly been made out of politeness. She could tell he would be delighted to come. She just hoped he didn't take it the wrong way. She wasn't sure how she felt about him yet. 'You could help me with the wine,' she added quickly as she took Robert's arm once more and gently moved them on.

When Sian called her half an hour later on her mobile

phone, for a moment Fiona couldn't remember why she was ringing. She moved away from the stand where Robert was studying some rather lurid statuettes.

'So, are you OK?' asked Sian, sounding as if she was bursting with curiosity.

'Yes, I'm having a lovely time. Why shouldn't I be OK? Oh – yes. Sorry! No, I'm fine.' She smiled.

'Well, I want every detail when you get home, or as soon as it's convenient,' Sian added, possibly thinking this might be a bit style-cramping for her friend. 'I won't keep you. Have a nice time!' And she rang off.

Fiona's nice time continued. Robert was companionable and unthreatening. He did have a penchant for things that Fiona felt were a bit twee and over-decorated, but he was pleasant enough. He took her for a delightful lunch in the orangery of the house.

'So, tell me about your house,' said Robert, topping up her glass. 'I think you said it was quite large . . .'

'It's lovely. A bit of a hotch-potch architecturally, but a lovely family home. I'd be very sad to leave it.'

'Do you have to?' Robert asked, as he tucked into his toast and pâté. (Everything in the café was locally produced.)

'Well, not immediately, but I do think my sons need their inheritance now and not after I'm dead. I don't think either of them would want to move in. The garden is massive. Although I love it.'

'I'm very much looking forward to seeing it.' His hand moved across the table and Fiona instinctively withdrew hers, but then felt a little rude. By now, though, she knew that although Robert was a perfectly nice man, she just didn't feel a spark. It was better not to encourage any intimate physical contact from now on, except a hand through an arm or something equally innocuous.

'My garden?' Fiona smiled. Her garden was out of control and lots of it a wilderness but it was her creation and she loved showing it to people – the right people.

'Actually, I'm not much of a gardener but I'd love to see the house.'

Although Fiona had ruled out anything more, even the flicker of hope for a friendship developing died an instant death. This was the second time he'd mentioned her house. Was he already envisaging himself sitting by the fire in his slippers with the paper? 'Oh. Well, it's no masterpiece but it is a big old family home, with lots of memories.'

'And lots of space?'

Fiona laughed. 'Oh yes, that too.'

'And in a very pleasant part of the world, obviously.'

Fiona regarded Robert over her fork full of chicken salad, wondering if she could detect pound signs in his eyes. Was it more than slippers by the fire he was imagining? she thought wryly. You did hear of men preying on 'rich' widows. Then she told herself not to be so silly.

Fiona had said she might pop in at Sian's house for tea on her way home to give her all the details, and so Sian made a cake. It was partly because Rory was getting tired of digging and wanted to bake. Sian often cooked with him as it was something they could enjoy together. They decided on a coffee sponge and Rory was just decorating it with Smarties when Fiona pulled up outside.

'I'll just let Fiona in. Rory, you don't need to put every single Smartie on there, you know. You could keep some to have after supper.'

'But it looks better with them all on!'

Sian sighed. With a four-year-old, there were some battles that just weren't worth fighting. 'OK, it's your cake.'

As she walked through the cottage she wondered if she

was too soft a mother, and if he did really need a father, and if marrying Richard would be the best thing for her. But as she had this thought several times a week, she didn't waste too much energy on it. Rory seemed fine; he was no worse behaved than any other children she knew and a lot better than some.

'Fiona! How did it go? What was he like?' she said as she opened the front door and ushered Fiona in.

'Fine. Nice, but not "the one". Not that I was necessarily looking for that but you know what I mean. Anyway, I found myself inviting him for dinner. I felt sorry for him.' She sighed. 'I must stop doing that. It's such a bad habit.'

Sian laughed. 'Well, come and have some tea. Rory's made you a cake. I helped, you'll be glad to hear.'

'Hello, Rory! How's my favourite boy?' Fiona kissed Rory, who accepted her gesture gracefully. Her mother was the only other person who was allowed to kiss Rory in that extravagant way. Sian was pleased he felt so at ease with Fiona. She felt as if she'd known the older woman for years, not just a few days, and Rory seemed to feel the same.

'We did cooking,' Rory said. 'And I put all the Smarties on even though Mummy said I should save some.'

'I think it looks brilliant, darling! I can't wait to have a slice.' Fiona pulled out a chair, hanging her bag on the back of it. 'It's bliss to be somewhere I can be myself again!'

Sian put on the kettle and found mugs. 'So? Tell all? Rory, go and wash your hands, there's a love. Then you can cut the cake.' Rory clambered down off his chair and went to the little downstairs loo.

When Fiona had her tea, Sian settled down for a gossip. Fiona filled her in on her day and then, changing the subject slightly, said, 'I do get stressed about dinner parties, but I sort of like the stress. It's part of it.'

Rory was busy picking the Smarties off his bit of cake. Once he was absorbed in something he wouldn't even notice a beloved train go by. 'So, who else are you inviting?' Sian asked, sipping her tea.

'Various people, including the Francombes, some old friends I have who are so brilliant at entertaining that they hire themselves out as a prize, to raise money.'

'Really! How does that work?' said Sian, intrigued.

'They're a prize for a promise auction. People pay to have dinner with them. They even produced a little booklet – again to raise money – on how to entertain.'

Sian was suitably astounded. 'These are people I must meet. They sound amazing.'

'And you shall meet them! I'll even show you their booklet.'

'You bought one?'

'Of course. It was a very good cause. Besides, I was dying of curiosity. I wanted to see if they used me as an example of how not to do it. I was slightly disappointed that they didn't.'

'So what do they say you should do?'

'Mad things like, "Sit married couples together so they can finish each other's anecdotes."' She made a gesture. 'And you can always tell the couples who have quarrelled on the journey over who then have to sit next to each other.' She paused, then went on. 'They hand-paint place cards – which reminds me, I bought some little holders. I've got quite a lot already but I couldn't resist them.' After much scrabbling she produced them from the bottom of her handbag.

'They're pheasants,' said Rory, having finished his cake and interested now there was something worth looking at.

'Yes. You're very clever to recognise them.'

'I had a book with them in,' he explained.

'I could hand-paint place cards if you like,' said Sian. 'I want to do everything I can to help.'

'There'll be plenty for you to do, don't worry. It's just a shame Richard is going to be away.'

'Yes, and Rory is going to be staying with Annabelle, aren't you, poppet?'

'But I could help in the morning if you want, Fona,' he said seriously, possibly suspecting he was missing out on some fun.

'Actually, Rory, I'd love it if *you* painted the name places. Mummy can do the boring peeling and chopping instead.'

'Oh yes, I like painting! Shall I get some paper now?'

'You could do, darling.' As he rushed away, Fiona mouthed to Sian, 'Sweet!'

'He's quite good actually,' said Sian.

'Takes after his mother, obviously.'

'So how will you explain your internet friend to everyone? Presumably you don't want people to know where he came from.'

Fiona was appalled. 'Good God no! People would fall in the pudding from shock. Heavens, I hadn't thought about that.' She paused. 'I know, I'll say he's an old friend of my husband's. Robert will understand. He's very nice . . .'

Another, less pleasant thought occurred to her. 'I feel I should warn you, I've invited Melissa's parents and felt I had to invite her too.' Sian had told Fiona about Melissa's visit and knew how she felt about her.

Sian hesitated for a second. 'You must invite who you want. And maybe it would be good for us to meet socially. "Know thine enemy" and all that.'

'And you might become friends. Her parents are very

nice.' Fiona had never really liked Melissa but as she could never think of a good reason why not, it was possible there was nothing wrong with her at all.

'I look forward to meeting them, too.'

Fiona got up, wiping her sticky fingers on the piece of kitchen towel Sian had provided. 'I'd better get back. So you and Rory will come down that morning?'

'Of course. Don't forget we agreed I was going to help clean out the barn before the dinner. Rory and I will come and do that, then I'll pop him over to Annabelle's in the afternoon and stay to help with the cooking.'

'Brilliant! I'm quite looking forward to it now. It's much more fun doing things as a team.'

Chapter Five

❧

On the morning of Fiona's dinner party the weather looked beautiful. A faint mist lay over the garden, the dew sparkled in the dawning sun and Tomasz Schafernaker had been optimistic when he'd made his forecast that morning. Alas, he had also been fairly vague and as Fiona was never quite sure where she lived, meteorologically speaking, she wasn't quite sure if the 'band of rain coming in towards the end of the day' would land on her or not. She'd just have to hope the gods were looking down on her kindly.

Her desire to have her dinner party in the conservatory with drinks outside overcame caution. Any doubts she might have' had about dragging the sofas and chairs out on to the paved area outside the conservatory when they might be rained on were subsumed by the desire to have a party that was beautiful and different. Her passion for candles, tea lights in paper bags and fairy lights wouldn't listen to thoughts of potential showers.

Sian and Rory were coming over soon to help her. She'd got suitable paper for Rory to paint place names on. She was just looking at her menu, wondering what to start on first, when there was a knock on the door.

She glanced at her watch. Just past nine. She wasn't expecting anyone except Sian and she'd come round the back way. Hoping it was a delivery and not a time-consuming caller she wiped her hands on her apron and went to answer it.

It was someone she recognised but only after he had smiled and said his name. It was the man from the bookshop.

'James,' she said. 'Do come in. I confess I'd completely forgotten you were coming today.'

He hesitated. 'If there's a problem, I could easily come back another time.'

'Oh no – no problem. It's just I'm having a dinner party this evening and your coming slipped my mind. Come through. Would you like some coffee? I'm about ready for a cup.'

She established James Langley in the library with a large mug of coffee and some home-made biscuits, rejects from the sables she had made to go with the gooseberry fool. She'd offered him a radio for entertainment but he'd declined. The books were more than enough for him; music or background noise would be a distraction.

Back in the kitchen, still feeling guilty for having forgotten he was coming, Fiona set about making chocolate brownies for her third pudding. She knew it was pudding overkill but she suffered badly from 'hostess anxiety' and decided she'd worry less if she could feed thirty people instead of the eight she was expecting.

There was a gentle knock on the door and Fiona jumped and dropped her knife on the floor. It was James.

'Sorry to startle you. I've brought back the mug and my plate.'

'Oh no need to do that.' She picked up the knife and wiped it on her apron.

'You're obviously a very good cook,' said James, looking round the kitchen at the signs of Fiona's efforts.

'Not really. I mean, sometimes it comes off OK, but I'm

not reliably good. Not like some people I know – people who are coming!' She winced and put her knife down of her own accord.

'I always feel that good cooks aren't people who can follow a recipe and make it look vaguely like the picture, but those who can make meals out of what's lying around in the refrigerator.'

'I can do that, actually. As a wife and mother you have to, most of the time. Are you married?' She could have bitten her tongue off but she managed to keep her expression bland.

'Not currently.' He smiled, apparently not offended by her question.

She nodded, approving of his good sense. 'Not sure I would go through all that again, to be honest. It takes so long to break a spouse in, don't you think? And I made such a mistake after my first husband died.' She paused. 'Why am I telling you all this? Why did I even ask you if you were married? I am so sorry! I think it's what people call over-sharing.'

He laughed again. 'It's because we were talking about marriage. It made you think about it.'

'I was talking, you were just being bored but not showing it. More coffee? Anything I can do to make up for the over-share?'

'No thank you, I'm doing very well.'

'I'll make you some lunch later.'

'No need to do that. I did bring sandwiches.'

'I'll be making soup anyway. I've got Sian, my young neighbour and her son coming. He's gorgeous. I'd marry him in a giddy minute.'

'And how old is he?'

'Four. Sad, isn't it?'

'Well, there's a danger that someone else might snap you up while you were waiting for him.'

Fiona chuckled. 'I doubt it, somehow.'

He smiled at her. 'I'd better get back to work.'

'And so should I.'

They exchanged looks for a second and Fiona realised she'd enjoyed chatting to him. He didn't seem that keen to rush back to the library either. 'Is it very boring, sorting out old books?'

'No. It's fascinating and I love it. But I mustn't waste any more of your time.'

'I'll tell you when the soup is ready.'

Just as James turned to leave, Sian and Rory entered the kitchen.

'I knocked and called but you didn't answer, so we just came in.' Sian looked at Fiona and then James. 'I hope I didn't interrupt anything.'

'No, no, not at all. I was expecting you.' She smiled and said, 'This is James – James Langley, bookseller.'

'Hi,' said Sian, shaking his hand and adding, 'Are you looking for first editions of James Bond with their dust jackets?'

James laughed. 'No. I don't think there's anything like that here. But there are many other treasures.' He turned to Fiona and said, 'Would you mind if I used the desk? For my record-keeping?'

'Use anything you think you need, of course!' said Fiona. 'Are you sure you wouldn't like another coffee? The soup will be a little while yet.'

'Don't make soup specially!' said Sian. 'You've got enough to do. Rory and I have brought some pasties we made. They'll be plenty for lunch.' She looked at James. 'And for you too, if you'd like.'

'I brought sandwiches,' James said to Sian. 'But a home-made pasty would be far nicer.'

Sian chuckled. 'Actually, you don't know that. Rory helped with them quite a lot.'

'Ah, the man Mrs Matcham would marry in a giddy minute,' he said.

Fiona laughed. 'That's right! And do call me Fiona. Please. Otherwise I'll have to revert to calling you Mr Langley, and you've been James in my head for a while now.'

A flicker of emotion crossed James Langley's face and Fiona suddenly realised she'd said something that sounded significant. 'I'll make some coffee,' she said quickly, 'to keep you going until lunchtime.'

'Well, I'll just settle Rory with some toys and I'll meet you at the barn, Fiona.' Sian moved towards the door. 'Don't be long.'

Chapter Six

When Fiona caught up with Sian at the barn door, wearing a determined expression, she suddenly felt a bit weak.

'Do we have to do it today? I know it was my idea but I can't believe I suggested it on the same way as a dinner party.'

'Well, you said you wanted it at least started before the dinner party. Why don't we just do a bit this morning and then this afternoon we'll concentrate on the house and the food?'

Fiona realised she wasn't going to be able to get out of it and she was quite well ahead with her menu already. 'OK, I'll just find my boiler suit.'

'Boiler suit, Fiona?'

'It was my husband's and I can still fit into it. It's also very warm, and has had so much paint splattered on it, it's practically waterproof.'

'Get it on, then!'

'And I'll find some gloves. I've got loads of pairs.'

Soon the two women had the barn doors open and were staring at the piles of furniture that confronted them.

'OK,' said Sian. 'We need to sort. A keep, sell, paint, chuck—'

'Or burn.'

'—areas,' Sian finished, laughing.

'Right!' said Fiona, trying to sound decisive, but not moving.

Sian glanced at her friend and saw she was frozen in indecision. She picked up a table that turned out to be a nest of tables. 'Keep?'

Fiona shook her head. 'You know I hate nests of tables.'

'Well, sell them.'

'Who on earth would want them? And how would I sell them anyway?'

'Just put everything you want to sell in a corner and get the local auction house along. They'll at least get rid of it. If it's got woodworm or anything, we can have a massive bonfire.'

'Oh yes! That sounds fun.' Fiona sighed. 'I'd probably be happy to burn all of it really.'

'Not at all!' Sian was horrified. 'You just don't know what's here, that's the trouble.' She paused. 'Tell you what, if you put the kettle on again, I'll make a start. It won't be so hard to make decisions when it's not all piled in a heap like this.'

Fiona was longer than she meant to be as she had to get the brownies in the oven. Eventually she went out.

Sian had got on well. 'Over there are nice pieces you might want to keep, if you don't sell them. Several of them would be good for me to paint but then they'd have to stay here until I did it.

'Now, what about those.' She indicated a fumed-oak dressing table with too-small drawers and a very spotted mirror and matching wardrobe.

'Burn or sell,' Fiona asked. 'Ghastly.'

'OK. But what about this?'

Right at the back, still partially concealed by odds and ends of furniture, was the most enormous cupboard.

'It's huge,' said Fiona. 'No one would want it. I'm not sure what it is, even.'

'I think it's wonderful!' said Sian.

60

Fiona turned to her, shocked. 'You do? Why?'

'It's a horrid dark, gloomy thing now,' she said, 'but imagine it a sort of distressed Scandinavian grey, with a red undercoat. Put it at the end of a huge kitchen. It would be an armoire.'

'I'm never sure what that means . . .'

'Oh, I think it's a posh cupboard, but this is lovely! It would swallow up an entire kitchen and have room for seconds.'

'Well, you have it, darling. I don't want it.'

'Fiona! Just imagine it finished.'

Fiona couldn't picture it, she just saw a monster, overpowering everything and probably full of spiders. 'I'm sorry, I just can't. But seriously, I'm more than happy for you to have it, to do what you like with.'

Sian considered, hands on hips. 'The trouble is, I'd have to work on it here. We couldn't move it ourselves and the reason I need a barn is to work on pieces like that. I couldn't do it at home.'

'That's all right. We'll get rid of everything we can, and anything we can't shift, you can paint.' Suddenly the task didn't seem so enormous now the first bit had been done.

They were both filthy and hot by the time they declared they'd done all they could. As well as the armoire, Fiona had given Sian a chest of drawers to work her magic on. For her part, Sian had insisted Fiona choose something she'd like painted for herself, and she'd found a small nursing chair which would be very pretty in her bathroom.

When they'd eaten pasties and sandwiches for lunch, Fiona turned her attention to her house and the imminent dinner party. Sian, refreshed, took Rory to Annabelle's.

*

A few hours later, James found Fiona in the kitchen dithering between wrapping little bundles of beans in strips of leek so she could steam them, or using streaky bacon and frying them. The first version would be fancier – and healthier – but she knew the bacon would add flavour and be delicious.

'Anything I can do?' he said. 'You sighed.'

She turned to him. 'Did I? It's probably because I can't make up my mind about these wretched beans and my wine waiter is going to be late.'

'Your wine waiter? That does sound grand.'

'He's not really a wine waiter, just a friend who was going to choose some wine for me from the cellar.'

'That sounds a very pleasant task. Can I do it? I'm not a bean expert.'

'Are you a wine expert?'

'Not in a professional way. I'd call myself more of an enthusiastic amateur.' He smiled and Fiona warmed to him yet more. He had a calming aura.

She returned his smile. 'That'll do for me. But you have to come to the dinner party. Otherwise I can't let you help.' She paused. 'Is that emotional blackmail?'

James considered. 'Possibly, but in a good way. And I'm very happy to accept.'

'That's such a relief. I'll show you to the cellar. There is a lot of wine down there. It needs drinking.'

'Would you like all the same wine? Or different ones?'

'Just one sort of each colour, I think. But nothing too strong. I think there's some Côtes du Rhône.'

'I'll find something. I think I know what's needed now.'

'The champagne is already in the fridge. I decided against cocktails. They're no fun unless they're incredibly strong and that can end up being a bit antisocial,' she said a little hesitantly.

'Good choice,' said James, possibly sensing that Fiona was wondering if she should chop a mountain of mint for mojitos, in case.

'Will the champagne be too cold, do you think?' Fiona was glad about the mint really. She did have enough to do without that, and she had insisted Sian go home after a long stint of helpful peeling and chopping and moving furniture out of the conservatory.

'I don't think you should worry about any of these things. After all, you'll take it out of the fridge to take into the garden, won't you?'

'Of course. I wish I could stop fussing.'

'You're not fussing, you're just preparing. Now, the wine?'

Fiona exhaled, allowing herself to relax just a little. It wasn't that she hadn't given plenty of dinner parties over the years, but for some reason this one was making her unusually strung out. 'The cellar's through that door and down some steps. Will you be all right or do you need me to show you?'

'I'll be fine,' he said firmly, disappearing down into the cellar.

'And I'll answer the door if anyone comes early,' said Sian who had just reappeared, showered and changed and looking fresh and pretty in a summer frock. She obviously sensed that Fiona was panicking. She took the apron from her and propelled her towards the door. 'Now, go and get dressed!'

Fiona got downstairs on the stroke of half past seven.

'You look amazing!' said Sian, kissing her. 'Really lovely! No one would ever know you'd spent all day slaving over a hot stove and moving furniture.'

'I totally agree,' said James, smiling. 'I hope you don't mind, Sian let me use the bathroom to freshen up a little.'

'No, of course I don't mind!' said Fiona, feeling expansive and generous. 'And if you want something different to put on, my son has some shirts here. Some of them are quite wearable.' She smiled. 'In fact, some of them are still in their packets. I'm always buying him clothes. He says, "Thanks, Mum, they're great," and never opens them. You might feel the same way about them, of course.'

'That would be kind. This shirt has expired, really.'

'Let me find them for you—' Fiona was about to lead James upstairs when Sian stopped her.

Sian was firm. 'No, Fiona, point us in the right direction and we'll find the shirts. You go and have a drink and prepare to greet your guests. There's a bottle of champagne open. James didn't think you'd want to do it just when you're greeting your first visitor.'

Obedient and grateful, Fiona went out to the garden where Sian had arranged candles and fairy lights round the paving in such a way that a performance of *A Midsummer Night's Dream* would have seemed appropriate. Perhaps it was just a little over the top for a dinner party – even a large, al fresco one – but there was an atmosphere of expectancy, as if magic was indeed about to happen, and Fiona was thrilled.

Honeysuckle perfumed the air and the jasmine in the conservatory wafted its contribution. A discerning sniff and Fiona detected roses. They were so lucky with the weather! Later in the summer this heat would seem oppressive and desert-like, now it was just wonderful.

As she sipped the glass of champagne that James had poured her before he and Sian went upstairs she decided she was glad Robert hadn't been able to come early. Now he could see everything perfect without having had to take part in the mechanics of getting it right. Then she remembered how many times he'd mentioned the house and hoped he didn't think it was all for his benefit. The other guests would appreciate it too.

The Francombes and Robert were both fashionably late. Sian insisted on acting as butler and letting guests in. Fiona wasn't at all happy about this until Sian said she found it quite easy to open a door and show people through, but not at all easy to make conversation with virtual strangers.

Sian had finished clearing up the kitchen (despite Fiona insisting she shouldn't and she didn't want her to ruin her own outfit) and was wondering if she should go and join the others in the garden when the bell rang.

'Oh! Where's Fiona?' said a large, well-dressed woman with a massive scarf wrapped round her. 'Are you the help?'

'Of course she's not the help, darling,' said a good-looking if slightly plump man who followed his wife. 'She's a helpful guest.'

'That's right,' said Sian, remembering that the 'how to entertain' booklet had referred to hiring the daughters of friends to be waitresses. They must be the Francombes. 'Now, is there anything you want to leave? Or shall I show you through?'

The bell jangled again, swinging to and fro on its coil.

'We'll find our own way, thank you, dear,' said the woman, whom Sian found herself warming to, although the word 'smug' had obviously been invented for her. She was so confident: a self-made woman completely satisfied with her creation.

Sian opened the door to a man who was tallish, quite good-looking with a decent amount of hair. She was sure this must be Robert and she could see perfectly why Fiona had said he couldn't be 'the one'.

'Hello?' he said, putting his hand in hers and squeezing it hard. 'I'm Robert Warren. Are you Fiona's daughter?'

'No, just her friend. Do come in. Everyone's in the garden.'

Robert Warren stepped over the threshold, looking about him. 'Good Lord! This place must be worth a few bob!'

Sian flinched but continued to smile. 'Follow me to the garden.'

'Do you know if it's mortgaged?' he asked in an undertone.

'I have no idea!' said Sian. 'Do come this way.'

Sian watched Fiona at the head of the table and felt proud of her. Everything was going brilliantly. There was enough room in the conservatory now half the plants had been removed, the table looked lovely and the Francombes were unable to hide their amazement at the elegance of the occasion. The food was delicious. Sian felt grateful that she'd talked Fiona out of parcelling up her green beans and just added crispy bits of bacon to them to make them special. She and James had helped clear away the asparagus and then James had carved one leg of lamb (perfectly pink) while Fiona did the other one. Robert, to Sian's private annoyance, just made slightly disparaging comments about the quality of the wine. If he'd actually been rude she'd have said something, but he was just dismissive. Fortunately Fiona didn't hear. Sian found she was enjoying herself. She didn't go to many dinner parties – when her parents held them she usually found herself out with friends for the evening – and despite the fact that she knew Fiona's wouldn't be a stuffy affair she had been concerned she might feel somewhat overwhelmed, but she didn't. And although her dress was a little frayed round the hem, she knew it suited her and she didn't feel too out of place amongst the peacock display of outfits around her. She'd had a long conversation with Margaret Tomlin who owned the boutique and whom she'd promised to visit with examples of her work. She even found herself able to converse with Melissa without wanting to wince.

They were on the cheese course, prior to the puddings, and Sian was just thinking how lovely Fiona looked when she heard a noise. Some sort of engine. It sounded terribly near, as if a vehicle was actually in the gravel drive, when usually people parked round the back.

She caught Fiona's eye. She had heard it too and obviously wanted to investigate. The noise got louder and more worrying. Sian was about to offer to go when there was a screech of brakes and the noise of metal against stone.

Sian would have run to check, but she was hampered by the chairs on either side of her. Fiona looked worried and then her expression changed as she saw the man standing outside the conservatory.

'Fuckity fuck fuck', said a male voice from across the lawn. 'Who put that bloody cherub there?'

There was a pause. Nobody spoke. Everyone looked expectantly towards the sound of the blasphemer. An intruder wouldn't have sworn so loudly, and would have probably done his research and known about the cherub. So who was it?

A tall dishevelled-looking man appeared in the doorway. 'Oh sod it. It's a dinner party. Hi, Mum!'

Sian, who had been trying to shift her chair to allow a bit of movement away from the table, hadn't seen the man who'd spoken. Now her view of him was obscured as people got up to make way for Fiona as she squeezed through to reach him.

She saw him wrap his arms round his mother and bend to embrace her. And then he looked up.

She thought she was going to faint. She thought she was dreaming. And then she realised she wasn't, and she wanted to run away.

A sip of wine gave her some thinking time. No one had noticed her reaction, they were all greeting the Prodigal, but Sian knew any second Fiona would start on introductions.

Fortunately, Melissa got up. 'Angus!' she squealed delightedly. 'Do you remember me? The last time you saw me, you pushed me in to the nettles!'

The commotion went on. Melissa was now hanging on to Angus, giving everyone the impression they had been childhood sweethearts, and his pushing her in the nettles was what boys did to girls they liked. For all Sian knew, this was true. Carefully, she pushed her chair back and was halfway out of it when Fiona called her name.

'Sian! Darling! This is Angus! Angus, this is Sian, my neighbour and helper. I don't know how I'd have managed without her, in fact.'

Sian forced herself to look up. Gus, the father of her child, looked back at her. He'd hardly charged. Tall, sun-streaked, dark-blond hair and a wicked, crooked smile.

'Sian?' he said, staring at her as if she was a statue come to life or something equally bizarre. 'Sian! What the hell are you doing here?'

Sian found that all the saliva in her mouth had dried up and her head was swimming. She felt a physical jolt. All the desire she had felt for him the first time round came back in a rush. How could her body betray her like this? She was in trouble. She took another sip of wine, hoping it might make it possible for her to speak.

'I . . .' was all she managed. She just couldn't believe he was here, in real life, the man who had taken her heart, her passion, her dreams, and run away with them, leaving her only with her much-loved son. Come on, brain, she implored it. Think of something to say! If only he'd got less attractive in the past five years, but he hadn't, he was the same, only more – of everything!

'Have you met before?' said Fiona. 'What an extraordinary coincidence! Why didn't you say you knew my son?'

'I didn't know!' Sian managed to speak at last. The wine had helped. 'I had no idea Gus was your son. You talked about Angus.' She frowned. 'And your surname is Matcham!' Just in time she stopped herself adding, 'Not Berresford.' His name shouldn't be engraved in her memory and the fact it was must remain a secret.

'So you two *have* met before?' asked Melissa, sounding proprietorial.

'Oh yes we have,' said Gus emphatically. 'We very much have. Although it's been a long time since we saw each other.'

The way he looked at her made it very clear he was remembering their time together in detail and Sian blushed as she remembered too. She was extremely embarrassed to be having such memories in a room full of people, all of whom seemed to be staring at her.

'How did you meet?' asked Melissa.

'At a party,' said Gus, 'just before I went away.'

The party. They met in the kitchen. Sian had gone in for some water and Gus had been there. He'd found a glass for her and filled it. When he handed it to her their eyes had met. Sian remembered the bolt of electricity that passed between them; it was seared on her brain. Sian had taken the water but didn't go back to the group she'd left. Gus had taken her hand and drawn her into the corner next to the table and then stood in front of her, as if cutting her off from the rest of the party. She remembered that she should have felt trapped but instead felt guarded, protected. And they talked. For hours. Eventually he said, 'Shall we get out of here?' and she'd nodded. Without saying goodbye to anyone they'd left the flat and got a taxi to his place. It was completely out of character for her, but she couldn't stop herself. They'd kissed in the taxi and could hardly tear themselves apart to get out of it. Gus had handed the driver a wodge of notes, probably to apologise for their behaviour and because he didn't want to waste time finding out how much he owed and counting the money.

Sian remembered tripping over some packed boxes as they got to the bedroom but she only found out he was leaving for a long, long trip the next day. By then it was too late, she was hopelessly in love, in lust, in thrall, whatever it was. Reluctantly she'd agreed that it was more sensible for them to part without promises to keep in touch, to remember this wonderful night as just that, with no regrets. After all, Gus didn't know when he'd be back.

'And you haven't seen each other since?' asked Fiona.

'No,' said Sian, dragging herself back to the present.

'I went away the next day,' said Angus. 'I mean, the day after we met.' He was looking at her just as he had then. When they parted, the Sunday morning, he had looked down at her with such sadness. He had cupped her cheek with his hand and held it. She knew then she would never regret that night of heavenly sex and she never had, even when she very first discovered she was pregnant. Now she cleared her throat, trying to think of something to say that would stop him looking at her like that, as if he might rush her upstairs to bed that very minute, ignoring the five years since they'd seen each other and his mother's dinner party.

At last reason took over. She'd grown up a lot since then and she had responsibilities. Much as her body would like that to happen, her head told her that she couldn't behave like the mad girl she'd been then. She had too much to lose. Her sanity for one thing. Her feelings were in turmoil, and she wished she could just run away, but she owed it to Fiona to try to carry on as if nothing had happened, as if she hadn't met a man she never expected to meet again, a man who still seemed every bit as dashing and carefree as he had been. She couldn't afford to admit – even to herself – how strong the attraction still was.

To Sian's huge relief, Fiona fell into mother-mode. 'Have you eaten, darling?' she said.

Gus turned to his mother. 'Um – no. I'm starving.' Then his gaze went back to Sian. She turned away quickly and busied herself with her napkin. His gaze was too piercing.

'Let's find him a chair,' Melissa said. 'Here, there's space by me.' She patted the seat beside her alluringly.

'Let the boy sit next to his mother,' said Margaret Tomlin firmly.

A chair was found, space made and Gus sat down.

'So, darling,' said Fiona. 'What took you so long to come home?' Then she put an anxious hand on his arm. 'Unless it's private . . . ?'

'Yes,' said Melissa, 'do tell. Have you got a wife and six children somewhere in Outer Mongolia?'

'Not that I know about,' said Gus, with a grin. He turned his head towards Melissa and while Sian couldn't see his expression, she could tell he was flirting.

Sian, who was still desperately trying to get her emotions under control, smothered a sigh. He was still able to charm the birds off the trees, she realised with a flash of jealousy, and admonished herself for such a thought. He could behave how he liked with anyone he wanted to. He wasn't hers, he never had been. And what on earth was she going to do about Rory? Gus was the

71

best lover she'd ever had, or would ever have, she was sure of that, but was he father material? That was the important point. From what Fiona had said about her son (much as she loved him dearly) and from what Sian had gleaned about him herself, she knew that he liked to take risks, he flirted with danger and he didn't like anything that might constrain him or take him away from doing what he loved best: taking off at a moment's notice to discovered and undiscovered lands alike. She'd have to make sure he wasn't going to take off again before she even thought about telling him he had a son. She couldn't put Rory through anything that might potentially hurt him; she couldn't put *herself* through that.

'So, if it isn't a deep dark secret, what have you been doing?' Melissa persisted. 'We've missed you!'

Gus turned to his mother with a look of triumph. 'I've been writing a book. Well, I've started anyway. I know you didn't believe me, but I have and I've got an agent. And he's going to send it out to publishers in the autumn – providing I've finished it by then, of course!'

'Oh, darling! I'm so proud!' Fiona beamed. 'I know that's what you planned to do but I thought with your dyslexia—' She stopped, possibly wishing she hadn't mentioned the thing that had made his school days so difficult.

'Lots of very creative people are dyslexic,' said Margaret. 'A friend of mine says it's a gift, not a handicap.'

'But why did you have to stay away to write it?' Melissa pouted, implying she had a right to demand he stayed near her. 'Surely the whole point of being a writer is that you can do it anywhere.'

'Probably easier to write about the place you're in,' said Fiona, a little briskly. 'Now, Angus darling, I'm dying of curiosity. How do you and Sian know each other? Did you know she's got a delightful—'

'Oh, don't bore him with that,' said Sian, 'I've got a little boy,' she said with the briefest of smiles, 'but other people's children are frightfully tiresome, aren't they?'

'Not necessarily,' said Gus, giving Sian a look she took to be stern – only that could have been her guilty conscience, she realised.

'Rory's not tiresome, he's adorable!' said Fiona, 'but maybe—'

'I've met him,' said Melissa, 'and he's a little angel, but maybe not all that interesting when we've got Angus here to tell us all about his adventures.'

Talking about Rory was the last thing Sian wanted to do and she should have felt grateful to Melissa, yet somehow she couldn't.

'Tell us about your adventures,' insisted Melissa. 'I'm sure we're all agog.'

Sian forced herself to stay calm, although all she wanted to do was go home and hide until she'd had time to take in the fact that he was here. But she couldn't leave now. She'd just have to wait it out a bit longer. She could go after the coffee, she promised herself. That wouldn't look odd. And she could help Fiona with it. That would speed things up and let her get away sooner.

She had to admit, as he regaled them with all of his adventures, Gus was very entertaining and she was sure that if he wrote as he spoke his book would be brilliant. While he talked he kept sending her meaningful glances. Sian couldn't acknowledge them. She didn't want her contradictory emotions to be stirred up any more. She caught his glance once, by mistake, and saw he was confused. He obviously couldn't understand why she hadn't greeted him as if they'd only just parted the morning before and she would be more than willing to carry on where they'd left off, in bed together. If it weren't for Rory, and to some extent Richard, and a whole host of other things, a part of Sian would have liked that too. But that was a lifetime ago, and she had been another Sian then.

It was a relief when she could get up and help Fiona clear the table.

Chapter Seven

Gus, thought Sian, for the hundredth time since she'd left Fiona's fateful dinner. What was she going to do about him? As Rory had been enticed with promises of a visit to 'Be Like a Monkey' – an indoor play area – to stay for the day after his sleepover, Sian had plenty of time to think without the distractions a four-year-old usually provided. She half wished Jody had called to say he was desperate to come home and she would be listening to his chatter right now instead of dwelling on the bombshell that had crashed Fiona's party. Still, Richard was coming to lunch so she could distract herself by thinking of him and being creative. There was nothing like looking through cookery books to calm the nerves. Then she remembered Richard didn't like adventurous food.

As she fried onions to garnish the top of the macaroni and mixed butter, sugar and flour to make a crumble, reproducing 'Good British Cooking' circa 1950, in fact even while she brushed her teeth and put on her makeup, rather than thinking about her guest, she found she couldn't help thinking about Gus – again. After all, she'd thought about him most of the night. She couldn't help it. But the more he filled her mind the more confused and unsettled she felt. She didn't have the time or emotional energy to get into a state over it. She just didn't know how best to deal with a situation she had never dreamt would happen. Here was Gus, living practically next door to a son he didn't even know existed. How did she go about telling him? Did she need to tell him? Could she risk telling him? Would he make a good father? Rory – and she – needed stability and someone who was reliable and who would be there for them. Someone who wouldn't just provide the fun and adventures in life, but someone who was there to deal with school and not getting into the football team.

She hardly knew anything about Gus, really, despite spending half that night – that wonderful night that seemed like a distant dream – talking to him. And although she knew she was still physically attracted to him she didn't know how she really felt about him; not now, not after nearly six years. No, she'd decided firmly as the blackbird heralded the dawn chorus outside her window, until she felt she – and Rory – were ready, Gus mustn't know that Rory was his.

The doorbell broke through her muddled thoughts. Richard was a bit early, she thought as she went to the door, but it wasn't Richard, it was Fiona and Gus.

Both Sian's heart and stomach seemed to go into freefall. She wasn't remotely ready to face him, but she didn't seem to have any choice. So, fixing what she hoped was a bright smile of welcome on her face, she said, 'Oh, hello! Fiona, I would have thought you'd have spent the day in bed after yesterday!' She kissed her friend, keeping up the chatter so she wouldn't have to speak to, let alone look at, Gus.

'Hello, Sian,' he said, following his mother into the cottage. He kissed her cheek. 'You left quite early last night.'

'I developed a bit of a headache,' she said, flushing. Heartache more like, but you couldn't take a paracetamol for that. She mustn't let either Fiona or Gus know how thrown she was. She must act as if it was the most natural thing in the world for the two of them to have popped round after the dinner party the night before – which of course it was. They didn't need to know what a bombshell Gus's arrival had been for her.

Gus didn't look convinced by her answer. 'So you weren't avoiding me, or anything?'

'Good Lord no!' said Sian, a little too expansively. 'Why would I want to do that?'

'Darling, don't interrogate her! Have we disturbed you, Sian? And where's Rory? I've been telling Angus all about him, and he's very keen to meet him.'

Oh the relief! 'He's not here. Annabelle's mum is taking them all off to an indoor play space where they go up and down slides and ladders and scream. I'm making lunch for Richard.'

Just at that moment, there was a knock on the door. Richard: bang on time. Sian took a step towards the door just as Gus, who had ambled into the kitchen called, 'I see you share my mother's habit of over-catering.'

'I'd better let Richard in,' Sian said nervously. Then she had a thought; it might be a good thing if Gus and Fiona stayed. Having Richard there would divert Gus, and having Gus there would stop Richard from asking her again if she'd changed her mind. What's more, Fiona had fed her so many times since she'd moved down here the least she could do was be welcoming and invite them to stay. 'Why don't you two join us for lunch?' she asked in a rush and then opened the front door and greeted Richard, reaching up to kiss his cheek, and saying, 'Do you mind sharing lunch? There's an old friend of yours here, and Fiona.'

Somehow when Gus came out of the kitchen to greet Richard, he was the man in possession. He looked very at home here in this cottage, as if he were the one who visited her regularly and Richard was the almost-stranger. Sian could see it wasn't right, but there wasn't anything she could do about it.

'Richard! Good Lord! Haven't seen you for years! What are you doing with Sian here?' Gus demanded jovially.

'I don't believe it!' said Richard. 'Gus! As I live and breathe! I think I should be asking you that! Sian is my—'

'Gus came with Fiona,' said Sian, cutting him off. She knew he was about to refer to her as his girlfriend but they'd made it a rule – well, she had – that they should always refer to themselves as just friends or, in Richard's case, a friend with aspirations. At least until Sian was ready to go public.

Fiona, who still appeared to find the situation quite amusing, was in the kitchen, checking on the crumble which was just the right side of burnt. She put it carefully on top of the stove and greeted Richard. 'Hello, Richard. I haven't seen you for ages. How are your parents?'

'Oh, they're fine.' Richard squeezed into the kitchen and kissed Fiona's cheek.

'It would be lovely if everyone could go into the other room,' said Sian. She'd managed to get most of her turbulent emotions under control. If she kept busy, she'd be absolutely fine. 'There're some beers and a bottle of wine,' she continued, and then noticing Fiona gathering up her handbag, she said, 'Fiona, Gu— Angus, do stay for lunch. Unless there's anything else you'd rather be doing?'

'Are you sure?' asked Fiona. 'We don't want to intrude.'

'I think we *should* stay for lunch,' said Gus firmly. 'There's loads and I can't resist crumble. Besides, Richard and I have a lot of catching up to do.'

'Well, could you do it in the garden?' said Sian, tension making her snappish. 'I need to set the table.'

'Men are like dogs sometimes,' said Fiona, spreading the tablecloth Sian had given her. 'Safer with lots of space around them.'

'Definitely. But they go back a long way, they'll need a good chat. Glass of wine?' Sian didn't wait for her friend to reply before pouring a couple of glasses and handing one to Fiona. 'Now, what have I got to do? Oh yes, dressing for the salad. So, what did I miss last night?' Keep it light, thought Sian as she collected ingredients.

'You missed Melissa making up to Angus as if he were George Clooney and she'd had his love child.'

Sian flinched at the word 'love child'. She knew perfectly well that Fiona was just making a lighthearted remark, but Sian suddenly realised that it wasn't just Gus she had to keep from finding out he was Rory's father, it was Fiona. And women were much more perceptive than men. She was lucky Rory had inherited her fairer colouring. That might fool the world for a bit. 'And how did Angus react?'

Fiona shrugged. 'I think he was quite amused. She's a pretty girl, after all.' She paused, obviously not wanting to be seen to pry but desperate for information. 'How well do you and Angus know each other?'

'Not well at all. We met just before he went away. It was years ago.

'But he remembered you.'

Sian nodded. 'Good memory, obviously.'

Fiona sighed.

'So,' said Sian, 'tell me about *your* love life. Did Robert kiss you goodnight?' Too late she realised that they had not, officially, been talking about her love life. She hoped Fiona wouldn't notice. She was going to have to be so careful. Every word was a potential minefield, it seemed.

'On the cheek, yes.'

'And James? Did he kiss your cheek?'

'Yes, but let's face it, all the men did. It's what people do.'

'True, even when you're just being introduced.' She added a teaspoon of mustard to her vinaigrette. A new anxiety occurred to her: supposing Gus had told his mother about their affair? Presumably he hadn't done it already or Fiona would say something, but he could at any time.

'You've put mustard in already,' said Fiona a few moments later, giving her a funny look. 'I think you want the honey now.'

'Oh yes! How silly! I was miles away.'

'Tired, I expect.'

'I've no excuse to be tired. Not like you. Now let's take this through and get the men in.' She didn't want to confess to Fiona about how little she'd slept.

'So, Gus, when did you turn up like the bad penny?' said Richard before putting a large forkful of macaroni cheese into his mouth and chewing vigorously.

'Last night,' said Gus. 'I didn't know my mother was having a dinner party and had put a cherub right in front of the garage door.' He sent his mother a mock-angry look which made her smile. 'My foot slipped off the clutch and the Land-Rover shot forward into it.'

'And he came into the conservatory, swearing loudly, Richard,' said Fiona calmly. 'In front of all my guests. It was such a shame you couldn't be there.'

'I know. I miss all the good invitations – well, almost all.'

Richard looked at Sian meaningfully. She smiled, feeling awkward. Why on earth had she thought it a good idea to invite Fiona and Gus to stay? How could she have ever thought she would be able to behave naturally? Looking at the two men now, she couldn't help comparing them. She was so fond of Richard but she knew her feelings for him had never been as strong as those she'd instantly felt for Gus all those years ago. Not only was Gus a very good-looking, easy-going man who drew everyone in with his enthusiasm and lust for life, they had a chemistry between them that defied logic. Richard was kind and thoughtful but they'd never have that essential connection. However, she knew that her feelings for Gus could so easily have been purely physical and were not the basis for a lasting, supportive relationship. She knew without a doubt that Richard could give her security and stability for Rory. She couldn't say the same about Gus.

'And what have you been up to while the rest of us have been making an honest living?' Richard spoke lightly but there was a hint of challenge in his teasing.

'Oh, you know, the usual. Writing a book, stuff like that.' Gus winked at Sian.

Not knowing why he had done this, Sian passed the salad to Fiona, wondering if she was the only one to feel tense.

'So, Richard, how was your trip?' asked Sian, ladling second helpings on to his plate without asking if he wanted it. 'Where were you, exactly?'

'Dubai, as usual.' Richard frowned slightly. He always went to Dubai and Sian knew that.

'It always sounds so glamorous,' said Fiona. 'Skyscrapers, shops, hotels, all springing out of the desert. I've always wanted to go to the desert, ever since those Turkish Delight adverts that were on when I was younger.'

Richard smiled politely. 'I don't get out into the desert, I'm afraid. I just get to see the skyscraper part.'

'Oh, what a shame,' said Fiona.

'I'll take you to the desert, Mum, if you want to go. You too, Sian.'

Gus smiled at the two women. Richard frowned. Sian didn't entirely blame him – Gus did look a little pleased with himself.

'So, what do you do in the desert, or wherever you happen to be?' said Richard.

'I travel, sometimes on my own, sometimes with indigenous people. I make observations, take notes. What I'm most interested in is learning ancient skills and crafts.'

'And can you earn a living from it?'

'Not really. It's very hard. That's why I've written a book.'

'So you'll go back to the wilderness when your book is published?'

Richard was behaving a little too like a firm-but-fair headmaster for Sian's liking. They were just having a casual lunch. If Gus took offence it could all get awkward. Although she had to admit Richard was asking the sort of questions she'd like to know the answers to.

'No. I'm home for a while now. I had an accident to my leg that took a long time to heal. If you can't trust your means of transport you don't want to be in the middle of nowhere.'

A rush of emotion – a mixture of relief, confusion and anxiety – caused Sian to give a little cough. Both men looked at her questioningly.

'Um, seconds – thirds, even – anyone? There's loads. Blackcurrant crumble to follow, courtesy of Fiona, who gave me the blackcurrants from her freezer.'

'I think pudding,' said Richard decisively. He smiled at Sian. 'And have you . . . ?'

She nodded. 'Yes, I've made custard. Otherwise I've got some ice cream if you'd prefer?' She looked questioningly at her other guests.

'Custard sounds lovely,' said Fiona.

'Are you another Bird's fan, Fiona?' asked Richard, smiling at her. 'Not many people seem to use it these days, but Sian makes it just as I like it.'

'So you're a good cook then, Sian? I didn't know that about you.' Gus smiled in a sexy way and Sian hoped fervently that neither of the others intercepted it.

'Making custard is a lost art,' said Richard, 'although I expect you can do it perfectly,' he added to Fiona.

'Thank you for the compliment,' she added, 'but actually, I always get lumps in it. It was one of the things that broke up my second marriage.'

'Surely not!' said Sian, getting up and beginning to clear the plates.

'Well, it's the little things, you know,' said Fiona.

'And those little things can make a relationship as well as break one,' said Richard, looking at Sian with undisguised fondness.

'I can't believe we're all getting so heavy about custard!' The plates gathered, Sian retreated to the kitchen.

Gus picked up the salad bowl and the remains of the macaroni and followed her out.

'You've got to love a girl who can make Bird's custard,' he said, taking the wooden spoon out of the saucepan and licking it.

Sian turned away so he wouldn't see her sudden smile. 'It's a lost art, remember. Right up your street.'

'I know,' said Gus. 'I know.'

It was such a relief when Richard got up to go that Sian hugged him goodbye more enthusiastically than she meant to. He hugged her back and she realised she'd given him completely the wrong message.

Annoyed with herself she went back inside to find Fiona washing up in the kitchen and Gus stalking about in the sitting room, picking things up and putting them down again.

'So you and Richard are good friends?' he asked, picking up a pen and taking it apart.

'Oh yes. He's been really helpful. He found me this house and his sister runs a nursery where Rory goes.'

'Just good friends? Or is there something more to it?'

She gently removed the pen. 'I don't want to talk about it.' It was the sort of question you only make up a really good reply to several hours later, she realised. And she didn't want to talk about Richard to Gus, it was none of his business.

Gus picked up a photograph. It was of Sian and Rory, taken about a year ago. 'So this is the famous Rory? He's very like you!'

'Yes!' She possibly sounded a bit too relieved as she said this but he didn't seem to notice.

'So do you see his father?'

'No. No, not for years.' She smiled, trying to indicate that this was fine. 'We're on good terms though. It's not a problem.'

'So Richard's my only rival then?'

He gave her a crooked, teasing smile and it sent Sian into a panic. She couldn't be sure if he was really teasing or not. 'Don't be silly!' She laughed nervously. 'Anyway, what do you mean rival?'

'I was kind of hoping we could carry on where we left off?' He raised an eyebrow in a comically suggestive way.

'God no.' Sian shivered. It was all getting far too personal. Memories of that wonderful night flooded back, and here she was alone, with Gus. She couldn't let him see the effect he was having on her.

'Calm down! I wasn't suggesting we rush upstairs right now.'

Sian was horrified to discover that she suddenly felt tearful. Part of her *wanted* to rush upstairs with him but the sensible, practical side of her knew she had to think of Rory now. She mustn't even hint to Gus she still found him infuriatingly attractive. And anyway, there was yet another part of her that wasn't sure how she really felt about him, she just knew his arrival had turned her ordered world upside down. Her emotions were in complete turmoil and she didn't like it. She bit back the tears. Her sleepless night had obviously made her over-wrought and emotional. 'Gus, please don't talk like that.'

She turned away from him so he wouldn't see she was upset but he came up behind her and put his hand on her shoulder, turning him round to face her. 'Sian, I'm sorry, I didn't mean—'

Like an angel sent from heaven, Fiona breezed into the room. 'OK, that's the big dishes out of the way. Come on, Gus, we must leave Sian in peace now.'

Sian collected herself, smiled at Fiona and said, 'Yes, actually, I'm expecting Rory home at any moment.'

'I'd love to meet him,' said Gus, concern still etched on his face.

'You will, darling,' said Fiona, 'but I expect he'll be terribly over-tired and ratty just now and Sian won't want you meeting him then.'

'That's right,' said Sian. 'That's exactly how it is.'

When she was alone she realised that not only did she not want Gus meeting Rory when Rory wasn't at his best, she didn't really want Gus meeting him ever. But of course she knew that wasn't possible, and even if she didn't tell him Rory was his son, she did want Gus to like him. A mess of contradictions, she slumped on the sofa. Why was life so complicated? Perhaps she should just marry Richard after all. There was more to life than passionate sex.

Richard would be much better at the really important things, like caring, providing and nurturing. Gus would be hopeless at that, she was sure. And Rory needed a proper father, not an adventurer who would disappear off at a moment's notice. She leant back and sighed. Then she heard Jody's car draw up and, pulling herself together, she headed to the front door to welcome Rory home.

Fiona and Angus walked back home together, the hoods of their waterproofs pulled up against the rain that was now pouring down. Whilst it was welcome for the gardens it was somewhat unexpected after the glorious weather they'd been having.

'Sian's a lovely girl, isn't she?' said Fiona, knowing she shouldn't, but unable to stop herself. She instinctively felt Gus and Sian had known each other a lot more intimately than either of them had let on. But she had to be careful. Gus would clam up the moment he felt his mother was 'interfering'.

'She is.'

She could divine nothing from her son's simple statement. 'And Rory's gorgeous! I love Rory.'

'Can't wait to meet him.'

'And she helped me so much with my dinner party. I must have them both over for a meal to say thank you.'

Gus glanced down and Fiona noted the playful smile in his eyes. 'I think that could start a weird pattern, couldn't it? You have a dinner party, Sian helps you, you have to have another one to thank her, she helps you . . . ?'

'But she doesn't need to help me any more,' said Fiona wickedly. 'I've got you.'

Angus laughed and Fiona thought how nice it was to have that rich colour in her aural world again. Maybe that was one of the reasons she'd tried internet dating; she missed male voices. Robert had a nice voice. Not a perfect voice, but still nice. James's was even nicer, she realised. 'So how did you and Sian meet again?' she asked, trying not to sound as if she was prying.

'At a party. As you do.'

'Only if you go to the right sort of parties,' said Fiona, aware that she didn't. (Hence the internet dating.)

They walked in companionable silence until they'd nearly reached the house, and then Angus said, 'Mum, I have to warn you, there's a van coming with my stuff in a couple of days. Have you got anywhere to put it?'

This was a bit of a surprise. Angus always seemed to travel light through life. 'How much stuff? I could easily stash your sleeping bag behind my couch, to quote an old song. But a houseful of furniture might be a problem.' She was trying to downsize not add to the clutter.

'It's not furniture, but there is a fair bit of it.'

'What is it?'

'Tents, yurts, equipment.'

Fiona considered. 'The barn has a bit more space in it now. Shall we go and look now or wait until the rain has stopped?' She'd promised Sian she could use it to paint her furniture in but it was a large barn – there should be room for everything.

They went in through the back gate to the courtyard. 'Here we are. It's quite a bit more organised than it was.'

'What's this monstrosity, Mum?'

'Oh, that's an armoire I've given to Sian. We couldn't shift it with just us, so she's going to paint it.'

'If you can't move it, paint it?' Angus raised his eyebrows.

Fiona laughed. 'Well, it seemed easier at the time.' She paused. 'Is there enough for what you need?'

Angus surveyed the few square feet that was empty and laughed.

'Not quite enough, Mum.'

'Oh.' Just how much stuff *did* he have, she wondered.

'Only if we get rid of more of this.' Angus made a sweeping gesture.

'We can do that, but where will Sian paint her furniture?'

'Maybe we can share,' he said after a moment.

Fiona shivered. 'Shall we go inside?' she said. 'It's raining, in case you hadn't noticed.'

'This isn't rain!' said Angus. 'This is the gentle tears of the gods, showing their disappointment with the world.'

It might have been a while since she'd last seen her eldest son, but Fiona still recognised when she was being teased. 'Let's go in and have another cup of tea. And for your information, this is rain. And we should be glad to have it.'

In spite of Sian's diligent clearing up, the signs of the dinner party were still evident in the serving platters piled up on the worktop, the rows of glasses, clean but not put away and an army of empty bottles lined up by the recycling bin.

'I think you'd describe that as a "serried rank" of bottles,' said Angus.

Not entirely sure she wasn't being reprimanded, Fiona put the kettle on. 'I do always wonder if people realise that refers to teeth.'

Angus leant against the worktop. 'So why such a big bash, Mum? It's not like you, is it?'

'Actually it is like me, but Jeff never let me have more than six, including him and me. Now I don't have to worry about what he thinks any more, I've gone expansive.'

'That can't be it. Jeff has been out of our lives for years and years.'

'I owed people,' she went on. 'And one of the reasons I gave the party was so Sian could meet Margaret. Do you remember her?'

Angus shook his head. 'There were several people at that dinner party I didn't know. And a couple of them were men.'

Fiona concentrated very hard on not reacting. If she didn't look guilty he wouldn't ask any more questions. It seemed silly to worry. She was a grown woman and could do what she liked, but after Jeff she was anxious not to do anything that might upset her boys. 'Oh? Well, I wanted to welcome Sian to the area, and meet Margaret, who might stock her furniture in her shop.'

'I see.'

Fiona laughed. 'I'm sorry so many of my guests turned out to be your old flames.'

He frowned and Fiona sensed tension in him, which surprised her. He was probably travel-weary.

'And it must have been quite a shock arriving to find the house so full,' Fiona went on. 'I still don't quite see why you didn't ring to say you were coming.'

'I thought you'd flap around getting ready and I just wanted to surprise you.' He looked at his mother quizzically.

'And you did. But you can't blame me if you were a bit surprised yourself.'

Chapter Eight

When Sian opened the door to Gus the next day her first feeling was relief that Rory wasn't there.

Then she noticed he was wearing shorts, old trainers and a T-shirt. He'd obviously been jogging and her body responded to the energy he exuded.

'Oh, hello,' she said as casually as possible. 'Couldn't you make it all the way home? Needed a rest?'

He smiled. 'No, but I saw your car, thought it must mean you were in and so called on the off chance.' He grinned. 'Just to be neighbourly, you know.'

Pleased and anxious at the same time, Sian opened the door and let him in. The smell of fresh sweat and after-shave caught her nostrils as he passed and she was sent dizzyingly back to their first meeting and what happened afterwards. Smell really was the sense that brought memories flooding to the front of one's brain, she realised, wishing he wasn't so loyal to Geo. F. Trumper West Indian Limes Cologne. She knew what it was because she remembered seeing it in his bathroom; he'd told her that he used it because it reminded him of his father. Afterwards, before she'd been sensible and worked on forgetting him, she'd sniff it in department stores, and remember.

She cleared her throat and led him through to the narrow kitchen. 'Would you like coffee? Or water? Or something?'

He threw himself down on to one of the two chairs drawn up to the tiny table. 'Water, then tea, if that's OK.'

Sian gave him his water and then clicked the switch on the kettle, wishing she could think of something to say. There were some of Rory's trains on the table and she gathered them up.

'So your kid likes playing with trains? We've got some up at the house.'

'We know about them. Rory plays with them often. I hope you don't mind.' She poured boiling water into mugs.

Gus laughed. 'What sort of a man would I be who minded if someone played with my toy trains?'

Sian laughed too, relaxing a little as she reached into the fridge for the milk. She could do this. They could have a perfectly easy conversation without it throwing her into a panic. 'Well, you know, some men are very possessive about their toys.'

'I'm possessive about some things, but not about play-things I discarded years ago.' He became serious suddenly. 'I do hope you don't think I discarded you. I never would have done that.'

'No. Oh no, I knew you were going away. I always knew the score. Listen, would you mind if we went through to the dining room? The kitchen is not the best bit about this cottage. The dining room is lovely and sunny.'

'It needs knocking through, really,' said Gus, following her.

'I know, but it's not my house. Sit there.' She pointed to the big armchair and put his tea on the table beside it. She didn't want to find herself sitting next to him. He was far too large and unsettling. She seated herself on the sofa opposite, pulling her skirt over her knees in an unconscious gesture of self-defence. Somehow she knew Gus wouldn't give up. He obviously wanted to talk about that night. She'd have to be grown-up about it and let him know that the past was the past. She'd moved on. He couldn't expect her to behave as if nearly six years in between their first meeting and now hadn't happened.

'So, Sian, I'm longing to know, what have you been up to since I went away? It's been a long time.'

'It has, hasn't it? Well, let's think.' It all seemed a long time ago. 'Was I working in a bar? While I was looking for something actually connected with my degree?'

He nodded. 'That's right. I remember you telling me about the man who always came and stood by you and it was only afterwards you realised he fancied you.'

'I'd completely forgotten about that.'

'I've got a good memory.' His look told her exactly what he was recalling; it made him smile.

'Of course, I've had a child since then,' she said, placing a hand on her stomach in remembrance.

'Oh yes.' His look altered slightly but the smile remained.

'Yes, that did take up quite a lot of the time,' she said briskly and then smiled, to indicate she was happy with the situation.

'But you didn't get married?' He frowned slightly, as if he'd assumed she would have.

'Oh no. It was quite a short relationship.'

'I'm sorry.' He leant forward as if to take her hand as a gesture of sympathy, but she sat back in her seat, avoiding his hand. He smiled. 'Do I gather you weren't left heart-broken?'

'Oh no,' she lied, smiling again. 'Nothing like that. I was very surprised to discover I was pregnant, but once I'd got over the shock, I was delighted.'

'I thought of you, you know. A lot. As I was walking across the frozen waste on snow shoes.'

'Did you? How strange. I can't quite imagine myself being thought of in such a wild terrain.'

'You feel I should only think about you when I'm some-where safe in England?'

'Yes, that sort of thing. Maybe while you're drinking tea, or something homely like that.'

He laughed. 'I'd never thought of people having special places to be thought about, unless you mean graves, or where ashes are scattered. But to tell the truth, I found it hard not to think about you.'

Aware she was blushing, Sian fiddled with her mug and then got up. It was getting awkward. She wasn't ready for this conversation, and might not be, ever. 'More tea?'

'No, I'm fine. Sian, please sit down, I want to talk to you.'

'Well, you are talking to me.' She knew she was blushing again and hoped he'd just think she was hot. Come to think of it, she was hot. She got up and opened a window.

'So, tell me, what brought the city girl you were to a little backwater like this?'

'I don't think of myself as a city girl. Not now, anyway. I've started growing my own vegetables and everything.'

'But why here? I know it's a lovely village but it's a bit of a coincidence, you moving practically next door to my childhood home.'

She was indignant. 'You're not accusing me of stalking you, are you? I didn't have any idea you were Fiona's son before you walked into the dinner party.'

'So if you're not stalking me, which is a bit of a shame, why are you here?'

Sian gave herself a couple of moments to answer. 'It was because of Richard really.'

'Oh, Richard.' He seemed to condemn Richard as being nice but not much more just by saying his name. 'You were rather evasive yesterday. Come on, tell me now, are you and he – you know – together?'

She should say yes immediately, without hesitation. After all, she and Richard might be together, one day. But she did hesitate and then found she couldn't lie.

'Well, not really. I mean, sort of. He's an old friend, of course, and he's been brilliant, but it was partly because his sister – who Rory knows well – was setting up a play-group, which meant if we moved here, he could be looked after somewhere he was happy while I worked. And it is a nice area, with a good school, a shop, post office, not too far from London.' She realised she'd gone on too long and had ended up sounding like an estate agent.

But Gus seemed not to notice. 'Come to think of it, we were at Richard's party when we met, weren't we?'

'Oh yes,' said Sian, wondering how much interest in their shared past she should admit to.

'But you must have moved on quite quickly after our – fling – if you've got a son who's about to go to school.'

'Not really. Well, maybe.' Sian picked at some paint lodged in the edge of her nail, aware Gus must think she was a slut by now. From a starting-school point of view, Rory could be a year younger than he actually was.

'I hope I didn't sound judgemental. I didn't mean to. There was no point in hanging round waiting for me, after all.'

'No.' Sian felt better. He didn't think she was a slut and he was right, they'd agreed not to contact each other after that night, to not even exchange mobile numbers.

'So how old is he? Rory, is it?'

'Um . . .' She went into a state of panic. She knew he was just being polite but she couldn't even hint that she might have got pregnant that night. 'I don't know!' she blurted and then felt a fool. 'What I mean is . . .' What she meant was, she couldn't instantly work out how old it was safe for Rory to be.

Gus was looking a bit bewildered.

'I'll make some more tea.'

Sian got up, grabbed their mugs and rushed to the kitchen, frantically doing sums in her head. She was in danger of making the situation worse.

'Hey, don't worry, it was only a casual enquiry,' Gus called from the dining room as Sian came back carrying two fresh mugs of tea, aware she would be horribly caught out if she lied. Rory would be having his birthday soon. Maybe she could put one less candle on his cake if Gus was likely to be around. No, she'd make it a children's-only party.

'So,' she said, deciding that only a complete change of subject would get her out of this mess. 'Shouldn't you be writing your book?'

The crooked grin that had first attracted her across a crowded kitchen had the same effect now. 'I've only just got back. I need some time off before I start work.'

'Don't you want to finish your book then?'

He shrugged. 'I've got to earn my living somehow, but will a book do that? I'm not sure. I'm a bit nervous about it, to be honest. I have an agent who says he can sell it for me if I do it right. I do have lots and lots of photographs. Perhaps it could be a coffee-table tome.'

Sian was surprised by Gus's uncertainty. He always seemed so assured and confident. She'd enjoyed his tales at the dinner party despite her anxiety that evening. She couldn't help being interested. The artist in her adored photographs. 'I'd love to see them,' she said, before she remembered she didn't want to have any more to do with Gus than she could help.

'Really? I'll bring my laptop over sometime and show

you. Or you could come up to the house. Mum's trying to make more space in the barn. She told me she's promised it to you to paint furniture in. I've got a whole load of gear coming that needs to go somewhere. I've wondered about the attic.' He paused. 'My mother seems to have got rather a lot of clutter.'

'I got the impression it's because people keep thinking they can store things in her house, because she has lots of room.'

'You don't mean you think I'm doing that too? Hey! Give me a break. She's my mum. It's my home. Where am I supposed to keep my stuff?'

Sian chuckled. 'At home, of course, but she might need – does need – help sorting things out. We've made a start on the barn, but I bet the attic and all the spare rooms upstairs are full too.'

'You're a good friend to my mum, aren't you? She told me.'

'Well, I am very fond of her and she's been wonderful to us.'

'Without her even knowing that we knew each other.' Gus looked across at Sian with an expression she couldn't read. 'Although we didn't know each other very long, did we?'

'No.'

'But quite well.'

Sian blushed fiercely again. It was wrong of him to refer to their time together, most of which they'd spent in bed. But he seemed to be determined to bring it up, again and again.

'Well, it was very intense,' she said firmly, as if trying to dispatch it to the past and imply there had been no leakage to the present. He mustn't know she had gone on reliving those hours for a long, long time, despite her head telling her not to.

'I thought of you continuously,' he said. 'I really wished we hadn't been so grown up about it; that we hadn't decided not to exchange contact details because we knew I was going away.'

'It seemed right at the time.'

'I know, but later, it seemed so wrong.'

Sian didn't know what to say. Not having contact details had made things easier for her in some ways; she couldn't tell him about Rory, or at least, not easily. At the time her mother had said this was an excuse: she knew his name, she could get in touch with him somehow. What was the internet for? Sian had replied it was for shopping, and eventually her mother had accepted that Sian did not want to track down the father of her baby and let the matter rest. She hadn't yet told her mother about Gus reappearing in her life. At least, she'd told her that Fiona's son had appeared at the dinner party, but not who he was. Of all the villages, why had she moved into his? And why had he come home?

She shrugged. 'Hindsight and all that.'

'Did you think about me, ever?'

Never had Sian been so grateful for a knock on the door. She ran to it, aware she was behaving completely erratically.

'Oh, Melissa! Now nice!' she said, inordinately pleased to see someone she didn't like very much. 'Do come in.'

Melissa was looking adorable in a flatteringly low-cut floral dress that would definitely qualify as a 'frock'. Sian, in her work clothes, was slightly less pleased to see her now.

'I hope I'm not disturbing you.'

'Oh, it's all right, I'm disturbed already. Gus is here.'

'You mean Angus? I always knew him as Angus. But how nice.'

The two women went through the kitchen into the dining room. Gus got to his feet. 'Hi, Lissa. Good to see you.'

'I went round to your house to thank your mother for a lovely dinner party,' Melissa said. 'I thought you were jogging? Your mother told me you were.'

'I was jogging. I called in on Sian for a drink.'

Melissa frowned slightly.

'So, would you like a cup of tea or something?' said Sian.

'Oh, yes please,' said Melissa with unseemly haste. It was obvious she intended to stay. 'Have you got green tea? I'm cutting down on caffeine.'

'I might have,' said Sian, going into the kitchen to look.

'I just love this little house!' she overheard Melissa saying to Gus. 'I want to buy it. Sian's only renting.' There was a giggle. 'It would be fun to live next door to each other, don't you think?'

'I'm sure it would be,' Gus agreed. 'But Sian and Rory live here.'

'But only renting,' said Melissa.

From the kitchen Sian couldn't quite tell how enthusiastic his response was. There was an unnerving silence from the dining room now. Were they locked in a passionate embrace? Or was Melissa measuring up for curtains? She made the tea as quickly as possible.

As she brought it through, adding some biscuits to the tray that she'd forgotten about earlier, she decided the guilty couple weren't exactly springing apart but they seemed easy in each other's company.

'Lissa tells me she's hoping to buy this cottage,' said Gus.

Sian forced a smile as she gave Melissa her mug. 'And I'm hoping Luella doesn't want to sell it. I love it here.'

'But you could find somewhere else to rent, surely?' said Melissa.

'I'm unlikely to find somewhere with enough garden to grow my own vegetables, convenient for Rory's playgroup, and later on, his school.'

'Oh,' said Melissa. 'I want to be near my parents.'

Not wanting to start an argument, or even a discussion about who had the greater need to live in her current home, Sian offered Gus a biscuit.

'I came round to see if I could have the full guided tour,' Melissa went on, while Gus crunched on his Hob Nob. 'If it's convenient.' She smiled prettily. 'Although of course, you're entertaining.'

'Just a bit,' said Sian, smiling weakly.

'But I'm sure Angus wouldn't mind, would you? By the way, your mother's dinner party was amazing! So elegant!'

There was just enough surprise in her voice to make Sian feel offended on Fiona's behalf.

'I know, I was there,' said Gus, smiling.

'Oh yes, so you were. Talk about arriving with a bang!' Melissa held his gaze and Sian looked away so she couldn't see how long they looked into each other's eyes.

'More tea, anyone?' she said after a few seconds.

'I'm cool, thank you,' said Melissa. 'So would it be OK to see round? I'm sure Angus would like to, too.'

'I'm sure he wouldn't! Why would he?' said Sian, looking at Gus, hoping he'd confirm what she'd said.

'Actually, that'd be interesting,' he said. 'I've always wondered about this little cottage.'

'Great!' said Melissa, getting up. 'Shall we go now?'

'Give me two minutes upstairs,' said Sian, giving in to the inevitable. 'You can show yourselves round down here.'

Sian barely had time to put yesterday's underwear in

the linen basket and resettle her duvet on her bed before she heard them coming up the stairs.

'Of course I'd gut the place,' Melissa was saying. 'That kitchen is horrible and I'd probably want to extend out the back quite a lot. But with work and money it could be rather darling.'

'I think it's rather darling now,' said Sian, meeting them on the landing, although she did agree about the kitchen.

'Of course it is,' said Melissa. 'It just could be so much better. So, is this the master?' She went into Sian's bedroom. 'No en suite? Still, you could knock through and make this single into quite a good one, I think.' Melissa peered into the room next door and then back again, obviously imagining herself already living here in style.

'That's Rory's bedroom. I'll just clear the floor so you can go in. You stay there!'

She scooped up some toys and stuffed a pile of clean clothes behind the curtained cupboard that was his wardrobe. She was just straightening the Thomas the Tank Engine duvet when Melissa and Gus came in.

'Yes! Perfect as an en suite-cum-dressing room!' said Melissa.

'But you'd be losing a bedroom,' said Sian, not wanting to think about Rory's bedroom being turned into a bathroom. 'Always a bad idea. It would reduce the value.'

'But you've got another bedroom,' said Melissa from the passage, pushing open the door. 'Oh.'

'Wow!' said Gus, over her shoulder. 'That's amazing!'

The room was bare apart from the chest of drawers that Fiona had given her, which stood on a piece of newspaper, drying. She joined the other two in her workroom.

'Please don't anyone touch it,' she said, feeling protective but also pleased by their reaction to her work in progress.

She'd sanded it back and painted it white. On top of the white were flowers, strongly reminiscent of Van Gogh's *Irises*. The top was plain, but it made a little artwork all on its own, Sian felt. She planned to offer it to Fiona as a thank you for making her so welcome.

'So this is what you do?' said Gus. 'It's amazing.'

'It is!' said Melissa. 'I'm really impressed! You can do art, not just decorating.'

'I try,' said Sian, also trying not to smile. 'I did go to art school.'

'Would you do something for me?' said Melissa, turning to her enthusiastically. 'I have some vile fitted wardrobes. You could paint them for me.'

'Not if you're planning to sell your house.'

'It's all right, I live with my parents!'

Sian smiled. 'Better check with them, then. It's quite a lot of money to spend on a room you're going to move out of.' Sian didn't want to do herself out of a commission but she always gave this caveat if she was asked to paint built-in furniture.

'Of course I'd check, but I think you should do something quite tasteful, like roses growing up or something. Mummy would *love* that,' said Melissa.

Sian glanced at her watch. 'Um, is there anywhere else you'd like to see? Only I've got to go and pick up Rory in a minute.'

This was a lie, but it would make them leave.

'I think I've seen enough for now,' said Melissa. 'The upstairs is bigger than I imagined. It is a sweet house.'

'Yes,' said Sian, forbearing to add, 'and possession is nine-tenths of the law.'

'Tell you what, come up for a drink later,' said Gus, who had been looking out of the window. 'And bring Rory. I'd love to meet him.'

'I'm not sure—' said Sian.

'You too, Lissa,' he said with the lazy smile any woman would find hard to resist.

'That would be lovely,' said Melissa with a little sigh. She hooked her hand through Gus's arm. 'What time would you like us?'

'About six?' said Gus. 'Sian? Would that be OK for Rory's bedtime, things like that?'

'Um, maybe. Can I get back to you on that?' No way was Sian going to be bringing Rory round for drinks with Gus if she could possibly help it – and certainly not if Melissa was going to be there too. On the other hand, Rory and Gus would have to meet sometime. She'd see what sort of mood her son was in when she picked him up. She wanted him to be feeling very sunny the first time he met his father, even if neither of them knew what was happening.

Later that day, when it really was time to pick him up, Rory emerged from playgroup with his arm round Annabelle. 'Mum!' he said. 'Can Annabelle come and play?'

'I should think so, darling,' said Sian and turned to Jody. 'Would that suit you? Rory's been to you so often.'

'Oh that's fine,' said Jody. 'It's as easy to have two as it is one, I often find.'

Once again Sian mentally thanked Fiona for introducing her to Jody. Not only because she helped out with Rory but because she was proving a very good friend. She was fun and it was good to have a friend her own age.

The two women walked back towards the car park chatting. 'So, have you got anything exciting planned for later?' asked Sian.

'Not really. There's footie on the box which means I not

only have to put up with spending all evening in the dining room, but with the yells and swearing as well,' said Jody. 'Men, eh. You're better off on your own. What about you?'

Sian suddenly felt it would be nice to have someone around, even to get irritated by. 'Oh, we've been invited out to drinks but I don't want to go really,' she said. 'It makes it so late for Rory.'

'Tell you what,' said Jody, 'why don't I come over and babysit?'

'I couldn't ask you to do that!'

'Yes you could. I'd love it. Home alone with the remote control all mine.'

'But it's early. Six o'clock.'

'Well, if you feed Annabelle with Rory, and then drop her off for me, at about five thirty, I can deal with the others and be with you by six. John can do bedtime before the match starts.'

'It seems a huge imposition . . .'

'No, really. It would be an escape for me.'

'OK,' said Sian, having thought for a bit, 'as long as you'll tell me if you want me to babysit in return. Rory could sleep on the sofa. We've taken advantage of your kindness often enough.'

'Deal! Although just having Annabelle to stay over would do. I can farm the boys out to other friends if we need a night out.'

'I could do a weekend if you wanted to go away.'

'You're a doll, thank you!'

As Sian wrangled the children into the back of the car and into their seatbelts, she wondered if she could confide in Jody about Gus, and then thought not. Much as she liked her, they hadn't been friends that long. It would be more sensible to keep her thoughts and worries to herself. That way they wouldn't grow legs. And, after all, she hadn't even told her mother everything.

With Jody happily ensconced in front of the television with the remote, a cup of tea and cupcakes made by the children, Sian walked up the road a few hours later, trying to pretend she was just going for a glass of wine with Fiona, and not that she was going to see the father of her child and if she was honest with herself, which she wasn't, a man she still found desperately attractive. She was also trying not to admit to herself that she was excited at the thought of seeing Gus again, because that made her feel guilty about Richard. Oh, she had to get her emotions under control.

Fiona met her at the door. 'No Rory?'

'No, Jody is babysitting. She wanted to get away from the football. It's very kind of her. Rory was a bit tired so better for him, really.'

'Sorry to miss him, but come on through. We're having champagne in the conservatory. You can stay for something to eat if you haven't got to rush back.'

She arrived just as Gus removed the cork from a bottle of champagne with a promising hiss. She gestured to him in greeting.

'Hi, Sian. Sit down, let me bring you a drink. You didn't bring your son?'

'No, he's in bed. He was tired after playgroup. A friend is babysitting.' She sank into one of the comfy chairs that had been brought back in from the garden. 'This is nice. I'm quite tired myself.'

'Here, have this.' He handed her a glass of champagne and smiled into her eyes. She looked away. Perhaps this wasn't such a good idea after all.

Fiona came in, taking off her apron. 'Give us a drink,

darling, there's a dear.' She sat next to Sian. 'Have you been busy?'

'Mm, I've managed to get quite a lot done though. Rory had Annabelle to play and after we'd made cakes, they got on so well I could really crack on. In fact' – she smiled, feeling a little smug – 'I've got something to show you I think you might like.'

'Oh, how nice! Have an olive.' Fiona handed Sian the bowl and then took a full glass from her son. She took a long sip.

The three of them were just settling into a companionable silence when there was a call.

'Hello! Anyone at home! I've been ringing but no one heard me.' Melissa came into the conservatory, smiling brightly.

Fiona jumped to her feet. 'Melissa! How lovely to see you.' Sian could tell this was the last thing she felt and wondered if Gus had forgotten to tell her he'd invited her. 'Do have a drink.'

Gus got up and handed Melissa a glass of champagne. 'Hey, you,' she said to him, kissing him. He kissed her back.

He hadn't kissed her, Sian realised, with a pang. The fact that she'd been sitting down and was hard to reach was no excuse. Then she reprimanded herself. He could kiss or not kiss whomever he liked.

'Hey, Lissa,' he said. 'What's up?'

'No one but you calls me Lissa any more, I love that you do that,' Melissa said delightedly and coiled her arm round his waist.

'So, Melissa,' said Fiona, 'how are your parents?'

'Oh, fine! Mum's organising something or other as usual.' She laughed charmingly. 'After all the lovely food you cooked the other night, she might rope you in!'

Sian sensed she wasn't alone in wanting to kick Melissa, who was clutching on to Gus like a drunk to a lamppost. She quite wanted to kick Gus too.

'You flatter me, Melissa. Your mother is a much better cook than I am.'

'Well, we won't fall out over it,' said Melissa. 'Anyway, I've come to issue an invitation of my own. I feel so grown up!'

She would have jumped up and down and clapped her hands had it not meant letting go of Angus, Sian could just tell.

'So what is it?' Gus disentangled himself and pushed Melissa gently into a chair.

'A picnic! Such fun. There's a fund-raiser for the local hospice, sort of like a gymkhana for adults, only with stuff for the littlies too, of course. I want you all to come. You too,' she said to Sian.

'Oh no, my mother might be staying,' said Sian, realising too late that as Melissa hadn't given a date, her excuse might not hold water. Although her mother was coming to stay, and very soon.

'You could bring your mum. She and Fiona can chat. I'm not sure if my parents are going to be around for chatting. They'll be running round like blue-arsed flies organising everything. We've got to get people to come so I thought it would be fun to get up a gang.' She looked at Gus in a way that told the world she would have preferred it to be a gang of two.

'It might not be suitable for Rory,' said Sian. She wasn't at all sure what a gymkhana involved, nor at all keen to find out.

'Oh no, it would be brilliant for Rory,' said Gus. 'Unless he hates horses.'

'He hasn't really met any,' Sian confessed.

'I'm sure he'd love it,' said Fiona. 'I'd have thought there'll be lots of things to do.'

'Oh, there will be,' said Melissa. 'My parents have been arranging it for months.'

'I'm surprised I haven't heard about it before,' said Fiona, a smile lifting the corner of her mouth.

'I don't think Mum and Dad thought you'd be able to do anything to help. But of course we need punters as well as helpers!'

'There's bound to be some sort of retail opportunity, isn't there, Melissa?' said Fiona.

'Oh, loads! Cashmere, crafts, jewellery – loads of stuff. Mum's pulled in all sorts of favours. It's at the castle.'

'Oh,' said Fiona, suddenly a lot more interested. 'It won't be open to the public, will it?'

''Fraid not. We tried, but they wouldn't do it. Can't blame them. Don't want civilians snooping around, even for a good cause.'

'I think it'll be fun,' said Gus determinedly. 'I think we should all go.'

'Sweetie!' said Melissa, jumping up from her seat and kissing him again. 'You're a doll.'

Sian sipped her champagne and suddenly felt deflated. Shortly afterwards she decided there was no point in her staying any longer. Gus and Melissa were happily reminiscing about their blissful childhood and Fiona had disappeared to prepare supper, whether *à deux* (mother and son) or *à trois* (mother, son and Melissa) Sian didn't know, or care. She knew she had no right to feel like this, but it seemed her jealousy couldn't be rationalised away. Watching girlie telly with Jody seemed a much better option.

Chapter Nine

❧

After Sian had gone home and Melissa had finally left too, Fiona went upstairs, leaving Angus slouched in front of the television. She checked her email; there was one from Robert. She opened it out of politeness but as it seemed to be about some item of furniture he was interested in and that should prove to be a real bargain, she didn't feel obliged to answer. If she hadn't already decided on their first date that she didn't want to see him again, the dinner party had confirmed this. He was perfectly pleasant but Fiona didn't need any more 'just' friends, not friends like him anyway, and if the spark wasn't there you couldn't manufacture it.

She found herself going to the dating website again. Luella had told her firmly (by email) that she was stark staring mad to stop doing it just because the first man didn't turn out to be a winner. Luella was right, it was time to get back into the ring.

To her surprise and delight there was indication of interest from someone else. She clicked through to his profile and he seemed gorgeous. Certainly more dashing than Robert.

She left a message to indicate that she was interested and went downstairs. Really life was a lot more fun when you took a few risks. Maybe she'd wasted the first forty-odd years of her life being safe? Maybe now was the time to break out?

Fiona checked on the dating website the following day. There was a message from Mr Dashing: *Fiona, lovely woman, would you care to come with me to a garden centre? I need some advice and I'm sure you're just the woman to give it to me. On Sunday? Yours, in expectation, Evan.*

Sunday, thought Fiona, that would be lovely. Something to look forward to. Helping other people spend money was always fun!

She typed an enthusiastic reply, and the arrangement was made.

Fiona was excited at the prospect of another date. It would be good for her to focus on her own life. Recently she'd found herself mentally putting Sian and her son together in her head, in spite of the exuberant Melissa, jumping up and licking everybody's face like an enthusiastic puppy. And there was Richard, of course, although Fiona wasn't sure how the land lay there. Sian didn't talk about him the way one did about a boyfriend, but then every relationship was different and he certainly liked Sian, that much was obvious.

Possibly a bit rashly, Fiona didn't alert Sian to her plans this time so she could text to make sure all was well. There were several reasons for this. For one thing she knew Sian's mother was staying with her and they might well be off doing something, and for another she was meeting Evan in a garden centre. What could possibly go wrong in a garden centre? She had been expecting a slightly more glamorous venue, but she'd mentioned her interest in plants so it was a good choice, really. Maybe he was just being considerate.

She found the address. It was one of those huge, out-of-town places that sold an awful lot of things besides plants and garden furniture and made Fiona sigh nostalgically for an old-fashioned nursery that only sold plants, not Christmas decorations and 'gifts'. However, a lot of them had very good cafés; a nice piece of cake might rescue a disappointing date. Evan was at a table by the coffee-shop entrance as arranged and he stood up when she approached. He had a silver, triangular beard – not a feature that appeared in his photograph.

'Fiona, dear lady,' said Evan, taking her hand and kissing it. She didn't know if she was charmed or horrified. Was he delightfully old-fashioned or a creep? No doubt she'd find out soon enough.

'Now, sit down and let's have coffee. Or would you prefer tea? Hot chocolate?'

Fiona sat. A tiny bit of her was relieved – there was absolutely no need to have alerted anyone to her where-abouts – the rest of her was disappointed. She could tell she was going to be bored within seconds. It had been a waste of time coming. Why she'd ever thought Evan was a bit dashing was now a mystery. He couldn't dash his way out of a wet paper bag. He made Robert look positively dynamic!

'So, dear lady, tell me about your garden? My own little bit of heaven isn't what you might call large, but nor is it small.' He laughed, a high, contrived sound that made Fiona wince. His 'dear lady' was now beginning to grate too. He went on to describe every bed, every border, every water feature (there were several, involving angels, doves and windmills). He had beds edged with cockle shells (scallops shells really, obtained from a fishmonger, my dear), wind chimes and a sweetly pretty 'arrangement' (pronounced the French way) of woodland creatures so lifelike, even the local squirrels were confused. Apparently it was the remote-control fairies that did it.

Initially the description had a gory fascination – she

had a secret passion for kitsch – but eventually she decided life was too short and she should make her polite farewells and go home to her own garden. Dealing with the convolvulus was a whole lot more fun than listening to Evan's description of removing duck weed from his pond, tiny plant by tiny plant.

Suddenly she was aware that he was looking questioningly at her. He had obviously said something she should have listened to. There was no way she could bluff her way out of it; she'd have to confess.

'Sorry, I was just a little distracted. Can you say that again?'

'I suggested,' said Evan, hurt, 'that we move on to a little nursery I know well where they have some rather special plants not generally available.'

Fiona opened her mouth to make her excuses. Although to her the thought of a special nursery was like a half-price sale at a designer outlet to many people, the thought of more precious hours of her life being spent with him was too much. But before the right words came to her he put his hand on hers.

'Dear lady, don't refuse me. I hate going to these places on my own. They make me feel quite vulnerable. Then I promise we'll have drinkies. I know a nice little place.'

Cursing her kind heart, Fiona weakened. 'OK.' She got to her feet, anxious to end the torture and get on to the good stuff. 'Where is it?'

'Well, I think it would be better if you just came with me in my car. I can drop you back here later. There isn't much parking there, you see. It's up a bit of a track. Much easier if we go in the one vehicle.'

Fiona hesitated. She wasn't worrying about breaking the rules of internet dating, they hardly applied to this courteous but boring person, but she didn't like being dependent on other people for lifts. She wanted to be able to leave when she wanted to. 'I'd rather take my car if you don't mind.' She was about to offer to take Evan but thought better of it. She'd lose her independence just as much if she gave him a lift as she would if she travelled with him.

'I think you'll find it would be better if you came with me. It's a little hard to find and if you lost me, we might never catch up with each other again.' Evan smiled and Fiona wondered what the downside of never seeing him again would be. She couldn't think of one.

'Please, dear lady,' he went on. 'Otherwise I'll think you don't trust me to keep you safe.'

Fiona sighed and gave in. 'Oh well, all right then, but I mustn't be late back. I've got my son living with me now and he's hopeless in the kitchen.' The fact he did find it easier to cook in the open air didn't mean he'd starve if she wasn't there, but she wanted her excuses built in.

'I understand. I myself am a competent cook, though, truth be known, not every member of the sterner sex can say the same.'

'Shall we go?' said Fiona. She was losing the will to live.

She got into the front seat of a Volvo and, having held open the door, adjusted her seatbelt and then shut her firmly in, Evan got in next to her.

'So does the nursery specialise in anything in particular?' she asked. 'I have limey soil, I'm afraid, so no rhododendrons for me.'

'Epimedium, Erythronium and ferns,' said Evan.

Although she was a fairly experienced gardener, the only one of these that Fiona recognised was ferns. 'Oh, I love ferns,' she said, hoping her ignorance of the other two would go unnoticed. She realised if she'd had any

112

chemistry with Evan she'd have just asked what they were. But if she did ask, he'd tell her. At length. She hoped she'd recognise the plants when she actually saw them.

It was quite a way to the nursery and the route was complicated. She could see the point of travelling in one car, although the more miles they covered, the more she wished she'd taken her own car and just got lost. She began to feel out of control, too far away from her car for comfort. She counted up in her head how quickly she could reasonably ask to leave. The further it was the longer it would take them to get back.

'Is there anything particular you're looking for?' she asked.

'Not really,' said Evan. 'I find it's better to just see what's there, although in my carefully crafted little plot, only the daintiest specimens are welcome.'

'Maybe we shouldn't go all that way if we're not going to buy anything.' Fiona had never managed to visit anywhere that sold plants without buying anything. 'My garden is full too.'

'I expect you're fortunate to have a much bigger garden than I have, but I find it a little oasis of green.'

'Oh.' Fiona had assumed because she lived in the country that Evan did too. 'Is where you live built up, then?'

'I'm surrounded by fields,' said Evan. 'But I like order. Nature is all very well but it needs to be controlled. What about yourself?'

Fiona wondered why he hadn't just said 'you'. 'I like a bit of wildness, personally.'

There was a pause. 'I picked that up in your emails,' said Evan.

Fiona began to feel a little uncomfortable, although she couldn't tell why. All she was really in danger from was a very long and boring afternoon. He was a man obsessed with his garden who tried internet dating. It didn't mean he was odd, just dull.

At last the car turned into a narrow lane that had a weather-beaten sign saying 'Squirrels Nursery' and Fiona instantly felt happier. Her overactive imagination had somehow created a sinister scenario and however hard she tried to stop herself she kept thinking this weird – or possibly just old-fashioned – man was taking her somewhere bad. But it was a nursery. They'd look at plants, they'd probably buy some, and then she'd make her excuses and he'd take her back to her car and she could go home – and never have to see him again. All would be well.

She got out of the car and stretched, looking around her. For a commercial premises it was quite run down. There were a few glasshouses visible behind a wall and a sign saying 'Sales' by a dilapidated hut, but Fiona refused to be disheartened. There'd probably be some really lovely plants here, the owners were obviously far more concerned with them than superficial things like signs and buildings. 'Oh, I can't wait to see what's here,' she said enthusiastically. 'You've been here before, which way do we go?'

'I think we should have a cup of tea first,' said Evan.

'But we've just had hot chocolate! Let's see what there is and then have tea.'

Fiona's objection was received with a look of hurt and rejection and her falsely inflated spirits sank. 'Oh, OK, whatever you think is best,' she said on a barely suppressed sigh.

Evan led the way into the house. There didn't seem to be anyone about although he called 'Shop!' in a way that made the place seem even more empty.

'Never mind,' he said, 'the tea shop's through here. They do lovely scones.'

'Really? It doesn't look as if anyone's been here for years! Don't you mean rock cakes?'

It wasn't a good joke by anyone's standards and it didn't even amuse Fiona. She was getting desperate. 'I really don't think there's anyone here to give us tea.' She was trying to sound firm and in control. 'Why don't we just look at the plants? It's why we came, after all.'

A slightly sinister gleam appeared in Evan's eye. 'I like a spirited woman but I think you really must do as you're told.'

Although appearing to be obedient went against every cell in Fiona's body she calculated that the date would end more quickly if she didn't argue and just went along with things. And she certainly didn't want to excite Evan by being 'spirited'.

Fiona found herself being taken by the arm and almost manhandled into a room containing half a dozen sets of tables and chairs. A thin curtain covered the window and there were flies on the sill. She resolved not to eat anything even if the scones were fresh out of the oven. Nothing here could possibly be remotely hygienic.

'I'll go and find Mrs Tibbs,' said Evan. 'You stay here, like a good girl.'

I'm now officially freaked out, thought Fiona. This is not a boring but harmless afternoon with a boring but harmless man, it's sinister. The moment Evan was out of the way she would try and leave.

But he was back before she could do more than shift in her chair. For a man no longer young, he moved with surprising speed.

For some reason they were sitting in the far corner of the room, as far from the door as they could be. Given that they were the only people there, there was no reason why Evan should have chosen this table. 'Why don't we sit by the window?' suggested Fiona. 'If we drew the curtain we could look at the garden.'

'Mrs Tibbs wouldn't like that,' said Evan. 'Very set in her ways is Mrs Tibbs.'

Probably stuck to the floor by grease, thought Fiona, if this room was anything to go by. She could see fly dirt beside the window and many corpses behind the curtain. 'Does she raise the plants? Or is there a Mr Tibbs?'

'Mrs Tibbs lives with her sister now. They raise the plants together.'

Knowing there were two women on the premises was a bit reassuring, and Fiona felt calmer. This was just a bad date; she hadn't been kidnapped.

A short time later an elderly woman wearing brown nylon trousers, a pink sweater and slippers shuffled in. She could have done with a new bra, thought Fiona, deliberately keeping her thoughts frivolous. Otherwise she felt she was in an episode of *The League of Gentlemen*. Mrs Tibbs had a tray on which were cups, saucers, a teapot, jug of milk and a plate of scones, which did indeed look very fresh.

'Those look delicious!' said Fiona, trying to make a friend of Mrs Tibbs. She might need her. 'Are they just out of the oven?'

'They are. Mr Lennox always calls ahead when he's coming. It helps with the arrangements.'

Fiona wanted to ask 'what arrangements' because getting a batch of scones into the oven didn't seem like 'arrangements' to her, but felt it was too difficult.

'I'll just go and get some hot water,' said Mrs Tibbs.

'Will you be Mother?' said Evan. 'I bet you're a lovely mother, Fiona,' he added.

Fiona poured the tea and then handed Evan the scones, the butter and the jam. She decided to risk food poisoning and have one herself.

'They're lovely scones, aren't they?' said Evan.

'Yes indeed. But I can't wait to see the plants,' said Fiona. 'If they're anything like as good as the scones they'll be wonderful.'

'Time enough for plants later,' said Evan. 'I've got other things in mind first.'

Just as she was wondering what on earth he could mean and, if it was what she thought it might be, whether fainting would get her out of it, her mobile phone rang. She burrowed for it like a terrier after a rat. 'Hello!'

She was aware of a wave of disapproval from across the table but she didn't care. 'James! How lovely to hear from you!'

'Fiona?' James sounded a little surprised at her enthusiasm.

'Yes! I'm so glad you've called. I need help!' She put as much expression into the word as she could.

Evan frowned and shifted his chair closer to her, blocking her exit. She had to be careful – and think fast!

'When you asked me what my favourite television programme was and I couldn't remember the name of it? Well it's come to me! It's *I'm a Celebrity . . . Get Me Out of Here!*'

'Fiona, are you all right?' James sounded anxious.

'Yes. I mean, no. Not at all!' said Fiona, aware she was sounding more deranged by the second. 'I just get in a panic sometimes. I'm in a lovely nursery with such a nice man. We're having tea and then we'll look at plants and then we'll go back to where I parked my car.'

James was silent for a moment, and then seemed to twig. 'Are you with someone you don't know without your car?'

'As usual, hit the nail on the head. It's called Squirrels and it specialises in ferns. Lovely place.'

'Do you want me to come and get you?'

'That's it! Now I must go. Evan will think I'm very rude for talking on my mobile. Goodbye! See you very soon, I hope.'

Fiona was aware that she was sweating. She disconnected and slipped her phone into her pocket. Then she stood up. 'I'm so sorry, I must visit the little girls' room.' She was aware she had never used that expression before in her life but nothing seemed normal here and it felt appropriate.

'I don't think they have one, it's a very small place.'

'They must have something,' she said firmly. 'If they serve tea, they must have a lavatory. It's the law!' She wasn't quite sure about this but it seemed like a good law to her.

'It's a small place. The law won't apply here.'

'Then I'll go out and pee behind a bush! And it's a nursery – they must have bushes.'

She stalked out of the room, glad she didn't really need a lavatory, and got as far away from the house as she could. She knew she had very little time before she would be found and brought back. She took out her phone, thanking God there was reception. 'James? Please rescue me! I'm with these mad people. Will you ever be able to find where I am?'

'I've had a look on the internet but I haven't very much information. Did you notice any place names on the way?'

'Etchingham, but we seemed to pass it several times. I got confused.'

'I'll come and get you. Don't worry.'

She had just disconnected when she heard footsteps behind her. She spun round. 'Now I need somewhere to wash my hands!'

Evan had the look of a headmaster disappointed in his favourite pupil. Before he could speak she said firmly, 'I'd like to see round the nursery now.'

'I thought you weren't interested in the plants,' said Evan. 'You didn't tell me very much about your garden. I thought you were up for some fun.'

Feeling hot and cold at the same time, Fiona shook her head. 'No, I want to see the plants. All of them.'

Followed by Evan she marched up and down the rows of benches, inspecting moss-filled and pot-bound specimens that wouldn't have endeared themselves to her even if she had been in the mood to buy plants. But she refused to go home. She wouldn't get in Evan's car again. She'd summoned help. It would be too galling, and worrying, for James if he found the place but her gone. Never, never, never again would she be so stupid as to go out with someone she hadn't thoroughly checked out.

Eventually, just as she was about to give up hope, she heard a car drive up. She hastened to the car park and was ecstatic to see James get out of an old Citroën. Ignoring Evan who was in the middle of telling her something she really didn't want to know, she set off at a jog.

'Fiona,' said Evan. 'Naughty girl! How dare you run off like that?' He set off in pursuit.

Fiona speeded up, terrified lest Evan catch hold of her. 'Get in, James!' she called as she approached the car.

He did and started the engine. Fiona reached the car and pulled open the passenger door and hauled herself in.

'Let's go! As fast as you can,' she said, panting hard.

James didn't speak, he just started the car, leaving the nursery with a satisfying spray of gravel.

Fiona looked back to see Evan, standing in the car park, looking amazed and affronted.

'Thank goodness you came,' she said, as soon as she could speak.

Chapter Ten

Fiona found herself giggling and unable to stop talking as James drove away, as if needing to exorcise all the fear and panic by describing, in every minute detail, the spooky Evan, the moss-filled plant pots and the surprisingly nice scones.

And when she'd finished that, she went on to castigate herself for her foolishness, for disobeying the most basic principles of internet dating, for letting herself be persuaded to abandon her car, for not having exchanged enough emails with Evan to find out how utterly horrible he was. Eventually, her mouth completely dry, she stopped.

'Internet dating?' said James.

He said this without any hint of criticism, just clarifying how Fiona had got involved with that freak. He was wonderfully non-judgemental.

'I know. It's mad. I wouldn't have had anything to do with it if my friend Luella hadn't put me on the site. I only wanted someone to go out with. I'm not hoping to get married again or anything.' She sighed, exhausted.

'We're reaching civilisation,' he said after a few minutes. 'We can either go back to your car and you can go home. Or I can take you home and arrange to pick your car up tomorrow, or I can take you to my home, the flat above the shop and give you dinner, and take you home later.' He shot her a glance. 'Have a think.'

Fiona thought. She didn't want to go back to the garden

centre, get into her car and drive home alone. She'd be fine tomorrow but at the moment she felt like a character in a thriller; she'd assume there'd be someone waiting to murder her on the back seat. Or that she'd be followed home by Evan, who would have gone there to wait for her.

Then she considered the being-driven-home option. It was a good one. She could pour herself a big drink, have a bath, watch some telly and go to bed. But at home there would be Angus, who would ask where she'd been and would wonder why she was behaving oddly.

'I'd have to ring Angus and tell him I'll be late back,' she said.

'So you're thinking about having dinner with me? I'm glad. I know you must feel a bit shaken but I hope you know me well enough to realise I'm not an axe-murderer, and being in a town, if you had to escape, it would be easy.' He paused. 'In fact, you could put a local taxi number into your phone before you have the first glass of wine. In case.'

'In case you have too much to drink to drive me home?' She chuckled. 'It's an idea.' Fiona realised how safe she felt with James. It didn't even cross her mind to wonder if he might be just as untrustworthy as Evan had been.

'I'm very happy to stay sober. I've been meaning to invite you out for dinner since your delightful party but I wasn't quite sure you'd want to come.'

'Why wouldn't I want to come? Golly, I've been through the whole internet-dating torture so I'll be asked out to dinner.'

'I don't think you realise quite what an attractive woman you are, Fiona. You have many friends, even if you did meet Robert on a dating site. People are drawn to you. I am drawn to you, but I didn't think I had much to offer you.'

'What do you mean? Any advance on beans on toast

would be welcome.' She paused. 'Of course at this moment beans on toast would be lovely. Anything would be lovely. But maybe nothing too carby. That scone has given me indigestion.'

'I've got some minty things for that in the glove box,' said James. 'Have a look.'

Fiona found them. 'Do you want one? No? These are a life-saver.' Another giggle came out of nowhere, probably because of the stress of her afternoon. She tried to suppress it.

'Why are you laughing?'

Being caught giggling made her laugh more. 'I'm not sure I can tell you.'

'I think you can. You've told me quite a lot since you got in the car.'

Fiona got herself under control. 'OK. Well, when I was finding the Rennies a thought went through my head that maybe things like that are what you need for dating as an older person. You know, in old films the hero always has to have a cigarette lighter, and probably a cigarette to go with it. Now if you're of a certain age you need indigestion tablets. Later on it would be a fold-up walking stick, or a Zimmer, handily in the boot.' She bit her lip. 'It's not really funny, is it?'

He was smiling. 'I do see what you're saying. And there are a lot of advantages to going out as an older person. I, for example, can offer you some very nice wine. When I was younger it would have been a bogof from the local supermarket.'

Fiona tensed briefly. 'I still drink bogofs.'

'So do I but I do know how to choose something a bit better.'

'Even in my cellar?' Her mind had gone back to the dinner party. 'Robert was very snooty about my wine.'

'I can't possibly comment.'

She could hear without looking that he was smiling and realised she hadn't felt so relaxed with any man except Angus or Russell for ages. 'So why were you ringing me?'

'I'd almost forgotten. It was about one of your books. I have a buyer. Quite a good price.'

'Oh, that's nice. And will you take a cut? I think you should.'

'Well, if you'd rather—'

'I'd much rather.'

'Very well, we'll keep it strictly business.'

'Except when you're rescuing me or offering me beans on toast.'

'I think I can do better than that.'

'You really don't have to. And I'll take a taxi home.' She raised her hand to stop his protest. 'No. I can easily ring Angus now and say I met a friend in town and we're going to have dinner, we want to drink and I'll take a cab home. He knows I never drink and drive so it won't seem unreasonable to him.' She paused. 'I could even say I met you.' She sighed. 'I don't want him to know about the internet dating. He'd just worry.'

'With good reason, if I may say so.'

'Please don't. No one could reproach me more than I'm doing myself and if you tell me off I'll start making excuses.'

'But you will be more careful in future?' James said.

'Of course! Now can we change the subject? I've been a complete idiot and you rescued me. I'm eternally grateful—'

'But you hate being ticked off and if I say any more you'll go right off me?'

She looked at him in wonder. 'You are remarkably perceptive.'

He chuckled. 'We're nearly there now.'

Fiona booked a taxi for ten o'clock, having decided that if she was desperate to go home by nine she could cancel it and book another. Then she went into James's bathroom to make running repairs.

Thank goodness for the mini make-up kit she kept in her handbag. Adopting her usual policy of not actually looking properly at her reflection until she'd done quite a lot of smudge-removing, hair-fluffing and lip-plumping, she applied the kit. Afterwards she hunted for the tiny phial of scent right in the bottom and added a squirt. It wasn't that she fancied James or anything, he was just a friend, but she had her standards. If he was going to feed her, it was only right that she should take a bit of trouble with her appearance. And she had looked a bit wild after her horrible afternoon.

James's kitchen was a galley half hidden behind a partition at the end of his sitting room, which was large, included a big fireplace and walls lined with bookshelves. The bookshop was in an old building and this room above the shop had wide wooden boards covered with rugs, beams and evidence of age in every inch. The furniture was old too: a battered leather sofa, a couple of deep but not matching chairs, an antique desk and enough little tables to house quite a lot of newspapers and periodicals.

'I do apologise for the mess,' James said, handing her a large glass of chilled white wine. 'My cleaning lady comes once a week, on Monday, so the dust has built up a bit.'

'I never notice dust.' She took the glass and smiled. 'I think this is a lovely room! Perfect, even. I've always fancied living above a shop – or rather, I'm always nosy about what the flats above shops are like. I like this very much.'

'I'm glad. Now will you be able to amuse yourself while I see what, if anything, I can offer you to eat?'

'Of course! I'll look at the books. Nothing nicer.' She shivered a little and he noticed.

'I'll just set a match to the fire. It won't take a second and it is a bit chilly in here.'

'It's not really, I'm just feeling a bit, you know . . . It may be partly shock. But the wine and a fire will cure me.'

Having lit the fire he said, 'Let me know when you want more wine. I'm going to rummage now.'

Fiona spent a lot of time reading every book title. She'd heard that you can tell a lot about people from their books but she suspected James's books were more to do with what had or hadn't sold in his shop. There weren't any paperbacks and all the titles were classics or very old.

'So where do you keep your pulp fiction?' she called through.

'In my bedroom,' he called back.

'Ah.' She extracted an old book of wild flowers and settled by the fire.

James reappeared with the bottle. 'I'm so glad I had this in the fridge, but it wasn't full, I'll need to open something else. Red? Or less than chilly white?'

'What are we eating?'

'Something with rice. I can't be more specific just at the moment. I may have to pop out.'

'Oh please don't! What would you have eaten if I hadn't been here?'

'I'd have popped out. I find having a twenty-four-hour supermarket quite wonderful. And it would supply a bottle of chilled wine if we wanted it.'

'I'd really hate to put you to the trouble.'

'No trouble. What about some lamb chops? They don't take too long.'

'I could peel potatoes—'

'If I had any. I'll buy ready-made mash. Honestly, one hardly needs to cook at all—'

'Which is a shame.'

'Yes. One day I'll invite you properly, but now—'

'My presence is a complete bore! I'm so sorry. Couldn't we just have toast?'

'Certainly not! I'm delighted to have you. Here.' He opened a cupboard Fiona hadn't noticed before and revealed a television. 'You find something soothing to watch while I shop.'

Having filled her glass he left her watching a property programme and, almost as soon as he'd gone, she closed her eyes. It had been a long day.

Chapter Eleven

Sian wasn't much looking forward to the gymkhana. She didn't want to spend a day watching Melissa flirting with Gus, and much more worrying was the fact that this was the moment she'd been dreading ever since Gus's arrival in the village: Rory and Gus would finally have to meet. How would they react to each other? Even though neither of them knew, it was important. How would it be for her, seeing them together? And she was sure her clothes would be wrong. She'd lived in the country long enough to know how mocked townies could be if they wore the wrong clothes.

However, it was a lovely day and she had a pretty dress to wear, so that was one problem out of the way. It was just her footwear she had to worry about, unless she was expected to wear tweeds and a deerstalker.

Rory was easy to dress in shorts, T-shirt, floppy hat and lots of sunscreen. He could wear sandals because his had thick, sensible soles. Sian just had several pairs of flip-flops, none of which had much in the way of sole.

Still, Fiona would put her right. She was taking them in her car.

'I've got a car seat from my grandchildren, for when they come over from Canada,' Fiona had said. Somehow the word seemed loaded to Sian, who felt a pang of guilt. Gus wasn't the only one who didn't know he was related to Rory. She'd been so busy worrying about how she could tell him and if she even wanted to she'd scarcely even given Fiona a thought. She knew how her own mother would feel if a grandchild had been kept from her. She was also feeling guilty about Richard. He was away on another trip and had hinted that he wanted to whisk her off for a romantic dinner for two as soon as he was back: they hadn't been able to spend much time together recently. What with everything else she'd given little thought to him. All this guilt and now a whole day of more worrying. She wondered how she was going to get through it.

Rory skipped along beside her as they went up to the Big House, looking forward to his day, convinced that he would get to ride on a pony. Although Sian did try to warn him this might not happen, he wouldn't listen.

Fiona kissed them both when they arrived. 'How lovely you look!' she said to Sian when Rory had gone to check the trains were still there. 'Angus has gone off somewhere. He's meeting us there later. He's being all mysterious. I could always tell when he was up to something when he was little.'

A strange mixture of relief, disappointment and anxiety about what he might be up to made Sian sigh and to cover it she said, 'I'm worried about my shoes. It's either these or heels. Neither of them are right for mud, and it might be a bit wet.'

'I've the very thing! I bought some of those flowery wellies and found I couldn't get my leg down them. You could have those. Put those in the bag in case it gets hot.' Fiona dashed off, obviously thrilled to be able to provide what was needed and get rid of an unwise purchase at the same time. Fortunately they had more or less the same size feet.

'OK then, got everything we're likely to need?' said Fiona, jangling her keys, scanning the hall for things that might be forgotten.

'I've got my bag,' said Rory. 'It's got a drink, some Babybels, sandwiches and an apple.'

'Very sensible. Although Melissa's parents are providing a picnic, they might not produce it soon enough for a young tummy. You know what men are like if they get hungry. They get grumpy. Now, come on, we've got a gymkhana to go to.'

Rory cheered and ran towards Fiona's car, his rucksack bumping on his back. Sian wished she felt half as happy to be going as her son obviously did.

'Well, we only got lost about three times,' said Fiona cheerfully, parking in the field, directed there by a straw-haired boy who sounded as if he went to Eton. 'I rate that as a successful journey.'

'So do I,' said Sian, who had enjoyed her tour of the local countryside, up and down several very narrow lanes she never would have gone down in the normal course of events. She realised how unadventurous she'd been since moving down. She'd hardly been out of the village. 'It was such a pretty drive.'

'Now all we have to do is find Melissa and her parents. It's such a luxury not having to lug a picnic for miles and miles. Except for Rory, of course.'

'I've got a rucksack,' said Rory. 'I'm fine.'

'It would be dreadful if we end up fighting Rory for his snacks because there's nothing else,' said Sian as they walked through the field to the gate. 'I wish I'd put more in now.'

'Oh don't worry, the Lewis-Joneses will do us proud. She's one of those competitive entertainers. Absolutely nothing will be forgotten and there'll be enough for the five thousand and their friends.'

'Well, you could be accused of that,' said Sian with a smile.

'I know, but with Veronica, you always feel guilty for not being able to eat more.'

'You do seem to feel guilty about a lot of things,' said Sian.

'Oh yes, it's part of my DNA.'

Although she spoke lightly, Sian thought she spotted Fiona blushing. Fiona wasn't the only one who felt guilty at the drop of a hat. If she only knew.

Mrs Lewis-Jones had indeed arranged a splendid picnic. Every special basket, flask, seat and glass-holder was provided. Everything was smart and clean, no musty thermoses with stained cups or melamine plates or plastic glasses. The waterproof rugs were big enough to pitch a tent on and the plates were Royal Worcester.

'This is wonderful!' said Fiona, seating herself in a chair that had an inbuilt glass-holder. 'Veronica, you have gone to a lot of trouble.'

'I do like to put on a good spread. If people have had a decent lunch they'll spend more money later and we mustn't forget this is a fund-raiser for the church hall.'

'And I've got a surprise for you all! Angus – Gus – and I hatched the plan.' Melissa was looking particularly adorable, her hair as shiny as a shampoo advertisement and her dress from Boden looking better than the catalogue. Looking at the two of them now Sian could see where Melissa got her looks from. Veronica was a very trim and pretty older version of her daughter. In the flurry of the dinner party she hadn't taken everyone in properly.

She sipped champagne from the silver collapsible cup she had been given 'because it's such fun to use these old things'. I must stop being jealous of Melissa, she ordered herself. She and Gus go way back. Of course they'll have plots and schemes no one else knows about.

131

'Rory, darling,' said Fiona, 'do you think you'll need your own packed lunch? There are lovely things here.'

'Those are little eggs,' said Rory, pointing at some miniature eggs on a rather fine bone-china plate.

'Quails' eggs, darling. Just like ordinary, but smaller,' said Fiona.

'Here, have a sausage roll,' said Mrs Lewis-Jones, offering Rory a large thermos. 'They're hot. Well, warm, anyway.'

'Let's get some more bottles open,' said Harold Lewis-Jones. 'I happen to know about a mystery guest Melissa has lined up and we'll need plenty of fizz.'

He refilled all the glasses and then placed the bottles in special wine holders that stuck into the ground. Rory was given one filled with elderflower pressé. Sian was impressed. They really had thought of everything.

'It's so kind of you to cater for Rory,' she said.

'I'll move on to the soft stuff soon myself,' said Mrs Lewis-Jones, 'or I'll fall asleep after lunch.'

'I'm afraid I often fall asleep after lunch,' said Fiona, 'with or without champagne.'

'Melly, when did you say your mystery guest was coming? I've got the game pie all ready to serve and I'd quite like to crack on with it.'

Melissa got to her feet and shaded her eyes as she looked across the fields towards the woods. 'I think I can see them coming now!'

Everyone looked in the direction she was pointing. 'Oh, it's Angus's Land-Rover,' said Fiona. 'Who's he got with him?'

'I think it must be a woman,' said Sian, 'unless anyone knows a man who'd wear a hat like that.'

'You'll know soon enough,' said Melissa smugly. 'Just be patient.'

Although Sian could see the hat, she couldn't make

out who was under it. But surely Melissa wouldn't import more competition and make such a production out of it?

'My goodness!' said Fiona as the Land-Rover approached. 'Melissa! What have you done? And why the secrecy?' She obviously recognised her son's passenger and was rather put out that she hadn't been in on it.

'Isn't it fun!' Melissa chirruped, apparently unaware of or immune to Fiona's irritation.

'Who is it, darling?' asked her mother. 'Oh! Good Lord! What a scream. It's Luella!'

'It's your landlady,' said Fiona to Sian. 'In case you'd forgotten.'

Sian appeared to be the only person not greeting the new guest with wild hoots of joy. Although she would be fascinated to meet her, she couldn't help suspecting that Melissa was up to something. Was she about to make Luella an offer in front of everyone so she'd force her hand and Sian and Rory would lose their home? For that was how she thought of the cottage, damp and all.

'Who is it, Mummy?' asked Rory.

'It's the woman who owns our house,' said Sian, trying to sound enthusiastic.

'And who's that man?' he said, as Gus pulled up the Land-Rover and got out.

'He's Fiona's son,' she said, taking a deep breath to steady herself. Luella's arrival wasn't the only thing that was making her feel wobbly.

'And he shouldn't be parking here,' said Veronica Lewis-Jones. 'I'll have to ask him to move that rattle-trap.'

'Don't let him hear you calling it that,' said Fiona. 'That Land-Rover is his pride and joy.'

'I'm sure, but all vehicles must be parked in the field,'

said Veronica firmly. 'Luella! How wonderful to see you! I thought you couldn't be dragged out of France without a coach and horses!'

Luella was dressed from head to toe in white linen, apart from her hat, which was straw and decorated with large fabric roses. She was the picture of an eccentric Englishwoman and played the part to perfection.

'Here, have this,' said Harold Lewis-Jones, having kissed Luella on both cheeks and handed her a beaker full of champagne. 'Get that down you, help you get over the journey.'

Veronica bustled forward, also kissing her. 'Yes, it must have been like a fairground ride being driven over the fields in that thing. Angus, I do hope you're going to move it. If you leave your Landy here everyone will think they can fetch their four-by-fours and park them.'

The moment had finally arrived. Gus was here and he was about to meet Rory. Sian's stomach was in knots and she just hoped the others couldn't tell how nervous she was. Even her palms were sweating. She took another deep breath.

'Don't worry, I'll move it in a minute,' Gus was saying, and then he turned to Sian. 'Hey!' He kissed her on the cheek, and looked down at Rory who was gazing up at him, big-eyed. 'You must be Rory.' Gus took his hand and shook it. 'I'm Gus. I'm a friend of your mum's.'

'Hello,' said Rory, retreating behind Sian, suddenly shy. She hugged him to her, needing the reassurance of his presence just as much as he needed hers.

'He's my son,' said Fiona. 'Hard to believe he was once your height.'

'Angus, darling, I hate to nag, but could you move it?' Veronica went on. 'There are some people over there looking daggers at me because I said they had to park properly. We can pretend Luella is infirm, so had to have a lift, but now you must put your car in the proper place. We won't eat all the lunch before you come back.'

'OK,' said Gus. 'Hey, Rory, would you like a ride in the Land-Rover? We can bring your mum!'

Rory looked up at Sian, his eyes full of longing, all shyness gone.

As a mother she felt it was best to say yes to everything it was possible to say yes to, and there didn't really seem a good reason to say no to this, especially as she was included in the invitation, even if her stomach still felt like a washing machine on full spin. It would look odd if she refused, much as she was tempted. 'Seatbelts?' She looked up at Gus, hoping against hope that the answer would be no.

'Full harness in the back.'

'Oh, OK,' she said, resigning herself to the inevitable. She could use the time to think of what to say to Luella when they were introduced. Luella's arrival was at least a good distraction from her turmoil about Gus and Rory.

Gus took a few minutes to settle Rory comfortably in the back seat, buckling the harness carefully. 'There you go, mate. Not even a charging rhino will get you out of that seat now.'

Sian heaved herself up into the passenger seat. 'Have you ever seen a charging rhino?' she asked Gus as he got in next to her.

'Yup. Prefer not to see one again though.'

'I'd love to see one,' said Rory with a sigh from the back.

'I'll show you a photo and you may change your mind. Now, all safely strapped in? Then off we go.'

As they drove they saw a row of stalls selling all sorts of things from riding clothes and paintings to mysterious items for arcane country pursuits Sian didn't want to think about. In the distance, on the hill, they could see where the cross-country course went.

'Look, Rory,' said Sian. 'Can you see over there? Horses! Jumping over what look like hedges.'

Just then, the Land-Rover was overtaken by a couple of girls on ponies. They had on cream-coloured jodhpurs, tweed hacking jackets, short boots and black velvet riding hats.

'That's the Pony Club,' said Gus. 'They're acting like policemen, making sure everything's all right.'

'I want to be a policeman on a horse,' said Rory dreamily. But as he was in the habit of wanting to be anything that he happened to see at the time, Sian didn't take too much notice.

'You could join the Pony Club if you wanted,' said Gus. You don't have to be a girl, although it helps.'

'I don't want to be a girl,' said Rory, worried.

'Really, it's not obligatory,' Gus went on.

'Boys ride ponies too,' said Sian, to clarify.

'Maybe later,' said Rory, sounding, thought Sian, worryingly like she did.

Just then a huge chestnut horse came cantering along. On it was a man in a black coat, white breeches and a top hat. He stopped when he got to the Land-Rover.

The horse, snorting gently, seemed enormous. The man leaned in. 'You know you shouldn't have a vehicle up here?'

'I do, and I'm sorry but I had a disabled relative to deliver to a picnic,' explained Gus. 'I'm taking the vehicle back now.'

'Very well.' The man touched his riding crop to his hat and cantered off again.

'Maybe I don't want to ride a horse,' said Rory, from the back.

'Darling! You'd start on a little pony! We'll try and find some later.'

'Or we'll track down a friend who's got something more child-friendly,' said Gus. 'You need something you can stroke.'

Sian looked out of the window suddenly. Gus seemed to have all the right instincts for fatherhood.

The field was now full of cars, but Rory enjoyed every bucketing moment of it. It was an incredibly surreal trip for Sian. Having thought for nearly six years that Rory and his father would never meet, and then having spent the last fortnight dreading their meeting, it seemed almost anticlimactic for them all to be bouncing happily along in the Land-Rover, but she realised that anticlimactic was probably a good thing at this point. And Rory's obvious enthusiasm for off-roading was so infectious that Sian almost found herself enjoying the ride too.

'Thank you!' said Rory ecstatically as Gus helped him down. He was clearly smitten. 'That was the best fun ever!'

Sian looked at Rory with pride. She did try to instil manners in him but sometimes he had to be prompted. This sincere gratitude meant she had not been wasting her time. And at least Gus and Rory's first meeting had gone smoothly, though she didn't want to even think about the next stage just yet. If ever.

'Yes, thank you, that was fun,' said Sian, 'although I sort of wish I didn't have to walk back up the hill in these wellies. They're fun but rather hot.'

'Take them off. Walk barefoot. I'll carry them for you.'

'OK.' Barefoot seemed as good as anything and the grass was wonderfully cool beneath her hot feet.

Somehow, when they got back to the picnic site, Rory was holding hands with both of them while Gus carried Sian's boots.

'What a delightful picture you make!' said Luella, enthroned on a picnic chair. 'Like a little family!'

The shock was like a bucket of water thrown over her. Sian turned away in case anyone noticed her reaction. For a moment she'd been in a happy little dream, but Luella's comment brought her back down to earth. Rory, oblivious to her confusion, had let go of Gus's hand by now and was pointing at the picnic and pulling Sian over to the rug.

'Luella, let me introduce you to Sian,' said Fiona. 'Of course you know each other by post and email but not in the flesh, so to speak.'

Sian came forward, wondering if Fiona had used the word 'flesh' because Luella had rather a lot of it on show. 'Hello. It is lovely to meet you for real. Rory and I do love living in your little house.' Might as well get her cards on the table as soon as possible, she thought.

'Oh yes! Love the thought of you living there! Hope you won't be heartbroken if I decide to sell?'

'Er . . .'

'I've got a confession to make,' said Melissa, materialising behind Sian with a couple of glasses of champagne. 'I arranged for Luella to come back so I could make her an offer – hopefully one she can't refuse! Obviously, me being a cash buyer means I can offer a smidgen under what you'd put it on the market for!'

Sian blanched.

'Oh, don't let's spoil this lovely day by talking business,' said Veronica, clearly realising her daughter's timing was less than perfect. 'Let's get on with the picnic.'

Sian was relieved. Luella would be distracted away from said business proposition for at least an hour.

The picnic was still magnificent, even if the others had been at it already. Apart from the sausage rolls and quails' eggs, which turned out to be just a sort of an *amuse-bouche* for Rory and others, there was a feast: little smoked-salmon sandwiches, triangles of toast with potted shrimps, tiny quiches and miniature brioches hollowed out and filled with scrambled egg and caviar. Gus helped himself from the proffered trays. Sian heard him muttering, but she couldn't quite tell what he said. It was something about 'a bit overdone' but she didn't think he meant the food. It was perfect.

After the starter there was a choice of a poached salmon with cucumber scales which must have been enormous or beef Wellington, also still huge, served cold.

'You see what I mean by competitive catering,' said Fiona to Sian behind her hand.

'I say, Harold, the beef was so absolutely delicious, I must have some more, but I'd appreciate a smear of mustard, Tewkesbury if you've got it.'

Luella's request caused a flutter of panic between the Lewis-Joneses.

'I've got wholegrain mustard, pickle, horseradish, ketchup and piccalilli,' said Harold Lewis-Jones grumpily. 'Only you would ask for something so obscure, Lu.'

'Pass me the mustard and the horseradish. I'll mix them. It's all it is,' Luella said. She seemed to be enjoying having caught her hosts out. 'And then maybe more salad. Ta.'

Rory looked first at Luella and then his mother. 'Mum,' he whispered. 'She said "ta".'

'She's grown up, she's allowed,' Sian whispered back. 'Oh. Is it like a swear?'

Gus laughed. 'No, mate, it's worse. It's slang.'

'Mummy, what's slang?'

'Slang is words people like to use instead of the proper ones, sometimes,' said Gus carefully. 'Some of it's Okay – like Okay. That's slang really. But if you said "bog" when you meant "toilet" your mum would probably tell you off.'

'I'd tell you off if you said "toilet",' said Luella. 'It's "lavatory".'

'That's not fair!' said Gus. 'You just said "ta".'

'I'm posh, I can say what I like,' said Luella, wiping her hands on her dress.

'Pudding, anyone?'

The way Veronica said this, it sounded as if she was offering a dollop of suet pudding and custard. Sian was not fooled. She suspected that something exquisite was going to emerge from the cool boxes, and she was right. Little pastry cases contained glazed summer fruits with dollops of clotted cream, small tumblers of goose-berry fool and chocolate brownies were held in Sian's direction.

'Just take one of each if you're wavering,' said Veronica. 'There's enough for everyone to have every-thing.'

After that she cut up hunks of home-made fruit cake. 'Now, Harold and I have got to go and do our duty in the committee tent. Mel darling, don't try and talk busi-ness over lunch, will you? It's frightfully rude.'

'As if I would, Ma!' Melissa giggled at the thought of such disobedience.

'Just checking. Oh, give me a hand up, Angus. I'm too old for this.'

Once her parents were out of the way Melissa took on the duties of hostess. 'Luella, are you sure you don't want anything else to drink? There's loads more fizz and it's such a bore to have to take it all home again.'

'Oh, all right then, if you're twisting my arm.' Luella waited until her beaker was full and everyone else had been offered. 'So this business we're not supposed to talk about. If it's about buying my cottage, I think I can say I'm definitely interested.'

Sian choked over the elderflower pressé she'd had instead of more champagne.

'Actually, Melissa, you wouldn't have some coffee there, would you?' said Fiona, having shot Sian an anxious glance.

'Oh yes,' said Luella, putting down her empty beaker. 'Only I'd prefer tea.'

'We're all set up for tea or coffee. Angus, darling, could you give me a hand? I'll do coffee first, if you don't mind, Luella.' A huge thermos with a pump appeared followed by another one marked 'hot water'.

Luella regarded it with distaste. 'In what parallel universe was tea made with hot water? We need boiling water!'

'Oh come on, Lu,' said Fiona. 'Don't make a fuss. We'll manage quite well with water in the thermos.'

'Actually,' said Gus, 'if Luella wants boiling water for her tea, she shall have it. In fact, I'll bring the tea myself.'

'How will you do that?' asked Melissa.

'Light a fire and boil it,' said Gus, winking at Rory as if aware he was about to be told off by everyone.

'Darling, there's no point in lighting a fire,' said Fiona, sounding as if she'd had this argument before and lost. 'We haven't got a kettle!'

'I've got a billy in the Landy. Come on, Sian, you and Rory can help me.'

As Sian had no desire to listen to Luella and Melissa discuss the sale of her home, she got up.

'Better put your boots back on,' Gus said.

He held her elbow as she poked her feet back into the boots and she felt supported, as if there was more to it than him just helping her keep her balance. Yet once she was safely in her wellies she edged away slightly, disconcerted by how welcome Gus's hand had felt. When they were a little way from the party and nearly at the woods, Gus said, 'I could tell from your reaction that was a bit of a bombshell. If I'd known what she was really planning I would—'

'Yes, well it was rather a shock. We're so settled here. It was all working out so well.' She heard her voice crack a little and suddenly realised she was tearful. 'Sorry, don't take any notice. It's the champagne. It's made me weepy. I'm fine really. It's not as if I wasn't aware that it was a possibility.'

'I don't reckon you are fine,' said Gus. 'Come on, Rory, mate, let's get some wood. Your mum needs a cup of tea.'

'The thing to do,' said Gus when they'd reached a suitable collection point, 'is to look up. Look for dead branches that haven't fallen on the ground yet.'

'OK,' Sian and Rory chorused.

'And if you want to check if a bit of wood is damp or not, put it to your lip.' He said this with a provocative grin, as if he thought Sian would die before putting a bit of stick to her mouth.

'That's cool,' she said, pleased to feel a bit annoyed by Gus rather than thoroughly upset by Luella.

'OK, you guys know what you're doing?' said Gus. 'I've got to sprint back to the Landy to get some kit. Back in a mo'.'

Sian watched him lope off and saw there was something a bit odd about his run. He'd talked of injuring his leg. It must have been quite serious.

Gus was back with them quite quickly and began sorting through the pile of sticks Sian and Rory had gathered in what Sian considered to be a rather brutal way.

'If it doesn't snap easily it's probably too damp. It's vital to prepare properly or it'll just smoke and we'll look like idiots. We want your mum to get her cup of tea, don't we, Rory?'

'Ladies like tea,' said Rory. 'All my friends' mums drink it a lot. When they're not drinking wine.'

'Rory!' Sian yelped in horror. 'It's not like that. We only drink wine when we're having a sleepover or people are taking a taxi home. And it was Luella who was so desperate for boiling water.'

Gus carried on snapping twigs, ignoring her protest. The ones he liked he put into a plastic carrier bag, which was part of the kit he had brought from the Land-Rover. The rest was hidden in a green sack.

'I hope you've got some matches and maybe some fire-lighters in there,' Sian said warily. 'I don't want my tea depending on your ability to rub sticks together to light the fire.'

'Of course I can make a fire like that – sort of – but we don't need to do it today.'

Rory dropped another bundle of sticks. 'Can you really make fire by rubbing sticks together?'

'It's a little more complicated than that, but basically, yes.'

'I'd love to see,' said Rory excitedly.

'I'll show you,' Gus promised, his face mirroring Rory's enthusiasm. 'One day soon we'll build a shelter, sleep in it, and cook our breakfast over a fire. If your mum agrees.'

A million thoughts flashed through Sian's mind. 'Well, maybe you wouldn't like to sleep in the shelter, Rory,' she said carefully. 'But if Gus can build one you could play in it.'

Gus was disdainful now. 'Madam, I'll have you know that the shelters I build are not for playing in!'

'Oh no?' Sian grinned at him. She found she was enjoying herself despite the day's anxieties. 'I think you'll find they are.' Rory, bored by this adult banter, ran off for more sticks. 'And while it's a lovely offer, I'm not sure Rory would really like to sleep out. He'd probably miss his bed and teddy and have to come in. You know what kids are like. Well – I mean—'

'I do remember camping out in the garden and getting scared in the night and running inside,' said Gus, helping her out.

'So you understand.'

'I think Rory would be fine if you slept in the shelter as well. We'll make a two-man one and Rory can sleep between us. For propriety's sake.'

Thank goodness the light was dim under the trees: he might not notice her blushing. She would have to train her mind not to continually rerun the time they had spent together: it was too unsettling. She had to admit, though, he was very easy to be with. She couldn't imagine Richard grubbing about in the woods. But that wasn't fair. Richard had many other good qualities; she was just having trouble remembering them right at this moment.

'OK, guys? Got enough fuel to make the ladies their cuppa?'

'Think so,' said Sian. 'There seems loads.'

'Let's go then.'

They returned to the picnic site with their burdens. Gus swung a backpack off his back on to the ground. 'Now, what have we got here?'

Rory peered in. 'Lots of things.'

'Why don't you unpack it for me, mate?'

Rory put in a hand and retrieved a billy can. Then there was a tightly bound pack of waterproof material.

'That's my tarp,' said Gus. 'Compass,' he went on as

Rory continued to unpack. 'First-aid kit. Head torch. Whistle. Can you test that one for us? Just give it a quick blow.' Rory obliged.

'Have you got everything you need to go hiking in there?' asked Luella, flinching as the whistle pierced the air.

Gus shook his head. 'Not really. I didn't bring my sleeping bag or my tent.'

'No knives?' asked Fiona, possibly speaking for all the women.

Gus shook his head. 'No. That's in my belt.' He grinned. 'I didn't bring an axe. That might be a mistake.'

Although he did mutter about the lack of his axe, Gus seemed to manage just fine without it. Surrounded by a growing crowd of people, he lined up dry sticks and criss-crossed kindling on top.

'Right, pass me the thermos with the hot water and we'll make it really boil. We could have filled the billy from a stream and passed the water through a cloth but I reckon the ladies are getting impatient,' said Gus, when he'd constructed his fire.

'I'd just stuff some newspaper under there and set fire to it,' said Sian, amazed at how much trouble Gus was taking. He was such an active person; to be taking such pains over a task seemed out of character. That and being a natural teacher. Rory was captivated. In fact they were all watching him in fascination, concentrating hard as if they were going to be asked to repeat the exercise themselves shortly afterwards.

'Newspaper would certainly work, but it's more fun to do it properly. I want to show Rory how to light a fire without matches.'

Eventually he reached into a pouch that was hanging from his neck. From it he produced a little cotton sack.

'Tinder,' he explained, withdrawing something white and fluffy. 'The cheating kind.'

'What do you mean?' asked Rory, sounding disappointed.

'When we go camping we'll do it with wild plants, but this is a quick way to make fire when your mum wants a cup of tea.'

Gus and Rory lay on their stomachs. Gus had a bundle of hay that he'd retrieved from his pack. 'This is really dry, Rory, mate. Now we're putting in this bit of very finely teased cotton wool – I stole one of my mum's cleansing pads but don't tell her.'

'I think she knows,' said Rory, who'd checked.

'Now, I'm going to make some very hot sparks with this.' He scraped a piece of metal against a column he'd produced from round his neck. A shower of silver sparks shot out, caught light to the cotton wool and then the hay. He picked up the bundle and dropped it on to the fine kindling where there was more hay. Soon the whole lot was crackling brightly.

'Not quite the orthodox way of doing it,' said Gus, adding some thicker sticks, 'but it'll get the billy boiling.'

'Oh,' said Veronica Lewis-Jones appearing a little while later. 'Was there something wrong with the water in the flasks?'

Everyone except Gus and Rory felt terribly guilty. 'It's just Gus showing off, I'm afraid,' said Fiona. 'He wanted to show Rory how to make a fire and boil a billy. Do have some of the tea. It's delicious.'

'Even if we did have to tear up the tea bags in order to put the leaves in the billy,' said Sian.

'Couldn't you have just put a tea bag in a cup?' asked Veronica, looking genuinely confused.

'That wouldn't be proper billy-can tea,' said Gus. 'You

need that burn-your-mouth-off effect. And of course you wouldn't have had tea bags in the old days.'

'Well, do make sure there's no trace of the fire,' Veronica continued disapprovingly. 'We're not supposed to have them.'

'I promise you, no one will know,' Gus replied with a grin that seemed to win her over.

Gus showed Rory how to gather up every scrap of unburnt wood, to pour water on the place where the fire had been until the ground was cool, even when you dug down into it, and was just showing him how to put earth over the scorch mark when Luella said, 'Who wants an ice cream?'

Both male heads turned in her direction and Sian felt pole-axed. Although one was fair and the other dark, their expressions were identical. Then she caught sight of Fiona and she went icy cold and then burning hot; she had seen it too. It was written all over her face. Fiona knew that her son Angus was Rory's father.

Sian stood up quickly, knocking over her cup of tea and stumbling in the process. 'Oh, I'm so sorry, Veronica, I . . .' She realised she was mumbling, trying to look anywhere but at Fiona. 'I think it's time we were getting home, Rory,' she managed to finish, feeling horribly weak and panicky.

'Yes indeed,' agreed Fiona briskly, standing up too. 'Rory, if you want ice cream we have some at my house.'

'No, really, Fiona,' said Sian in embarrassment, desperate to escape the situation, 'you don't need to leave on our account, I'm sure we can get a lift to—'

'Not at all. It's not remotely a problem.' Fiona smiled, but beneath the smile there was a determination that made Sian shiver. 'I wouldn't have it any other way.'

Chapter Twelve

Fiona glanced in her mirror to see if Rory looked like going to sleep. She wanted to talk to Sian, to check she was right in her suspicions, but Rory was resolutely awake, allowing no time for discussion. Sian sat beside her looking tired and a bit pale.

'So did you enjoy yourself, Rory?' said Fiona cheerfully.

'I liked the fire but I didn't ride a pony,' he replied after careful consideration.

'Oh, we can arrange that for you another time,' said Fiona. 'That would be easy.'

'Would it?' said Sian. 'I keep meaning to check out a riding stables and give him a trial lesson.'

'I'm sure Melissa will know someone to do with the Pony Club who'd be only too happy to let you have a go,' said Fiona, keeping things light. She was pretty sure that Sian had guessed she suspected Gus was Rory's father, but until they had a moment alone she didn't want any awkwardness, not in front of Rory. 'She owes you, after all,' she went on. 'Fancy bringing Luella to the picnic like that and getting her to say she'll sell! And I can't believe Luella didn't tell me she was coming over.'

Sian sighed deeply. 'It was a bombshell.'

'What's a bombshell?' asked Rory from his car seat.

'It's when something's a big surprise,' said Sian.

Like discovering you've got a grandson, thought Fiona.

'This isn't anything you need to think about,' she said out loud.

'Oh. OK,' said Rory, and turned his head towards the window.

Fiona's own bombshell flooded her mind with questions. Do I love Rory more now than I did before, now I know there's a blood tie? And how do I feel about Sian? She's a lovely woman but she kept a grandchild from me for nearly five years. Although, Fiona reasoned a moment later, she didn't know anything about me then. She wouldn't have known that until Angus appeared at the dinner party. What an utter shock that must have been! No wonder she's seemed a bit distracted lately. You bring up a child on your own all that time and then the father, who presumably you thought you'd never see again, turns out to be the son of your friend next door; a father and a grandmother for your son in one hit. Such a weird coincidence.

But was it really a coincidence? She came down here because of Richard, and Angus and Richard had known each other for years. Maybe she thought she might see Angus again through Richard? Maybe it was a plan?

Fiona turned on to the main road with relief. Soon they'd be home and she'd find out if Sian was manipulative or just strangely lucky – or unlucky. She glanced at her friend again. No, not manipulative. It hadn't occurred to her that she might meet Angus again, that much was clear from her reaction at the dinner and she'd obviously had no inkling that her new friend and neighbour was the mother of her ex-lover.

It was a relief to know that. Fiona had grown really fond of Sian, she might even say she loved her. She didn't want to think that their friendship had some hidden agenda. Sian would have to tell Angus now though. It would be wrong not to.

'Fiona.' Sian interrupted her musing. 'I know we said we were going back to yours, but would you mind coming to mine instead? Then if Rory gets tired I can put him to bed.' Sian figured that if she was going to have an awkward conversation, it might as well be on home ground.

'Fine,' said Fiona, 'but have you got ice cream?'

'I have. Also wine and nibbles. I could even knock us up a quick pasta and salad if we want it.'

'I don't think I'll ever need to eat again!' Fiona replied with a sigh.

Later, when she'd settled Rory at the table with a bowl of ice cream and two wafers, Sian asked, 'Where will Gus be? At home getting himself something to eat?'

'I've just spoken to him on his mobile. He's got to take Luella back to her hotel and then he muttered something about taking Melissa out for a drink.' Fiona looked at Sian, feeling apologetic and then cross with herself. Her son had every right to go out drinking with whomever he liked. 'They are free agents.'

'Of course,' said Sian looking stung. 'I just wondered. Now, what would we like, apart from a very big drink?'

'We shouldn't really.'

'Well, I shouldn't because I've had loads already but you only had one glass of fizz, and you didn't have the mugs that some of us got.'

'No. Trust Veronica to have those antique folding beakers. For shooting parties no doubt.'

'They're very grand, the Lewis-Joneses, aren't they?'

'But fun.' Fiona suddenly felt bad talking about them when they'd been such generous hosts, and even worse for being about to say they weren't really grand, just rich. 'And very kind,' she added.

'Definitely. And brilliant planners. Think of the organisation involved in that picnic, even if you had it catered.'

'Absolutely!' Fiona agreed wholeheartedly. 'The last picnic I had anything to do with was a bottle of pop for the kids and some curling sandwiches.'

Sian nodded, obviously recognising such picnics. 'So, a drop of Pinot now, then?' she added.

'Fine! Lovely! I can walk from here if I overdo it.'

Fiona was determined to make things easy for Sian. She was looking dreadfully tense.

Rory, having finished his ice cream, asked if he could go and play in the garden. 'I'm going to make a pretend fire and boil a billy.'

'As long as it's pretend,' Sian said, and then opened the fridge.

Fiona watched Sian hunting in the fridge for olives and wine. It's my fault she's strained. She knows I'm going to ask her about it and she doesn't want to talk about it. But she's got to. Fiona was very sure about this. They couldn't just leave the matter unaddressed.

Sian produced a bottle of wine, some olives and half a packet of Kettle Chips, which she tipped into a bowl.

'Let's go into the sitting room. We can hear Rory from there and it's comfortable.' She paused. 'Might as well make the most of it, while the house is still mine.'

Both women sat down with glasses and snacks to hand. Sian filled the glasses. 'Cheers,' she said a moment later. Both women took a big gulp of wine.

'OK,' said Fiona. 'Elephant in the room: how did it happen?'

Sian sighed. She was obviously not going to pretend she didn't know what Fiona was talking about. She settled into her chair and adjusted a cushion at her back. 'Well,

151

we met at a party – Richard's party – I can't remember if you know that.' She paused.

'Not important. Go on.' Fiona didn't want to get side-tracked.

'Well, I'd gone into the kitchen for a glass of water. Gus was there – do you mind me calling him that?'

'Not at all. Go on.'

Sian seemed to feel a certain amount of relief at being able to talk about that night with someone else, even if that someone else was Gus's mother. Maybe she'd been trying to forget, which could have been causing her almost as much heartache as remembering. And she seemed to realise there was no point in not telling Fiona everything; she'd only prise it out of her at some point anyway.

'Honestly, Fiona, it was like magnets. We just flew together. He gave me the water and that was it. We talked for ages. Then he asked me back to his flat. And I went. I knew what would happen and I still went.'

'I understand.' Fiona found herself almost envious. There was something magical about that sort of connection. She couldn't blame Sian for following her instincts. And of course she didn't blame Angus. Men were programmed to behave like that.

'To be honest, even if I'd known I was going to get pregnant, I'd still have gone.' Sian blushed, as if she'd just remembered she was talking to her ex-lover's mother.

'I don't blame you at all. You wouldn't want to be without Rory.'

'Well, not now, obviously, but when I first realised, I did panic.'

'I'm sure.'

'I couldn't say the P word.'

'Which P word?'

'Pregnant. I still blush when I say it.'

152

Fiona sipped her wine as the tension she hadn't realised she'd been feeling ebbed away. This conversation wasn't as hard as she thought it might be. Sian was being very honest with her, and brave. 'So what did you say to your parents, if you couldn't say the word?'

Sian made a face. 'I said I'd done a test and it was positive.'

'And how did they react?'

'Well, Mum hugged me and made out she was delighted but I knew she was a bit worried.'

'And your father?'

'Oh well, I was dreading telling him. I didn't want him to know that I was sexually active – and I wasn't, very. There had only been a couple. But your dad . . . You know, I was his little girl, not a grown woman.'

'But you did tell him? Or did you get your mother to?'

'I told him. He was fine – seemed to be. Concerned, of course, but they didn't reproach me or say I'd been careless or anything.'

'Not much point, really.'

'Well, no, that's what they said when I asked them about it. And they rallied round. Dad's always been brilliant with Rory.'

'Angus is pretty good!' Fiona felt defensive on her son's behalf. She wasn't quite sure why.

'He is. And he doesn't even have to be. I mean, he doesn't know who Rory is.'

'He will have to know though, Sian. I appreciate it isn't going to be easy but you have to tell him.' Fiona was firm. She topped up their glasses and waited for Sian to speak.

'Does he?' Sian seemed to be pleading. 'I mean, I've brought Rory up on my own – with my parents and lots of other people's help. I don't want anyone interfering and—'

'You don't have to let him interfere, but he has a right to know. He's Rory's flesh and blood. Besides that, Rory would like having a dad, wouldn't he? All boys need a male role model.'

'He's got Richard and my dad for that,' said Sian.

'It's not the same.'

Sian sipped her wine as if she agreed, but didn't want to admit it.

'And you're going to have to tell him quite soon.'

'Am I?'

'Yes. He deserves to know. He's got eyes in his head. He might see the likeness like I did. Like you did.'

'Unlikely,' Sian said quickly, as if trying to convince herself. 'We only saw it because they were together. He won't see himself and Rory like that.'

Fiona pressed on. 'There are mirrors, old photographs. You can't rely on him not recognising his own facial characteristics and mannerisms. Now I think back I wonder if I warmed to Rory so quickly – straightaway really – because there was a familiarity about him.'

Sian shook her head and bit her lip. 'I suppose it's possible. But I don't want to tell him. I think life is difficult enough at the moment, with me struggling to get work, having to find somewhere else to live – all those things.'

Fiona was sympathetic but resolute. 'Listen, Rory's got a birthday coming up, hasn't he?'

Sian nodded.

'It'll give you a little time to psych yourself up to do it, but you'll have to tell him by then.' Seeing Sian was about to argue she went on: 'Honey, he could easily work it out for himself. He can do sums. It would be much, much better if you told him than if he found out on his own. I know it's difficult for you, but I can't let you not tell him and the longer you leave it the harder it'll be. '

'OK,' said Sian in a small voice after a few moments.

Satisfied that she'd got Sian to see sense, Fiona said, 'When did you find out Angus was going away, for such a long time?' Fiona remembered when she had found out. Of course, as a good mother, she had pretended to be pleased, rather as she imagined Sian's mother had pretended to be pleased about Sian being pregnant. But in her heart she'd wondered how she'd manage without him in her life. There were postcards and the odd snatched phone call and email but it wasn't the same. She had got used to it though. And better a happy son across the other side of the world than a bored and edgy one close at hand.

'He told me sometime during the evening. Not quite sure when.'

Fiona nodded. 'Just to reassure myself about my son's efficiency, can I ask how you got . . .'

'Pregnant?' Sian wrinkled her brow as she worked out how best to put this. 'I can't really say it was a "wardrobe malfunction" but . . .'

'Condom split?'

'Condom split.'

Fiona laughed, glad to lighten the mood.

'Hello, Mum, hello, Fona,' said Rory, who appeared at that moment, obviously wondering why his mother and his friend were laughing. 'These flowers are for you.' He handed Fiona a bunch of flowers, including two dandelions and a sweet pea, before running back out to the garden to put more sticks on his pretend fire.

Fiona said, 'When Rory becomes my open-and-aboveboard grandchild – and I insist that soon he will – I never want him to call me anything but Fona.'

Sian got up out of her seat and kissed her cheek.

Chapter Thirteen

Sian had just settled down to work one morning the following week when the phone rang. She was not thrilled to hear Melissa's voice at the other end.

'Sian, it's me, Melissa.'

'Oh, hi. I was just writing to your mother to thank her for such a wonderful day.' As she talked she made a note on a bit of paper to do just that.

'It was fun, wasn't it?' Melissa paused. 'Actually Angus told me off a bit.'

'Oh? Why should he do that?'

'He said it was unfair of me to bring Luella and spring on you that she's going to sell your house to me. I am sorry. I just didn't think.'

'It was a shock, I must admit, but not entirely unexpected.' What was surprising was that Melissa had rung up to apologise.

'Angus was quite cross with me in fact.' Melissa giggled. 'He can be quite – masterful – when he wants. Not a bad thing in a man.'

Sian didn't really feel able to comment. 'I hope it didn't cause you to fall out.'

'Oh no, it was huge fun being told off by lovely Angus. But in order to make it up to you, I wonder if you fancy coming round to Mum's to see those fitted wardrobes I was talking about? Although I'm moving out, she did say she quite fancied having a revamp. What do you say?'

Sian didn't think she could say no, really. Veronica Lewis-Jones knew a lot of influential people. She certainly didn't want to offend her and she wasn't responsible for her daughter's behaviour. 'OK. When do you think would suit? Mornings are best because I've got Rory some afternoons.'

'Oh! That's another thing. Angus – can't think of him as Gus really – was saying what a nice child Rory is. And he is! I'm sure he'd look after him one afternoon while you came over here. Mummy's rather busy in the mornings.'

'Oh.' Sian was rather taken aback at the idea of Gus babysitting for Rory. 'Well, I'm not sure that will be necessary. But have you got a preferred day?'

'As soon as poss, really.'

'Tomorrow?' Having your fitted wardrobes painted wasn't usually such an emergency but provided she worked after Rory had gone to bed, she should be able to finish the piece she was working on and be free the following afternoon. Fiona would have Rory if necessary.

'Fabbo. About two o'clock?'

'Fine.' Or maybe she could ask Jody, if she hadn't used up all her childminding brownie points with her yet.

'OK, now the address. Have you got Sat Nav?'

'I have a map.'

'Oh good. Sat Nav is absolutely no use in finding my parents' house. Have you got a pen and paper?'

Eventually Sian got the information she needed and managed to get all the telephone numbers she could too, in case she got lost. Working in the country was more difficult in some ways. London might be big and sprawling but you usually got to your destination eventually. Now she had to negotiate narrow country lanes with grass growing up the middle and hedges that scraped the sides of your car.

Still, she was pleased to think she might get another commission. When she'd finished the child's wardrobe she had on the go at the moment there was nothing much else in the pipeline apart from the monster cupboard in Fiona's barn, and the little nursing chair. She really needed some paid work. She was going to go and visit Fiona's friend's shop to see if she was interested, but Margaret was away on holiday at the moment. She also planned to visit other similar shops to see if she could drum up some business, but private commissions were best really. She was looking forward to something she could get her teeth into. It was always exciting to have a potential new project. She enjoyed all aspects of her work, even the painstaking, fiddly bits, but the initial stage was the most exciting. The planning, the drawings, the choosing of colours. With luck Veronica would be happy to let her imagination run riot (within limits) and recommend her to all her friends. She smiled. It would also give her a proper focus for her thoughts – something she badly needed!

She buttonholed Jody when she went to pick up Rory later and asked her favour. 'I really wouldn't ask you but for some reason they can't see me in the morning.'

'Oh no, that's fine, but you can do something for me in return.'

'Anything! You've done so much childcare for me. Do you want me to have Annabelle for a weekend? I'd be more than happy to. Or I could move in here and look after all the kids.'

Jody laughed. 'Nope, although that's a good offer. I want you to do a farmers' market – well, craft market really – with me.'

'Why?'

'I've made a shedload of cushions and I booked a stall ages ago with another girl but she can't make it. It would be so much more fun if there were two of us. You could bring some samples of your work and hand out leaflets. It might be a really good way of getting yourself known locally.'

Sian considered. 'It's not the sort of thing I'd think of doing usually. I mean, people don't sell furniture at farmers' markets, do they?'

'Well, as I said, it's more of a craft market really. It's on when the farmers' market isn't. Come on! It would be great publicity for you and loads more fun for me. John will look after the kids.'

'It does sound fun, I must say. It would be something completely different for me. OK, I'm in.'

Sian drove home, her mind whirring. Would leaflets and photographs be enough? People liked to watch people working. Should she take a piece of furniture with her? There might not be room with all Jody's cushions. And it might get a little boring for people if she was working on one piece the whole time. What could she do so that they could see the results immediately and have something to take away with them? A plan started to form in her head.

'Rory, I've got it!' she said as they pulled up outside the house. 'I'll do children's names for people while they wait. There are always loads of names you can never buy anything personalised for.'

Rory sighed. 'What are you talking about, Mummy?'

'Oh, nothing really. I'm just thinking aloud.' She'd have to prepare lots of boards ready, primed and with a bit of decoration – half for girls and half for boys – or maybe more for girls? Some that could go either way, she decided, as she released Rory from his seat. She found herself looking forward to the craft market rather than dreading it. Jody was right, it would be fun, especially now she had a plan. Two new projects in one day: things were definitely looking up. At least on the work front. Richard would be thrilled for her. She would tell him next time he phoned.

The next afternoon, with Rory safely and happily at Jody's house, Sian set off for the Lewis-Joneses. She found Melissa's parents' house eventually but she was late. 'I am so sorry!' she said, as Veronica kissed her and ushered her into their huge house made of reconstructed Cotswold stone. Sian had just had time to take in how large it was and to feel impressed before she was whisked inside. And she'd thought Fiona's house was big!

'Don't worry,' said Veronica. 'I still get lost all the time if I haven't been to places before. Now, would you like some coffee? Harold's got an amazing machine that'll produce a cappuccino for you in seconds.'

Sian laughed. 'No thank you, I think I should have a look at the wardrobes straightaway. I've wasted enough of your time already.'

They went up some stairs thickly carpeted in a shade of eau-de-Nil Sian knew would stay clean for about five minutes in her house. Maybe the Lewis-Joneses replaced it every few years, just because of unsightly stains. Oh, for that sort of money!

Melissa's bedroom was perfect. Huge, with windows on each side, it had an en-suite bathroom twice the size of the bathroom of the cottage she was so eager to buy and a wall of wardrobes that could have housed the entire spring collection of one of the smaller fashion houses.

'This is amazing! I can't believe you'd want to change it,' she said, looking at the room with awe.

'Yes, but it needs an update. I'm a little bored with it. Lissa said you did wonderful work. I'd like the room to be unique.'

'Isn't it already? Dual aspect, en suite, fitted wardrobes: an estate agent's dream property! Anyone's dream property! Painting it could reduce its value.'

'But we're not moving.' Veronica smiled. 'Show me your portfolio, I'd love to see what you might make of it.'

Sian smiled back. She hadn't intended her warnings to work as reverse psychology, but they'd obviously done the trick. 'Oh, OK.'

'Let's go and have a cup of tea if you don't want frothy coffee. I can't wait to see inside those books!'

An hour later, Sian drove away happy. She and Veronica had devised a plan that would be pretty and different but not so fantastical as to put people off. They had toyed with the idea of having a unicorn emerging from a forest of snow-covered birches but had concluded that wild roses winding in and out of the wardrobes would be better than a full-blown *trompe-l'œil*, although, now she'd got the idea, Veronica was seriously considering something like that in the dining room. 'I've got rather bored with all that William Morris wallpaper. It's a bit gloomy.'

Sian had had fun. She liked Veronica even if she was rather forceful. She might have enough work to last her all year!

That evening, with Rory happy in the garden for a bit and no need to feed him, thanks to Jody, and plant-watering done, Sian went into her wood store (previously a potting shed) and found some suitable planks. She'd spotted them when she'd first arrived and thought they looked useful. They were off-cuts from some flooring, but new and therefore splinter free. Her father had donated his table saw to her when she moved and now she cut as many potential door names as she had wood for. It was twenty, and she debated if she should get hold of some more timber or if that would be enough. It was hard to say, but she felt it probably would be.

She had put a coat of primer on most of them when the phone rang. It was Fiona.

'Would you and Rory be up for a quick drink? I need a rest but Angus is on a mission and I feel obliged to help. If you and Rory came I could stop.'

It would have been so easy to make an excuse – not even an excuse – and say Rory had had a long day. But Sian found herself saying, 'That would be lovely.'

As she and Rory walked up the road she acknowledged she was looking forward to seeing Gus. It would be safe now, after all. He'd met Rory and although she knew she had to tell him, she didn't have to do it tonight. And with Fiona there he couldn't tease and unsettle her quite so much.

They found Fiona's house in organised chaos. The barn, which had been fairly clear before, thanks partly to Sian's efforts in starting the operation, was now full of neatly stacked items, which, according to Fiona, were yurts.

Fiona handed Sian a gin and tonic. 'I felt the need for strong liquor. I'll tell Angus you're here. He's obsessed with clearing out the attic. God knows why. If he wants to turn out my cupboards, there are plenty that need doing.'

Sian laughed as they walked into the house, Rory running ahead, having been told the trains were in the conservatory now.

'Yes. Melissa's been helping him most of the day. She's gone now.'

A pang of jealousy gripped Sian and made her nearly choke on her drink. She caught herself in time. 'I went round to Veronica's this afternoon,' she said. 'She's got some fitted wardrobes she wants roses on and is thinking

162

about a full-blown mural for the dining room.' She took another sip now she felt it was safe. 'I haven't actually done one before.'

Fiona shouted up the stairs, telling her son that Sian was here, before answering. 'But it would be like painting furniture wouldn't it? Only bigger?'

They reached the conservatory and Sian sat in her favourite place. 'That's what I'm relying on.'

'Hello!'

Gus, covered in dust, appeared in the doorway and then swooped on Sian, in order to give her a kiss.

'Hello back!' said Sian, slightly startled by his effusive welcome. 'What have you been up to?'

'Well, my stuff all arrived so I've been putting that away. And there's the attic. You would not believe how much junk my mother has stored in there. I think we should have a sale in the garden to get rid of it all.'

'Some of it I want to keep!' protested Fiona.

'Honestly, the space is much more valuable than all that stuff, even if some of it is antique.'

'Hmm. If you say so, dear.'

'I do. Now, do you two want another drink before I jump in the shower? I won't be long.'

Sian quickly dismissed the vision of him in the shower that popped rather disconcertingly into her head at this point.

Fiona said, 'Why do people always "jump in the shower"? I never would! I'd be far too worried about slipping and falling over.'

After Gus returned, Rory played happily in the corner with some of Gus's old toys whilst Sian and Fiona discussed her commissions and the merits of village life versus the bright lights of the city, with Gus firm in his opinion that the best life was out in the wild with only your wits to protect you. It gave Sian a pang to think he might want to go travelling again soon.

After an hour Sian took a sleepy Rory home. It was well past his bedtime but she felt a mother's pride at the way he hadn't interrupted the grown-up chat or demanded juice every five minutes. He really was a very good little boy.

Once Rory was fast asleep (he'd only needed one story tonight) she finished priming the planks and propped them up to dry against the side of the cottage. She just hoped the weather forecasters were right and they were in for a fine night.

As she got ready for bed, she realised she had enjoyed chatting to Fiona and Angus this evening, just the three of them, at ease with each other, nothing said to cause any alarm, no guarded looks. It was a moment of rare tranquillity before the storm, she thought. Because somehow she knew a storm was inevitable, and that there wasn't much she could do to protect herself from the battering. For now she was just thankful for the lull that came before.

Chapter Fourteen

❧

On the morning of the craft market Sian delivered Rory to Jody's house before any reasonable person was awake. Jody came out eating toast and peanut butter, looking showered, relaxed and ready to go. Rory ran under her arm into the kitchen without a backward glance at his mother.

'Tea?' said Jody. 'Or shall we wait till we get there? There'll be a café.'

'Let's get on. Rory's obviously fine, and I've got a bit of setting up to do. Can I follow you? You've been there before.'

'Fine, I'll just get the keys. It's a shame we can't travel together.'

Sian grinned. 'It's good we've got enough to fill two cars though, or our stall might be a bit empty.'

The craft market was partially covered and the stalls were already set up. Jody drove right to the entrance and found out from a woman in jeans and a very shaggy top which one was theirs. She came to Sian's window.

'We can dump stuff here and then go and park. Annie will keep an eye on it if you've got anything nickable.'

Sian had accumulated quite a few little painted pieces, footstools, tables and small chests, as well as a larger dressing table – another one donated by Fiona and done in rather a hurry. As the place was already busy with people setting up, intent on making their pitches look interesting and good value, she emptied the car, trusting that everything would still be here when she came back.

'Wow, that all looks amazing!' said Jody when she'd filled her half of the stall with cushions, plumply inviting and sumptuous.

'Your cushions look heavenly. Maybe we should do something together. You find a lovely fabric for the cushions and I could paint the bed head to match.' Sian adjusted where she was to do her paint-on-demand name signs for doors for the fifteenth time. 'I just hope I get some customers. It would be so embarrassing if I don't.'

Jody laughed. 'Have you ever sold your own stuff before?'

'I've got commissions, but I don't think that's quite the same. They've asked me round because they probably want to buy my work. I haven't actually had to say, "Roll up, roll up, come buy."' Doubt crept over Sian and it felt like getting into a cold bath.

'What's the matter?'

'I don't think I can do it. I don't think I can actually sell my work like this.'

This aspect of doing a craft market hadn't occurred to Sian. She'd just thought of having things to sell and things to be a bit entertaining, like the name boards. She hadn't thought she'd have to speak to people and persuade them to buy. 'I suddenly think I want to go home.'

'Well, you can't.' Jody was firm. 'Go and get us a hot drink and a bacon butty and you'll feel better.'

'You think?'

'Yup. And if you're still windy when you've refuelled, we'll swap.'

'What do you mean?'

'I'll sell your work and you sell my cushions.'

This idea was appealing. 'So I tell the passing woman

166

that new cushions are just what she needs to revamp her sitting room and you have the very ones?'

'Exactly! Now run along and get us a hot drink. Do you want some money?'

Sian was already on her way. 'No, I'm fine. Ketchup on the butty?' she called over her shoulder.

Jody was a brilliant salesperson. She caught a passing woman of late-middle age who foolishly paused for a second in the vicinity of the stall.

'I bet you've got a child you have to buy a present for?'

The woman stopped and nodded, cautiously.

'And I bet they've already got everything any little heart could desire – far more toys than is good for anyone?'

Pleased to be given a platform for feelings she usually felt obliged to keep private, the woman took a breath. 'Well, I'm afraid I do think that! Children don't need all these expensive toys to make them happy. A few, good quality, sturdy toys should last their childhood.'

'So is it a grandchild or someone else you're looking for?' Jody was shameless. Sian was now hiding behind the pile of cushions.

'It's my goddaughter's little girl. She has everything, including a pony. Really, there's nothing left for me to buy her.'

'Well, why not a name for her door?'

Sian tensed, waiting to spring into action, mentally calculating how to fit something like 'Mellasina' on to one of her prepared boards.

'She's got one,' said the woman.

Sian relaxed, half disappointed, half relieved.

'Ah, but my colleague here could put her name on one of these boxes. How about that?'

Oh golly, thought Sian, I hope this child has got a really short name.

'Ah, now that is a nice idea. It would last her for ever, wouldn't it? But these boxes are all painted. There's no space for a name.'

'Sian!' ordered Jody, 'come out from behind there and help this lady!'

Sian, blushing and sweating, came out. 'Sorry, I was just doing something. How can I help? You'd like a name on one of these boxes? I can do that for you. Which box and what name would you like? I can just blank out some of the decoration and paint in the name. Although you would have to come back a bit later.'

The woman shook her head, but then spotted a larger box at the back of the stall. 'This hasn't got too much on it. Maybe you could fit the name in there without blanking anything out? I'm in a bit of a hurry.'

'What name would you like?'

'Zoë. Do you think you could do that while I wait?'

Sian took a breath. It shouldn't be a problem at all, but somehow the thought of painting a name in front of her customer's very eyes was daunting. 'Why don't I practise on one of my blank name boards so you can see if you like the lettering and then you could go round the rest of the market while I do it?'

Fortunately Sian's hand kept steady, she remembered how to do a zed and there was room to further customise the box with a few poppies, which apparently were Zoë's favourite flower. Even the umlaut on top of the 'e' went well. The woman went away a bit later with the box under her arm and a satisfied smile on her face.

'You should have charged her extra for putting the name on,' said Jody, ever-practical.

'I know, but I didn't like to.'

But it turned out to be a loss leader. Several people had spotted her painting the name and wanted name boards. She began to relax and was soon producing unicorns, sea horses and dragonflies without hesitation or a need to rough anything out first. She also sold a lot of cushions, discovering she was in fact a demon saleswoman as long as it wasn't her own work.

By lunchtime, the early crowds had drifted away and Jody and Sian were beginning to get tired and hungry. 'I reckon we've done a day's work by now,' said Jody.

'How many more people are we likely to get?' Sian rearranged her remaining stock yet again, and then plumped Jody's stock of cushions, which had been replenished twice from her stash in the car.

'Not that many. Milly over there is packing up.' Milly sold soaps and bath oils and did a brisk trade with the going-to-a-dinner-party-need-a-gift trade.

They were just about to give each other permission to do the same when Fiona and Gus strolled up.

'Oh, look at that old dressing table! What an improvement!' said Fiona. Then she kissed Sian and introduced Gus to Jody.

'Lovely cushions, I must have one, but, Gus, look at that dressing table!'

'Must I, very pretty and all that, but dressing tables aren't really my thing.' He kissed Sian and then kissed Jody too.

'But it was ours! I gave it to Sian to decorate. It was that horrid orange oak.'

'Fiona, I was planning to give it back to you. If you'd like it, I'd be thrilled.'

'No,' said Gus firmly. 'Unless you want it in your bedroom. We're getting rid of the crap, not adding to it.'

He winked, trying to imply he was teasing, but not quite making it.

Fiona shook her head slightly in irritation. 'Gus, honestly!' She looked at the two younger women. 'He's on this purge, getting rid of all the things in the attic that have lived there happily for years.'

As Sian knew that Fiona had wanted to get rid of all the surplus furniture, she guessed the problem was just that Gus was making her do it a bit faster than she would have done on her own.

'Gus, maybe I could interest you in a name board?' she said, feeling his high-handed attitude to the dressing table should be punished. 'I could do a Gus – or Angus even – in two ticks. I've really got my hand in.'

Gus stood over her, pretending to contemplate the idea, stroking his chin with his fingers.

'Or maybe have a cushion, Fiona. They can't be considered clutter, can they?' Sian went on. 'This one would look lovely in the conservatory.'

'So it would. I'll have it.'

While she was paying, Gus inspected Sian's remaining stock intently, picking up the pieces and inspecting them. 'Yes,' he said suddenly. 'I do want you to do a name board for me.'

'Oh, great,' said Sian, slightly surprised. She hadn't expected him to really want one. 'Which name do you want? Gus, or Angus?'

'Melissa,' he said. 'It would make a great present.'

'Oh,' said Sian, when she could speak, which took a second or two. 'Is it her birthday?'

'Yes, and she's being quite helpful to me at the moment. I'd like to give her something nice.'

'Well, I'm flattered and a little surprised that you consider my little offerings "something nice",' said Sian, fighting a losing battle with waspishness. 'After the way you reacted to the dressing table,' she added, so he wouldn't think she was in any way jealous of Melissa.

'I just don't think we need it,' he said firmly. 'Now, any chance of some little ponies on Lissa's name? I always think of her on a pony, somehow.'

'I tell you what, I'll do a much better job if I do it at home,' she said, her pride demanding that Melissa's name was perfect and the ponies pure Thelwell, barrel-shaped with their tails sticking straight out behind. 'I could drop it round to you. When do you need it by?'

'Friday, if possible. I'm taking her out for a birthday drink.'

'Fine! No problem.' She smiled brightly, as if he was just another customer.

'Great. Sian, I was wondering—'

'Oh look,' said Sian delightedly. 'Here comes Richard!'

She'd been expecting him back in time for Rory's birthday – he'd promised – but he must have been able to get away earlier. And he'd arrived at just the right time!

'Hi, girls, Gus,' said Richard. 'Would anyone mind if I took Sian out for lunch?'

Lunch out with Richard wasn't actually all that exciting although he was pleasant enough company. They'd had many lunches out together before, after all. But even if it had been the dullest thing ever it would have been worth it to see the expression on Gus's face. With a grin, she happily strolled off with Richard in the direction of the local bar.

Although she knew it had lots and lots of advantages, Sian rather wished she hadn't accepted Fiona's offer to have Rory's birthday party in her garden. She discussed it with her mother.

171

'It's an awful upheaval for her. I should tell her I'll have it here.'

'Don't do that! She'd be terribly hurt. Besides, I'm longing to meet her. Why don't you want to have it at her house?'

Sian couldn't tell her mother why. She knew she'd have to sooner or later, and probably would when her mother came down for Rory's party, but she couldn't do it on the phone. 'I don't know really. It just seems an imposition.'

'She had no reason to offer if she didn't want to have it,' said Sian's mother firmly.

Sian bit her lip to stop herself saying, 'Oh yes there is,' in a pantomime way.

'Anyway, I want to see her house,' her mother said. 'And yours is too small for a party if it rains. Oh, and I presume Richard is coming? He's such a nice man.'

He was, Sian acknowledged, if only he took up half as much of her thoughts as Gus seemed to do these days. He would be the perfect husband: reliable, dependable, loving; everything that Gus wouldn't be. She could see that Rory liked Gus but even if she felt he'd be a good father she still wasn't sure reliable and dependable – or even faithful – were words to best describe him.

She and Rory were baking together when Gus knocked on the back door and walked in.

Seeing him was a shock. She'd managed to avoid him, apart from brief moments, quite well since she'd delivered the name board for Melissa. Then she'd just stood on the doorstep, refusing to come in, and handed it over. Now he was in her kitchen, filling the space with his energy – and she was horribly aware that Fiona's deadline to tell him about Rory was looming. In fact it was the very next day.

'Hi, guys,' he said. 'Come on. I need you.'

'Actually I'm quite busy here,' said Sian. 'Baking for Rory's birthday party.'

'We're going to ice the biscuits in a minute,' said Rory. He still had the remnants of chocolate from where he'd licked the bowl round his mouth and flour on his sleeve.

'Cooking's for girls!' said Gus, glancing at Sian, obviously hoping for a reaction. 'I need help with some men's stuff.'

'Then you don't need me,' said Sian tartly. 'And Rory, though obviously a big boy' – she looked at him encouragingly – 'could hardly be described as a man.'

'Obviously neither of you are men, but you're all I can get at short notice. Come on!' He wasn't going to accept any excuses.

'What do you want us for?' asked Rory, obviously keen to be a man, if just for a little while.

'Need help building the shelter for your party! Mum and I thought it would be fun to have something different. Kids always have clowns or entertainers or something and we – well OK, it was my idea – thought having a shelter to play in would be much more fun.'

'Oh,' said Sian. 'Well, I do have quite a bit to do here. Can't you manage on your own?'

'Nope! It would take too long and also, why should the birthday boy miss out on a treat like building a shelter?'

The birthday boy looked at his mother, obviously wanting to help Gus very much. Gus also looked at her and Sian found herself unable to resist two pairs of eyes – mostly because they matched; she found Rory hard enough to resist. Gus, who was a giant version of her son with different colour hair, was just as appealing, only in a worryingly different way.

'OK, I suppose so.' She took off her apron, feigning

reluctance. 'I'll have to ice these after you've gone to bed, Rory. Are you sure you wouldn't rather stay and do them now?'

'Mum!' Rory's meaning was plain. In a little while – probably shortly after he'd started at school – he'd add 'duh!' to indicate how ridiculous her question was.

As she cleaned them both up and found Rory's wellies and the ones she'd appropriated from Fiona, as well as a pair of gardening gloves (as suggested by Gus), she realised how pleased she was to see him again. Was this a good sign or not? she wondered.

'I got a proper child seat put in the Landy, you'll be glad to hear,' said Gus. 'This should do you until you're about eleven, the man in the shop reckoned.' He strapped Rory in.

'Oh that's kind!' said Sian.

'Well, I did it because it's better than the racing harness really. More practical.'

This was a relief. Although Sian trusted Fiona as much as she trusted anyone, there was always the fear that she might let something slip by mistake. Sian didn't want him to have put a child's seat in his car because he knew he was Rory's father, but Fiona clearly hadn't let anything slip. Gus would scarcely be making such relaxed, casual conversation if he'd just heard from his mother that Rory was his son. Sian couldn't even begin to imagine the uproar that would result from Gus getting that particular bit of news in that particular way, but knew she'd find out soon enough. If she hadn't told him by tomorrow – D-Day – then Fiona surely would. She climbed into the passenger seat with a sigh.

'So where are we going?' she said after a moment's silence.

'To some woods I've known all my life. We need to get

the right kind of timber. Mum's garden is OK for little twigs but we need serious sticks and leaf litter. Lots and lots of leaf litter.'

Sian wanted to ask if it was OK to just go to random woods and take serious sticks and leaf litter but didn't. Gus would scoff at asking permission for anything he wanted to do.

After a few miles they bumped down a track and stopped at the opening to a wood.

'Here we are, my favourite spot in the entire world,' said Gus, jumping down from his seat before going round to help Sian.

'Really? And you've seen a lot of world. This bit is your favourite?'

'Yes. "East, West, Home's Best." My brother and I used to have Scout camp up here and then drag our parents with us as much as we could. When we were old enough to come here on our own on our bikes, it was the only place we ever went, nearly.'

'I can't imagine letting Rory cycle all this way on his own,' said Sian. 'But I have come down from London. I'm sure things are different in the country.' Were they all that different? She hoped so.

'Well, our parents did know where we were. It was before every kid had a mobile phone, but they knew we were safe enough.' He chuckled. 'Although there was one time when I fell and split my leg open. My brother helped me out of the wood. We limped along until we came to a house, knocked on the door and they took us in. They were great. Rang the folks, gave us squash and biscuits, washed my leg.' He looked at Sian, suddenly stern. 'Honestly, most people are good and kind and do the right thing. The weirdos, the ones you read about in the paper, are the exception.'

'I know that!' said Sian lightly.

'OK!' said Gus when they'd got to the part of the wood he thought was best. 'We're looking for two long sticks with a fork in the top. I can cut off a bit if necessary. Ah! Found one! See, Rory? We need another, just like this. Yell if you need a hand carrying it. Remember, always drag if you can. No point in carrying more weight than you need to. We'll get all the stuff we can and put it here then we'll go and get the Landy.'

Sian was pleased and surprised at how Rory got into fetching sticks, working hard to bring bigger ones. She got into it too, finding unexpected satisfaction in the task.

'OK, that might be enough. Nearly, anyway. Now, Sian, will you be frightened in the woods on your own? Rory and I'll get the vehicle and we can start loading. Here.' He reached into the back pocket of his trousers and handed her a couple of black bin liners. 'Fill these with leaf litter. We need a good amount of it. I've got more sacks that I'll bring up.'

Rory was thrilled to be going off with Gus. He took extra long strides to keep up with his new friend.

Watching them marching off together she asked herself, not for the first time, how it would go when she told Gus about Rory. Surely it would be all right? He liked Rory. He couldn't object to finding out he was his son. It would be fine. It was the fact that she hadn't told him until now that was really worrying her. Would he understand why, or never forgive her? She didn't know if he was the forgiving type. But Fiona had been brilliant; surely he would be too?

Convinced, even if just for a little while, Sian happily gathered up leaf litter, trying not to think what she was gathering up as well in the way of bugs and creepy-crawlies. She was glad of her gloves. She filled the bags, squashed down the leaves and got quite a bit more in. She was pleased with herself. She'd make a country girl yet.

Rory was obviously having the best time he had ever had. Sitting in the front seat, well strapped in, Sian was pleased to note, driving up through the wood in the Land-Rover, his complete and utter joy radiated from every inch of him. No birthday present anyone ever gave him could match up to this.

'Right, guys, now we pile the timber into the back.'

It was tiring work, especially as Gus produced more black sacks for Sian to fill. Neither Gus nor Rory thought that leaf litter was their concern. She had to go further and further afield to get it, having used up all the stuff nearby. She could hear Rory laughing, probably at some-thing naughty that Gus had said and consoled herself that Rory would soon have all the benefits of a father without her having to have a husband. Maybe it would be the ideal solution. She'd coped on her own for so long she knew she could continue to do so but seeing how much Rory enjoyed being with Gus she couldn't deny him his father. It looked as if Gus was here to stay, at least for the foreseeable future – his leg and his book would see to that – so maybe she could risk letting Rory grow attached to him. As for herself – and Richard – that was for another day.

They drove back to Fiona's house and Gus swung the Land-Rover into an entrance Sian hadn't seen before, right up the end of the garden.

'We'll unload, take stock and then see if we need to go back for some more,' said Gus.

'I'm hungry,' said Rory.

Sian looked at her watch. 'It's nearly his suppertime,' she said. 'And I could murder a cup of tea. That means I want one very much,' she explained to Rory, who looked confused at her expression.

'OK, we can have a brew and then crack on,' said Gus. He got a day pack out of the back of the Land-Rover and pulled out a billy.

Sian considered insisting that they go back to the house and not do the bushcraft thing but didn't. Rory was so happy and she could wait for her tea. It was fun playing at camping. She knew this was child's play for Gus but for Rory it felt like an adventure knowing she could go back to the comfort of the cottage afterwards made it fun for her too.

She sat down on the grass. She wanted to lie down really, but it was a bit damp.

Gus was teasing out the inside of a cotton wool pad, having built up a fire of sticks as fine as string and all the sizes up to the thickness of his thumb. He was well practised at it and it didn't take long. He looked up at Sian and smiled. Then he put down his sticks, straightened up and went back to the Land-Rover. He came back with a rug, waterproof on one side, wool on the other.

'Here, something to sit on.'

'I was expecting you to produce a tarp and a pile of kapok or something,' she said, arranging the rug and settling on it.

'We don't have to rough it all the time. Rory? Will you go to the house and ask if we can have some milk? We've got everything else. And if Mum wants to come up here for a billy-can tea, she's welcome.'

'OK!' said Rory.

'Oh, and bring some biscuits,' Gus added.

'OK!' said Rory again and shot off.

'He's a lovely kid. You've done a great job with him.'

'Thank you,' said Sian, wondering if maybe she should

tell him now. Then she decided no, Rory would be back at any moment, and she might not have finished explaining. And Gus might (as she worried he would) react badly. She didn't want to disturb this happy moment and spoil Rory's day. And truly, she should tell her son first. She'd leave it. As long as possible. Even if she knew she couldn't put it off for ever.

Rory came back bringing milk, biscuits, a bottle of wine and Fiona.

'I didn't think you should have all the fun on your own,' explained Fiona. 'So I thought as it was wine o'clock we'd bring it.'

Sian jumped up and kissed her. 'That's so kind. Although how I'll finish icing the biscuits if I have a glass of wine I don't know. With all this fresh air I'll just go to sleep.'

'You'll be fine. It's not the birthday cake, after all.'

'No, Mum's bringing that tomorrow.'

'It's a shame your father can't come.' Fiona unscrewed the bottle of wine and produced three tin mugs from her pocket.

'I know but it's this Old Boys' thing he goes to every year. He's only ever missed one.'

'When was that?' Fiona handed Sian a rather full mug.

'When Rory was born. But we've spared him birthday parties since if we haven't been able to make it when he's home. They're something he endures really. Parties are best for little boys.'

'Indeed,' agreed Fiona, looking over at her own 'little boy'.

Rory had devoured a packet of crisps and Sian had had a cup of billy-can tea and a glass of wine and now felt it was time they left. She got up and stretched her legs. 'Come on, Rory, we should get going. Big day tomorrow.'

'Hey! We have a shelter to build! You can't go home yet!'

'But, Gus, Rory's tired!' protested Fiona.

'I'll let Rory off, after all it's nearly his birthday, but someone has to help me build this shelter.'

'How long will it take?' asked Sian, worried about the un-iced biscuits and other preparations she still had to make for the party.

'It's OK,' said Gus, 'I'll go down the pub and get some of the lads up. We'll have it done in no time.'

'Gus, darling, do you know any of the lads "down the pub"?'

'Not yet, but I will do soon enough.' He put a hand on his mother's shoulder. 'Don't worry, Mum! I'm an expert at getting indigenous peoples to help me. It's my stock in trade!'

The two women exchanged exasperated glances but as Sian was very glad not to have to help him build a shelter when she wanted to get her tired boy into a bath and then bed she smiled warmly at Gus. 'It's so sweet of you to do this for Rory, isn't it, Rory?'

Rory nodded. 'Yes. Thank you.'

'No worries, mate, it's the least I can do.' He addressed Rory but afterwards he gave Sian a look that tore at her heart. Suddenly him not knowing was a terrible burden.

Chapter Fifteen

❧

'Come on, birthday boy,' said Sian to Rory the following day. 'We're going to take these things up to Fiona's and then go back and wait for Granny to ring. She's got your cake.'

'Is it a dragon cake?'

'Let's wait and see.'

Sian and Rory walked up the road towards Fiona's house. Sian was carrying a basket full of plastic boxes. In the boxes were biscuits in the shape of Peter Rabbit, their coats the very same blue, toasted sandwiches cut into shapes – she had a big selection of cookie cutters – and tiny tomatoes hollowed out and filled with finely grated cheese. Her mother said that in her day no one bothered about healthy eating at birthday parties, but Sian didn't want to take the chance. There were going to be mothers there she hadn't met yet. Jody had said she'd distribute invitations at the playgroup for her as she knew everyone. And Fiona had invited a few more young friends of her own.

'Fona's made a cake but she wouldn't let me see,' said Rory, grumbling gently.

'I know. It's very kind of her.'

'She said Gus didn't want interesting cakes any more. I like Gus. It was fun getting the sticks for the shelter, wasn't it?'

'It was, darling.'

'And Annabelle's coming? And her big brothers?' Ever since he had spent the day they went to the craft market at Annabelle's, he'd been obsessed by her brothers.

'I'm not sure, actually. But I know Fiona has invited some people we don't know, just to make it more fun.'

Actually Sian was a bit nervous about meeting Fiona's friends' sons and daughters; she was sure they'd be 'Yummy Mummies', tanned and slim and so would despise her.

'Are they bigger than me? The children?'

'I'm not sure. They will be nice though and you'll know lots of them from playgroup. Anyway, Fiona would only invite nice people.' Although Fiona had a tendency to see the good in people, Sian reflected, which might prove a problem. She could tell that Rory was a bit anxious too.

Once they arrived they felt better. Fiona embraced Rory and kissed him. 'Happy birthday, darling!' she said.

Gus swung him into the air. 'Hey, mate! What's it like to be five years old! Very much like being four and seven-eighths, I expect!' He put Rory down and ruffled his hair. 'Hello, Sian,' he said.

'Hello! Hello, everybody!' Sian sounded impressively carefree, she thought. She was glad she hadn't tried to fudge Rory's age. Quite apart from anything Fiona wouldn't have let her and her mother would have said, 'Don't be so silly.'

'Is it OK if I take Rory to show him the shelter I've built? I'd like him to see it before the other kids arrive.'

One glance at Rory told her how much he wanted to go and a second later she realised it was unlikely that Gus would find out he was his father from Rory given that Rory didn't know himself. Also, if the party was too much for him, at least he would have had a nice time first.

'That's fine,' she said.

'It's nice for them to have bonding time together,' said Fiona, when their sons had gone. 'You will tell him, won't you?'

'Yes! I said I would.'

Sian had actually rehearsed what she was going to say whenever she woke up in the night, which seemed to be every hour on the hour. Sadly, none of the versions were fit to say out loud. 'Gus, you know you were wondering who Rory's father was? Well, it's you! How about that!' Or, 'Rory was asking who his dad was the other day, so I told him it was you. He was thrilled! And, you'll never guess, I wasn't lying! It is you!' Or, 'You know when the condom split all those years ago? Well, I got pregnant, and it's Rory!' Nothing seemed right although she had her reasons for not telling him all sewn up: she'd had no way of getting in touch with him. It was the rather long gap between meeting him again and telling him now that was making it so difficult.

'You seem a bit on edge. Is it the thought of telling Gus, the birthday party, or what?'

'I am worried about telling Gus, about how he'll take it. Of course I am. And children's parties are very stressful. Although you've taken most of the stress out of it . . .' She faltered and chewed her lip.

'But there's something else?'

Sian sighed. 'It's the thought of having to up sticks and move somewhere else, just as we're getting settled here. I'm beginning to have a network of friends. I loved doing the craft market, there's you and . . .'

'There's Rory's dad,' Fiona prompted her gently.

'Yes.' This wasn't on Sian's list of reasons why she didn't want to move – officially, anyway. But Fiona wouldn't see it like that. She knew deep down that telling Gus was what was preying on her mind most today but of the two it seemed easier to worry about the roof-over-her-head issue right now. In fact, it was time she did give some serious thought to it. It was clear Luella did want to sell and if she didn't look for something soon it would be September, Rory would be starting school and they'd have nowhere to live. She shuddered.

'Well, I don't think you should worry too much about it.' Fiona took Sian's hand and gave it a squeeze.

'Why not? Even if I don't worry, I should start to look for somewhere else. I don't want to settle Rory into school and then move him after only a term. I should get on with house-hunting.'

'Just trust me. Don't do anything rash like registering Rory's name for a different school. I feel in my bones that it will be all right.'

As Sian had quite a lot to think about just then, she decided to try and forget about imminent homelessness and trust Fiona's bones. 'OK.'

'Shall we have a glass of wine, just to get us in party mood?' said Fiona, possibly feeling bad for nagging.

'Better not.' Sian smiled, to show she forgave her. 'Will you keep an eye on Rory if I go back home and wait for Mum?'

'Really, Angus is very responsible. Rory doesn't need me too.'

'I know, but I didn't tell Rory – although he might remember – that I've got to go back.'

'It'll be fine. Off you go.'

Fifteen minutes later, Sian ran out of the cottage, extremely pleased to see her mother. 'Hi, Mum!'

They embraced fondly and then checked the cake was OK. They decided they should drive to Fiona's with it, although it would be quicker to walk. It was such a beautiful creation Sian was terrified something might happen to it if they risked trying to carry it and walk at the same time.

She had just ushered her mother out of the back door so she could lock up when she had a terrible thought. She stopped. 'Mum!'

'What?' Her mother turned round, surprised by the sudden urgency in Sian's voice.

'Mum, there's something I should tell you.'

'What? Spinach in my teeth? Visible dandruff? What's so urgent?'

Sian was still standing with her hand on the door knob. 'It's Rory.' She saw her mother go pale. 'He's all right! No, this is about his father.'

Penny didn't look much happier on hearing this. 'Have you heard from him?'

She'd realised she couldn't let her mother go to the party without telling her first. Fiona would assume she had told her and might mention it. Her mother would be so hurt to find out from a stranger, even if she was a fellow grandmother.

'Sort of,' she said. 'He lives next door. He's Fiona's son, Gus.'

Penny put her hand up to her mouth, coughed and then rubbed her forehead. 'Right. And this is just coincidence?'

'Nearly. I met Gus at Richard's party.'

'Ah.'

'But Gus doesn't know. Fiona does, she spotted the likeness and she made me promise to tell Gus soon. Today is the deadline. She says he has to know, that it's not fair on him for me to keep it from him.'

Penny chewed her lip. 'I think she's right.'

'But don't say anything, will you? I mean, I've got to tell him, I accept that, but—'

'Of course I won't say anything, but, darling, you did pick your moment rather, to tell me.' Penny looked utterly bewildered.

'I know. If I didn't feel I had to tell Gus today I would have chosen a better time. But I thought you should know first, somehow. And I wanted to tell you in person.'

She felt horribly guilty for not having told her mother sooner, especially when she and her father had been such a support over the years. She should have known her mother wouldn't judge her or think her a bad person.

Penny went up to her daughter and hugged her. 'Come on, let's go. They'll be waiting for us.'

Fiona was as welcoming to Sian's mother as she had been to Sian and Sian was proud of her mother's ability to behave as if she hadn't just received startling news.

'So where's the birthday boy?' asked Penny, when she'd been given a glass of wine.

'Playing dens with my son, Angus,' said Fiona. 'They'll be back in a minute. I just sent them a text saying they must appear.'

'I thought Sian said your son's name was Gus,' said Penny.

'Lots of people do call him that but I prefer Angus. He answers to both, thank goodness.' The doorbell rang before Penny could indicate that she knew that Gus was Rory's father. 'Ah, the first guests!' Fiona said. 'I'd better let them in. Where are those boys?'

Fiona went to the door and Penny mouthed to Sian how lovely she thought she was. Sian could tell that, as the news sank in, her mother was beginning to be pleased. With such a charming mother, Rory's father must be a 'nice boy'.

Fiona came back with Richard at her heels. 'Help

yourself to a glass of wine and then you all go through to the conservatory. As it's such a nice day, we're having the food outside.' The bell jangled again. 'Why does everyone come at once, and where *are* Angus and Rory?'

Richard kissed Sian. 'Hello, Penny,' he said to Sian's mother and kissed her too. Sian felt she could see him turning into a son-in-law before her very eyes. She didn't know whether having him here today would be a help or a hindrance. Would she get a moment to tell Gus alone and what would Richard say when he found out? She'd have to tell him too at some point.

Angus and Rory appeared, filthy, and were dispatched by their respective mothers to clean up. They still hadn't reappeared by the time Jody and Annabelle had come – without the big brothers. Rory would be disappointed but they were having a boys-together day with their father.

'I must say I'm a little nervous about meeting all these new people,' Sian admitted to Jody and Fiona. Penny and Annabelle had gone to shout up the stairs after Gus and Rory.

'Oh, no need to be anxious!' Fiona handed Jody a glass of wine. 'They're all lovely and – big coup – I've asked the head teacher from Rory's school! She hasn't got children herself but was very happy to come.'

'Why would anyone go to a children's birthday party if they didn't have children?' asked Sian. 'I asked Emily, you know? Who runs the playgroup? She had a "prior engagement". I don't blame her!'

'You'd be surprised who's agreed to come. Melissa couldn't be kept away.'

'You asked Melissa?' Sian couldn't keep the horror from her voice.

'Well, not really, but I was talking about it in the shop while I was buying things for Rory's cake. She invited herself. I did stress it was an outdoor party and Angus would be doing lots of very dirty things with the children. She laughed and said she didn't want to be left out when Angus was doing dirty things.'

'She sounds fun,' said Jody.

Sian frowned. She found it hard to admit that Melissa could be fun, really, because she was still annoyed about her stealing her house and not even seeming to think Sian might find that a problem. But Melissa had got her a very good commission. She wondered how Gus and Melissa had enjoyed her birthday drinks and then brushed the thought aside. It was none of her business. 'At least I know her,' she said.

'The head teacher?' said Jody. 'Do you mean of Fillhollow School? Miss Andrews? She's a very good head. The boys love her.'

'Felicity, that's right,' said Fiona. 'And then there are two other families. Tom and Meg, who've got Cassandra who's going to be in Rory's class, and Immi and Peter. Their eldest is at school already and their little one will start next year. They're lovely.'

'And that's it?' Sian felt relieved. There wouldn't be too many new people to cope with. And although she hadn't met some of the other mothers from the playgroup properly yet she knew them by sight and Jody said they were all lovely. It was silly, after all these years, to be embarrassed to explain she was a single mother but when meeting people for the first time she always had a frisson of nerves.

'It'll be fine, darling, honestly,' said Penny. She knew how Sian felt. 'Just be yourself. They'll love you.'

The conservatory was the perfect party venue. People spilled out into the garden and the children ran out to play with the various wheeled toys and the small paddling pool that Fiona had borrowed. Sian was both impressed and grateful. She wouldn't have been able to produce such an ideal set-up. She wouldn't have had the space for a start, or the contacts.

At last Rory and Gus appeared, both with rather wet hair, but looking very clean.

'Sorry we're late,' said Gus.

'We had a shower,' said Rory. 'We were *so* dirty!'

'Better late than never,' said Penny. 'You must be Gus.' They shook hands before Penny turned to Rory. 'And hello, birthday boy!'

'Hello, Granny!' screamed Rory. 'Is Grandpa here?'

'No, darling, he couldn't come. But I've got a very special surprise for you later, when you open your presents.'

'Oh, presents!' said Rory, who in the excitement of seeing the shelter and playing with Gus had obviously forgotten all about them.

The children were outside and Gus was gathering them together, making them wait until everyone was present and correct before taking them to the shelter. Sian had forgotten her shyness and everyone was chatting happily, drinking wine and eating crisps. Even Richard, who wasn't used to being around so many children and parents, seemed to be enjoying himself.

'You and Richard must come to dinner with us,' Immi was saying. 'Not that I can cook or anything, but we always drink a lot so no one cares.'

'We're not actually alcoholics or anything,' said Peter, 'and if the children get on, Rory could sleep in Hamish's bottom bunk, and then you don't have to worry about babysitters.'

'It sounds great fun,' said Richard. 'Sian, Rory and I would love it.'

Sian tried not to feel irritated by his proprietorial tone.

'Oh, here's Melissa,' said Immi under her breath. 'She always makes me feel fat and frumpy, which is what I am, but I don't like to be made to feel like that.'

'You're not at all fat or frumpy!' said Sian, warming to her new friend even more.

'Hi, guys!' said Melissa, looking more gorgeous in her 'rough-tough' outfit than Sian ever felt dressed in her best. 'I got my legs out for the occasion.' She held one up for inspection.

'The trouble with shorts,' said Immi, 'although they look lovely if you've got the legs, is that you do have to slather on the fake bake or something.'

Something about the way she said it implied that Melissa hadn't got the legs for shorts, although Sian could see nothing wrong with them.

'I went for a St Tropez the other day,' said Melissa, now looking at her legs more critically.

'They look great!' said Sian, trying not to grit her teeth.

'No streaks? Good-oh.' Melissa checked that every man present was looking at her and then said, 'Oh! Sian! Angus gave me the name board you painted for me! It's to die for! So sweeeet!' She turned to the others and giggled. 'It's got the cutest little ponies on it, like the Thelwell ones. I loved those cartoons when I was young; I loved anything to do with ponies, still do. It used to drive Mummy mad.'

'That sounds interesting,' said Felicity Andrews, the head teacher. 'Do you think you might be interested in doing some name plates for the Reception class? We usually have cardboard ones but it would be rather fun to have wooden ones. We've got a bit of money raised by parents for just that sort of thing. The children would love something more than just bog-standard ships and trains. I must get your telephone number, Sian, and we can arrange a proper time to get together to see what you can do for them.'

The conversation about name boards and what range of designs would work best continued for a few moments before Melissa got bored now she wasn't the centre of attention.

'What about this shelter then?' she said. 'Angus told me all about it and I can't wait to see it!'

'Come on then,' said Gus overhearing her. 'Whoever wants to come, can.'

'Hardly worth having a shower,' said Penny as she and Fiona watched Angus lead the troop of children accompanied by Peter and Melissa. 'They'll get just as filthy again.'

Sian followed them. Richard had gone to fetch Rory's present from the car, rather to Sian's relief. He'd been a bit too possessive for her liking, but she hadn't known how to stop him without appearing rude.

Seeing the shelter completed for the first time, Sian was amazed. It looked like a hillock, covered in leaves, with a dark entrance. The leaf litter was so thick she realised Gus or someone must have gathered a lot more. You had to crawl to get into it, although it turned out to be big enough for two. She was really impressed, but didn't tell Gus. Plenty of other people were doing that for her.

Gus and the others clambered in and out of the shelter, instantly covered in dirt, just as Penny had predicted. It was as well they'd all dressed appropriately for the occasion – well, some of them had. There had been a little too much leg and shapely bottom on display as Melissa crawled into the shelter and out again for Sian's liking.

Gus now had Rory on his shoulders. As he was putting him down Rory fell off on to the rug, giggling almost to the point of hysteria. They both ended up rolling on the ground.

'Oh you two!' said Melissa. 'You look exactly alike. Both filthy.' Then she suddenly stopped and stared. 'You *do* look alike. Why is that, I wonder?'

'They're not at all alike,' said Penny quickly as Sian held her breath and Fiona glanced anxiously at her son. 'Rory is so blond!'

'No, seriously, Angus, what were you doing nine months before today five years ago?' Melissa looked intently at Gus.

The others all turned to look at the tableau on the rug.

Sian couldn't bear it. She shook herself free of Richard's hand and set off towards the house, but not before she saw Gus look down at his son and recognise him.

Sian hurried into the downstairs cloakroom, locked the door and spent a long time washing her hands and splashing her face. Should she take Gus aside and tell him, as she'd told Fiona she would? Or could she just leave it? After all, he knew now. He didn't need to be told. She knew this wasn't an option really. She had to face him. She braced herself and opened the door.

Unsurprisingly, he was waiting just outside. 'Well? Were you going to tell me? Ever?'

He was furious. Absolutely furious. And it suddenly seemed to Sian that this reaction was totally irrational. It gave her courage. 'Calm down. I was going to tell you, when the time felt right. And I really can't talk about it now. There's a birthday party going on.'

'Oh? And when would that right time be? When he went to university?'

'It was today actually. I was going to tell you today,' she said defensively.

'Oh? Odd choice! There's a birthday party going on!'

'I promised Fiona—'

'Oh, so my mother knows, does she? And your mother knows, judging by how guilty she was looking just now. The whole bloody world knows I'm Rory's father except me!'

He towered over her as she stood with her back against the cloakroom door. Suddenly Sian felt very foolish and very vulnerable. Everyone else had wisely, but unfortunately, stayed outside. There wouldn't be any convenient interruption.

'I didn't tell Fiona, I promise,' she said quietly. 'She saw for herself. And I only told my mother just now, before we came.'

'I'm still the last to know. I should have been the first. You should have told me years ago. Five years ago!'

'I had no way of getting in touch with you. You know that. You're being unreasonable.' She was on firmer ground again.

'I'm not being unreasonable! I find out I'm the father of a child that you've kept from me for five years! And I'm angry. Well, I have every right to be angry.'

'No! Gus, I had no way of telling you. I didn't think I'd ever see you again. We decided that was for the best. You agreed.'

'But you did see me again. You should have told me then.'

'Oh, really? "Hello, Gus, how amazing to see you after all this time, by the way I've got a little boy and he's yours." That would have been good, wouldn't it?'

'It would have been fine and if you didn't tell me immediately there was no reason to wait until now. Why did you? Were you deliberately trying to keep us apart? It's been weeks!'

'No!' It was the first time in the conversation that she

lied to him and then she realised she owed him the truth. She let out a long breath, trying to avoid his piercing glare. 'Gus, I didn't know you. I didn't know how you'd react, what sort of a dad you'd be. I didn't want Rory getting attached to someone who was likely to just go off exploring again.'

He smouldered at her and she edged away slightly

'You're an explorer,' she said gently. 'It's what you do. It's not unreasonable for you to do it.'

'I'm not an explorer any more!' he said, still angry.

Sian was just marshalling her arguments again when Richard appeared.

'What's going on?' he said. 'I heard raised voices.'

Sian didn't know if she was pleased to see him or not. Nor did she know what to say to him.

'Sian was just giving me some news,' said Gus. 'A piece of information I should have had a long time ago.'

'Gus, that's completely unreasonable—'

'I don't think a children's birthday party is the time to discuss anything serious,' said Richard. 'Sian, darling, Rory wants to open his presents. I think you should be there.'

Gus pushed past them both and went out through the back door, slamming it.

'What's up with him?' asked Richard. 'What on earth were you talking about?'

Sian turned to him. 'Not now, Richard. I can't talk about it now.'

He frowned. 'It sounds important. Why can't you just tell me?'

'It's complicated,' she snapped. And, feeling almost as guilty about hurting Richard's feelings as she did about Gus, she pushed past him and went to join the group of people round the table where the presents were.

'And this is from me and Grandpa. It's tickets to Euro Disney,' her mother was saying.

Richard came up behind her, obviously having forgiven her for her brief outburst. He put his hand on her shoulder.

Somehow Sian managed to comment appropriately and to encourage Rory to say thank you if he forgot as the presents were opened. She observed her mother writing down who had given what so thank yous could be written later. She was thankful her mother and Fiona had taken charge. She didn't know whether the others knew the truth but she was grateful that no one was giving her strange looks or behaving awkwardly.

Her brain and her emotions whirled together, leaving her unable to think clearly. Richard's hand kneading gently at her shoulder was comforting. The fact that Gus was missing was helpful. Then she noticed that Melissa was absent too. At least that meant she wouldn't be asking questions as well, even if Sian was sure she was interrogating Gus for details and providing comfort when he gave them.

'Right, now for the cakes!' announced Fiona when the last of the wrapping paper had been folded and Rory's breathy gratitude had been expressed sufficiently. 'We're very lucky we've got two!'

At least no one said, 'One from each grandma,' thought Sian, which might easily have happened if Melissa had been there. Everyone else seemed willing to gloss over what had happened earlier.

'What fantastic cakes!' said Jody. 'Look, Annabelle! A dragon! And a shelter, just like the one Gus made where you played! These are amazing!'

'Yes, Mum,' said Sian, pulling herself together somewhat, and going round the table so she could hug her mother. 'That's utterly brilliant! And Fiona! That shelter is just the best. You've even got a little fire in the entrance, and a kettle.'

'I had such fun making it! Those long thin minty things were good for the branches, along with some cut-up Curlywurlys.'

'Not chocolate fingers? They're my standard cake-making aid,' said Immi.

Fiona shook her head. 'I started with them but they were too regular. It was awful, I had to eat them.'

This was greeted with chuckles. 'The things you have to do as a grandmother – proxy-grandmother,' said Fiona quickly. 'It's all self-sacrifice.'

'And how did you do the leaf litter?' asked Peter. 'Is it just chocolate shavings?'

'*Just* chocolate shavings? Huh!' said Fiona. 'I had to spend hours shaving and chopping and when the bits got too small, I had to eat them too. It was a real labour of love.' She hugged Rory. 'Now let's inspect this dragon. It's very beautiful. A sort of Fabergé dragon.'

Penny stood proudly over her cake. 'Well, as you can see, I used lots of those little jewel sweeties, in diamond shapes. Brilliant for a spiny back.'

'It's a dinosaur,' said Annabelle.

'No, it's just a bit like one,' said Sian.

'I did sort of base it on a dinosaur,' Penny acknowledged with a smile. 'And I probably did get carried away with the sweets.'

'Where are the candles?' said Rory, obviously worried that this vital part was missing from both his birthday cakes.

'Here,' said Fiona. She produced two plates. On one, five stripy candles were fixed with icing. On the other a big number five, made out of cake, was studded with five indoor sparklers.

'What's all this?' demanded one of the dads. 'That's cheating!'

'When I was a little girl we just had the candles stuck in the cake,' said Felicity Andrews. 'But at school we don't. We practically have to have a fire extinguisher poised over it if we have candles at all.'

'Penny and I both decided, separately, that we didn't want our works of art spoilt by candles,' said Fiona.

'Right, Rory, you blow out the candles and we'll cut the cakes,' said Penny, taking his hand and guiding him over to the table, now covered in napkins and plates and the two magnificent cakes.

'Yeah!' yelled the other children crowding round.

'I've never been happy at the thought of the birthday boy spraying the cake with spit and germs as he blows them out,' muttered Penny to no one in particular.

While the men stood around chatting, the women cut the cake and served it out. Most people wanted to take theirs home and Sian was put on wrapping duty. Unfortunately her ability to cut complicated geometric shapes was hampered by emotional overload.

When the last man, woman and child had taken away a piece of cake – in some cases two pieces, one from each – Richard said to Fiona, 'Do you mind if I take Sian and Rory home now? Sian looks exhausted and Rory probably is too.'

'Oh, but I can't go without clearing up,' said Sian, wishing she could with all her heart. 'I'm fine and Rory can always go and watch television if he needs to slump.'

'Absolutely,' Fiona said to Richard, ignoring Sian.

'Yes,' agreed Penny. 'I'll help Fiona here and let myself in later. You take Sian off to bed.'

'Yes,' repeated Gus, appearing from nowhere. 'You take Sian off to bed, *Richard*.'

Chapter Sixteen

When at last her clock showed it was five thirty in the morning, Sian got up with a sense of relief. She no longer had to battle the night to try and force herself back to sleep; she could just give in and be awake. After all, it was nearly six o'clock. That was a more or less sensible time to get up.

She made herself a cup of tea and went into the garden. She'd pulled on an old cashmere cardigan, fluffy from too much washing, over her nightie. It promised to be a beautiful day, but she still shivered slightly, whether from cold or from misery she couldn't tell.

The dew on the garden gave everything, even the weeds, a softness, like velvet highlighted with sparkles. Everything, from the roses on the pergola to the bean plants, the first of which Rory had picked a couple of days ago, to the compost heap, looked beautiful and new and full of possibility.

It almost made Sian cry when she'd resisted tears all night.

She hugged her mug for warmth and pulled her feet up under her, smoothing her nightdress over her knees. Would life ever be normal, peaceful, again?

From the corner of her eye she noticed movement over the garden wall and realised there was a dark head bobbing up and down; someone was running. Even without seeing his face she knew it was Gus. When he came up the hill a bit he would be on a level with her and if he looked up, he would see her.

She almost went inside to avoid him but then she wondered why she should. She was in her garden enjoying the early morning. She wasn't going to be driven away by someone who probably had no idea she was there. It wasn't six o'clock yet. If she kept very still he might not notice her.

The head stopped. Two seconds later Gus had come into the garden. He was wearing shorts, trainers and a torn T-shirt.

'Hello,' he said.

She shrank back. She wasn't dressed, which made her feel vulnerable, and he was obviously just as furious as he had been the last time she saw him. He was sweating and with the sweat he was radiating something she read as deep hatred and anger.

'Hello,' she said cautiously.

'Is Richard here?'

She frowned. 'No. Why should he be? Do you want him?'

He put his foot on the edge of a box full of flowerpots and seemed to relax a tiny bit. 'I just thought he might have stayed the night, having "taken you to bed".'

'It wasn't like that. As you know perfectly well. Besides, my mother's staying with me. Honestly.' Why must he always jump to the wrong conclusions?

He shrugged. 'I realise I don't know very much about you, or what you might or might not think is acceptable behaviour. Nothing I thought I knew perfectly well is true any more. My life has been completely turned upside down since yesterday.'

She felt the same but didn't say so. However much turmoil she'd been going through, it must have been worse for him. 'I'm sorry.'

She wasn't going to be allowed to get away with such a simple statement. 'You should be, you should be bloody sorry. And we need to talk.'

She sighed, sure she was just as sorry as he wanted her to be but not sure she could express it in a way that he would ever accept. 'We are talking.'

'I mean, we need to talk without having to keep our voices down.'

He was right. He couldn't express his indignation and she couldn't explain all the decisions she'd made since she found she was pregnant in whispers. She considered what best to do. She didn't want to have to make a date with him, better get it all over with now.

'OK. I'll tell my mother I'm going out so she can look after Rory when he wakes, and I'll get dressed. We can go for a walk.'

'Don't be long.'

She left him pacing like an angry bear in the garden and went to wake her mother.

'Mum?' she whispered. 'Gus is here,' she went on, in reply to her mother's murmur. 'He wants to talk. I owe it to him. Will you look after Rory if he wakes before I get back?'

'Of course, darling.' Her mother sat up and then shook herself awake. 'Good luck.'

Sian pulled on her clothes quickly. Jeans, a T-shirt, trainers and her cardigan on top. She might get too hot but the softness of the cardigan comforted her and she needed comfort right now.

She pushed her hands through her hair in lieu of a brush, did her teeth and smeared on a bit of moisturiser and she was ready. Make-up wouldn't help her now. Better face Gus just as she was.

'Where are we going?' she asked when she stepped into her garden again.

'We'll go round the village. It doesn't matter. We're not going to be looking at the scenery.'

Sian braced herself for a difficult hour. She didn't think she could cope with any longer than that and she didn't think she could get away with any less.

They went out of the gate and set off down the road towards the village, away from Fiona's house. They had only got a few yards before Gus began.

'OK, what I need to know is, why you didn't tell me as soon as you reasonably could?' Gus sounded as if he was trying hard to be calm but not finding it terribly easy.

Sian felt he would never understand, however long and hard she tried to explain, but she had to do her best. 'I had a lot to think about. I never expected to see you again. I had always assumed I'd bring Rory up on my own, without a father.'

'But what about Richard? I don't think he assumes any of those things.'

'Richard is nothing to do with this!' Sian caught at a bit of loosestrife flowering on the verge as she passed so she could keep her hands occupied.

'Isn't he? I think he is. I think he sees himself as your husband and Rory's stepfather.'

Sian didn't reply immediately. She knew he was right and she knew she hadn't properly considered Richard in all this. Knowing she didn't love him, not like that anyway, she'd set his feelings aside. But was that wise? She recalled the look of hurt and confusion on Richard's face when she'd told him last night, when he'd taken her home. Hurt that she hadn't felt she could tell him earlier and confusion because he wasn't sure what that now meant in terms of his relationship with Sian and Rory. She had been relieved that he hadn't pressed her for more details and left shortly afterwards 'And why wouldn't he? Boys need a male role model,' Gus went on.

'Oh, not you as well! Everyone keeps telling me boys need a male role model. It doesn't mean I have to get married. And Richard wouldn't marry me just so he can provide Rory with a role model.' She'd had enough of being told what was and wasn't good for her son. The son she'd raised perfectly well on her own for the last five years – well, with a little help from her parents, of course.

'Oh no, he wants you,' Gus growled. 'He'd take Rory because that would be the only way he'd get you.'

'That doesn't make him a bad person!'

'Oh, I know exactly how saintly bloody Richard is! But whatever other virtues he's got, he's not Rory's father!'

'I do know that,' she said quietly, hoping his volume would lower, to match hers.

'But I was the last to know, wasn't I?'

'Rory doesn't know.'

'But you will have to tell him. And soon. I've missed five years of his life, I'm not missing any more, and I'm not going to be palmed off to him as a "friend of the family"!'

'I didn't actually deprive you on purpose! You were out of reach – I knew that you would be! We have actually had this conversation. In fact we had a similar conversation nearly six years ago!'

She was getting out of breath but she didn't want to ask Gus to slow down. It might just tip him over the edge. She hurried along beside him, doing her best to match his long, angry strides.

'It's all very well to tell me you couldn't get in touch, I know that. But I'm in shock. I have a five-year-old son! One I might never have known about it if chance hadn't plonked you down here next to my family home!'

'I know. It was a shock for me too, seeing a man I

thought I'd never see again appear at a country dinner party. For goodness' sake, I was – am – Fiona's friend! I didn't know who her son was. Why won't you believe me?' She put her hand into the hedgerow again and caught a nettle. A moment later she found the sting a good distraction.

He wasn't prepared to cut her any slack. 'Yes, but you had time to get over that. If my mother hadn't given you an ultimatum you might never have told me.'

She didn't reply.

'In fact, you didn't bloody tell me! You let me find out for myself!'

'I would have told you. If Melissa hadn't seen the likeness and made that stupid remark—'

'Don't blame Melissa for this. She's actually been incredibly supportive.'

'Oh good.' Sian picked up her pace, as if she could outwalk him. She felt her own anger ignite.

He lengthened his stride a fraction and was level again. 'So why didn't you want me to know about Rory?'

'I don't – didn't – *not* want you to know about Rory, I was just picking my moment. Not that there ever would have been a good moment, I now see!'

'Are you blaming me for being angry?'

'No! But I do wish you'd see how hard it was for me to find the right time.'

He didn't reply immediately. 'It was shock as much as anything.'

He seemed to be calming down. Maybe they could talk about this in a civilised way. 'Honestly, I went through something very similar.'

His anger was still driving him. 'It's hardly the same! You knew I was Rory's father. I had no idea I had a son.'

Sian stopped and looked up at him. 'What do you want

me to say? I can't go on saying sorry, it doesn't mean anything any more, but I *am* truly sorry: that it was all such a shock, that I didn't find the time to tell you before you found out. But I can't apologise any more!'

They walked on in silence. Sian was wondering when he would stop feeling so aggrieved and they could turn back and she could go home.

'We need to discuss me seeing Rory on a regular basis.'

Sian looked down and for the first time she spotted a scar on his leg.

'You mean access?'

'No! I don't mean bloody access! That sounds like we're divorced, having to spend every second weekend at some damn theme park or McDonald's! I want to see my son. And I want him to know I'm his father.'

'I'll tell him—'

'When? When he's eighteen? When he asks? I want him to know now!'

'He's only five years old.'

'I'm not likely to forget that.' He paused. 'Listen, I'm very fond of Rory but I'd like to get to know him, as a son.'

'You will. Although if we move too far away from here, it might be harder.'

'Don't worry about moving away, it'll be all right.'

He was so dismissive of this real threat her anger flared once more. 'We don't know that. Unless Melissa's told you she doesn't want the cottage any more?'

'No, she still wants it.'

'Well then, we'll have to move. And I don't know if we'll be able to find anywhere else in this area I can afford. I think we should go home now,' she added, turning round. 'Rory will wonder where I am.'

'I could come back with you—'

'Look, I said I'm not going to deny you access or anything, but Rory will be tired after his party. We both need to think about this carefully.'

'I have thought about it.'

'Listen, I can't cope with this any more. Not now. I need a moment to think. You go home, get a shower, have breakfast. I'll do the same. We'll work something out.'

Although obviously not happy, Gus clearly realised he wasn't going to get any further at that point and, face softening a little, agreed. They headed back down the lane in a silence that was a long way from companionable but at least wasn't completely antagonistic, until Gus strode off towards his mother's house, without even nodding goodbye.

Well, that went well, thought Sian as she walked towards the cottage, her shoulders hunched.

'Hey! Mum! Have you been for a walk?'

Sian took off her cardigan – so much for a comfort blanket! – placed it on the back of a kitchen chair and kissed Rory's cheek. 'Yes, darling. What did you have for breakfast?'

'Eggy bread with syrup.'

'Very sticky, I'm afraid,' said Sian's mother. 'What can I get for you?'

'Oh, just toast and Marmite as usual, I think. And tea.' She sat down at the table and gave her mother a grateful smile. 'It's lovely to be waited on.' What she meant was it was lovely to be mothered.

She was just on her second cup of tea when the phone rang. It was Richard.

'Sorry to ring so early but I've got to be at the airport in an hour. We need to talk.'

Not him as well!

'We are talking.' She laughed gently, hoping she hadn't snapped. It wasn't fair to let her feelings about Gus be transferred to Richard.

'Yes, I know, but I want to talk seriously, about the future. Finding out that Gus is Rory's father has changed things rather.'

'Has it? I mean – between us?'

There was a pause. Sian could almost hear Richard considering his next sentence. 'I think we should regularise things. For Rory's sake.'

'What do you mean?'

'I mean, if you're going to have to move . . . if we got together maybe you wouldn't have to? Rory could still go to the same school and everything.'

Was this a proposal of marriage, or the offer of a house share? 'I'm sorry to be dense, Richard but—'

He broke in quickly and nervously. Sian guessed he'd known that this wasn't the way to talk things through with her, but couldn't bear to leave the country again without having at least tried to say his piece – or stake his claim. 'We'll talk about it when I get back. I've got to go now. Take care!'

Sian went back into the kitchen feeling tired and bewildered. She seemed to have two men, both fighting to be the father of her child, if she interpreted what Richard had implied correctly. She knew how much he wanted them to be able to put their relationship on a more permanent, public footing, and she knew he was very fond of Rory, but he'd never actually forced her hand and she'd been happy to let things drift along as they were. Was he about to finally do so? Force her to make yet another decision she didn't want to make right now? Why couldn't she just go on bringing up Rory on her own? But she knew this wasn't possible – at least as far as Gus was concerned. He would be in Rory's life now whether she wanted him to be or not. And she did want him in her son's life, really. For Rory's sake, even if Gus's presence in her life did nothing for her general state of mind.

She went back into the kitchen, but before she could sit down again she heard the letter-box flap, indicating the post had arrived. She went to get it, hoping for a confirmation of a commission, a cheque or even a jolly catalogue that she could read while she finished her tea.

There was a thick cream envelope with her name typed on the front. She could tell it was bad news, even before she picked it up from the mat.

'What's that? Anything nice?' asked her mother, who'd produced a damp cloth for Rory's fingers and was wiping hard.

'Don't think so.' Sian opened the envelope and read the contents. 'Nope. It's just confirmation that Luella is selling the house. She wants me out by October. I could stay until December, but she'll pay me a bit to go early and who wants to move at Christmas.' She slumped down on the kitchen chair. Could today get any worse?

'That's very soon!' her mother said, looking over at Sian with concern. Having satisfied herself her grandson was now clean, she ruffled his hair and pulled his chair out for him to get down. 'Rory, why don't you go and paint me a picture before it's time to go to playgroup?'

Rory regarded his womenfolk. 'You want to do talking, don't you?'

'Yes. Very boring talking,' said Sian. 'Do a lovely picture, darling. I know, paint your birthday cakes! You could give one to Fiona, as a thank you.'

Inspired by this idea, Rory went off to the dining room to find his paints.

A little while later, Penny put down a fresh mug of tea

in front of Sian, who sipped it, glad of an excuse not to have to talk, or make a decision, or anything, for a few moments. She'd given her mother a rough outline of her conversations with Gus and Richard.

'Tell you what,' said Penny. 'Why don't you and Rory come and stay with us for a few days? Dad would love to see you both and it would give you a little break to think about your options.'

Suddenly, Sian yearned to go home – home home, where she'd lived as a child. 'I've got a bit of work to do and I must help Fiona clear up after yesterday,' she said half-heartedly, waiting for her mother to dismiss these as mere excuses.

'I'll do that. Rory can go to playgroup, you work and I'll help Fiona. I like her so much and I'm sure she wouldn't mind me doing it instead of you. Then, this afternoon, we can drive back. You needn't take your car, you can go back by train, or I'll drive you.'

Sian suddenly felt like crying. She was so glad her mother was here. She knew exactly what she needed. 'It wouldn't look like I was running away, would it?'

'What from? No, it's perfectly reasonable for you to visit your parents. Then when you're with us, we'll scour the internet for somewhere to live nearby. And I'm sure Mrs Florence said something about wanting that table you painted for her touched up. I think the leg got a bit chipped.'

'So it'll be work! Oh, Mum, thank you!' She came round the table and hugged her mother.

'You don't need an invitation to come and stay, you know that.' Penny patted her daughter's back.

'I know, but you had the idea and made it seem OK.'

She went off to find Rory to take him to playgroup, feeling a glimmer of hope for the first time since Gus had found out about Rory. Perhaps everything would work out OK after all. And time away would help put some perspective on it all – she hoped.

Rory slept in the back of the car and Sian used the time to think. Her mother, aware of what was going on, didn't chat except to ask for a peppermint from time to time.

What was she to do for the best? Should she let Richard take away her problems, be a good stepfather to Rory and a prop to her? He'd be brilliant. He'd never forget an anniversary, he'd take her on holiday to nice places with good hotels and they'd never miss the plane.

If she let herself have anything to do with Gus apart from a fling, she'd be clambering up mountains in the snow, Rory frozen and moaning along behind, and expected to make meals over tiny fires using only tin cans, peeled birch twigs and maybe a pair of socks to get the bits of lichen out of the water.

And it wasn't just the trappings, it was the commitment. Richard could commit, no problem. He'd commit to her, to Rory, to their family life.

But Gus? What were the chances? What was his attention span when it came to women? Hard to say, but she didn't think it would be long. He'd seemed quite interested in her when he first appeared but now it was Melissa who was 'incredibly supportive'.

And it would cut both ways. She hadn't been supportive, she'd just kept him from his son for five years. And if he forgave her for the first four and three-quarter years, because she'd had no way of getting in touch with him, the fact she hadn't told him the day after he returned home would always be a provocative thorn between them.

That she'd never felt about Richard the way she'd felt about Gus when she first met him wasn't really a problem.

It was just pheromones and madness anyway. Nor was the fact that she still felt that way towards him. It would fade. It had to.

Then there was the house question. 'What are the chances of finding somewhere nice to live that I can afford and yet stay in the same area?' she said aloud, glad Rory was still out for the count and envious of his childish ability to sleep.

Penny didn't answer immediately, giving the impression it was because she was overtaking a huge lorry but Sian knew it was because she was thinking up an optimistic way of saying, 'Not good.'

'It will be a challenge,' Penny acknowledged. 'But you know me and the internet, I can find anything on it.'

'But Luella's cottage was amazingly cheap. I didn't realise quite how cheap until I'd lived there for a bit.'

'You will have to compromise, not have such a big garden perhaps, but you might get a nicer kitchen.'

'It's the area that's most important. Rory's made friends, I have too, and there's the school. The head was brilliant. It would be perfect for him.'

'You could drive there. It wouldn't be the end of the world.'

They drove on in silence for a while. Then Penny said, echoing what she'd said when she first found out about Rory, 'What about Gus. Utterly gorgeous, of course, but is he the man for you?' There, her mother had voiced her own thoughts. It was out in the open.

'I don't know if he even wants to be the man for me. He wants to be Rory's dad. I'm not sure I'm necessarily part of the deal.' Everything was such a muddle. She couldn't think clearly about anything and it wasn't just a simple question of 'Do I love him; does he love me?' any more. She knew that what she'd felt that night had been amazing, but she also knew that sexual desire could disguise itself as proper love. She had to put all that passion behind her for Rory's sake and think what was best to do.

'How do you feel about that? Rory's father taking an interest in Rory?' her mother said carefully.

'Of course I'm happy for him to see him.' She could truthfully say that. 'There's no reason why I shouldn't be. But . . .'

Penny glanced across. 'But?'

'There's also Richard. Now he does want me, and Rory, and he'd be brilliant. Reliable, committed, caring. If I moved in with him – married him even – I could stay in the area. He's away a lot, so I'd have plenty of time to myself, which I do value. He'd let me work. He'd be perfect!'

'You're not selling him to me.'

'What do you mean?'

'I mean you're telling me about all his virtues but not the most important thing: do you love him?'

'I like him! I respect him. He's a friend – he could become my best friend. I could come to love him. People do.'

'You know how your father and I feel about Richard, we're very fond of him but why would you compromise? Why live with someone you don't love? Even if they love you – and I think he does. Watching him at the party, he couldn't take his eyes off you. He's a good man.'

'I know.'

'Which is not to say that Gus is a bad man. But would he be a good husband?'

Sian didn't answer. That was the million-dollar question.

Chapter Seventeen

When Sian and Rory went back on the train a few days later, Sian felt stronger and better able to cope with her problems. Nothing like a few days being looked after for restoring optimism and positive thinking.

She had restored Mrs Florence's chipped table leg (by adding a cherub to hide the repair) and picked up another couple of jobs. One, painting a vine over a window, turned out so well and looked so pretty, she took photos so she could add it to her portfolio. The other job, still to be designed, involved something similar to trail over an old-fashioned lavatory cistern and included a snake. This would be fun to do, but Sian doubted if it would turn out to be a popular line.

Penny had also tracked down a couple of properties. Close to the school and affordable, just, Sian was looking forward to seeing them.

And Rory had loved his time with his grandparents, being spoilt rotten and taken on day trips by his doting grandfather whilst his mother worked. They'd both enjoyed their visit.

Fiona picked them up from the station but refused to come in for a cup of tea afterwards.

'I won't, darlings,' she said. 'You'll want to settle in.' When Rory had run into the garden to inspect the beans Fiona had watered for them while they were away, she said carefully, 'Sian, if Gus came to see you, could you let him in? He's got over his shock a bit and promised not to shout at you. He wants to get to know Rory better so that when you tell him, when the time is right, it's not a shock.'

Sian put her shoulders back. She was a stronger woman now than she had been when she and Gus had parted after their walk. She was a grown-up; she could handle this. Plenty of people did. She'd read about such a woman in the paper at her parents' the day before.

'Fine! I think that sounds very sensible. But Rory already really likes Gus.'

'I know, but Gus wants to see him knowing who he is, rather than just a nice little boy.'

Sian smiled. 'As long as he goes on thinking he's nice.'

So one afternoon a few days later, while Rory was playing with Annabelle, Gus came round.

'Hi! Is Rory here?'

'No, I'm afraid he's out.' Sian couldn't help smiling. It was as if Gus had said, 'Can Rory come out to play?'

Gus gave a rueful smile. It had probably sounded like that to him, too. 'Well, can you spare the time to make me a cup of tea? I promise I won't shout.'

Sian opened the door wider, suddenly aware of how pleased she was to see him, in spite of all the tension between them. 'You're in luck. I was just about to take a break. I've been painting.'

'Can I see?'

She led him upstairs to where she was covering a small chest of drawers with tiny ponies, their tiny riders looking quite like Annabelle. 'I got the idea after I did Melissa's name board. Moving to the country made me aware of pony-mad girls and how I could exploit them.'

'You're good at this, aren't you? Do you never yearn to paint pictures?'

Sian shook her head. 'No. It's illustration I love. I don't think I could express my inner turmoil with paint and canvas.' She smiled quickly, wishing she hadn't mentioned 'inner turmoil'. 'But I had a great time in London.'

'Yes?'

She nodded. 'Apart from spending time with Mum and Dad, I picked up a very nice commission.' She described the vine and the snake. 'I also found a couple of properties to view on the internet.' She paused. 'They won't be as nice as this of course, but the kitchens might be better. Let's go down and I'll make us tea.'

'You'll need space to work in any property you found.'

'Of course, but thanks to you and Fiona, there's the barn for bigger pieces.' She stopped suddenly. 'Unless you want to use that space for anything?'

He shook his head. 'Not at the moment. It's all yours.'

Sian made tea and they took it out into the garden. It was a relief that things seemed a little calmer between them. It wouldn't do for there to be too much tension; it wouldn't be good for Rory.

'I'm going to miss this,' she said, looking at the space where she'd dug and planted and recently picked beans and strawberries.

'This garden in particular? Or just having a garden?'

'This one a bit. I've put so much into it. But I think if I had a bit of ground – somewhere Rory can play and I can potter about – it would be OK.'

'So,' he said when they'd sat in silence for a while, 'the reason for my visit. Do you think Rory would be up for sleeping in the shelter tonight? I promised him on his birthday that we would sleep in it, and I had a look at the forecast and this weather isn't going to last for ever. It's pretty much tonight, or not at all.'

Panic struck Sian suddenly. She was supposed to be

being reasonable, allowing him access, but this seemed too much, too soon. 'That would be a shame,' she said cautiously. 'What will happen to the shelter if it gets rained on?'

'The shelter would be fine but it would be very muddy all around it. That does make it all a bit more difficult for inexperienced shelter-dwellers.'

'I'm sure!' Silently she struggled, turning away from Gus so he wouldn't see her expression. She couldn't be sure it wasn't tortured. She saw a way out and took it. 'The thing is, I'm not sure if Rory would actually make it through the night in the shelter. Even with you there,' she added.

Gus had obviously thought of this. 'Then you'll have to come too. We'll arrange it with Mum that any or all of us can come back into the house if we don't like it any more.'

This was almost worse. Spending the night with Gus and Rory in a very small space hadn't been what she'd thought of as 'access' when she offered it so freely before she went to London.

'Oh, go on,' Gus persisted. 'I'll buy sausages and things and we'll cook dinner on an open fire.' He paused. 'I promised Rory. I don't want him to think I've forgotten. It's important he sees me as someone he can rely on.'

There was no arguing with that. 'OK. I'll bring some-thing for pudding. Will Fiona be eating with us?

Gus shook his head. 'She's going out. It'll be just us. No chaperone.'

'You may joke, but what would people think if they found out we'd spent the night together?'

'In a shelter with Rory? Not much, I don't suppose. And what people?'

Sian relaxed, surprised she was able to joke with Gus. London really had been just what she needed, she realised. 'You're right,' she said.

'And it might be a good opportunity to tell Rory I'm his father,' Gus continued tentatively, a question in his voice.

Sian didn't reply. Stronger though she undoubtedly felt, and willing though she was for her and Rory to join Gus in the shelter later, she wasn't ready to acknowledge that particular issue just yet. She looked at her watch and stood up. 'Well, we'll see, shall we? I'm going to have to get Rory now. What shall I bring with us?'

'A sleeping bag for Rory but otherwise I've got every-thing, including a very expensive sleeping bag for you that my mother used once.'

'OK, that sounds good. See you at about seven? Or is that too early? I like to get Rory to bed soon after then.'

'I'll be ready.'

Rory was thrilled at the thought of spending the night in the shelter, especially when he knew his mother was going to be there too. 'Can I take my torch?'

'Definitely take your torch. We'll pack your rucksack with useful things.'

'Teddy?'

'Yup. Can't leave him behind, I'd never hear the end of it.'

'Book to read?'

'Gus might read to you. Put it in.'

In the end the rucksack was quite heavy with things Rory thought essential for a night away. Sian, who wasn't intending to change out of the old tracksuit – a bit paint-spattered – which she'd put on, took very little. Her bag did include a torch, some night cream for her face and a packet of baby wipes. She didn't think she'd have to actu-ally sleep in the shelter all night. She was quite sure Rory would get fed up and either want to come home, or sleep in Fiona's spare room. Sian was sure she could borrow a nightie and a few essentials from Fiona if they didn't come back to the cottage.

She did have a blackcurrant crumble with her. It was still hot from the oven as she'd had to make it while Rory was getting ready. Rory had already been fed at Annabelle's but Sian was sure he'd eat a sausage or two if given the opportunity.

Gus had made a trail of tea lights to the top of the garden (possibly Fiona's idea) where he had a campfire burning. Despite herself, Sian had to admit that it did look utterly magical.

'Hey! Rory!' Gus picked him up and swung him in the air. 'Sian!' Having replaced Rory, he kissed her cheek. 'Great to see you both. Rory, I had to light the fire without you or it wouldn't have been ready to cook on before we'd all fallen asleep.'

'It's hot!' said Rory, hopping from one foot to the other in excitement.

'That's what we like. Sian, sit down, have a glass of wine. Do you want a chair or the ground?'

'Oh, the ground,' said Sian and immediately sat down on the cushion he thoughtfully handed to her.

Gus had gone to a lot of trouble to make everything comfortable. Apart from a fire, nearly big enough to roast an ox on, she felt, there were sleeping bags and cushions to lie on and a log with a slice off it to make a table. There were candle lanterns hanging from nearby trees and Sian could see bottles of wine, with soft drinks for Rory.

'Wow!' she said. 'All we need is some soft music playing in the background and we look all set for a night of—' She'd been going to say 'passion' but managed to stop herself in time. 'Well, for a party.'

'Music is just the touch of a button away. I always take my iPod with me when I'm on a journey.'

'Oh no, don't let's have music. It doesn't seem right, unless you can play the guitar or something.' Sian laughed at herself, beginning to relax. 'I think my idea of what's right at a campfire is based on a lot of old Western movies.'

'Then you shouldn't have wine then,' said Gus, pulling back the glass he was holding out to her.

'Just coffee,' agreed Sian, taking the glass anyway.

'And swigs of red-eye straight from the bottle,' said Gus. 'Rory? You want some elderflower or something?'

'In *Swallows and Amazons* they call it grog,' said Rory.

Sian settled herself more comfortably, sipping her wine and slightly wishing she'd dressed up more; her old jeans and a hoodie seemed rather casual for such a beautiful setting. 'That's down to my dad,' she said. 'He won't read Rory stories that he doesn't like himself so Rory gets read a lot of things that are really a bit old for him.'

'I love *Swallows and Amazons*,' said Gus. 'Now your granddad's not so handy, I could read those books to you.'

'Cool,' said Rory, sipping his grog.

'Now, tucker.' Gus leant back behind the log-table and produced a large oblong metal container with a lid. 'We have chops, sausages, steak and homemade burgers. My mother made those. She also made salad.'

'Oh, and I've got pudding, in my bag,' said Sian.

'I thought we were going to cook the things,' said Rory.

'Well yes, but it's late, nearly bedtime – for me anyway – and I thought it would take a bit long. I do have some we could cook though, but I thought your mum might be starving and need something to eat straight away.'

'I am quite hungry, actually. You ate at Annabelle's, Rory, you can probably wait a bit longer.'

'OK, Mummy can have something now but I want to cook my own sausage.'

'Fair enough.' Gus handed Sian a roll. 'What would you like in that? Chop? Sausage?'

'Oh, a sausage please and no ketchup or anything.' A moment later she bit into it. 'This is heavenly!'

'Nothing like food cooked outdoors for good eating. It's better if you've been for a bit of a hike first, of course. Now, Rory, you cook this.' He produced a peeled stick with a sausage speared on it. 'Hold it over the bit where there are no flames, just glowing embers. Let me know if your arm gets tired and we'll rig something up.'

'My arm's tired,' said Rory after a matter of seconds.

'OK.' Like a magician, Gus reached behind the log and produced two sticks with forked ends. Choosing his position carefully, he stuck them into the ground. Then he pushed Rory's sausage further down the stick, added another couple, and then propped the stick on the forked ones. 'There! A rotisserie that doesn't actually turn round.'

Rory looked at him questioningly.

Sian explained. 'A rotisserie goes round and round so the sausages, or whatever's cooking on it, cooks all over. Gus will have to turn over the sausages when one side is done. But that's no great problem. He's used to it.'

'Did you cook the chops on the fire?' asked Rory. 'Did you put them on a rohteessry?'

'No, I put them in this.' He produced a hinged barbeque griller.

'That doesn't look like something you'd have in your pack when you're on the trail,' said Sian.

'No, but you try to cook chops on a fire without some sort of grill, and see how you get on.' He turned the sausages. 'Of course I could cook a haunch of venison, no problem. It's these little namby-pamby cuts that are more tricky. More wine?'

'I must say this is a very luxurious camp,' said Sian, allowing him to fill her glass. The furthest she and Rory had to go was the house, and she was enjoying herself. One of the downsides of being a single parent was always having to be the decision-maker, the responsible one, the driver. She enjoyed the times when she could let go a bit. And even if it only lasted the evening, it was such a relief to be sitting here with Gus, talking naturally, no tension between them to ruin the atmosphere. Rory's presence seemed to act as a balm. They could be an ordinary little family, as Melissa might say. Sian stopped herself; she didn't want to think about Melissa and she didn't want to think about the future or what it might or might not bring. She just wanted to enjoy this moment of harmony.

'I thought Rory might appreciate something realistic and manly but that you might prefer a few comforts,' Gus was saying. 'Me and Rory will go off on the trail together some time. If that's all right with your mum, of course.'

'Mum?' Rory, who had been getting drowsy and was in danger of falling asleep before his sausage was cooked, sat up, all attention. 'Can I go with Gus?'

'Of course,' said Sian. After she'd spoken she realised that she did feel that Rory would be perfectly safe with Gus. Maybe having a father for Rory might not be as hard as she'd always thought. As long as it wasn't all the time, of course.

It was nearly dark and it wasn't easy to read Gus's expression but Sian was aware of the warmth in it. 'Thanks, Sian,' he said. 'I'm glad you trust us guys to go off together.'

'Well, Rory's been brought up to be sensible and,

knowing Fiona, I expect you have too. I'm sure you'll be fine.' She chuckled. 'Honey,' she said to Rory. 'I think you should think about getting into your sleeping bag. Then you can eat your sausage and go to sleep.'

'I am tired,' he said. 'Can I have ketchup and a roll?'

'Of course.'

While Gus dealt with the sausage Sian got Rory into his sleeping bag. 'You can sit up and eat and then wriggle into the shelter. Gus will help you.'

There was a fair amount of giggling and wriggling and pretending to be a caterpillar but once inside the shelter, which now had a ground sheet, Rory decided it was very dark. 'You won't go away, will you?' he asked nervously, still her little boy.

'No. We're both here,' Gus reassured him. 'You can see us, by the fire. And later, we'll be sleeping in the shelter with you. You won't be on your own.'

'I want a story!'

'Darling, it's a bit difficult to read stories in this light,' said Sian.

'Did you pack a book in your bag?' asked Gus.

'Oh yes,' said Rory. He burrowed in his rucksack and produced it. 'Mum said I should bring one and you might read to me,' he added hopefully.

'Come out of the shelter then.' Gus was doing some burrowing of his own. 'What book is it?'

'*Brer Rabbit*,' said Rory, emerging from the shelter, still in his sleeping bag. 'It's one of Grandpa's.'

'He means one of the ones that Grandpa will deign to read,' said Sian.

'Here.' Gus handed Rory what seemed to be a bit of thick elastic. As he put his own on, Sian realised it was a head torch. 'Head torches are essential in the dark when you're on the trail. You need to see where you're putting your feet and keep your hands free. That one's yours, by the way,' Gus said casually, helping Rory to tighten the strap to make it fit.

'Oh, Gus, that's very kind of you!'

'Thank you, Gus, that's very kind of you,' echoed Rory, filling his mother's heart with pride and relief that he said it without being prompted.

'I'll switch it on for you this first time. It's a bit tricky.'

Sian lay back and watched, nibbling on a burger, while father and son lay snuggled up together with their head torches. Who wouldn't melt at the sight of them both? Sian found herself suddenly feeling rather emotional and took another bite of her burger. It wouldn't do to get all soppy now.

Gus read aloud very well and did all the voices. Rory giggled and then became more drowsy, his head dropping and rising again as he woke himself up. The story came to an end and Gus eased off Rory's head torch. 'Come on, mate.' Then he picked up Rory and wriggled back into the shelter with him.

Although he seemed to be fast asleep, he mumbled, 'Can I keep the torch on?'

'Sure, if you want to,' said Gus. 'But you can see the fire and it's a nicer light. Your mum and I are just here. And when you wake up we'll be next to you.'

'OK.' Rory sighed and slept.

'I have to admit you're very good with him,' Sian said quietly as Rory drifted off.

Gus acknowledged this praise with a grin.

'And I don't believe being his father has anything to do with that,' went on Sian. 'You're just good with children. I noticed at Rory's birthday party. You're a natural.'

'I do feel a great connection with Rory, but I like kids.' He sighed. 'I have a dream . . .'

Sian felt she needed to lighten the mood. 'What, raising a "passle o' kids" out West?'

Gus chuckled ruefully. 'Well, that too, but my more immediate dream is to run bushcraft courses for children. I love showing them the proper way to do things, but making it fun. Lots of children – city kids in particular – never know there are more fun things to do with a knife than stab your mates with it.'

'Wouldn't children of Rory's age be a bit young for that?'

'Probably. When you're one to one you can do a lot more, but I'd plan to do courses for children of maybe nine or ten – before they get too sophisticated to want to play in the woods.'

'I think it sounds a brilliant plan. It would use your skills and do a good thing for the world too.' She shrugged. 'Well, you know what I mean. Getting children to appreciate nature and wildlife and not to drop litter – it's important.'

'I certainly think so.'

'So what's stopping you?' she asked. There was such passion in his voice when he talked of his plans. She felt flattered he was telling her about them and was sure that whatever he set his mind to he'd achieve. She suddenly remembered the barn full of his stuff and smiled. 'You certainly have enough yurts to put them up in.'

'That's true.' Gus stretched and shifted his position. 'Sadly yurts are only one of the things I might need. The first thing is a bit of land. I could possibly rent it, to get me started, but you can't start a business if you're underfunded. It's why so many of them fail.'

Sian thought for a minute. 'I'm sure Felicity at the school would help. Maybe you could take her top class on a trip. That would give you practice. You could see if they like

223

it, what they can manage and what they can't. She'd tell other heads of schools, get you more children.'

'That's a great idea! I'd have to have lots of parents to join in and help but I'm sure that wouldn't be a problem.'

'Where would you do the course? If you could?'

'In the woods where I took you and Rory for preference. The trouble is, I have no idea who they belong to.'

Sian chuckled. 'Well, get my mother to find out. She's a wiz on the internet. Just give her an address, or the nearest you can come up with, and she'll find out, I'm sure.'

'How did she get to be so good at internet snooping, then?'

Sian shrugged and rested her arm on a cushion. 'Practice. And she says herself, she's terribly nosy. If the information exists, she wants to have it.'

'Oh well,' said Gus, 'that would be a great place to start. If I could rent, or borrow, those woods for a weekend, we could try it all out. But I'll still need capital.'

'Wouldn't Fiona help you?'

'Certainly, but I'm past the age when it's acceptable to take handouts from your mother.'

Sian sighed. 'But it wouldn't really be a handout, would it? You'd pay her back. I really couldn't have done without my parents when I had Rory. They supported me in every way possible.'

'It is rather different,' said Gus, obviously still a bit spiky on the subject of Sian's single parenthood. 'You were a girl and there was a baby on the way. I don't have those time constraints and I need to get the money without her help.'

'Right,' said Sian after a second, taking his point. 'Let's think. Have you got anything you can sell? All those yurts, the canoe, stuff from your travels? Do you need to keep it all?'

'Not really. But they wouldn't raise much and I made that canoe! Took bloody for ever. I'm not going to sell it.'

'Fair enough. What about this book you're supposed to be writing?'

'I don't think I'd get enough money from that to start a business with.' He picked up something, which turned out to be a spoon he'd been whittling. He produced his knife from his belt and started shaving away. He was just like Rory, he couldn't just sit still, he had to be busy with something. She was starting to see just how alike they were even if she wasn't quite sure how that made her feel. 'Eventually it might make a bit but not immediately,' Gus went on.

'Have you asked the bank for a loan?'

'You're joking! No bank would lend me money, not in the current climate – probably not even if I put Mum's house up as security, which she suggested and I utterly refuse to do.'

'A rich benefactor?'

'Where would I find one of them, then?'

She chuckled.

'I'll get backing from somewhere, eventually. I just have to keep positive, and keep my nose to the ground.'

'That sounds uncomfortable!'

He laughed. 'Fortunately, as an explorer, I'm used to discomfort. Come on, you've hardly eaten anything. Have a chop.'

'Maybe it's time for pudding? Rory will have to have it for breakfast.'

'Oh no, I've something much better in mind for breakfast. It's a sort of damper, you know, like they make at Scouts.'

'Hmm, think I'd prefer crumble. Do we want to heat it up? Or shall we just have it as it is?'

'As it is.'

'Here we go then. Richard would want custard. I have brought some cream.'

'I like cream,' said Gus, giving her a funny look.

'Well, at the risk of being misunderstood,' said Gus later, when the wine was finished and most of the food, 'I think it's time for bed.'

Sian sighed. She didn't know whether it was the wine or the flickering firelight and the air of romance, but a part of her – the woman in her rather than the mother – would have loved to have just gone to bed with him as she had done all those years ago. It had been fantastic. And he was in his element out here, at his best, his rugged, handsome features all the more appealing in the half-light. But she was a mother now; she couldn't be spontaneous any more, not when it might have an adverse affect on Rory. And it could all go horribly wrong. What if Gus got bored with her and left her? Possibly for Melissa Lewis-Jones? She would find it hard to let him see Rory if she fell for him all over again and he threw her aside. Admittedly he hadn't thrown her aside last time but could she trust him? Really trust him? Her mind wasn't at its clearest – they'd finished the wine between them – but she knew that sleeping with Gus was out of the question, even if she did now accept she wanted to. At least they had a five-year-old chaperoning them, which made the whole question irrelevant.

'I'll just go back to the house and wash and things,' she said. Gus helped her to her feet; she was a bit unsteady on them.

'It's because you've been sitting in a cramped position,' said Gus, 'it's made you a bit wobbly.'

Sian smiled in the darkness. 'Nothing to do with the wine, then?'

'No, nothing at all! Do you want me to come with you to the house?'

'Certainly not. I'll be fine!' She set off down the path, still lit by tea lights. 'I'll be back shortly.'

Her washing included a lot of cold water to her face and not just because it had smuts from the fire on it. She wanted to make sure she was fully in control before she went back. She did add a squirt of scent after all her ablutions though. Was it for her or for Gus? She didn't know – and didn't care to enquire.

She crawled into the shelter and then posted her feet into the sleeping bag that Gus gave her. She shuffled around until she was comfortable, glad of the proper pillows he had also provided. She could hear Rory's breathing and knew he was fast asleep.

'OK? Comfy? Still room for me?' Gus asked.

'There's still room. Rory and I don't take up much space.'

But Gus took up quite a lot of space and not just the physical kind. Sian heard him settle himself and then it all went quiet.

Although she'd been sleepy and possibly a little bit drunk when she got ready for bed, now she was wide awake and very aware of what she was surrounded by – leaf litter – and what leaf litter was full of – insects. I can't believe this, she thought, I'm here to protect Rory from bogeymen, he's fast asleep and I'm lying awake frightened of earwigs.

Although she lay as still as she could, trying to relax, Gus was aware she was still awake.

'Are you all right?' he said, as if he sensed she was getting more and more tense and further from sleep.

'Think so. But I'm worried about things dropping on me.'

'What sort of things?'

'Wriggly ones.'

'I don't think there are any or we'd hear them landing on us.'

This was perfectly logical and Sian tried to take comfort from it. 'OK. I'll put my head under my sleeping bag hood,' she said. Why hadn't she thought of that before?

'Won't you be too hot?'

That was probably why she hadn't thought of burying herself in goose down on a hot summer night. On the other hand . . . 'I can't risk the wriggly things. Oh, God, something dropped. It definitely did.'

'Hang on. Keep calm. I'll sort it.'

'I am calm!' she whispered, fooling neither of them.

'OK. Hide under your hood for a moment, I'll see what I can do.'

It seemed to Sian she was there for hours but she knew it was really only a few minutes before Gus came back. She risked a peek out of her hood. He was wearing his head torch and carrying something.

'It's a tarp. I'll make a lining for the roof. I do sort of wish you'd mentioned your fear of things dropping on you before. It would have been easier to fix without having Rory to trip over. He's amazing the way he can sleep through all this.'

'I'll get out,' said Sian. 'That'll give you a bit more room.'

Ten minutes later, protected from bits of leaf and twig and centipedes, Sian got back in the tent.

'I thought Rory might be scared but I didn't think I would,' she said apologetically.

'No need to be scared, you've got me to protect you.'

'And the tarp.'

Gus gave a low chuckle. 'Oh yes, the tarp.'

'We'd better not talk, we might wake Rory.'

'OK. 'Night, John-Boy.'

Sian laughed. 'I don't see you as a *Waltons'* fan somehow.'

'Oh yes. Saw all the reruns.' He paused. 'So, goodnight, sleep tight and don't let the earwigs bite.'

'Oh shut up!' she whispered.

He laughed.

Sometime during the night Sian was aware of shuffling. She and Gus had put their sleeping bags one each side of Rory. It had taken her a long time to get to sleep and Gus had started to snore gently long before she finally did. Now she felt too deeply asleep to wake herself and allowed the shuffling to go on without her. A little later she woke properly. Rory had gone and Gus was curled round behind her sleeping bag.

'Where's Rory?' she asked, suddenly guilty for letting herself sleep when her child had needed her.

'Calm down! He woke and wanted to go inside. I've tucked him up in the spare room. He's fine in there.'

'Yes, but—

'He's got my mobile and can ring you if he's worried. But he went back to sleep straightaway. I waited until I was sure.'

Sian's brain accepted that all was well and she waited for her body to catch up and her breathing to steady.

'I don't think we should leave him alone in the house, though.'

'He's not. Mum's home and I told her she had a guest.'

'Oh.' With her son obviously safe, Sian couldn't think of a reason why she should go back into the house, at least not one she could admit to. She was still in a state and although she knew it wasn't Rory that was causing it, she clung on to her motherhood like a lifebuoy. 'I think I should go—

229

'There's no reason for you to go. He's perfectly fine.'

She couldn't say that she wasn't fine, or that it was for her sake she wanted to go into the house; she might as well just come out and say she found being alone in the dark with Gus just too – well – too erotic. She was all too aware his body had been curled around hers only moments before.

She started to speak and found her voice had become husky. She cleared her throat and tried again. 'That's really kind of you to look after Rory. Thank you very much.'

She sensed him wince. 'He's my son. It's not kind at all.'

'No, it is kind! Lots of dads would expect the mum to do the night shift.'

'I'm obviously not lots of dads.'

'No.' The word 'dad' was so domestic Sian tried to focus on it. She tried to visualise him in stripy pyjamas and slippers, a tartan dressing gown over the top. That's what dads were like, not – well – not like Gus.

Sian tried hard to relax, to steady her breathing, but it seemed to make her worse.

Eventually Gus shifted and said, 'You're very strung out all of a sudden. Did an earwig get into your sleeping bag?'

She made a sound somewhere between a giggle and a squeak. 'If one had I wouldn't be tense, I'd be leaping round the lawn and screaming.'

He patted her through her sleeping bag. 'Now that I'd pay good money to see.'

'I'm not giving you the opportunity. I'm getting up and going into the house. I'll get into bed next to Rory.'

'Why does Rory get all the fun?'

'There won't be any fun! We'll be asleep! It's mad to stay here when—' She stopped. She wasn't sure what exactly she had been going to say but she knew very well she couldn't say it.

'When what?' His voice has hardly louder than a breath.

'When Rory's not here.' It didn't sound very convincing.

'It's not that, is it?'

'What do you mean?'

'Don't be disingenuous. You're not happy being alone here with me.'

'No—'

'Because you're not sure what might happen. You can't guarantee that what happened six years ago won't happen again.'

The fact that he was right didn't make her a jot less indignant. 'That's silly! I'm not worried that you might leap on me, Gus! For goodness' sake—'

'You're not frightened of me. You're frightened of yourself.'

'That's the most ridiculous thing I've ever heard. Now I'm going to sleep. Goodnight.'

The truth has never been a good soporific, Sian discovered. She lay there, tense, curled up in her sleeping bag, listening for earwigs dropping on the tarpaulin above her head.

Chapter Eighteen

To be fair to Angus, thought Fiona, as she left the house, he did give his overnight guests breakfast, even if the breadknife was almost more useful for the atmosphere than for the toast. If only they could get past all the rubbish that kept them apart, they'd be perfect for each other, she knew it! Young people were so silly sometimes. Still, at least Gus now knew Rory was his.

She pointed the car in the direction of town and the bookshop. It was her day for returning James's kindness and she was looking forward to it. 'Milly-Molly-Mandy Keeps Shop' always was her favourite story.

But she was still nervous. She opened the door of the shop feeling exactly as if it was the first day of a new job. In a way it was, although of course it didn't really matter if she did well or not. But she wanted to do well for James. He was so nice, had been so kind. He deserved her very best efforts.

'Good morning!' said James. 'You're wonderfully punctual. Early even.'

'Well, I had campers overnight. Angus made a shelter for Rory's birthday party and last night they all slept in it. Not terribly well, going by what time they got up.'

'Camping is a skill I've never acquired, I'm ashamed to say,' said James, squaring up papers on the desk and checking there were sharpened pencils available.

'Nor me, but Angus loves it. It meant a lot to him that

Sian and Rory spent the night – or some of the night in Rory's case – in the shelter.'

'So he and Rory get on, do they?' She'd told him that Gus was Rory's father when he'd asked if she could do him a favour and mind his shop for him. It had been a relief to talk to him about it as Gus was being frustratingly unforthcoming on the subject and although she and Penny had got on well, she didn't feel they knew each other well enough yet for confidences.

'Oh yes. I don't think Rory's noticed any difference in his behaviour but I can tell Angus is determined to be a brilliant dad.' She put down her bag on a chair. 'It's such a relief that he knows, I can't tell you.'

'I could tell it was worrying you when we spoke the other day.'

'*I* felt guilty, as if it was my secret. Anyway, maybe we should press on? I don't want to hold you up but nor do I want you to have to rush off before you've taught me how to use the till and things.'

'We're unlikely to be very busy. Most of my business is done via the internet. I only really keep the shop on for some locals and because I can afford to.' He gave a rueful smile. 'And I suppose I'm old-fashioned.'

'I'm glad you are,' said Fiona. 'I think I am a bit, too. Although not in a bad way,' she added hurriedly.

'Well, let me show you where you can put your things. I have an office. Full of junk and terribly untidy. I do apologise.'

'Of course my house is immaculate. I'm shocked by seeing a few things knocking about the place,' she said dryly and he laughed.

'Well, there are women who would be horrified. I have a cleaning firm that does the shop but I never let them in here. Right,' he went on briskly. 'Hang your jacket over there unless you want to keep it on. The shop does warm up later when the sun comes round but it's quite chilly first thing.'

'Yes, I'll hang on to it for now. It's also part of my look. I'm not sure the outfit works without it.'

He studied her for a moment. 'It is very attractive. But I'm sure if you were hot, it would work without the jacket.'

'Thank you. I don't know why I mentioned it really. Something about you makes me say things I wouldn't normally.'

'I hope that's a good thing.'

'I don't know about it being good but it must mean I trust you. And I hope you trust me!' Really she wished she could just chat normally to him and not go off at a tangent every time or get deep. Stick to the point, Fiona, she told herself firmly.

'Of course I trust you, Fiona. I wouldn't leave you in charge of my shop if I didn't.'

Fiona felt she'd better come clean. 'I am totally honest but I'm not desperately good at sums and the till is terrifying me.'

'OK, we'll get to that. There's a kettle, all sorts of tea bags, coffee, hot chocolate sachets – essential in winter, I find – and biscuits. I bought some nice ones specially for you, so you must eat them. And a little fridge for the milk.'

'How lovely. I can sit here reading and eating biscuits all day!'

'You can. And if you run out of biscuits, when you close for lunch you can buy some more out of the petty-cash tin, which is here.' He indicated a wonderfully old-fashioned black tin which would have seemed archaic when Fiona was a girl.

'Oh, I love this!' she said, fingering it. 'Is it secure?'

'Not really. But it doesn't have a lot in it and when I go out I fling it in the safe and lock that.'

'I don't think I'd want to do that. I'll take it with me when I go out, I think.'

'It would be heavy and bulky.'

'Really, I'd prefer to do that.'

He didn't press his point any further. 'Well, now the till.'

The till did seem rather daunting but James provided her with a pad and a pen so she could write down the details of every purchase if anything went wrong.

'And will I have to learn the card machine?' Fiona hardly dared to ask this.

'No. I think for today we'll refuse to take cards. If they're a regular customer just write down their details and we'll sort it out later. If they're strangers, they can come back.'

'But I might lose you a valuable sale!'

'No. If they're real collectors they'll come back. Really, don't worry about it.' He smiled kindly at her. 'I could close the shop of course, but you were so insistent that you wanted to repay me for rescuing you, and I don't like closing it. If people come and can't get in, they don't come again.'

'I know. I once went to a tea shop – a tea shop, mind – and they were closing. It was just after half past four. I didn't think, OK, must go back there again when they're open. We asked for tea and the woman said she was just about to turn the sign round and refused to let us in.' Fiona sighed at the memory. 'I wouldn't have minded if it had been later but it was the middle of the afternoon!'

'Bad service is always disappointing when good service is so easy.' He smiled again. He had a lot of shy charm, she realised. There must be people who came here to buy a second-hand book rather than search the internet, just because James was so pleasant.

Eventually James had to go and Fiona was on her own. She walked about the shop, up and down the rows of shelves, trying to familiarise herself with where things were.

She found the cookery book section, which seemed larger than the others. He must specialise in them. She thought with fondness of the little book he had posted to her after the dinner party. Books were lovely gifts. She took down an early edition of Elizabeth David's *Mediterranean Food* and remembered how, when her mother had her books in the fifties, you couldn't buy olive oil except in chemists and garlic was horridly seasonal. Now even the smallest corner shop seemed to have several varieties of olive oil as well as all the other kinds.

Further along were the gardening books, which took quite a lot of time to examine. There was a wildflower book which gave the flowers their old country names as well as the Latin: 'sneezewort', 'stinking goosefoot' and 'shaggy soldier'.

She found herself walking slowly round every section. Partly she was fascinated and partly she felt if she'd at least visited every section she had some chance of being able to direct people to the right place. This was what most people wanted, James had told her, where to find their particular passion.

Eventually she extracted a book called *Mrs Beeton's All About Cookery*. It had no date on it, but from the advertisements inside – one was for a stuffing mix called Stuffo – she reckoned it to be from the thirties. She flicked it open and found a recipe for ox palates and three ways of cooking tripe. She moved swiftly on to the soufflé section: there were eight of those.

She had deliberately not picked out a novel for herself. She felt she couldn't risk disappearing into another world when she was supposed to be minding the shop. Although she had noticed a clutch of Ethel M. Dells that were almost irresistible. Although well out of date – almost for her mother's generation – she had always loved them. Maybe she could buy them later.

Her first two customers wandered round, bought nothing and gave her no trouble. The next needed to find a present for an aunt and Fiona was able to point her in the direction of the gardening and cookery books. The woman was pleasant, paid with cash and Fiona managed to make the till work. Fiona settled into her job with more confidence. She glanced at her watch. In another two hours she could break for lunch.

She was just wondering if it was worth going out for lunch – the whole locking-up procedure was a bit daunting – when a woman came in.

About her own age, she was attractive and well dressed and was bearing a foil-covered pie dish.

'Oh,' she said when she saw Fiona. 'Where's James?' She sounded extremely put out not to find him where she expected him to be. 'He's always here.'

Fiona smiled apologetically. 'He's gone to an auction. I'm minding the shop for him. Is there anything I can do to help?' The dish, which appeared to be hot, was disconcerting.

'Oh,' the woman said again. 'I've bought him a pie. Chicken and mushroom. For his lunch. He's very fond of my pies. He says I have a very light hand with pastry.'

This seemed charmingly old-fashioned and James-like. 'Well, I could put it in the fridge for him. He could have it when he comes home, heated up.'

The woman considered. 'It won't be nearly as nice as it is fresh out of the oven.'

Fiona forbore to suggest that the woman took her pie

to the auction then, to ensure he got it fresh. The pie was giving out delicious smells, reminding Fiona that it was lunchtime. 'But it would still be nicer than any pie he could buy. Do you really make your own flaky pastry?'

'Oh yes. Most people buy it ready-made these days.'

The snooty way the woman said this made Fiona say instantly, 'I do. I even buy it readyrolled.' She paused. She was incurably truthful. 'I do make shortcrust.'

'I don't know what to do with it now,' said the woman. Really, her day had been ruined by James's absence.

Although she found this woman extremely irritating, Fiona didn't want her to be even more upset and tried to be kind. 'Well, I could make us some tea or coffee and we could eat it?'

The woman couldn't have been more appalled if Fiona had suggested they stole the contents of the till and went on a bender with it. 'No! It was a present for James!' The woman frowned crossly. 'Excuse me, but who are you? I've never seen you in the shop before.'

Fiona felt horribly guilty, although she knew it was silly. 'I'm a friend of James's,' she said apologetically. 'He asked me to mind the shop for a day.'

'Well, why didn't he ask me?'

As Fiona had no idea who the woman was, what James's relationship was to her, or indeed anything else about her except that she had a light hand with pastry, she couldn't really help. Perhaps he hadn't asked her because she was so possessive and odd? 'He asked me because I owed him a favour.'

'Oh? What?'

Fiona certainly wasn't going to tell this woman the details but she didn't have much time to think up an answer. 'Well, he just did something for me.'

'I'm sorry,' the pie-woman went on, meaning she wasn't sorry in the slightest, but was in fact rather cross. 'I thought I knew all James's friends.'

'I'm Fiona,' said Fiona, hoping this would be enough. She was suddenly aware of how little she knew of James's private life. She really hoped this woman wasn't James's girlfriend or anything. Partly because she seemed to be barking mad, but also because Fiona realised she didn't want James to have a significant other.

'But how do you know him?' She indicated it was impossible for James to have friends he didn't meet through the correct channels.

'He sorted out my library for me. I know him professionally.' This sounded good and also as if she were minding the shop because of the library, not because of anything else. She was aware that Pie-woman was asking all the questions. She should ask her some in return. 'So, how did you get to know James?'

'Oh, I've known him since he first moved here.'

Well, that definitely gives you first dibs on him, Fiona thought. Out loud she said, 'Would you like to sit down? And do, please, put down the pie. I'm sure it'll be wonderful heated up, just what James will want after a long day at an auction. I'll put it in the fridge.'

'I didn't know he had a fridge here.' The woman sounded indignant, as if she should know the whereabouts of all James's white goods.

'It's only very small. It's in the office. For keeping the milk for tea and coffee. Are you sure you wouldn't like something?' Fiona now wanted to eat the pie more than she'd ever wanted to eat anything.

'When is he going to be back?' The woman held on to the pie. She was not going to be seduced into letting go of it by the offer of hot drinks.

'I don't really know. He wasn't sure. I think it depended on what, if anything, he wanted to buy.'

'So he was selling?'

'And buying. He wouldn't need to go if he was only selling, would he?'

Pie-woman frowned. 'I suppose not.'

'Listen, it's lunchtime. I was about to put the kettle on. Do join me in something.'

'Lunchtime? Do you want to go out? I could mind the shop for an hour.' She seemed eager.

Although she wasn't a possessive person and she had no right to be possessive over James, Fiona found herself unable to allow this pie-maker control over James's shop, even for an hour. After all, if James really knew this woman that well, why hadn't he asked her to mind the shop for him? He obviously never had. That was probably for a reason. 'That's very kind but the alarm system is very complicated. I couldn't possibly explain it to you. I'd decided not to go out.'

The pie-woman spotted the flaw in this argument at the same time as Fiona did. 'Well, if I was here you wouldn't need to lock up. I'd look after everything.'

There was something a bit avid about this woman's desire to look after the shop, which gave Fiona a hint as to why James hadn't asked her. 'I'm sure you would but really, I can't do that.'

'I don't see why not. I've known James far longer than you have!'

'How do you know?' The fact that this was very probably the truth didn't make the question any less impertinent. 'Where did you meet him? You didn't say.' Fiona was being quite impertinent herself but she was getting desperate. If this woman didn't either put down the pie or leave the shop, or preferably both, she thought she might do something violent.

Her saviour came in a very unexpected form. The shop bell jangled and in walked Robert Warren.

Fiona and Robert looked at each other, she with relief and he with surprise.

'Oh, Fiona. Er, hello!'

'Hello, Robert!' Fiona was much more pleased to see him than she should have been. 'How lovely to see you!'

The pie-woman looked at Robert with the same accusing stare she had been directing towards Fiona all this time. 'Are you a friend of James's too?'

'Er, no. I came here to look for a book about antiques,' said Robert.

Fiona debated whether she should remind him that actually, he had met James, or just leave him in ignorance. A look from the pie-woman helped her decide. 'Actually you have met him, Robert. He was at my dinner party.'

'Oh! Oh, I remember now. He helped with the wine. I forgot he said he had a bookshop.'

'That's him,' Fiona confirmed, earning herself a look of dislike from the pie-woman.

'You must know James quite well if he's had dinner at your house and he helped with the wine,' the pie-woman said. She didn't add that it was tantamount to leaving his boots under Fiona's bed but she obviously felt it was.

'He was working in my library,' said Fiona primly, reading her subtext with no problem.

'I remember him now,' said Robert. 'He was quite interested in old buildings.'

'We met at the local history society. He gave us a talk on old books,' said the pie-woman, softening a little.

'So you're a friend of Fiona's?' Robert knew how to be charming and looked genuinely eager to know the pie-woman.

'Oh no,' said Fiona quickly. 'I don't even know your

name.' She smiled, encouraging the woman to introduce herself. 'I'm Fiona Matcham.'

'Miriam Holmes,' said the pie-woman, as if disclosing classified information.

'And this is Robert Warren,' said Fiona. 'Miriam – may I call you that? – has a very light hand with pastry. She tells me.'

'That's nice,' said Robert, giving her his intimate and flattering smile.

'So,' asked Miriam, softening further. 'How did you two meet?'

'On the internet,' said Robert before Fiona could chip in with something less incriminating.

Miriam paled, taking in the horror. 'You're not telling me – are you? – that you met James over the internet? That's disgusting!'

'It's not disgusting!' defended Fiona. 'That's how I met Robert.' She forced the picture of the vile and evil Evan she had also met that way aside with an effort. 'And I told you – keep telling you – I met James because he's sorting my library for me.'

'You don't think James looks on the internet for women, do you?' Miriam didn't seem at all reassured.

'I'm sure he doesn't,' said Fiona firmly. 'He has lots of other ways of meeting women, as we can both testify. Now, would you like me to put the pie in the fridge for later or do you want to take it home?'

Reluctantly, Miriam let go of the pie. 'No. I made it for James. I want him to have it. Have you got a pen and paper? Then I can leave him a note.'

Fiona handed these over with alacrity and then turned to Robert. 'Is there anything I can help you with? I'm in charge of the shop today.'

'Er, well, yes. Do you have an antiques section?'

'We certainly have. Follow me,' said Fiona, glad she could remember where it was.

'I didn't realise you and James were such close friends,' he said, sounding disapproving as he followed her between the shelves.

'We're not,' she said smoothly. 'I'm just returning a favour he did me.'

'What favour?'

'Really, Robert, it's nothing to do with you.' She smiled, wishing simultaneously that she'd thought of an acceptable favour that James could have done for her, and that she hadn't been so rude. It wasn't her style.

Once she'd established Robert in front of the antiques books she went back to the desk in time to receive the note, which was long. She resolved that the moment both Miriam and Robert had left her alone she would eat the pie.

'I didn't eat all of it,' she said apologetically to James a couple of hours later, 'but I was starving.'

James thought the whole thing hilarious. 'Come upstairs for a drink. I'll close the shop and you can tell me again, without leaving out any of the details.'

Once she had a large glass of white wine in her hand and seen the rest of the pie safely put in the kitchen area, Fiona began to see the funny side too. 'I didn't leave out many before. She was just so cross to see me here! She'd murder me if she knew about the pie. Who is she?'

James ushered her into the sitting part. 'Miriam? She's that rather scary thing, a woman of a certain age looking for a husband.'

Fiona had been heading for the sofa but she stiffened. 'I could be described as that myself!'

'I know, but I don't think you are looking for a husband and no one could think of you as scary.'

'I don't find that remotely flattering!' She was indignant. 'I can be positively daunting if I put my mind to it!'

'And if you don't, you're positively adorable.' Swiftly and quite without warning, James took the glass of wine out of her hand, set it on a convenient table and kissed her.

It took Fiona a couple of seconds to realise he really was kissing her and not just giving her a friendly peck, but no, his mouth was on hers and his arms were very tightly around her.

She had time to wonder how long it had been since she'd last been kissed like this and if she still knew what to do when she stopped bothering to think.

'Oh my goodness,' she said when she was released. 'That was very unexpected.'

'But not unwelcome?'

Fiona shook her head a little and sank down on to the sofa. She retrieved her glass and took a sip.

'I'm sorry if I shocked you,' said James. 'I've been wanting to do that for a long time.'

'Really?' Her second sip was almost a gulp, she was so surprised. 'I had no idea.'

James seemed to find this hard to believe. 'Oh come on, surely you must recognise the signs. It must happen all the time.'

'No! It doesn't. And I thought we were just friends. I had no idea you wanted to kiss me.'

James picked up his own glass and sat next to her. 'And the rest . . .'

Fiona found herself blushing and, foolishly, trying to remember what sort of underwear she had on.

'Ever since you first walked into the shop I've wanted you. It was one of the reasons I've spent so long sorting through your books. Oh! I've got quite a nice cheque for you, by the way. That little collection of books did very well.'

Fiona clapped her hands. 'Well done. I am pleased. And you've taken off your commission and everything?'

'All the expenses, yes.'

'Thank you so much. I'm so grateful.' She was nearly at the bottom of her glass now.

'Fiona, I sense I've thrown you rather. I'm sorry, I just couldn't resist.'

'No, that's fine. I didn't mind you kissing me at all.'

He put her empty glass in a safe place. 'Then you won't mind me doing it again?'

She didn't reply.

'Snogging on the sofa is vastly underrated,' said Fiona a little later.

'Mm,' said James, not quite so sure. 'It makes me wish I had a chaise longue.'

'Why?'

'Well, after the hurly-burly . . .'

'Oh! You mean the deep, deep peace of the double-bed?'

'No wonder I love you. You understand my literary references.'

Fiona chuckled. 'You mean by Mrs Patrick Campbell? That is the advantage of women of a certain age.'

'But you're not taking the hint?' James pushed Fiona's hair off her face with a tender hand.

Fiona swallowed. 'This has taken me terribly by surprise, James.'

'I know. I'm rushing you.'

'Just a bit.'

'Supper then? I don't suppose I can interest you in some chicken and mushroom pie?'

Wine, relief of tension and the fact that it was funny, made Fiona giggle, just a bit hysterically.

'I haven't put you off altogether though?' James refilled her glass.

'No. Not at all. I just need to get my head round the idea, that's all.'

'Let's look in the fridge to see if there's anything to go with the remains of the pie.'

'Frozen peas would work,' said Fiona, opening the tiny freezer compartment in the top of his fridge. 'What?' He was looking at her in a rather strange way, as if he wanted to laugh, but not quite.

'Sorry, I just have to do this.' He took her into his arms and kissed her very thoroughly indeed.

That's what that look meant, she realised as she kissed him back.

James drove Fiona home after supper. She didn't ask him in but she did kiss him, fairly comprehensively, as she said goodbye. She felt giggly and happy and the minute she entered the house and was away from the situation, she wished she had just gone to bed with James, whatever the state of her underwear. She'd probably never have the chance again – or the nerve. She went to make a cup of tea, feeling that her evening could have ended in a much more exciting fashion, were she a little braver.

Chapter Nineteen

Sian was sewing on name tapes in the garden. The light was going and the large citronella candle that she had put on the table wasn't really giving out much light. And although she was wearing a cardigan and jeans, she was also a bit cold. It had been warm earlier and she was just clinging stubbornly to the last of the summer, knowing she'd have to go in soon.

'Hey!' said Gus, letting himself into the garden.

'Hey back.' She carried on sewing, hoping he couldn't discern the little leap her heart had given when she'd seen him.

'What are you doing out here? It's not really warm enough.'

'You can see what I'm doing. It was warm earlier and for some reason I didn't want to go in. It's such a lovely evening. What are you doing here?'

'I thought you might be lonely, with Rory away.'

She bit off the thread. 'I miss him, but I know he's having a really good time. Mum rang earlier and we spoke.'

'So how's your dad coping with Euro Disney?'

'Resigned, I think. But he'll do anything for Rory, so it's probably fine. You can at least get wine in Paris.'

'Talking of which.' Gus produced a bottle from behind his back. 'Do you fancy sharing it?'

'I do have to do these.' She indicated a large pile of sweatshirts, socks and T-shirts and a smaller pile of name tapes. 'But I suppose I can't be done for being drunk in charge of a needle.'

He laughed. 'Let's go in. You can't see what you're doing and these chairs you've got here aren't all that comfortable.'

'OK. I give in. The summer's nearly over, isn't it? Once Rory goes to school . . .'

'That's one of the things I want to talk to you about.'

Although his voice had that tone that people used when they were going to say something that might not be good news, Sian was calm. 'I think I can probably guess what, and I agree with you.'

'You do?' Gus was obviously very surprised.

'Yes. Bring the wine, I'll get some glasses.'

'I'll light the fire, if you don't mind. I know it's only August but it feels damp in here.'

A few moments later she'd joined him in the sitting room, holding two glasses, a packet of crisps and Rory's school clothes. She'd put the thread in her pocket and the needle in her lapel. The fire was crackling and she saw that Gus had lit the candles on the mantelpiece and switched on the lamp on the table next to the sofa.

'This cottage is a bit damp,' she admitted as she sat back on the sofa and arranged her sewing. 'Everyone kept telling me so but I've only just started to notice. Maybe this is a house for summer only.'

'Maybe.'

'It's irrelevant anyway. Pour the wine, why don't you?'

'Have you eaten?' he asked.

She shrugged. 'Toast and Marmite. It's my default meal when Rory's not with me, I'm afraid.'

'I'll make you something.'

'No, I'm fine. We should discuss how to tell Rory. Should we do it together, or should I do it on my own?'

'You mean tell Rory I'm his father? Is that what you meant?' He seemed surprised.

Now she was confused. What else could he be talking about? 'Yes, isn't that what you wanted to discuss? I decided myself he should know before he goes to school.' She frowned. 'What did you mean?'

'Let's not start an argument until we've had at least one glass of wine.'

'So it's going to start an argument then? I'd better gather my resources.' She allowed herself a quick, flirty smile and picked up another sweatshirt.

'You can't,' said Sian firmly when Gus had made his statement of intent. 'Everyone will think you're his father—'

'Which I am!' insisted Gus. 'What's your problem?'

'I know you're his father and I dare say half the county knows it too, but when I registered Rory, I didn't put your name down.'

'That's ridiculous. No one's going to know or care what you put down on any damn form. You're just making problems where none exist!'

Sian was determined to remain calm. 'No I'm not. The school won't want random people turning up. I bet the first day of the school year is merry hell!'

Gus got up and fiddled with the fire, rearranging the logs so that the end bits burned. 'Rory wants me to come. He asked me if I would.'

Rory had told Sian this and she had spent a long time explaining that it wasn't possible. Rory hadn't been convinced by the argument but he did eventually accept that his mother had said no, and meant it. 'He can't have everything he wants. It's the first rule of life.'

'Maybe, but it's not unreasonable for him to want his dad there when he starts school.'

'He doesn't know you're his dad! That doesn't make sense.' She frowned. 'And we must tell him, before someone else does by mistake.'

'I know.' Gus sighed.

'And I know I will have to tell him. I just haven't worked out when.'

'So it's you doing it now, is it? Not "we"?'

She'd always been the one to tell Rory important things, on her own, without a partner. 'I know he'll be thrilled, but you have to let me decide when the best time to tell him is. I'm his mother.'

'Hang on! Don't I have any say in any of this? I'm his father!'

'I hadn't forgotten!'

'OK, then we'll tell Rory about me being his dad and take him to school together.'

'I've told Rory it has to be just him and me going.' But she spoke with less conviction now.

'You can tell him things have changed. Things do!'

'But we're not together. If we turn up in the school playground with Rory on the very first morning, people will see us as a couple. And we're not.'

'You're worrying about nothing.'

His sudden smile made her heart lurch. And perhaps she *was* worrying about nothing. She was certainly tempted by the idea of having Gus there; sending Rory off to school was going to be a special day, but also a strange one for her, and she was sure that Gus would make it feel celebratory rather than slightly lonely. She turned away and picked up another sweatshirt. 'Tell you what, you can come if you sew a name tape on. Here. Do it on a sweatshirt, it's less fiddly than a sock.'

Gus narrowed his gaze and looked threatening, and then he picked up the garment Sian was handing him, and the needle and thread. He turned away from her and hunched over so she couldn't see what he was doing.

'I'll get some more logs in,' she said, unable to sit and do nothing while he struggled with a needle.

In the woodshed, filling the basket with logs that had been there since last winter and were wonderfully dry, she wondered if she'd been unkind setting him such a challenge. After all, men could never sew.

Just as she got back into the house, the phone rang. It was Melissa.

'Hi, Sian, how are you?'

'Fine. You?' Sian tried to inject a bit of enthusiasm into her voice, for politeness' sake.

'Frightfully excited actually. The sale of the house is going through swimmingly, probably because I'm a cash buyer and there's no chain.'

'Oh.'

'Sorry! That was a bit tactless. Of course it's not good news for you, but you'll find somewhere. There's loads of rental property about at the moment because no one can sell. I checked that the rental market is still buoyant in case I want to rent out the cottage.'

This was twisting the knife. 'I did think you wanted to live here yourself. Although I suppose if you don't, I could just rent it from you and not move.' This would have been a solution but she didn't really believe it would happen.

'Oh no, that wouldn't do. I want to gut the place. So much needs doing to it. Of course if I did decide not to live in it you could rent it afterwards.' She added hurriedly: 'But I'm afraid you'd have to pay quite a bit more.'

'Right, so that's not a solution.' Sian paused. 'Why were you ringing again?' She knew perfectly well that Melissa hadn't told her and wanted to get this conversation over as quickly as possible.

'Oh, sorree! Didn't I say? I want to come round with a builder and an interior designer, possibly an architect. My father knows one who'll do it for me for nothing.'

'How lucky for you.'

'Yes, isn't it?' Melissa had no notion that Sian had been sarcastic. 'Anyway, I can only get everyone together next Monday week. Is that all right for you?'

Longing to say it wasn't, Sian sighed. It was Rory's first day at school. She would be feeling odd and possibly miserable anyway, so she might as well have her home invaded by Melissa and her team of eager helpers. She didn't have to stay. She could go and cadge a cup of coffee from Fiona while they tore her home apart, possibly literally. 'You can come at half past nine.'

'Not before? Builders start horrifically early, you know. Half eight?'

'Absolutely not. It's my son's first day at school, we'll both be very busy at half past eight. Now I must go. See you a week on Monday.' She put the phone down a little more forcefully than she meant to. Damn Melissa.

She went back into the sitting room with the logs. The sweatshirt with a beautifully sewn name tape on it was on her chair. A T-shirt was on top, also marked. Gus had just picked up a pair of PE shorts and had cut a name tape from the ribbon of them that curled on the table.

'Oh. So, you can sew,' said Sian, pretending not to be impressed and fooling neither of them.

'Which means I get to come with you when Rory goes to school.' Gus was firm.

'Oh, OK.' She sighed, feeling defeated. 'Although I would have made you do all of them if I'd known you were so handy with a needle,' she added more briskly.

He frowned. 'You're not miffed that I can sew, are you? What's up?'

'Your friend Melissa. That was her on the phone just now.' She relayed the conversation to him.

'Well, it's a pain, but it's not really a surprise, is it?'

'I suppose not. I knew she wanted to redo the kitchen.'

'I think you're hungry,' Gus said, getting up. 'Top tip: never try to argue with a hungry woman. I'm going to make you a snack.'

She tried not to laugh until he was out of the room.

The name-tape sewing was finished by the time he came back with two loaded plates. She'd been wondering what he'd found to eat in her currently poorly stocked fridge, but apparently there was something.

'No wonder you're in a bad mood. There is no food in your house!'

'What's that then, if it's not food?'

'Beans on toast with melted cheese, but I had to slice a crust of bread sideways.'

'You did very well.' Now she saw and smelt the beans she was suddenly starving.

'Tuck in then.' He poured more wine into her glass.

As he ate the second slice of beans on toast she said, 'You were hungry too.'

'I'm always hungry.'

'Like Rory.' Then, wishing she hadn't said that, she got up. 'I'll find us some pudding.'

'Hah! Bet you can't!'

Fortunately, after this rash offer, she did have ice cream, and the makings of chocolate sauce. She toasted some flaked almonds briefly and then assembled everything in tumblers.

'Ta da! Chocolate nut sundaes,' she announced proudly when she brought them through.

'Oh wow. My favourite.' Gus took the glass and the spoon and inspected it. 'No jelly?'

'No. It would have taken hours to set. Be grateful for what you've got. And eat it before it all melts.' It was rather like having an older version of Rory in the house. Father and son were frighteningly alike.

When she'd dug her own spoon carefully down the side of the glass so only a small amount spilt over the side she noticed her sketchbook on the table. 'Oh, you've been nosing about.'

'Yes,' he replied, unabashed. 'You're really good! I mean you can draw and not just paint.'

She took a moment to consider a reply. 'Well yes. Often one comes before the other. Although not always, not for everyone,' she added, a stickler for accuracy.

'Drawing always seems a black art to me. I just can't do it. Anyone who can seems like a magician.'

'We all have our different talents. I feel like that about maths.' She picked up her sketchbook and flicked through it. 'After all, you can write.'

'Can I? Although my agent was very enthusiastic, I've got cold feet. I mean, writing about bushcraft is so different from doing it.'

'But there'll be photos? You said you had loads.'

'Oh yes. The book will look pretty, lots of colour shots of beautiful sunsets and things, but the technical stuff – which is what I really want to get over to the reader – is going to be lost in my incompetent prose.'

'Well, then you need line drawings!'

He looked at her. 'I do!'

Too late she realised she might have volunteered for something. 'And you'd like me to do them?' She tried to hide her excitement at the prospect.

'Well, if you've time. I know it probably seems a bit boring.'

'Not at all! I think it'll be stunning and I'd absolutely

love to do the drawings for you!' Suddenly it seemed silly to pretend she wasn't keen.

'I can't pay you—'

'Oh, honestly, Gus! You don't need to worry about anything like that until you've sold the book and got some money yourself.'

'I will try and repay you in kind.'

'You're so silly!'

Gus took offence. He left his chair and came and sat on the arm of hers with a terribly familiar look in his eyes. 'You think I'm silly, do you?'

Sian got up. He was too near. She didn't want him noticing that she was now breathing rather fast. But it was a mistake. He got up too and caught her. She found she could hardly speak. 'Yes!' It came out very breathily.

'Well I think you're silly too.' Then he wrapped his arms around her and kissed her, long, hard and with a lot of attention to detail.

As they kissed, Sian's defences melted. She was no longer a single mother, fighting for her independence, she was a woman, in the arms of a man she not only wanted but loved. She could finally admit to herself that she'd never stopped loving Gus, all these years, even though she'd tried to. When later he said, 'Would you like . . . ?' Without any hesitation whatsoever she said 'Yes,' and led him upstairs to her bedroom.

All the chemistry they'd shared six years before was still there, made more intense for Sian because there'd been no one else since. The first time was fast, hot, passionate and somewhat lacking in finesse, but after that they took their time, exploring and rediscovering each other's bodies.

'That's the first time I've felt properly a woman and not just a mother for ages.'

'For how long?'

'Nearly six years.'

He kissed her naked shoulder. 'That's very touching.'

'I know.' She didn't tell him that he'd spoilt her for other men. Some things are best kept to oneself.

They woke slowly and late, both starving hungry. 'There's nothing to eat,' said Sian. 'No bread, anyway.'

'What have you got?'

Sian lay back and tried to focus on food. 'I'm got milk in the freezer. Things like flour, sugar. Jam. Marmite, peanut butter. All stuff that goes with toast, really.'

'Eggs?'

She nodded. 'But no bacon. Or tomatoes, mushrooms, or anything else you need for a cooked breakfast.'

'Not at all. I'll make pancakes, the fluffy kind,' he said. 'You go back to sleep.'

She didn't think she would sleep but she plumped the pillows and snuggled up, feeling she just wanted to revel in what had gone on in the past few hours. The next thing she knew, she was waking up as Gus placed a tray on the bed. On it was a pile of pancakes, a cup full of golden syrup, the butter dish, and a couple of plates and knives.

'I'm going to get the tea now,' he said and disappeared downstairs. He seemed not to feel the chill and was quite happy wandering about in his boxers. She surveyed the feast before her. She could get used to this.

After they had taken a shower, together, they decided to go out for lunch. Wrapped in a towel in Gus's case, and a dressing gown in Sian's, they discussed where to go.

'Not locally,' said Gus. 'Let's make the most of the weather. It might be the last day of summer.'

'And we've spent most of it in bed.' Sian sighed happily.

'Don't look at me like that or I'll take you straight back

there,' said Gus with a look that made Sian feel that wasn't a bad option.

'If there was a single thing left in the house to eat I'd take you up on that, but you need to keep your strength up.'

Having indicated that his strength was not at all diminished, he let her go and Sian was free to get dressed. While Gus went home for clean clothes she pulled on her jeans and a Breton-style stripy top. It was a casual outfit but she knew it suited her. Then she put on a careful amount of make-up: the kind that Gus would never notice but she knew would enhance her eyes and lips. Her skin didn't need anything on it apart from a bit of moisturiser. She was glad she'd been so quick because Gus was back before she'd stuffed her feet into her sneakers.

'So where do you want to go?' he asked. 'Stately home, theme park, garden centre?'

'I don't want to go anywhere with lots of people. Just take me somewhere nice.'

'OK, I can do that. And do you want to buy a picnic? Light a fire, boil a billy? Or have lunch in a pub?'

'Lunch in a pub,' said Sian, hoping it wasn't so completely the wrong answer that he would go right off her.

He laughed. 'I even know where a good pub is. Come on!'

'So where are we going?' she asked after they'd been driving for a few minutes.

'To my favourite spot. Remember, the woods I took you and Rory to. We'll go in further than we did last time. There's something I want to show you.'

'Oh. How lovely. Maybe we should have brought a picnic.'

'No, waste of time. We'll have a bit of a walk, find the

pub, have a bite of lunch, couple of beers and then go back for . . . a siesta.'

'Oh yes. A siesta. Good idea!'

She spent the rest of the journey alternately looking out of the window and looking at Gus's thigh. It was a happy time.

'Here we are,' said Gus, having driven a little way into the wood and parking up. They climbed out of the Land-Rover and Gus hooked his arm around Sian's waist. She tried to keep pace with him, stride for stride, but after a couple of yards she had to stop.

'It's no good, my legs are just not long enough.'

'Your legs are the perfect length. I'll fit my stride to yours.'

Mention of legs reminded her. 'So what about your injury? You never talk about it,' she said.

He shrugged. 'It's a lot better now and mostly it's OK. I wouldn't want to trust it on a long expedition though.' He looked at her. 'My heart's not in exploring any more – not the way it was.'

She looked up at him and smiled.

They walked through the woods and up a hill to a large clearing. 'This is where I'd like to set up my bushcraft school, the one I was telling you about. It's big enough for a few tents or yurts with a main camp in the middle.'

'It is a lovely spot.' She looked around her. It was magical, as if it hadn't been touched in centuries, except to clear it of course. She doubted many people came up here.

'Yes. It would be absolutely perfect if it had a stream running through it, but there is one not too far away,' Gus said.

'So what do you want to do most? Write a book or set up a business?'

'You know? If you'd asked me a couple of months ago I'd have said the business, no question. But I have been cracking on with the book and the more I get into it, the more fun it is to do. I've nearly finished it. In fact I sent some of it to my agent and he loves it. He's even got a publisher lined up.'

'I'm so glad. I think it's going to be wonderful. I'd love to read it – or part of it if you didn't want me to see it all,' she added hurriedly. 'I know some authors don't like to show anyone their work, not even their family or friends, until it's published.'

'You'll have to see it if you're going to illustrate it.'

They walked on in silence for a bit. Gus stopped suddenly. 'Would you – would you come with me to the meeting? When I go to see the publishers?'

'Why would you want me there? I don't think it's at all usual. After all it's not a picture book for children.'

'I know but . . .' Words seemed to be failing him a bit.

'What? Tell me!' She turned to face him so she could get him to look at her.

'I know it's silly, you're just a girl' – he grinned quickly to make sure she knew he was joking – 'but I'd feel more confident if you were there. I can do a lot of things, but one of the things I can't do, apart from draw, is sell myself. With you there, I think maybe I could.'

Sian was touched but still wasn't quite sure he really needed her to come. 'You'll have your agent. He'll do that,' she said.

'Yes, but if the publishers don't believe in me they won't buy my book, will they?'

'I suppose not. And if you want me there, of course I'll come.' She'd do anything to help Gus. And she knew how much harder it was to sell your own work than it was to sell someone else's. If she could sell Jody's

259

cushions, she should be able to help sell Gus's book. As they walked and Gus told her of the things he and his brother had got up to, Sian thought what an idyllic childhood it sounded. Was Rory's childhood anything like as perfect?

'Penny for them,' demanded Gus, when she hadn't spoken for a while.

'I was just thinking what a wonderful childhood you had with your brother, roaming the woods and fields.'

'It wasn't all perfect, if you must know. When Mum married the wrong man it was awful for all of us. Worse for her, I think. She'd thought she'd done the best for us but it was the worst. He was a bully. But all this' – he indicated the woods around them – 'that made up for a lot.'

'I want Rory to have that sort of childhood, where he doesn't spend all day on a computer or hanging out on the streets. It's one of the reasons we moved. He'd had a bad time in school in London. I had to take him out of it after a term. He just sort of shrivelled.'

'He won't shrivel here!'

'I know, which is why I don't want to move away. The school here seems so lovely. Jody, Annabelle's mum, says it's brilliant.'

'Well, you won't have to move away, far, anyway,' said Gus firmly, 'so he can still go to that school.'

Sian sighed. 'Even if that's true, even if one of the houses Mum found for me is OK . . .' She stopped.

'What?' He was demanding but not impatient. He really seemed to want to know what was troubling her.

'I feel this past summer has been an idyll that's all going to end when Rory goes to school. It's been so lovely here. The weather has been so perfect, your mother has been so welcoming. I feel settled here. I have friends, I have work, I live in a cottage I love. And on the first day of term it's going to be measured for demolition and Rory starts school. It's the end of everything, really.'

Gus's arm came round her shoulders, heavy and reassuring. 'No it's not. Rory's going to go on needing you for years and years. It'll still be idyllic.'

He sounded so certain.

Chapter Twenty

'Mum,' said Rory, early one morning. It was the week before he was due to go to school and Sian had stopped sending him to the play scheme so they could have some quality time together. She also wanted to look at the houses her mother had found on the internet.

'Yes, darling?' They were having a leisurely breakfast, Sian very aware that such breakfasts would be confined to weekends very soon.

'School won't be like it was in London, will it?'

Rory's foray into school in London had been traumatic for everyone. It was hard to decide who had suffered most, Rory who actually had to endure the huge school on a huge site with a less than sympathetic Reception teacher – one of several – or Sian and her parents who spent each day he was in it worrying and wondering how he was getting on, hoping they wouldn't be walking a silent, sometimes weeping child home.

'Absolutely not. Annabelle's brothers love it, don't they? Jody says they do. And it's smaller for one thing, remember. And you've met your teacher already.'

The head teacher, Felicity, had arranged a little party in the holidays for children new to the area who hadn't already met their teacher, and so neither she nor the other children were completely strange to Rory. Sian had been enchanted by the welcoming quality of the classroom, the interesting and varied material on the walls and the warm and nurturing attitude of the staff. She'd worry about the complete lack of racial and cultural mix such a cosy environment could provide another time.

'And I do know the children, don't I? From play scheme?'

'You do. Annabelle is your best friend.' Sian didn't say it, but she recognised Annabelle as the sort of feisty little girl who would protect Rory should he need it.

'And I'm good at lessons. I can nearly read!'

'So there's nothing whatever to worry about, is there?' she said, giving him a reassuring hug.

After this little chat, Rory seemed to think that school was going to be brilliant. She was glad Rory now felt excited about the prospect but she also felt a little sad. While she relished the prospect of having more time to work she knew she'd miss him. She would appreciate not having to pay for the play scheme though. And now Rory seemed happier she could concentrate on worrying about Gus – again.

She hadn't heard from him since the weekend, which was slightly unsettling. She'd been sort of hoping he'd check out houses with her and then there was the more important issue of when to tell Rory about Gus being his father. They'd been so caught up with each other over the weekend they hadn't really talked about more serious issues. They'd planned to tell Rory together and he was going to school next week – but where *was* Gus?

In the end Sian gave up waiting and rang the house. Fiona answered and said he wasn't in and how busy he'd been lately. Sian waited a day and then, sacrificing her pride, she rang again. This time Fiona had said he couldn't come to the phone. She sounded almost guilty and Sian didn't press her or leave a message. Suddenly there didn't seem any point.

She tried to convince herself it was fine. Of course he was busy! He was finishing his book and goodness knew what else. She wouldn't be neurotic about it. Why should she mistrust him?

But somehow, like a tiny splinter, hardly visible to the naked eye, the doubt festered in her.

She wouldn't have worried so much if she hadn't been sure she heard Melissa's laugh in the background when she'd been on the phone to Fiona. Suddenly she couldn't help worrying that history was about to repeat itself. She couldn't talk to Fiona because she wasn't sure if Gus had told her about the weekend. Men weren't as open about such things with their mothers as women tended to be. Then she told herself she was getting herself into a state unnecessarily. There would be a perfectly reasonable explanation. She had plenty of things to keep her mind occupied: she was due to go over and make a start on Veronica's wardrobes that afternoon whilst Rory was at Annabelle's, who was also spending time at home before school started.

And then Sian had another thought. Richard. What was she going to do about him? She suddenly felt terribly guilty. He was away for another fortnight, but then he would want to talk about things, and possibly ask her to marry him. How could she explain to him that she didn't love him, and so couldn't be with him? She couldn't tell him that she'd fallen in love with Gus (not that she'd told Gus that and he certainly hadn't mentioned the 'L' word), that would just add salt to the wound. And anyway, could she be absolutely certain she had a future with Gus either? And what was best for Rory? Just when she thought life was getting simpler again a coachload of worries and questions had arrived demanding answers.

Now, sitting with Rory in the garden, she had another

wobble. She'd just had a blissful weekend with Gus, but where was he now and why wouldn't he come to the phone? Had he perhaps seduced her just to prove that he could? It certainly hadn't felt as if that was what was going on, but presumably men who treated women like that were very practised at ensuring that their seductions felt genuine.

Sian was brought back to the present by a tugging at her sleeve. It was Rory asking her if he could show Annabelle his new name tags and could he try his uniform on one more time? Thank heavens for Rory and something practical to do – although if it hadn't been for him she wouldn't be in this predicament, she thought wryly.

In the end it was Fiona who rang Sian.

'I thought, if you'd like to, it would be fun if you and Rory came up here for tea on Sunday? A little pre-school celebration?'

'Is that like people having a celebration of someone's life, rather than a funeral?' Sian wasn't sure why the prospect of Rory going to school suddenly seemed so gloomy, but it did.

Fiona made sympathetic noises. 'Well, it is the end of an era, isn't it? And cake always makes everything feel better.'

'Will Gus be there?' Sian concentrated on sounding nonchalant, as if they hadn't spent two days in bed together, more or less, and then had no contact with each other.

'Yes.'

'Oh good. We decided we should tell Rory about him being his dad before he went to school. Sunday will be the last opportunity to do that.'

'Of course. I'm sorry he's been so—'

'Oh, you don't need to apologise! It's no big deal.'

'It is quite a big deal and I must say I think it's very bad of him to leave it so late but, in his defence, he has been—'

'Busy, I know. It's all right.'

She must have made a good job of sounding light-hearted and relaxed because she heard Fiona sigh with relief. 'Till Sunday then,' Fiona said. 'About three thirty? Then if Angus decides he needs to make a fire or something, there'll be time.'

That Sunday, Gus galloped down the stairs to join Fiona, Sian and Rory in the kitchen where they were eating tea. At least he's here, thought Sian. He'd come out of hiding for his son, even if he wouldn't even come to the phone for her.

He swooped on Rory, picked him up, tossed him in the air and generally threw him around until he was squealing. 'Who's the big man then? Going to school, are we?'

'Yes,' said Rory, giggling hysterically.

That's not father behaviour, thought Sian, that's wild younger uncle behaviour. Richard would never be so rough with Rory. And then a pang of guilt assailed her, adding to her growing doubts.

'Sit down, do,' said Fiona, possibly feeling the same as Sian did. 'Rory will bring his tea back up if you're not careful.'

'In a minute. Got to say hello to my best girl.' Then Gus kissed Sian on the lips, giving her a look that made him seem even more like a wicked uncle than a responsible father. Sian ducked out of the way before it could go too far. How much did Fiona know? Probably everything, the way Gus was behaving. But she wasn't going to let him think he could act as if nothing had happened and he hadn't been ignoring her for the last week.

While Fiona was tending to her son and grandson Sian found herself asking: which would she rather sleep with? The wicked uncle or the dad? Then she sighed at her answer.

'Gus, we need to have a quick chat, on our own,' said Sian, while Rory and Fiona were pre-occupied with the cake, which was a miniature version of the dragon that Penny had made for his birthday party. Fiona had made it, she claimed, 'to give her the chance to play with all the pretty sugary things'.

'We do? Well, let's wait until we've had tea. Hey, Rory? I've got something for you.' He handed Rory a small parcel wrapped in tissue paper.

'It's a dragon!' said Rory when he'd opened it.

'Did you make that?' said Fiona, sounding incredulous. 'It's lovely!'

'It is,' said Sian softly, admiring the perfectly carved scales, claws and nostrils on the wooden creature that her son was turning over and over in his hands. 'You can do carving, why can't you draw?'

'It's whittling really and dragons are supposed to be rough and scaly. I know where I am with a knife. Talking of which, are you going to cut that cake or just look at it? Here, use this.' From his belt he produced a knife that no woman would ever let a child use. Neither Sian nor Fiona said anything.

Rory managed very well, using the knife carefully, helped by Gus. He gave everyone a slice.

'So, are you going to give your dragon a name?' said Gus, just as Sian was trying to catch his eye so they could discuss when to tell Rory about his father.

'Yes, that would be a good idea,' said Sian. 'You could take it to school with you, tucked away in your bag.'

'Then you'd have a friend with you,' said Fiona.

'I've got lots of friends at school already,' said Rory

proudly. 'But I will take my dragon too,' he added, anxious not to offend Gus.

'You can leave it at home or take it with you, whichever you like,' said Gus. 'No pressure.'

'So, are you going to give him a name?' asked Fiona.

'Don't know,' said Rory, fingering the little toy lovingly. 'What should I call him?'

'That's up to you, mate,' said Gus. 'You could call him Bill, or something. Or think of something dragony.'

'What's dragony? I mean, what's a dragony name?' asked Rory.

'Please don't feel obliged to call him Puff,' said Fiona. 'We'll be singing the tune all evening.'

'Not Puff then,' said Rory, accepting it was not a popular choice. 'I think Bill. Bill the dragon.'

'I like that!' said Sian. 'None of that poncy alliteration for you.'

Rory looked at her. 'Is that one of Grandpa's big words?'

'Yes,' said Sian. 'It means having words that begin with the same letter but don't worry about it. You won't have to know that until you're much bigger.'

'I'm bigger now.'

Sian, despairing of getting Gus alone, decided to plunge in and say what was on her mind. There was no time like the present. She took a deep breath and launched straight in, before she had time to change her mind. 'You are! And because you're such a big boy, Gus and I have decided to tell you something.'

Fiona made to get up but Sian put her hand on her arm to keep her at the table. She caught Gus's eye and he nodded slightly.

'You know how lots of people have a mummy and a daddy and you've only had a mummy?'

'And your grandparents,' put in Fiona.

'Yes?' Rory was playing with his dragon, not greatly interested.

'Well, you have got a daddy—'

'And it's me!' Gus interjected, clearly – and understandably – keen to be part of the announcement. 'How about that?'

'Cool,' said Rory, still fiddling. 'Does that mean I can have a knife?'

Sian didn't know whether to laugh or cry. Quite how she expected Rory to react she didn't know, but this hadn't been one of the scenarios she'd run through in her head.

'Next birthday, mate, if you're really, really careful with it,' said Gus.

Fiona and Sian looked at each other and laughed.

'I think it's time for a glass of wine,' said Fiona.

Gus walked Sian and Rory home later. When Rory ran ahead into the house, Gus kissed her. When he let her go he said, 'See you tomorrow. Eight thirty?'

Sian nodded and then watched as he turned and went home. What was really going on with him? She was more confused than ever. He'd virtually ignored her for the last week and then acted as if nothing had changed. Had he just been taking advantage of her when they'd spent that time together? Or was he really the nice and thoughtful man he sometimes seemed? It was so sweet of him to give Rory the dragon and he'd made it so much easier than she thought it would be telling Rory about his father. He seemed serious about being a good dad, but what about the two of them? How did he really feel about her?

Once she'd fed, bathed and popped an excited Rory to bed and they'd discussed again how great school was going to be, she decided to finish painting a toy chest she'd started as a 'thank you' present for Jody. It was just what she needed to keep her mind off things.

Gus called for them the next morning promptly at half past eight, and the three of them set off together. It was a lovely day but Rory was happy in his school uniform of grey shorts and blue sweatshirt. He had a new satchel on his back, bought for him by Penny and hidden away until this morning, and at the bottom, under his packed lunch, was Bill the Dragon.

Sian carried his PE kit in the bag with his name embroidered on it. She had considered embroidering a little dragon, to match the one she'd painted on his name board, but had decided it was too fiddly, and he might grow out of dragons. Although she hoped not, for Bill's sake.

'The thing about school is, there are girls there,' said Gus.

'I know that. Annabelle's a girl. She's my friend.'

'My brother and I thought girls were weird,' Gus went on, not perturbed by Rory's casual attitude to the opposite sex. 'We didn't know any until we went to primary school, and then we were sent away to school, where there weren't any. It explains a lot.' He looked at Sian meaningfully.

She smiled, as she was supposed to, glad that Gus was there to stop either her or Rory getting too serious about this going-to-school business.

Rory saw his form teacher waiting with some of the children in his class. He ran towards her, giving his parents a casual wave. 'Laters!' he said.

Gus and Sian looked at each other. 'Where did he pick that up from?' said Sian.

'Not from me, mate.' He took her hand. 'Do you want

me to come with you when Melissa and her wrecking crew come round?'

Sian was a bit embarrassed by this public display. The mothers she'd met knew she was single; now here she was, in the playground, holding hands with a gorgeous man. She didn't want anyone thinking she was the sort of woman who couldn't do anything without her boyfriend. Thank goodness for Jody!

'Hey, you guys! Gus, how nice of you to support Sian, and how typical of the little beasts that they just run in and take no notice of us! Are you coming for a coffee?'

'No thanks,' said Sian. 'I've got Melissa coming round to measure up the house.'

'Gus? You'd be welcome too?' said Jody.

He shook his head. 'I've got work to do. Thanks for the offer though.' He turned to Sian. 'Can you pop in and see Mum, quickly? She'd like to hear how it went, from your point of view.'

Sian glanced at her watch. 'OK, but don't let me accept coffee or tea. I've only got half an hour.'

'How did it go?' asked Fiona when they appeared in the kitchen.

'Fine! He hardly looked back. It helped that Annabelle was there and he'd met his teacher and the head.' Sian felt a little emotional but didn't want to show it. Rory's first day at school was a growing-up experience for her as well as for him. She didn't count that terrible first attempt in London.

'Would you like a bit of cake?' suggested Fiona. 'Something to cheer you up? You probably feel a bit strange.'

'I haven't got time for cake, I'm afraid. Melissa's about to descend on the cottage with builders and decorators and things.' She put on a positive expression with an effort. 'She's really cracking on with buying the house.'

'Oh, poor you!' said Fiona. 'How utterly ghastly, a whole load of strange people tramping over your home, deciding how to bash it about. Come back the moment they're gone. We'll have lunch.'

Sian walked briskly down the road, thinking how much she'd miss having Fiona so near, always ready with tea and cake, wine or food.

She just had time to clear the breakfast and make the beds before the onslaught arrived.

Melissa kissed her fondly, as if they were close friends instead of deadly rivals for the same house. 'Darling! So sweet of you to have this crowd, first thing on a Monday morning too!'

'That's fine.' Sian didn't bother to say she hadn't really had a choice and that she might as well have a whole load of strangers cluttering up the place as mooch about missing Rory on her own.

'Let me do the intros. This is Philip, the architect.' Sian nodded at an amiable man in spectacles. 'Bob – the builder, obviously! If you're called Bob you have to be a builder these days.' Sian smiled at the joke. 'And this is Wendy, an interior designer.' Melissa announced this as if it was a lovely surprise. Sian smiled again, this time more weakly.

'Well, I'm not going to offer to make you all coffee,' she said, 'nor am I going to show you round. The cottage is far too small for all of us, so I'm going to be in the garden if you need me.'

'Oh, that reminds me! I've got a garden designer coming in a moment. I really want a lot of decking and a hot tub.'

'But not vegetables?'

'Darling, let's face it, it's only mums at home who can grow veggies. Unless you're a retired granddad, of course.'

That put her in her place. 'Oh well. It seems a shame, but there you are. I'll go and potter around outside.' Sian really did try to smile but she knew it came out as a sickly grimace.

She was hoeing the last of the lettuces that were starting to bolt, wondering if she should pick them all and make soup, when Wendy, the interior designer, came out.

'Hi!' she said. 'Do you mind if I join you? The builder and the architect are arguing about the best way to handle removing a supporting wall and I don't think they should do it.'

'Oh.' Sian looked up. 'Of course I don't think anyone should do anything, really. I just want to live here.'

'I think you would find that kitchen gloomy and damp in winter, not to mention small, but that wasn't why I came to find you.'

'Oh? What was it then?' Sian could see the woman was trying to be friendly, but she couldn't quite match it.

'I saw your amazing furniture!'

Sian considered the bits and pieces she had acquired from relatives, auction houses and, occasionally, new-from-Ikea that she'd added to Luella's basic supply. 'Really?'

Wendy laughed. 'Not that furniture! I meant the stuff you paint.'

'Oh, that!' Sian relaxed. 'I'd forgotten about that for a moment. I've only got the small stuff here. Larger pieces I paint up at my friend's barn. That's one of the reasons I don't want to move away.'

'Melissa said you wanted to stay really.'

'But if Luella, my landlady, wants to sell, I can't really stop her.'

Wendy paused tactfully. 'Do you take commissions, for painted furniture?'

'Of course,' She brightened. 'I do stuff on spec because my mother keeps buying bits and pieces at auction and I can't resist doing it. But commissions make most sense really. I'm doing something for Melissa's mother.'

'Fantastic! I've got this client, she has a massive bedroom absolutely full of furniture. You can get rid of the furniture but she won't get rid of the fitted wardrobe, which does actually take a lot of stuff, but I just thought, you could paint it like a mural and blend it into the other walls. She said she fancied a mural but I didn't know anyone who could do it.'

'Brilliant. That would be a lovely job.' Veronica was delighted with the start she'd made on the wardrobes and couldn't wait for her to get going on the mural in the dining room, so she felt it was something she could confidently agree to do again. She hesitated, her middle-class reluctance to talk about money kicking in. 'Is she a good payer? This woman?'

'Absolutely. I'd make sure you got really well paid. Give me your details and we can arrange a time for you to go and see the job and meet Mrs Wilkinson. She's quite local.'

Now she had a very good commission to think about, when Sian walked up the road to Fiona's, she was feeling slightly less pessimistic.

'I thought I'd take the children into town for pizza,' said Jody when they'd greeted their children and the first day of school had been deemed a success. 'Otherwise they'll fall asleep in front of the telly while I cook tea, won't eat anything and won't go to bed. Fancy coming?'

Rory was jumping up and down like a jack-in-the-box next to Annabelle.

'Oh, OK,' said Sian. 'I was going down the fish-fingers-and-oven-chips route but it's all still in the freezer. Pizza would probably be healthier, really.'

'As well as more fun,' said Jody. 'This going-to-school

business is all very well, but Annabelle is my baby. I don't know about you, but it's a big growing-up moment for me too!'

'Absolutely! Although this isn't really Rory's first day at school, it's his first successful one, so I'm over a hurdle and we should celebrate.'

'Come on, we can all pile into the people carrier,' said Jody. 'You can even have a glass of wine.'

'This is a brilliant idea,' said Sian as they set off, Annabelle and Rory arguing happily in the back about who was the best at sums and Annabelle's brothers chatting about football. 'I wouldn't have thought of it. We used to go out for tea sometimes in London, but somehow because you can't actually see Pizza Express, you forget it exists.'

'I don't forget,' said Jody.

As they drove, Sian regaled Jody with tales of Melissa and her crew. Telling her about her morning, with Melissa mentally knocking down walls and installing hot tubs, made it all seem less horrible somehow. But of course she couldn't tell Jody what was really gnawing away at her, even with all the distractions of the day: the Gus issue, which seemed to be preoccupying her even more than ever. OK, so he'd been friendly yesterday afternoon and this morning, but he'd behaved more like an overgrown puppy, bouncing all over her, than someone who was serious about the future. It was so difficult to tell with him and she daren't risk getting all serious herself and asking him what his intentions were. She squirmed at the thought; it was something a father would demand in a Jane Austen novel. She suppressed a sigh. Maybe she should have just come out with it and asked him the old question: 'Will you respect me in the morning?' Perhaps she had just been a notch on the bedpost, a bit of fun, and he wanted to keep her sweet in case she changed her mind about letting him be a part of Rory's life. Now she wondered if he'd be talking to her at all if it wasn't for Rory.

She sighed. In some ways it was very tempting to just let go and live for the moment, as Gus seemed to do, but she couldn't. She had too many responsibilities and she couldn't risk getting hurt all over again, not now she had Rory to think of. A heartbroken mother wasn't what any little boy wanted or needed. Gus had told her that himself about his own mother's disastrous second marriage.

The children's singing broke into her jagged thoughts, and she noticed they had now arrived outside the restaurant. Jody parked the people carrier – the size of a small bus, as far as Sian was concerned – and the children were extracted from the various seats. An experienced mother, Jody marshalled them all into the restaurant safely.

'Ooh, look,' she said, children filing under her arm as she held the door open. 'They've got a cocktail bar in the old County Hotel. What's it called?'

'The Boca Loca,' said Sian. She'd noticed it the other day when she'd popped into town for some more paint.

'One day we'll get the girls together, leave the kids with the chaps and go there. I love cocktails.'

'So do I,' said Sian. 'But they have to be strong, otherwise they're just like Alcopops and you drink too many and get hideously drunk.'

'Not an option now, sadly. OK, kids, what are you all going to have?'

They were just shepherding the children out of the restaurant after a very happy and noisy meal when Rory said, 'There's Gus!'

Sian looked at where he was pointing. She saw Gus, in

a suit, ushering Melissa, also wearing a suit and a smart little hat, into the Boca Loca. He had his hand on her waist and was laughing down at her. Sian looked away quickly before she could see his hand go down to her bottom, where she was sure it was headed.

Sian felt suddenly and violently sick. She cleared her throat and wiped her forehead, which was damp. The pieces of the jigsaw seemed to fly around her head and then fit into place. Fiona's cageyness when she'd rung and asked for Gus; the fact that he had hardly spoken to her; the suspicion that she'd heard Melissa laugh in the background when she'd phoned. It all made sense. Melissa and Gus were going out with each other. What she and Gus had was just sex – fantastic sex, but apparently nothing more. Not for him, anyway.

'Are you OK, Sian? You look like a goose walked over your grave.'

Sian shook her head quickly. 'Oh, I'm fine. I just – I just felt a bit odd.' And with one quick look back at the doorway they'd so happily disappeared through she climbed into the car, all the excitement and fun of the evening destroyed.

Chapter Twenty-One

'Are you sure you're all right?' asked Jody as she let Sian and Rory out at their front door. 'You still look a bit pale.'

'Oh, it's just a bit of indigestion. I always forget the effect that jalapeño chillies have on me. I like them—'

'But they don't like you,' said Jody, 'as our grandmothers used to say.'

Sian managed a laugh. 'I'll find something for it when I've got Rory into bed. It'll be a quick shower in the morning for him, I think, rather than a bath now.'

Rory, tired and full of pizza, obligingly agreed. After teeth-brushing and one story, he was happy to be tucked up. Sian went downstairs and put the television on without taking in what the programme was. But she couldn't concentrate, couldn't even work, which had always distracted her from the biggest of problems. So in the end she gave up and went to bed, haunted by the image of Gus and Melissa together.

In the morning, when she'd taken Rory to school and sidestepped offers of coffee with other mothers, she came straight home and picked up the telephone. She couldn't just hang around waiting for Gus to get in touch, wondering if possibly she'd got it wrong about him and Melissa – although how she could have, she didn't know. No, she would be brave and ring Melissa, ask her about it. She had plenty of excuses to get in touch with her, after all.

'Melissa! Hi! It's Sian.'

'Oh. Sian!' said Melissa after the tiniest pause, which was long enough to make Sian wonder if Gus was with her.

'Hi,' she said again, 'sorry to ring so early, but I just wanted to check dates with you. When did you say the architect was coming round again?'

'The architect? Oh! Sorry, wasn't sure who you meant for a minute there. I'll just check my diary.'

Sian strained for sounds of whispering while Melissa went for her diary but could hear none. She pushed aside the image of Gus in Melissa's bed, waiting for her to come back to him.

After she had told Sian the date she said, 'Right, sorry to be so dippy. I was out last night and drank far too many mojitos.'

Playing into my hands thought Sian. 'Oh yes. I think I saw you, going into the Loca Boca or whatever it's called.'

'Did you?' Melissa sounded embarrassed.

'Yes, what was it like?'

'What?' She sounded almost panicked now.

'The cocktail bar?'

'Oh, lovely! You should definitely try it. Really nice. Cute guys working there too. They juggle and everything. Like that film.'

'Cool!' Sian found herself imitating Melissa's girlish tones. 'And was that Gus with you?'

'Angus? Er, yes! We had a great evening, he's such fun.'

'He can be, can't he?' This time it was harder to keep the acid out of her voice. Hearing it, Sian decided it was time to ring off. 'Anyway, got to dash. I'm *sooo* busy!'

She was busy, but she couldn't work properly. Thinking to give herself a nice project, she started refining the designs for Melissa's mother's wardrobes, but that just made her think of Melissa and Gus, wondering what they'd get up to in Melissa's bedroom. Eventually, despite knowing it was probably completely the wrong thing to do, she emailed Richard.

Sian felt terribly guilty about Richard. After sleeping with Gus she had meant to tell him, gently but firmly, that he couldn't expect anything from her except friendship. Yet somehow she hadn't done it. Was it because she'd been so swept up in Gus she just put Richard to the back of her mind? Or was it cowardice? Or, and this felt the truest reason, was it simple indecision?

Contacting him might help. He could be so reassuring. And so without overanalysing it any further, before she could decide whether or not it was sensible to add Richard into the unhappy mix right now, she typed:

Dear Richard, Just checking to see when you're back. It's been ages. I've missed you.

She stayed on the internet for a while, looking at her website and wondering if she should update it again when she heard a ping. Richard had emailed back.

Hey! Funny you should email just then, I'm about to set off for the airport. I'll be back tomorrow. Can you get a babysitter? I'd love to invite you to dinner.

There were a million reasons why she should refuse. It was Rory's first week of school, it was terribly short notice to get a babysitter and she needed an early night herself. And she knew she would only have more decisions to make when she did see him again. But somehow after seeing Melissa and Gus together and Melissa confirming her worst fears she felt she needed to see someone who cared about her, really cared, and who wasn't related to her or Rory in any way. She hadn't realised how much she had secretly hoped Gus had changed, that she could rely on him and that he might, just might, consider a future with her, not just with Rory. That he might be ready to settle down. How wrong could she have been? He was still the risk-taking, grab-each-opportunity-as-it-arose guy she'd first met. All very attractive in its way but not what she wanted or needed any more. She felt as if she'd been punched. She'd given him everything and he'd just taken it. Perhaps seeing Richard might help clarify things for her. He was always good in a crisis, even if this time she couldn't tell him what her crisis was.

She checked with Fiona first that she could babysit and once she'd confirmed she could, she replied to Richard that she'd love to, she was looking forward to it. The alacrity with which Fiona said yes when she'd called had only compounded her belief that Gus was now with Melissa and Fiona felt guilty.

Richard insisted on picking Sian up so she wouldn't have to worry about drinking and driving. She'd taken a lot of trouble with her appearance. Richard was so nice and kind and dependable, he deserved her best outfit and careful make-up. She put on her favourite black dress. It was above the knee and had a flattering cowl neck that showed enough cleavage to be interesting but not so much as to be tacky. Then she realised she'd have to wear tights. It would just look wrong with bare legs, so she found a pair of sheer black tights, and as she eased them on, she felt it was symbolic. She was preparing to step away from the casual clothes of summer and dress like a woman again. High-heeled shoes added to the feeling. She was a strong woman, in control. Not a confused, vulnerable one in danger of falling to pieces.

'You look pretty, Mummy,' said Rory from his bed, with Fiona lying next to him, prepared to read a mountain of stories.

'Yes! You look amazing!' said Fiona.

'Well, don't sound so surprised. I can scrub up well if I try.'

'I know,' said Fiona, 'but you just look, well, different.' Something about the way she said it made Sian wonder if she meant that was a good thing.

As Sian got into Richard's car – new and very luxurious – she thought different was indeed what she wanted to be. She didn't want to be who she had been. That woman was foolish, romantic and idealistic. Now she wanted to be a bit more pragmatic and sensible. The whole 'in love' thing was overrated anyway. It was only a chemical reaction after all. It would soon wear off. She didn't remind herself that it hadn't worn off after nearly six years apart.

'You are looking absolutely stunning!' said Richard, handing Sian into the car and getting in beside her.

'You're looking pretty hot yourself,' she said brightly, and then she looked at him again. He *was* looking good. He had on a nice suit and looked groomed and prosperous. Not in a horrible way, she added mentally, in a good way. 'New car?' she added. She was doing well. She could be that sophisticated woman, having dinner with an attractive man, whom she liked; she knew she could.

'Yes. I thought it was time to have something a bit more luxurious. And there's plenty of room for a car seat in the back.'

Sian thought briefly about Gus's old Land-Rover and decided she much preferred Richard's new Audi. She chose to ignore his comment about the car seat.

'I can't believe I've never been to your house before,' said Sian, looking up the drive to where a red-brick building with a tiled roof stood somewhat smugly at the end.

'Well, you haven't been down here that long and I've

been away so much. Do you like it?' He had stopped the car just after they went through the electronic gates.

Sian found herself laughing. She felt like Elizabeth Bennet on her first sight of Pemberley. 'I've always been fond of this period of architecture. I think it's underrated.' She hoped he wouldn't ask what she was laughing at.

'Mm, Edwardian. I agree with you. I wanted somewhere I could really spread out.'

'So you haven't had the house that long?'

'I've had it about five years but I've only recently taken back possession.' He pulled on the handbrake. 'It was rented. I've had it all redone though.'

He unlocked the front door and ushered her inside.

He gave her a glass of champagne. He'd retrieved the bottle from a very smart designer fridge that just happened to be standing in an alcove to the side of the front door, surrounded by racks of various wines. Picking up his own glass he took her on a tour.

They started in the large panelled hall. It was a little dark for Sian's tastes but the parquet floor gleamed, showing off a large Persian rug. 'And this is the sitting room,' he continued, opening a door to the right.

It was vast and had a bay window at the far end draped with luscious brocade curtains, fringed and swagged and matching the cushions on the benching. The fireplace was brick, surrounded by leather sofas with more cushions. There were candles ready to light and the fire was laid.

'We'll light it later, if we're chilly. Come and see the kitchen.'

The kitchen was occupied by a young woman who was cooking. 'This is Joy,' said Richard. 'She cooks for me sometimes.'

'It smells delicious,' said Sian and smiled, looking round at the marble surfaces, the island unit, the tiled floor. It was all beautifully done but somehow it wasn't to her taste.

'I won't tell you what you're having,' said Joy. 'But I am quite pleased with it.'

'Oh, I hope you get to eat it too!' Sian said.

Joy smiled. 'Don't worry. Richard, don't forget to show her the walk-in larder.'

Richard didn't forget. Nor did he forget to show her the guest wing, the games room, including a pool table, and the indoor pool. From the pool he indicated a small stable block. 'Is Rory interested in ponies?'

'He is, actually,' said Sian, remembering how disappointed he'd been that he hadn't had a ride on one at the gymkhana. If Richard had hoped to impress her, he certainly had.

'Well, there's space for you both to have something to ride if you want to.'

'Richard, I don't know what to say!' Sian felt genuinely lost for words.

'Just say yes to another glass of champagne,' he smiled, 'and don't worry about anything else just now.'

They went back to the sitting room and found that someone, presumably Joy, had dimmed the lights, lit the candles and put a match to the fire, which now crackled merrily. It wasn't really cold but it did look cosy.

She allowed Richard to refill her glass. 'I had no idea you were so . . .'

'Affluent? Rich?' He laughed. 'Don't worry about it. I don't. I work hard, and I get paid well.'

'Obviously. This is delicious champagne.'

'Sian, darling, you look uncomfortable. Is that cushion too big? Let me find you a smaller one.'

'No.' She put her hand on his wrist to stop him leaping to his feet. 'I'm fine. Just a bit overwhelmed.'

He smiled. 'But in a good way, I hope?'

'Well, it's a beautiful house!' she said tentatively.

'But you don't know what, if anything, I've been trying to hint at for the last half-hour? I'm sorry,' he said, looking suddenly rather uncomfortable. 'I'm not very good at this.'

Sian hid behind her glass. Somehow she just knew what was coming.

'I was going to wait until after dinner, but I might as well make my proposition now.'

Oh, please don't, thought Sian. Don't say anything that means I have to make a decision I'm not ready to make. She wished they could just sit here, like old friends, chatting comfortably about everyday things. He was looking at her, his kind, handsome face smiling at her in the candlelight and all she wanted to do was run. She forced herself to smile back. She could do this, she told herself, gripping her champagne glass as if it was the safety-bar on a roller-coaster. She felt worryingly spun around by life.

Richard took a sip of champagne and announced, 'I'd like you and Rory to come and live with me here. As you've seen, there's plenty of room. You could have your own room and everything, I wouldn't expect anything from you.'

That wasn't quite what she was expecting but she feared Richard hadn't finished yet. Did he really mean he wanted housemates, was he really just offering her a roof over her head?

'Do you mean that? That we could be quite separate?'

'Well, I mean . . . Of course, in time . . .' He took her hand and Sian willed herself not to withdraw it. He was being so kind.

'If you weren't about to be thrown on the street,' he went on, smiling, 'I would have courted you a bit longer, but I can't bear the thought of you and Rory living in some hovel when I have all this I could share with you.'

'But we would have been all right. We *will* be all right,' she said quietly.

'You will be if you come and live with me. Let me look after you, Sian – and Rory. There's a wonderful big shed where you could work. Or you wouldn't have to work. You'd never have to work again if you didn't want to. I can give you everything, Sian, if you'll take it.'

She looked across at this kind man who'd done so much to make life easier for her. Now he was offering her a home in his house and, if she wanted it, more than that: himself.

It was a hugely generous offer. But could she accept it? It had so many advantages, for Rory particularly. And she was extremely fond of Richard. Maybe that fondness would develop into proper love, given the chance. She didn't think that what she felt for Gus was 'proper love', it was just lust, a lethal cocktail of hormones that affected her brain in the worst way. And Gus, well, he was a chancer, an adventurer who took his pleasures where he could. At least with Richard she'd know exactly where she was. Maybe she should follow her head for once, instead of her heart, which had let her down so badly before.

Richard put his hand on hers. 'This is a great house, I know, but it needs a family in it to make it come to life.

Sian put aside her feelings about how great the house was but found herself wincing slightly at the word 'family'. She could quite easily see Richard and Rory getting on fine but herself left out of the trio, because she couldn't really commit to someone she was just very fond of.

But perhaps that would be fine. Perhaps she should carry on doing what she'd always done and hadn't failed her: put Rory first. Give him a secure and financially more affluent future. She and Richard were both sensible people, they'd give each other space and the homelessness thing was getting more and more serious.

Maybe they could just move in and live together platonically, and see how it worked out. She took a deep breath and another sip of champagne.

'You're so kind! Can I think about it? It's a lot to take in. And I'd have to be able to work, make a contribution, or I'd be a kept woman.' She smiled to disguise the horror this thought created. She mustn't let Richard give in to his instincts to pay for everything. She must hang on to her independence.

'Whatever you like, you call the shots. And in return . . .' He paused.

There had to be an 'in return' or it just wasn't fair. She waited for him continue.

'In return, you promise you'll learn – try to learn anyway – to love me.' He got up from his sofa and came to sit on hers. He took her into his arms and kissed her.

It's nice, thought Sian in surprise. She leant into him as he kissed her again. Really, kissing him is nice. And if kissing him is nice, maybe the rest of it would be. Maybe living with Richard would be more than OK. Maybe she really would learn to love him as he wanted her too. 'And if you do find that I'm not a bad bet,' he said a bit later, 'then we'll talk about getting married, and maybe me adopting Rory. Make everything regular. At last. I know I'd make a good husband, and a good father.'

Sian didn't like to remind him that Rory already had a father. She didn't want to remind herself. She hugged Richard closer to her, blocking out all such thoughts.

When they were in the car a little later, driving her home after a delicious dinner and a bit more kissing on the sofa, he said, 'I've never told you this, but I've wanted to make a proper home for you and Rory ever since I found out you were pregnant.'

'But, Richard, you never said anything,' Sian said in surprise.

'I know. I was shy and I had nothing much to offer you then. It's different now.' He chuckled. 'You know, I put money into my sister's business to make it possible for her to open sooner, to encourage you and Rory to come down here.' He paused. 'I hope you don't think I'm devious and stalkerish. I just felt I had to give you time to get over Rory's father – Gus.' He looked at her quickly as if to see how she reacted to his name. 'You were in love with him, weren't you?'

She nodded. She couldn't actually speak.

'I knew you wouldn't have slept with him unless you were. You're not that sort of girl.'

She nodded again. He was so right. She wasn't that sort of girl. And she'd slept with Gus again. But that was something Richard must never know. He didn't need to. It was over between Gus and her, if it ever really had begun again. It was no good being in love with someone who couldn't commit. They'd just break your heart over and over again.

'So will you think about it? You and Rory coming to live with me? I'll arrange it so I'm not away quite so much.'

'I'll think about it,' she agreed. 'Definitely.' And she realised she meant it.

After they'd kissed goodnight in the car and Sian finally got to bed – Fiona had thankfully wanted to get straight off so there was no danger of a potentially awkward cup of tea with her where she might have asked questions Sian didn't want to answer – she decided that whatever happened, if she went to live with Richard, he would never know she still loved Gus. He must never, ever feel second-best. And she would learn to love him properly, of course she would; how could she not?

Sian really wished she had someone she could talk things over with, but she didn't have anyone locally she was close enough to. Jody was lovely and wouldn't be judgemental, but this was heavy stuff and Sian didn't feel she knew her that well. And maybe she would be horrified at the notion that Sian was considering moving in with a man she didn't love, just because he loved her and had a large house and a swimming pool.

It wasn't a terribly nice house, thought Sian objectively. It was probably worth millions but she didn't really like it. Did this make her less of a gold-digger if she decided to live there?

Not really, she decided. It made her *more* of a gold-digger, because if she did agree to marry him, she'd ask him to move. Really, she was despicable!

But was she? Would she be? She'd play the role of wife with everything she had. She'd cook for him, make him custard, entertain his friends, sleep with him. She'd put on an Oscar performance if necessary. He need never know that she loved someone else, never guess. She'd make absolutely sure of it.

Sian made her decision sometime during the night. On the morning following her dinner with Richard she decided that going to live with him was the best thing she could do for herself and for Rory. And as they only had a month before they had to leave the house, she'd better get Richard and Rory better acquainted fast. So she invited him to dinner – only it would be tea really – with Rory, after school. It would all be perfectly natural.

Richard was delighted when she called to thank him for a wonderful evening and to invite him to tea that afternoon. She knew he was working from home today and wouldn't mind dropping by. She didn't actually say anything but he picked up that she wanted Rory to be there too. She didn't mention his offer the night before. There'd be time enough for that.

Richard arrived promptly at five with a present for Rory.

'I missed your first day at school, so here's a belated happy-first-day-at-school present.'

It was a large box of Lego making it possible to build a fixed-wing helicopter. Rory was overwhelmed. He looked up at Richard with big eyes.

'Richard, it's amazing!' said Sian, touched to see how well he'd chosen for Rory. 'And I do hope you'll be able to help Rory with it. I can't follow plans – at least, not easily.'

'Would you like me to help you with it?' asked Richard.

Rory looked up at him and nodded. 'Thank you,' he whispered.

'After we've eaten then,' said Sian. 'Richard, I hope you don't mind eating so early.'

'I'm happy to eat at any time, especially if it's your cooking,' he said, and patted her shoulder.

They were just eating their pudding, syrup sponge and custard, when there was a small noise and Gus appeared. 'Hello! Anyone at home! Oh.' He stopped abruptly. He had a jiffy bag under his arm.

No one moved for a few moments and then Sian lowered her spoon. 'Hello, Gus. Richard's here for tea,' she said brightly as if it was the most natural thing in the world for the three of them to be cosily sitting down together at five thirty.

'So I see,' said Gus, apparently not at all pleased to see his old friend sitting next to his son.

'Can I get you some? It's syrup pudding. With custard.'

'I don't like custard.'

'You don't know what you're missing,' said Richard.

'We have ice cream,' said Rory helpfully.

'Or would you like a cup of tea or something?' said Sian, on her feet and feeling desperately uncomfortable.

'Actually, I'd like a word with you, Sian. On your own if that's possible,' said Gus shortly.

'We're eating,' said Sian, wishing that Gus would just go away and leave them in peace. She wasn't ready to speak to him just yet.

'I'll wait.'

He waited, accepting nothing in the way of food or drink and looking as impatient as he could without actually drumming his fingers on the table.

Richard tried to engage him in conversation but Gus gave one-word answers and didn't make any effort himself. He was behaving incredibly rudely but there was nothing she could do about it.

Eventually Sian said, 'Why don't you tell Gus what you've been up to, Rory?'

'Oh! I've been at school! Richard brought me a happy-first-day-at-school present, a big Lego set. And he's got a swimming pool!'

Sian knew it was just Rory chattering on and whilst she was pleased for Richard, she wished Rory hadn't mentioned his present and his swimming pool; she could tell it had upset Gus.

'And do you like school?' Gus asked.

'Oh yes!'

'You got on OK?'

'Yeah. Oh, and after our first day we went to Pizza Express with Annabelle and her brothers and Jody.'

'I was there too,' said Sian, to clarify.

'What sort of pizza did you have?' asked Gus.

'Well, I had the one with . . .'

While the men discussed pizza, Sian went back to her pudding. She ladled more syrup sponge on to Richard's plate without asking, and handed him the custard.

'Actually,' he said, 'could I be a nuisance and ask you to whack it in the mike for a couple of seconds? I don't like cold custard.' He smiled sheepishly and Sian instantly suppressed any irritation that might have been forming. Gus made no such attempt; he snorted, clearly annoyed at Richard's presumption.

'Oh!' said Rory to Gus. 'I saw you!'

'When?' asked Gus. 'When did you see me?' He was frowning.

'When we had pizza. You were looking smart!' There was just a hint that his father looking smart was a bit of a betrayal but Rory was generous enough not to make too much of it.

'I'm still confused, mate,' said Gus.

'You were going into the cocktail bar opposite the pizza place,' said Sian. 'With Melissa.' She really wished she could have avoided saying that, but the words emerged without consulting her wishes.

Gus looked startled. 'I didn't notice the pizza place.'

'Why would you when the Boca Loca beckoned?' Sian sipped her wine. It tasted horrid with her pudding but she had to stop herself sounding as if she cared. He hadn't even had the grace to look guilty when she'd mentioned the wine bar.

Gus cleared his throat. 'Sian, there is something I want to tell you, in private.'

Richard raised his eyebrows. 'We're still eating.'

Gus drew in a breath, but before he could say anything Sian intervened. She didn't want to be private with Gus but she didn't want a row in front of Rory either. 'I've had enough,' she said. 'Why don't you two finish up and make a start on the Lego?'

'OK,' said Richard. 'We'll clear up first though.' He looked at Gus and smiled. 'We've got a helicopter to build.'

Gus looked at the enormous box on the worktop. 'I see.'

Sian felt a pang of sympathy. He was in no position to spend nearly a hundred pounds on a toy. She wasn't herself. 'Come on then. Let's go through to the sitting room.'

'You and Richard are very chummy all of a sudden,' Gus said icily once Sian had closed the sitting-room door. 'He's invited you both to his house and bought Rory expensive presents?'

'Rory didn't go to dinner with Richard, I did that on my own. I told him about the pool.'

'So you had dinner with him, did you? And it was just you and him, was it? And has he got a circular bed with black satin sheets?'

'Gus what is this?' Really, he was being absurd! 'How dare you come here and interrogate me about Richard. What I do with my time is nothing to do with you.'

'Since you ask, I am a bit confused.' Gus's eyes glittered with anger. 'I came here to tell you something and it turns out that you've got news of your own! You saw Richard's house and suddenly thought, What a nice chap! What a good provider he'll be with his regular income and flashy car! Let's get cosy with him!'

Sian flushed with anger. Who was he to accuse her after what he'd done! 'Richard just came round for tea, that's all. Anyway, I don't think you're in any position to question who I see!'

'No? Even when the person you're seeing might become *my* son's stepfather?'

'Now you're being ridiculous. I would never stop you seeing Rory. You can have all the access you like—'

'Oh, very generous of you!'

'Actually, it is quite generous of me as you've proved yourself to be completely unreliable!'

'Have I? How do you make that out?' He glared at her.

Suddenly Sian couldn't bring herself to talk about him and Melissa and how desperate she was when he didn't get in touch after they'd slept together.

'I think you know! Anyway, that's all in the past.'

'Is it?'

'Yes. Now what is it that you wanted to say?' She was getting impatient. All the hurt and betrayal she'd felt at seeing Gus and Melissa together was giving her the courage to stand firm and not break down in frustrated, angry tears.

Gus laughed and shook his head. 'Not going to tell you. It's no longer relevant.'

Now he really was being childish.

'In which case there's nothing to keep you, is there?'

'Except Rory.'

'Do say goodnight to him, but let me make it clear, if you make things difficult for me, in any way, like not leaving the minute you've said goodnight, access will have to be on a formal basis, by appointment. None of this just swinging by when it suits you.' She couldn't have Rory upset, no matter how upset and angry she was.

'You'd stop me seeing my own son?'

'Not if you're reasonable, but I have my own life to consider.'

'And I see exactly in which direction you've been considering it!'

'And why shouldn't I look out for myself for once? I've put my own needs second for five years and been happy to do it, but I'm a person with needs too!'

'And I'm sure Richard is more than capable of fulfilling them! Except in the one way that matters!'

'What are you talking about?'

Gus had stopped pacing and was looking at her with such intensity she almost flinched. 'I'm talking about sex! What we have together—'

Sian didn't want to think about what she and Gus had – had had, she reminded herself – together. As she'd said, that was in the past. She had moved on now. She'd made her decision and she damn well wasn't going to be bullied by someone who had absolutely no right to get all high-handed with her.

'There's no need for you to worry about that,' she said, aware she was sounding prim but determined to remain in control of the situation. 'There are absolutely no problems in that area, thank you for your concern!'

'I see! You've checked that out as well as the bank account, have you?'

How dare he! 'If you don't leave my house now—'

'Oh I will! Just as soon as I've said goodnight to Rory.'

'I don't think that's a very good idea. You're not in a fit state to see him.' She could almost see flames in his eyes and she stepped back. 'Another thing – if you think I'm coming up to London with you to help sell your bloody book, you're in for a surprise! Now please leave!'

'Oh, I'm going. And if you want a laugh, you can read that!' He slammed the jiffy bag down on top of a small cupboard and then flung himself out of the cottage.

Chapter Twenty-Two

ﾟ๛ะ

Fiona was in the garden, trying to find some solace in dead-heading the roses, a job that she usually found soothing. Nothing was worse as a parent than seeing your child suffer from heartbreak. Well, she was sure there *were* lots of worse things to watch your child doing, being ill, for example. But just now it was seeing her light-hearted, flippant boy so miserable.

When he came back from Sian's a few nights previously she couldn't tell if he was just so angry he could hardly form words or so devastated he didn't want to speak, but the combination was horrible to see and very difficult to live with.

She gathered that Angus had gone round to give her his news and she had been having a cosy meal with Richard, who, instead of being the nice man she had known vaguely since he was a schoolboy, had morphed into Croesus and Sian into a gold-digging little tramp.

Fiona had instantly offered to go and see Sian, to find out what on earth was going on, but Angus forbade her, in such a way she felt obliged to promise that she wouldn't. She was sure there must be some mistake but she couldn't interfere. Since then she'd just had to watch him suffer, although she hoped that the long periods he spent in his study meant he was writing his book.

She had just snipped off a rose that hadn't really finished blooming when she heard the telephone ringing. She ran in, hoping it was Sian, hoping everything would be normal again.

It was James.

Suddenly she found it hard to breathe. She was a little breathless anyway, from having run in from the garden.

'Oh, hello!' she said, trying not to let him hear she was short of breath.

'Hello. Fiona, I'm calling to ask you to dinner.'

'Well, dinner would be lovely.' Fiona's breathing was easier. She seated herself on the little bench that was next to the telephone in the hall and imagined a nice little restaurant or pub that backed on to a river.

'At my house,' James went on.

Fiona got up. Now she had severe butterflies in her stomach as she heard the subtext. 'Right.' She didn't feel up to elaborating.

'I want to cook you a really special meal, not just what happened to be in the fridge.' He paused. 'Will you come?'

Fiona rubbed her lips together and snatched a breath. It would be lovely to see him again and it would get her away from the house and Angus's misery for a while. 'If you tell me when, possibly.'

'When would suit you? Would during the week be suitable? Or is it easier for you at a weekend.'

'During the week would be fine,' said Fiona. 'I know weekends are busy for you.'

'I could manage but I don't want to wait until the weekend if I can help it,' he said. She could hear that he was smiling.

'So – when?' She worried she wasn't sounding as enthusiastic as she felt at the thought of seeing him again, but nerves were making her keep to the point. She didn't want to gush.

'Wednesday?'

'Fine,' said Fiona. 'What time?'

'Is half past seven good for you?'

'Yes. Very good for me. See you then. '

When she sat down she realised she hadn't felt like this for many, many years. She also thought that if there was a drug that sold that feeling she'd buy it on the street corner with no qualms at all.

Of course she wasn't in love. She couldn't be. She didn't know James all that well really. It was lust. But along with the lust came a very large dollop of sheer terror. It was an exhilarating combination and for a moment it swept away her feelings of sadness about Angus and Sian. And soon after this came guilt. That was a woman's fate, she concluded. No joy without guilt about some bloody thing or other.

Now she only had to worry about what to wear. But what a worry! Supposing they carried on from where they left off? She not only had to think about what to wear on top but her underwear.

She went upstairs to inspect her knicker-drawer. A quick rummage produced several pairs of Sloggis, comfy and reliable and as sexy as cold porridge. Then there were the attempts at something slightly less homely, lacy but scratchy and so never worn, and then the huge selection of the make-you-thinner type. Fiona bought these often but usually decided they made her so hot it was better not to actually wear them.

Anyway, she couldn't let James see her in something resembling an old-fashioned, long-legged bathing costume, only very tight and mercifully not stripy. She would have to think of something to wear that wouldn't require strong elastic to flatter her.

She decided she had nothing suitable and went to her little study to go on the internet to visit her favourite catalogues on line.

Another dilemma: what sort of event was she attending? 'Special Occasion'? 'Mother of the Bride'? She shuddered. Eventually she found a couple of things she thought would do. One was a simple button-through sleeveless dress in linen that went with a very pretty, slightly floaty, long shrug. She would never ever usually show her bingo-wings in public, but provided it was dark – or darkish – she could whip off her top and hope he would be distracted and not notice her arms.

She went through the long and tiresome process of 'adding to her basket', finding her credit card, typing it in wrong a couple of times and forgetting her password until eventually she had managed to place her order. Then she decided it was far too 'dressed up' and would look as if she was trying too hard.

She stomped down to her bedroom cupboard, determined to find something she already owned. Everything came out and was put back as not being right. Eventually, she went downstairs for a cup of tea.

At least having to worry about what to wear for dinner with James meant she wasn't worrying about Angus and Sian, thought Fiona when Wednesday arrived, standing in front of her wardrobe for what seemed like the millionth time in the last three days. She'd suggested to Angus again that she should talk to Sian but his response had been the same: she was not to do that under any circumstances.

She stared at the clothes she should have known by heart and then, on impulse, she pulled out a favourite dress, very old and much washed. It was linen and used to have a pattern of roses on it. The pattern was faintly discernible but faded and subtle. The colour was like spilt tea and brought out her own colouring; it always made her feel good. And, far more by luck than design, it went perfectly with the shrug part of the outfit Fiona had bought specially for this dinner.

Relieved to have the decision made, she went to her bathroom.

She'd done a major exfoliate and moisturise the night before, so she just had a quick shower, reasonably confident that her skin was as good as it could be. She'd tackled her armpits too, bewailing the fact that recently developed near-sightedness meant she couldn't see to use a razor properly and had to use vile-smelling hair-removing cream. But now she felt she'd done her best and was not entirely displeased. Remembering what she'd heard Gok Wan say on the subject once, she applied scissors and some colouring mousse to her pubic area, but utterly refused to contemplate his advice with regard to wax. She'd rather die without ever having sex again than go through that amount of pain.

She took stock of herself in the mirror, pulled her shoulders back and her stomach in and decided, if the lights were suitably low and James didn't have A1 vision either, she'd pass muster. She started on her make-up.

When she finally set off to town to James's flat, possibly a bit before she really had to, she still thought the likelihood of having sex with him was low. It wasn't that she didn't want to, but she couldn't see herself getting through all the embarrassment that would go before. Although she was as groomed and buffed and depilated as she could be, she couldn't actually imagine taking her clothes off with anyone else present. She didn't think she could get into bed without her clothes on and wait for him to come to her either. In fact she had to stop thinking about it altogether because every scenario seemed to offer more opportunity for humiliation than the last. Far better to die a chaste old woman than go through any of it!

She felt good in her old dress though. She'd ironed it carefully and with the new shrug it looked very pretty. Being linen it would look crushed fairly soon, but as long as she looked her best when she turned up, that was OK.

She'd brought a bottle of wine with her, one from the deepest part of the cellar where the good stuff was. She didn't know what it was like really, just that it was red. She didn't expect James to open it, it was a present. She'd have brought champagne but she didn't want Angus to see it chilling in the fridge. It would have seemed wrong to have something so celebratory when he was so sad.

She had felt a little devious as she left the house. She'd told Angus that she was having dinner with a friend and if it looked like they were going to finish the bottle she might stay over. She wasn't asking his permission or anything, she was just being considerate to the other adult she shared the house with. That was what she told herself, anyway.

She didn't really want to think about how Angus might react to the news that she had a boyfriend. She'd messed up their lives so much when she got married again too soon after her husband died, in the mistaken belief – among the other reasons for doing it – that it would be good for the boys to have a father-figure.

Her confidence and pleasurable anticipation grew as she drove. It was a lovely late summer's evening, and while the anxiety she had felt ever since James's phone call was still very much there, it had almost become indistinguishable from desire.

She was too early. She parked where she usually did when she came to town and sat in the car, tweaking her hair in the driving mirror and trying to control her breathing.

She checked her mobile to make sure he hadn't phoned to cancel and then decided she might as well go. She was just working herself up into a state. She would walk slowly and look in the shop windows. James was a very punctual person, he wouldn't mind if she arrived dead on time.

He must have been waiting for her in the shop because he opened the door almost immediately. He stood with the door wide looking at her, smiling. Her own smile grew and grew as she looked up at him.

'I am so very pleased to see you,' he said. 'Do come in.'

She stepped over the threshold and into the shop, which seemed full of shadows. He put his arms on her shoulders and kissed her on the cheek. Then he took her into his arms and kissed her again, this time not on her cheek. When they broke away she looked up at him and wondered how she'd never noticed how sexy and twinkly his eyes were. Her nerves subsided somewhat but her desire didn't.

'Come upstairs.'

She preceded him up the narrow, twisting staircase to the flat above, liking it all over again, with its wide polished floorboards that undulated slightly, old rugs, crooked windows and dark furniture.

She looked about her, preparing to sit on the sofa in front of the fireplace.

'No, not there,' he said and ushered her to a corner she hadn't been aware of before. A little crooked door stood open. 'Come to what passes for a garden for me.'

He led her to a balcony, just big enough for a small round table and two chairs. On the table was a plate of blinis with smoked salmon and something that looked like sour cream. There were two glasses and nudging up against an urn filled with lavender was a wine-cooler with a bottle of champagne in it.

'This is lovely!' she said. 'So unexpected!'

'Yes. It's just a bit of extra roof really, which goes over the landing downstairs, but it had already been made into a balcony when I bought the premises. I think it's what convinced me it was the right property.'

He poured the champagne and handed Fiona her glass. 'Here's to you,' he said. 'I can't tell you how much I've been looking forward to this.'

But what was he looking forward to? The mental coin-flipping that had been going on in her head started up again; desire warring with fear. Fiona sipped; the bubbles helped. The coin came down firmly as a 'no'. She was not going to sleep with him. She was just too scared.

Having made this decision, convinced it was final this time, she relaxed a little and accepted a blini. It was delicious.

'What are we celebrating?' It wasn't the wittiest remark ever devised but she couldn't think of anything better.

'Being here, tonight, on this lovely evening. With you.' He seemed unaware that she'd just decided he wasn't going to see the underwear the sale of the books had financed even though it had been far more expensive than everything else she was wearing put together.

'It is lovely to be here, I must say.' She sighed a little, possibly regretting her decision. 'I brought a bottle of red. I left it on the table. I'm not sure what it is – I just grabbed it from the cellar. Obviously we don't have to drink it – it's a present really.' Aware she was gabbling, she sipped her champagne. I must be the worst sort of date, she decided, too old to be girlish and too inane to be a sophisticated older woman.

'Just relax, Fiona,' said James, causing her heart to give a little flip. 'Nothing is going to happen that you don't want. Just concentrate on us having a pleasant meal in not-unpleasant surroundings. Although I do admit to wanting a garden on nights like this.'

'But this is lovely too.' Fiona looked about her at the roofs and chimney pots, the view of the streets, cafés and bars, people doing evening things. 'It's just different.'

'Most of the time I'm very happy with my mostly urban existence. Look. There's the spire of the parish church and just beyond that you can see the river. It's a town but it's old and I like that. Just now and again I'd love a bit more greenery.'

'You could grow a honeysuckle in a pot or something, add a bit of trellis, make it seem more like a garden.' Then she stopped talking, aware that she'd fallen into her old trap of trying to solve everybody's problems even when they didn't want them solved.

'Sit down, darling, and eat the blinis. I've got to fiddle about in the kitchen.' She liked the way he said 'darling'. It reminded her of her first husband.

James had definitely changed since she'd known him, Fiona decided, or was it just that she was looking at him in a different way? When she first met him he'd been charming and polite but not particularly dynamic. Now he was taking charge in a way she found very attractive. She wondered if all motherly people liked to be bossed about, just a little bit.

He came back quite quickly with a big bowl full of asparagus and a smaller one with hollandaise. 'I know it's not really in season but it's such a short season, I think it's all right to extend it.' He'd brought napkins but no plates. 'I thought we could just dip into the sauce and eat.'

Fiona plunged a spear into the hollandaise. 'Did you make this?'

'I did. It's not that hard really.'

They ate their asparagus and sipped champagne in friendly silence. But although she hoped she looked calm, she was still nervous. It had been such a long time since she'd been alone with a man like this.

He moved to refill her glass, but she stopped him. 'I'd better not have too much. I have to drive home.'

He put down the bottle and took her hands to ensure he had her full attention. 'Fiona, I know that you're worrying but you don't need to. This flat isn't huge but there is a second bedroom. I use it as an upstairs office mostly but it has a single bed in there. If you have too much to drink to drive safely, you can have my bed and I'll sleep there. Just relax.' He paused. 'I've put clean sheets on, just like I would if my sister was staying.'

'OK!' Knowing she could stay over, chastely, was definitely helpful. It meant she didn't have to get through the whole evening counting alcoholic units in her head. She took quite a large gulp of champagne and relaxed again. James was being so understanding. Just as well she always had moisturiser and make-up in her handbag.

After the asparagus came salmon cooked with pesto and parmesan and new potatoes.

'You'll notice that it's the sort of meal that you can prepare mostly in advance and all the last-minute cooking is very quick and easy,' said James, pouring some Pinot Grigio into her glass.

'I just thought it was a nice summery menu,' said Fiona, who also thought it was just the sort of supper she'd provide for a friend: simple, delicious food that wasn't too heavy.

'Good old Delia, is what I say.'

Fiona laughed and relaxed fully. They were just two friends, having supper on a lovely evening. She would stay the night, as she would with any woman friend if she didn't want to drive home. All that nonsense with the underwear and colouring foam and scissors was just – well – nonsense.

'A drop more wine?' asked James a little later.

'Oh go on, why not?' Fiona put her knife and fork together. 'That was absolutely delicious,' she said. 'I'm guessing that you made your own pesto.'

He nodded. 'It's so easy. At least it is since my sister gave me a food processor for Christmas.'

'Angus makes lovely pesto with wild garlic leaves,' Fiona went on. 'He uses Cheddar instead of parmesan and sunflower seeds instead of pine nuts. It's delicious.'

'I'm sure, but it wouldn't go well with what's coming next.'

'Which is what?'

James smiled. The twinkle was back in his eyes and Fiona felt another surge of desire. He got up and took her hand so Fiona got up too. 'I'm going to take you to bed.'

She didn't say anything, she just let him lead her back through the little door into the flat. She was still dithering, any minute now she would say: Thanks but no thanks. Then the mental coin flipped again; this time it came down as heads: she did want to sleep with James, very much indeed.

The only light in his bedroom came from a candle he must have lit sometime during the evening. He kissed her once they'd reached the bedroom and as he did so removed her shrug. She kicked off her shoes. He unzipped her dress. She suddenly wanted to have all her clothes off, very quickly, and feel his skin against hers.

Glimmers of worry did penetrate her passion. Supposing her body had forgotten what to do? Supposing it was all too late? It had been years and years since she'd last made love. And yet somehow her fingers flew down his shirt buttons and her hands smoothed against his skin as she put her arms around him.

Her underwear didn't get much appreciation, she realised, as it was shrugged off and they were both naked and lying on the bed.

Quite a while later she said, 'My goodness, you are good at this, aren't you?'

James, who was panting, lay back on the pillow and laughed. 'You are an amazing and very wonderful woman.'

She sighed ecstatically as she flopped back next to him, pulling the sheet up over her breasts. 'You did all the hard stuff, I just . . . went along for the ride.' She giggled. 'Please be a gentleman and ignore the pun.'

He leaned up on one elbow and kissed the top of her cleavage, which was just visible. 'I'll be a gentleman and bring you a drink. Wine? Tea? Water?'

'Water, I think. That would be lovely.'

'And maybe pudding?'

She sat up a little bit. 'I thought that was pudding.'

He developed a rueful expression. 'No, that was an inter-course . . .'

She threw a pillow at him.

'I'm sorry, I couldn't resist. You set it up for me. I'll go and get it. Water and crème brûlée.'

A little later, while they were sitting in bed eating their pudding, she said, 'I was really quite worried that I'd have forgotten what to do, and then I realised you don't actually have to remember.'

'If you were making it up as you went along, you did a very good job.' He took away her empty ramekin and spoon.

'I was so worried. Just the thought of – well – you know.'

'I knew you were worried. I hope I didn't make you anxious.'

'You did make me anxious but it somehow made it all the more exciting. And lovely.'

'I'm very glad to hear it. I was anxious too.'

'I'm surprised. You seemed – very assured.'

'You made me feel like that. Fancying you as much as I do made it easy.'

She chuckled. 'Well, who'd have thought it, two old people like us having an amazing time in bed together.'

'I have to confess I have been thinking about it, almost from the first time I met you.'

'That's such a blissful thing to say. When you're a pillow of the local community—'

'Don't you mean pillar?'

She chuckled. 'I suppose I did, but pillow seemed more appropriate in the circumstances. But as I was saying, I'm a good woman, I do church flowers, make cakes . . .'

'Have dinner parties.'

'Sometimes. And although I tried the internet dating thing, I didn't expect to have sex again.'

'Did you mind the thought of not having sex again?'

'Yes, because it's an important part of life, but I was perfectly resigned to it.' She frowned a little. 'I just wish my darling son and Sian could realise that and get on and sort out their relationship.'

'So, would you like to do it again?'

'Have sex again? What, now?' Fiona was a little shocked – and tired.

James laughed. 'No, not now. I'm not as young as I was, but in the future? The near future?'

'Oh yes.' Then she was overcome by a pang of guilt. 'But I don't want to get married. You don't, do you? I mean, I know it goes against my image, but I don't want to disrupt my life . . .' Her voice trailed off as she realised she'd just made a rather huge leap, from sex to marriage in one enormous bound. But things felt so instinctively right with James that it was hard not to think of him as someone who could become a very permanent fixture in her life.

Luckily James smiled. 'It's all right. I'd like it if we were a proper couple, could do things together and stay in each other's houses, but I don't want to get married again.'

'It's just that I'm suddenly worried,' Fiona explained.

'Why? What have I said to worry you?'

'Angus! And Russell – that's his brother. What will they think about their mother—'

'Pillow of the community—'

'Having a shit-hot lover?'

James began to laugh until tears emerged from between his eyelids. 'I'm sorry, that just got to me. I'm an antiquarian book-dealer. I don't really see myself as a shit-hot lover.'

'No, but I do! I wouldn't usually use a word like that, but it seemed appropriate.'

'Are you really worried about what they'll think? Angus and I got on well at your dinner party.'

'I know, but boys and their mums . . . you know what they're like. And I messed them up terribly before.'

'But you're not getting married this time and they're adults anyway.'

'I don't think you're ever adult enough to be happy with the thought of your parents having a sex life. Sex is only ever for one's own generation, don't you think?'

'To be honest, I'd never really considered it.'

'I probably worry too much.'

'I'm sure you do, and I'm perfectly happy to just be a friend who stays over—'

'In my bed!'

'Yes. After all, your house is so small, you couldn't possibly find room for me anywhere else.'

She punched him gently on the arm and then snuggled down and put her head on his chest, hearing his heart go thump, thump, thump under her ear. 'Let's not think about it now.'

He kissed her shoulder. 'No. But I would like you to know that I not only fancy you, very much indeed, I think I'm also in love with you.'

Fiona drove home in a cloud of bliss. Because of James having to open the shop at ten, their morning had to come to an end, but James had gone on being the perfect lover throughout. He'd lent her a shirt to sleep in, brought her tea and croissants in bed and later, run her a bath. They'd kissed like teenagers before she left and they planned to see each other again, very soon.

When she got home she found Angus in the kitchen, staring at the wall, still looking like a thunder cloud with depression. Her own happiness gave her insight: sometimes you had to sacrifice your honour and break a promise. If she had the opportunity, she'd sort out Sian and Angus. She couldn't stand by and watch them ruin their lives.

Chapter Twenty-Three

Quite why Sian had suggested the Boca Loca as a place to have lunch with Richard, she didn't know. The trouble was, when he'd rung she'd been a bit distracted and just said the first name that came into her head when he asked where she wanted to go. Now, parking where Jody had parked when they had all gone to the pizza place, she felt she must have been mad to suggest it. She spent every waking moment trying to forget Gus, and the place where she'd seen him with Melissa was rubbing salt into a very tender wound.

She spotted Richard already seated at a table, reading a newspaper. He'd obviously got here early, but somehow his over-promptness irritated rather than cheered her. She made her way over to the table, trying not to feel like a lamb going to slaughter.

Richard saw her and smiled, rising to greet her.

'Hi, Princess,' he said and kissed her cheek.

Calling her Princess seemed to be a new thing of his, and Sian wasn't sure she liked it. 'Hello, Richard.' She couldn't quite bring herself to call him Prince.

He pulled a chair out for her and she sat down.

'So, cocktails?' he asked. 'Or shall we just have wine with lunch?'

'Just a spritzer or something for me. I'm driving.'

'Well,' he perused the menu. 'You could have a virgin cocktail.'

'Without alcohol? That would be nice. Choose me something.' For some reason being with Richard always sapped her energy, perhaps because she felt she had to work at making him happy, and making herself feel happy with him. Or perhaps it was the ever-present guilt. Often she wished she could go back to how they had been before, just friends, before she'd more or less told him she'd move in with him; but then they'd never really been just friends – not as far as Richard was concerned.

They sat opposite each other, Richard gazing across at her adoringly while she thought up something to say. Why was it all such an effort?

'Rory's started bringing reading books home from school. He's very good at reading,' she said, deciding to keep to talk about Rory. Rory was a safe topic.

'That's because you've always read to him. You're a very good mother, Sian. And I hope you might like more children.' He put his hand protectively on hers.

She looked into his eyes for a minute and saw all his yearning for children. She knew he'd be a brilliant father, not only to a boy like Rory, but to babies, toddlers, even difficult, constantly demanding children.

She did want more children, probably. Because Rory took up so much of her time she didn't think about it often, but she was far too young to give up thinking about babies altogether. Giving Richard a child would be the best reward for him. If she did that, she could stop feeling guilty. Her debt would be paid. But how horribly clinical that sounded – even to her.

'Hmm?' Gently he squeezed the hand he was holding and Sian realised she hadn't replied.

'Oh yes, I would like more children,' she said, smiling, 'but let's have lunch first, shall we?' She wanted to steer the conversation away from anything too deep and mean-ingful. She wasn't ready. She ignored the little voice that was nagging away inside her saying, 'You'll never be ready.'

Richard laughed. 'Of course, it's early days and we haven't set the date for you to move in with me, have we?'

'I just don't think we should rush things. It will be a big change for everyone, us being a couple.'

'I know, but the sooner the better, surely. Rory needs a proper family, now he's at school.' He obviously saw Sian stiffen. 'I know you've been a family, you and Rory, with your parents helping out, but I mean a proper family, mother and father living under one roof. And being married, preferably.'

Sian put on an expression she hoped looked willing and attractive, and fiddled with her cutlery to give herself time. She realised now what a very conventional person Richard was at heart and how much of this aspect of his character he was willing to suppress for her. It wouldn't have been hard for him to find a nice, unattached, un-encumbered girl to marry, who would have loved him wholeheartedly. He really was a very good man, but everything he was saying made her want to sink further down in her seat. It's not that she couldn't appreciate how much he was offering her, how much he loved and wanted her – it just all felt so suffocating.

'I think I'll have the salmon,' she said, focusing on anything but the look of devotion on Richard's face.

He chuckled gently. 'You really are very unusual. I prac-tically propose to you and you tell me what you want to eat. I've known women who can't do that even when they haven't got anything else to think about.'

The truth was, Sian had so much else to think about, it was nice to have an easy decision to put her mind to.

At least she was sure she liked salmon. Nothing else in her life seemed so certain at the moment.

'I think it's early days to talk about marriage,' she said. 'But it's never too early to talk about lunch.'

'Very well then. I'll join you in the salmon. Do you want a starter?'

Suddenly Sian felt a rising tide of panic build inside her. She saw her future flash before her: a life of perfectly pleasant lunches like this one. She'd be trapped in a perfectly pleasant life full stop, and she couldn't bear it.

'No, I don't think so,' she said, getting up. 'In fact, I suddenly feel a bit sick. I'll just go to the Ladies, if you'll excuse me—'

When she was in the Ladies Sian looked at her reflection and realised why she felt sick. It was the thought of sharing the rest of her life with a good, kind man, who bored her rigid. How could you learn to love someone who bored you? Why hadn't she noticed before? Was it because when they'd been just friends, with no other agenda – or no terribly pressing agenda – he hadn't been so boring? Was it because he was looking at settling down with her, as a happily married couple, that he became so dull, so lacking in possibility? Gus had his faults, in fact he had every fault ever invented, but he wasn't dull. With him there would always be something new over the horizon.

It wasn't really that she had a choice – Gus was clearly not an option any more – but did the fact that she still thought of Gus, constantly, every conscious and unconscious minute, mean that she couldn't go on pretending with Richard?

Yes, she realised, it meant exactly that.

She took several long deep breaths and then went back into the restaurant to break Richard's heart.

*

Sian drove back to the village with tears streaming down her face. Richard had been so good about it, so noble, so utterly self-sacrificing. She had almost been tempted to take it all back and throw herself into his arms, but having got the words out, having spoken her mind, she couldn't.

'I always knew it was too good to be true,' he said. 'I knew that bastard Angus would get you in the end.' He had paused, while Sian gulped back the sobs. 'Let me know if he lets you down. I'll be here.'

She hadn't actually mentioned Gus, she'd just said she couldn't live with him if she didn't really, really love him, and not just as a friend. She knew in her heart she'd made the right decision but somehow that didn't make her feel any better.

As she came to the village, she decided she couldn't face being alone in the cottage right now. It had been her haven, but it was full of boxes and packing cases ready to move to Richard's, and now she'd told Richard she couldn't live with him, finding somewhere new was even more urgent. But where? Not even her mother's demon internet searching had found anything affordable in the same area – even if she wasn't fussy about having a garden and three bedrooms so she could work.

She decided to go and see Fiona. She hadn't seen her for ages, possibly because they were avoiding each other, neither of them knowing how to be with each other since she and Gus had had that huge row.

But she and Fiona had been friends before Gus had appeared: their friendship might survive the differences between Sian and Fiona's son.

She drove past Fiona's house to check if the Land-Rover was there and when she couldn't see it she parked at home and walked up. As she waited for her knock at the door to be answered, she wiped her nose and hoped the fact she had been crying wasn't too obvious. She should have gone into the cottage to fix her make-up, really, she thought.

'Is Gus here?' she asked when Fiona came to the door.

'No, I'm afraid not. But—' Fiona began.

'Thank God for that. Can I come in?' Sian asked anxiously, suddenly unsure of her welcome and sniffing.

'Of course,' Fiona said, opening the door wide and ushering her in. 'You're obviously dreadfully upset, but I kind of wish you weren't pleased that Angus isn't here. I was hoping you'd come to see him.' She led the way to the kitchen and Sian followed, still hiccuping and wondering what Fiona meant about Gus.

As she got to the kitchen table Sian made a big effort to calm herself. She wiped her nose on the back of her hand and then said, 'Sorry, that was disgusting.' She got up and helped herself to a sheet of kitchen towel.

'Do I put the kettle on or open a bottle of wine?' Fiona asked.

'Tea, please. I've got to pick up Rory soon.'

Fiona made tea, a process which allowed Sian to pull herself together a bit.

'So,' Fiona said, putting a mug and a packet of Jaffa Cakes down in front of Sian. 'What's up?'

Sian sighed and clung to her mug of tea as if it could keep her from more crying. Seeing Fiona sitting there, so kind and concerned, it was all she could do not to put her head on the table and start sobbing all over again. She just hoped Fiona wouldn't hate her.

'I've just broken the heart of a very good man,' she said.

'Oh? That would be the second this month then. Getting to be a habit.'

Sian looked up at Fiona, not entirely surprised. 'Fiona, I presume you mean Gus – Angus – but I haven't broken

316

his heart. He was angry about Richard for some reason, but he had no right. I doubt he's broken-hearted! In fact, I'm sure he's fine.'

Fiona shook her head. 'He's not! I live with him, I know exactly how "unfine" he is!' Fiona got up and found a knife to open the Jaffa Cakes, but it was obviously more to give herself something to do than because it was necessary.

'That's not my doing. And if anyone has a right to be broken-hearted it's me!' Sian said. Trust Gus to have made out that he was the one who was aggrieved and it was all her fault. As if he hadn't been brazenly taking Melissa out for a romantic meal just hours after he and Sian had had a wonderful weekend together. And he'd even got his own mother believing him! She was the one who was broken-hearted, Sian thought indignantly.

She took a deep breath to calm herself. She wasn't upset with Fiona, any mother would take their child's side.

'I promise you I didn't break his heart, and I can't believe that Melissa's let him get away this soon in their relationship!'

Fiona looked bewildered. 'Sian, what on earth are you talking about? Angus and Melissa aren't together, they're just friends.'

Sian considered, re-ran what she had seen in her mind and concluded that Fiona was mistaken. She didn't want to tell her something that maybe Gus wanted to keep secret but she had to stick up for herself too. 'I don't think so. I saw them together, going into a cocktail bar. They were definitely more than just friends. They looked like a couple.'

Fiona shook her head. 'Honestly, they're not.'

'Really! They are!' She'd love to be wrong about this but she wasn't. She'd read the body language and she hadn't got the wrong message. 'If they're not why did they go into the bar together, all dressed up, laughing into each other's eyes?' Seeing Fiona wasn't convinced she went on. 'And why didn't he get in touch with me . . .' She couldn't say 'after we'd had all that amazing sex'. Fiona was Gus's mother. That would be way too much information.

Fiona didn't say anything; she sipped her tea. Sian watched her friend, who was obviously chewing over something difficult. 'What?' said Sian at last, bracing herself for the truth to finally dawn on Fiona – that Sian was right. 'What are you thinking?'

'I'm thinking that I have to break a promise. Possibly more than one.' She took another sip of tea. The decision was obviously giving her some difficulty. 'When do you have to get Rory?'

Sian glanced at her watch. 'In about half an hour.'

'We'll have to hurry then. Come with me.'

Not at all sure that her friend hadn't gone slightly mad, but feeling she had to humour her, Sian followed Fiona up the stairs to the first floor and then up to the attic. Fiona opened the door at the top of the stairs and said, 'You go first.'

The smell of fresh paint, sawn timber and a tinge of new carpet hit her as she went in. She remembered this suite of rooms from before, when it had housed mountains of unwanted possessions. Originally the servants' quarters, they had been left untouched for years.

Now, it was so different that it hardly seemed the same place. An old skylight was uncovered and now filled the space with light. A window she hadn't noticed before meant light came in from both sides. She went to it and looked out, seeing the tops of trees, hills and fields beyond. The view was magnificent. But why had Fiona brought her up here?

'This is the sitting room, obviously,' said Fiona, 'the bedrooms are through here. This one is a tiny double.'

Sian followed her into a room that had a double bed in it, an old dressing table that Sian recognised and a chest of drawers. This room also seemed light and airy when it had seemed so cramped when full of furniture. The window was smaller and when Sian looked out she saw the opposite gable. A new Velux was on the opposite slope of the ceiling. 'I kind of hope no one ever finds out about that window,' said Fiona, 'but you can open it completely and get to the fire escape from it, so while it's probably wrong from an architectural point of view, it is safe.'

Sian hardly heard her. She went into a little single bedroom, small but done up like a ship's cabin with built-in furniture. It even had a round window.

'This would be a perfect room for a little boy, obviously,' Fiona went on, 'and the bathroom, if you've time to look at it, is through here.'

Sian glanced at her watch and saw it was a quarter to three. 'I should get Rory—'

'Just glance.'

Sian glanced and saw a small room with a corner bath and a shower over it. A washbasin and a loo took up the rest of the space.

'And kitchenette,' said Fiona, opening some double doors revealing a sink, cooker and cupboards. 'It's tiny, but it's independent.'

'This is wonderful,' said Sian, still not quite sure why Fiona wanted her to see it right now. She could have shown it to her another day, when they had more time. 'Are you going to let it?'

'No, you ninny! It's for you!'

Sian looked at Fiona in confusion, but she didn't have time to ask her what on earth she was talking about. She

319

had to pick up Rory. 'I must go, or I'll be late.' She headed for the stairs.

'I'll come with you,' said Fiona, hurrying after her, 'so I can explain.'

In the end they rushed so much they got to school early and had a few minutes sitting in the car.

'Angus did it for you,' Fiona explained. 'It's why you haven't seen him. He's been working so hard to get it ready. It's not quite done, but good enough. He didn't want you to have to worry about having somewhere to live.'

'I don't know what to say,' said Sian confused. Why couldn't Gus have just told her that's what he was doing? And why would he do such a thing anyway, now he and Melissa were together? Then she realised: it was for Rory. He didn't want to see his son on the street and obviously had to include her. 'That's kind of him,' she went on. 'Of course, I'd pay you rent.'

But it was hardly ideal, sharing a house with the man she was trying so hard to forget, possibly bumping into Melissa in a scanty nightie – or, God forbid, no nightie at all – as Sian went up to the attic.

'You still don't understand, do you?' Fiona broke into her waking nightmare.

What was Fiona trying to say now? 'I'm sorry to be dense, Fiona, but I don't think I do. Perhaps you could explain?'

'It really isn't for me to tell you.'

'What isn't? Please, Fiona, just tell me whatever it is.' It wasn't like Fiona not to come to the point.

'I think Angus intended—'

Just at that moment, Sian caught sight of a group of children heading towards the school gates. 'Oh, they're coming out. I'll have to go and get Rory.'

'Come back to tea then. You need to know the truth.'

But Sian had already hurried across the playground towards her son.

'Fiona's here,' she said to Rory, having intercepted his book bag, lunch box and coat before they fell to the ground. 'I've got the car. Do you want to go back to Fiona's for tea?' She was hoping he'd say no so she could just run Fiona home and concentrate on feeding Rory and not have to think what to do with her life – at least for the time it took to feed, play with, bath and read Rory a bedtime story.

'Oh goody! Can I go in the shelter? Can I? Is Gus there?'

Rory's enthusiasm meant Sian couldn't get out of the tea invitation. She wished she hadn't mentioned it but knew that Fiona would insist anyway. It was interesting that after their revelation that Gus was in fact Rory's daddy, he carried on calling him Gus and looking on him as his fun big brother, she thought distractedly as they headed towards the car park.

Fiona had got out of the car and Rory ran towards her. 'Is Gus there? I want to see him!'

Fiona caught him and swung him in the air. 'Goodness me, you're heavy! I'm afraid Gus is in London.'

'Oh.' Rory was put out but not for long. 'Can I go in the shelter? Is it still there?'

'Darling, that depends on your mum. You've got your school clothes on and the shelter will make you filthy.' Sian was torn. She could tell that Fiona was unlikely to let her leave until she'd got whatever was bothering her off her chest. She was desperate to tell Sian something and might even resort to making a fuss if Sian didn't sit down and hear her out. She had a feeling it was to do with Gus but wasn't sure she wanted to hear it, and whatever it was she certainly didn't want Rory listening. But the shelter would make him filthy, there was no doubt about it.

'Tell you what,' said Fiona, 'we'll find you some things of Angus's – Gus's – for you to wear instead. They'll be huge but at least they'll keep you cleanish. And whilst you're playing in the shelter, Mummy and I can have a nice long chat.' She looked pointedly at Sian.

Sian resigned herself to the inevitable.

Fiona was a woman who could provide what was needed quickly. An old sweatshirt of Gus's went down to Rory's knees. She looked at Sian.

'Oh, never mind about his trousers. We've got another pair,' she said, 'but, Rory, don't you need a drink and a snack?'

'Banana?' he said hopefully.

'I have a banana and you can take it with you. Do you want to go on your own or shall we come up and watch you?'

'Come and watch me,' he called, running off.

'And bring the banana,' muttered Sian.

The two women watched Rory rush off up the garden and followed more slowly.

'What's Gus doing in London?' Sian asked.

Fiona sent her a glance, which felt a reproach. 'He's going to see his agent, and a publisher.'

Sian's teeth clamped down on her lip. 'I'd forgotten.'

She felt a slight pang when she realised that if things had been different she'd have been there with him, helping him impress the publishers. Then she remembered that Gus had only himself to blame for her absence. She still wanted his book to do well though, she felt she could allow herself that.

'Yes, but you weren't going anyway, were you?' Fiona said. 'You and Gus quarrelled.'

'Yes.'

'He told me you'd taken up with Richard.'

So that was what this was all about. He had no right to be cross about that! He was all loved-up with Melissa, mere hours after climbing out of her bed, and he had the gall to question who she saw. And she had only kissed Richard! She could imagine what he and Melissa had got up to. They'd probably had a good laugh about her too. Poor Sian, so easily seduced – and twice! And now he'd got his own mother fighting his battles. He was priceless!

'Well, he'd taken up with Melissa,' she explained, trying to be calm. 'And don't say he didn't, I told you, I saw him – them, together.'

Fiona sighed. 'Honestly, that was perfectly innocent.'

'Was it? How do you know?'

'Because—' Fiona was just going to explain when Rory came flying back looking for his banana.

'It's still there! It's still fine!' he said. 'We could sleep in it again.'

Once he'd run off again, clutching a banana, Sian muttered, 'You didn't actually sleep in it the first time, but hey.'

'Sian, you need to know the truth about what's going on with Melissa and Angus.'

'I'm not sure I want to.'

'Yes you do. Don't be silly. She set up a meeting with someone who's got some land. She knows – or her parents know – everyone. This man has land and he wants to invest. Angus could set up his school for bushcraft, when he's got a bit of capital.'

'Oh God,' said Sian very quietly, realising that Fiona's explanation could actually have some truth in it. 'I do know how much he wants to do that,' she admitted.

'But he won't get that bit of capital unless he sells his book tomorrow,' Fiona continued. Her voice was urgent now she saw that she was finally getting through to Sian.

'He'll do that, no problem. It's a great idea, with marvellous photos, all that stuff.'

'He might not.' Fiona was looking at her with an expression Sian couldn't read. Was it disapproval? Disappointment? Or possibly hope?

'What do you mean?'

'He needs you there, Sian.'

'But why?'

'You give him confidence, you're a team. He needs you to be there!' Fiona repeated.

'Well, he should have said! He should have communicated with me! And why couldn't Melissa go with him?' But Sian's anger and hurt were starting to morph into guilt at how wrong she'd got things.

Fiona took Sian's arm and gently brought her round to face her, obviously heartened by the fact that she didn't immediately pull away.

'Sian, darling, why do you keep going on about Melissa? There is nothing going on between them except friendship. Never has been.' She paused. 'I'm not saying Melissa wouldn't have liked there to have been – she made a play for him the moment he arrived home. But he just sees her as a jolly childhood friend, and recently a useful business contact.' She took a breath, possibly giving Sian a chance to speak. When Sian didn't, she ploughed on. 'I must say Melissa has been a very good sport about it. When she realised Angus wasn't interested in her as a girlfriend she set out to help him as an old chum. Once he'd confirmed that he was Rory's father, it pretty much settled it.'

Sian nodded, beginning to accept what a hideous mistake she'd made.

'Angus told me that you and Richard were together. I know you're not, any more, but it was a hell of a kick in the teeth for him. He did that whole flat for you. Not all on his own, he got builders in and everything, which he paid for, so you would have somewhere to live. He had to pay huge overtime too, to get it done so quickly.'

Sian felt as if she'd been at the bottom on a deep lake and was slowly making her way to the top. 'I didn't know.' Maybe she had jumped to conclusions and the evidence against him was only circumstantial. 'But why didn't he tell me? Speak to me on the phone?' A lump of sadness was forming in her ribcage.

'He wanted it to be a surprise. You know what he's like.' She paused, possibly deciding whether or not to pour more coals of fire on to Sian's head, and then doing it. 'He invested all his savings into making a home for you. Money he could have put towards setting up a business.'

'Oh God, that's awful. I thought he – I thought he wouldn't – he didn't call once – he never said he loved me!' She was biting her lip hard, fighting back the tears.

Fiona put her arm around Sian's shoulders. 'He may not have said it in words, but he's shown it. Actions speak louder than words, and all that. And if you love him—'

'I do. I know I do. It's why I had to break up with Richard.'

'Then you show him, like he tried to show you.'

'But how? And to be fair to me, I would have thought he'd have guessed how I felt about him.'

'And to be fair to him, you didn't guess how he felt about you.'

Sian nodded and then turned away and walked up the hill, away from the shelter, Rory and Fiona. She needed some moments on her own, she needed to think what to do next. She stopped and suddenly knew what that was. She hurried back towards Fiona.

'I need to go. I need to go to London. I need to be there with him, to show him I care – and to help him get his deal.'

'How are you going to do that?' Whilst obviously pleased that Sian had seen sense at last Fiona was ever practical.

For the thousandth time that day Sian looked at her watch. 'I could put Rory in the car, take him to my parents. If we set off now we'll be there before bedtime.'

'But Rory will miss school in the morning.'

'Yes – and I'd forgotten, he has a date with Annabelle – but that doesn't matter.'

'Why don't we ask Rory if he'd be happy to stay with me? Then you could go on the train.' Fiona was now focused on helping the mission as much as she could.

'Could I? Have I got time?'

'Let's ask Rory. We'll tell him that you're going to London to get Angus back.'

Rory was delighted at the prospect of staying with Fiona, more because she had several Pixar movies on DVD than because he wanted to help his mother. But Sian didn't care either way, just as long as she got to the station on time.

'You go home and pack,' said Fiona, 'and then Rory and I will take you to the station, and pick up some fish and chips on the way home,' she added *sotto voce* to Rory.

'Fish and chips!' squealed Rory, making Sian glad they'd always been such a treat or they wouldn't be making her trip so much easier now. She had a sudden thought.

'Oh, God. What shall I wear? What do you wear to meet a publisher?'

'Honey, I have no idea! Just look pretty. You always do. Whatever you wear will be fine!'

Sian was just about to rush out of the house when she spotted the package Gus had left. It had been moved several times as she'd tidied up but she hadn't ever looked in it. She didn't have time to look in it now, but she stuffed it into her bag as she left. She could give it back to him.

It was only when Sian was on the train to London, having waved goodbye to a very happy Rory, who was focusing on eating chips in front of Buzz Lightyear, that she realised she didn't know what time the meeting was or which publisher he'd gone to see. She rang Fiona from the train. Unfortunately whilst Fiona could tell her the publisher's name, she didn't know what time the meeting was being held.

'I know it's in the morning,' she said helplessly. 'And I shouldn't think too early. About ten seems likely. You could ring them up and ask.'

'Would they tell me? It's probably against privacy laws or something.'

'You could quote the freedom of information act at them, that might help.'

Neither of them thought this was really an option. 'Never mind, I've got all night to think of a way of finding out. Thank you so much for having Rory.'

As Sian had already said this at least a dozen times, Fiona just repeated her side of the dialogue, that her son's happiness was involved too, so no thanks were needed.

Her parents, although a bit confused when she rang them, were delighted at the prospect of her coming to spend the night with them.

It had been a bit of a rush to get on to the train and what with having to first fling some bits and pieces together for Rory and herself on the way and ring Fiona for details once the train had set off, she'd hardly had a chance to get her breath back. As she put her phone away now and sat back in her seat she considered her own packing. She hadn't had time to plan it and she'd probably brought all the wrong clothes. But that wouldn't matter. She wasn't the focus and even if she had been, illustrators could be arty, or wear mismatched clothes – it went with the image. It was her work they'd be interested in.

She rummaged in her bag and got out her sketchbook. She hadn't wanted to bring a huge A3 portfolio on the train, so she'd just brought her A4 Moleskine. She flicked through it, and as she did so, her heart sank. There were pictures of flowers, both realistic and imaginative, fairies, sea horses and fleur-de-lis, lots and lots of dragons, but there was nothing, as far as she could tell, that proved she would be the right person to illustrate a book about bushcraft. She and Gus had wasted so much time with their silly misunderstandings. If they hadn't fallen out so spectacularly she'd have had time to read some of his work and do some preliminary sketches.

She looked at her notebook again. This was no good; this wouldn't help Gus. In fact it would hinder him. They'd think she was just some deranged ex-girlfriend stalker turning up with an assortment of drawings that had no relevance to the project whatsoever. Knowing he had such women in his life they'd send him away, not wanting to risk taking him on.

Her clothes didn't matter but her work did. She had to do something about it. She found her pencil case and selected a pencil and then realised she couldn't draw properly on a train. She'd have to put something together once she got to her parents. She'd work through the night if necessary. Gus's career – his book, his bushcraft project, everything – was at stake.

Then she remembered the package and took it out.

Inside were fifty pages or so of typing. She read the first page and realised it was his book. She read the second page, and then the third. She started to smile, partly from relief and partly because the book was funny! He could write, he could really write! She didn't have to be professional to know that. She knew she was swept along, intrigued, amused, entertained. His personality was on every page, in every line, teasing, anarchic but informative. She realised she'd want it to succeed even if she had no feelings for Gus, even if he was just a casual friend, it was so good.

Later that evening, after a homely and necessarily quick meal with her parents, she cleared the table in her old bedroom and started to draw.

She couldn't draw from life, but only from memory. Gus's hands as he scraped a piece of birch bark with a knife, producing a tiny pile of tinder; the shelter with its thick overcoat of leaf litter, making it look like a cave; Gus whittling, creating curls of wood so fine they resembled the ribbons on a gift, him standing with an axe high above his head.

When she'd run out of things she'd seen Gus doing she read through his book again, picking out scenes she thought would make good drawings. She smiled as she drew, her enthusiasm increasing as she brought the incidents to life with her deft pencil marks and shading in. She added in a picture of Rory running with a forked stick, partly for fun, partly to show all ages could enjoy the bushcraft. She longed to have time to add colour but her paints were in the country and line drawings were probably what was required. When she finally zipped up her pencil case she was satisfied she'd done some of her best work, enough to impress even the fussiest of publishers. She closed the notebook, stood up, stretched and went downstairs to have a cup of tea with her parents before everyone went to bed.

They admired her work and kissed her goodnight. Her mother had obviously put a gagging order on her husband on the subject of his daughter's love life. It was a huge relief to Sian. She wasn't clear of her own feelings or how Gus thought about her; she really didn't want to have to justify her actions. She wasn't at all sure how her father would react to Gus anyway. He was still trying to come to terms with the fact that he was Rory's father. Her mother had thought it best to tell him. If there was any likelihood of them seeing Gus whilst Sian was in London – which she wasn't at all sure *was* likely – it was better to be prepared.

Chapter Twenty-Four

The receptionist was very kind. 'I'm terribly sorry but you're at the wrong place. We're the head office but Emmanuel and Green are in Park Street.'

Sian would have liked time to cry. She'd set off early, her mother's Oyster card in one pocket and her father's *A-Z* in the other and all should have been well. Sadly the tube was chaotic because of an electrical fault on one of the lines and she wasn't sure enough of the buses to try one of them. She was already running late. At least she assumed so – she didn't actually know what time the meeting was.

'What's the quickest way to get there?'

'Bicycle, frankly, but otherwise, take a cab. I'll ring them to say you're on your way if you like. What's your name and who were you going to see?'

'I don't know! I mean, I do know what my name is, obviously, but I don't know who I'm going to see and they won't have heard of me.'

The receptionist regarded her kindly, possibly relieved that she wasn't going to have to deal with a madwoman for very much longer. On the other hand she was a bit curious. 'What's your plan?'

'I'll think of something when I get there. Thank you!' Sian called as she ran out of the door.

In the taxi she tried to calm down and stop worrying about the meter, which seemed to be going up alarmingly quickly. Fortunately her father had thrust some notes into her hand and now she came to examine them, she realised she had sixty pounds extra. At least that was all right. And as they got nearer she realised it was in a part of London she knew a bit from having had a job there once, which reassured her a little.

At last, having gone through horrendous traffic, the cabby pulled up. 'Here you are, love.'

She leapt out, said, 'Keep the change,' and ran up the steps to the entrance.

It was a much smaller building than the previous one had been and Sian felt this was a good thing. There wouldn't be quite so many meetings; she had a better chance of tracking down the right one.

Moments later she was at the door and then realised she had to speak into a microphone, another tiny nail in the coffin of her self-confidence. She hated these at the best of times; she could never make them work and as she wasn't on any list, even if they heard her properly they might not let her in. With a supreme effort of will she made herself sound calm and professional.

'I'm here with Angus Berresford and I'm a little bit late?' The raised inflection at the end might help, she thought.

The door clicked, she pushed and it swung open. 'Hello!' She was rather hoping to find Gus waiting in the foyer. 'I'm even later than I thought. Has the meeting started?'

The woman, wearing a telephone headset, looked rather startled. 'Er, yes it has,' she said.

Relief that she didn't say 'which meeting?' caused Sian to smile. 'If you could just point me in the right direction?'

What she really wanted was to be taken by the hand and led to the right room, but the telephone started ringing just then. The receptionist waved a hand. 'Second floor, third on your right. Er, the lift's that way.' The girl pointed as Sian set off in the wrong direction.

The lift was slow and Sian had time to count her blessings. She hadn't left her sketchbook in the cab, it wasn't raining and she didn't need to go to the loo. Lots of blessings really. Another blessing would be if they had water in the meeting. Currently all the moisture that should have been making her mouth work seemed to be running down her spine leaving her mouth incredibly dry. The scarf she'd added to hide the paint stain on her shirt was adding to the stress by making her far too hot.

She fell out of the lift into a corridor set with many doors. What was it the receptionist had said? Third on her right? Counting the door in front of her as number one, she counted two more doors, knocked boldly and went in. It was the Gents. Fortunately no one was in it. Why wasn't it marked? Indignant, she came out again and saw that it was marked, she just hadn't noticed the symbol. She then spotted another symbol on a door that indicated the Ladies. Should she take time to sort herself out a bit? She was already late, would a few more moments make a difference? She was through the door before she could answer her question.

The Ladies did have someone in it. A young woman was washing her hands. 'Oh, thank goodness,' said Sian. 'I'm late for a meeting and I can't find it. I don't suppose you'd know where it is?'

The woman went to the towel and pulled down a section and went about the drying process. Then she added hand cream from the dispenser. For Sian time seemed to have stood still but she realised that it must only have been a few seconds.

'Who's it with? Your meeting?'

'I don't know.' Sian gave a probably insane-looking smile. 'It's with Angus Berresford. Any ideas?'

'Oh yes. They're in the committee room at the end. I'll show you.'

'The receptionist said third on the right.'

'That's Edward's office but what with the agent and the art department and head of publicity, they thought it would be too small. It's in there.' She paused. 'Would you like me to announce you?'

Sian considered. 'Yes please. I'm Sian Bishop. The illustrator,' she said with more confidence than she felt.

The young woman knocked and went in. 'This is Sian Bishop, the illustrator,' she said, and abandoned her.

'Sorry I'm late!' said Sian brightly. 'You just carry on. I'll pick it up.'

Everyone in the room was staring at her, most wondering who on earth she was and all wondering what the hell she was doing there. She hardly dared look at Gus as she crept round the table. Fortunately there was a vacant chair, and she sat down.

Gus was staring – glaring possibly – from across the table. She couldn't meet his eye, not until she'd got her breath back and put on the façade of being a normal person, perfectly entitled to be where she was. It would take some doing.

If she'd hoped she could just disappear into the background she was to be disappointed. The meeting was called to a halt.

'Excuse me?' said a youngish man in a crushed linen suit. 'Who is this? Who are you?' He smiled at Sian, obviously trying not to be rude, but needing to know.

'This is Sian Bishop,' said Gus firmly. 'She's my illustrator.'

'Don't mind me,' said Sian, heartened by the fact that

Gus hadn't denied he even knew her. 'I'll just make a few notes. You carry on.'

There was some shifting and shuffling and then the young man said, 'As I was saying, what this book needs is total passion and commitment.' He looked anxiously at the woman sitting at the head of the table.

The words fell into the room like stones when they should have been feathers, dancing around to be picked up and tossed playfully about.

Gus was looking down the table in front of him. The man in the linen suit was drawing a naked lady on a pad, and everyone else was looking embarrassed and disappointed. The woman at the end looked tired.

Sian had to do something.

'Oh, I've got that!' she said, launching straight in. She'd made a complete fool of herself simply by arriving. With her dignity gone she might as well carry on without it. 'Absolutely. In spades! I know this book is going to be bloody brilliant! Because Gus – Angus even' – she allowed the quickest smile ever smiled to shoot in his direction – 'is fabulous. A fabulous writer, really knows his stuff and is a brilliant communicator.'

'Those are my lines,' said another man in a striped shirt and pin-striped suit. 'I'm his agent.' But he didn't sound aggrieved, rather the reverse.

'But I've had the privilege of seeing him in action,' went on Sian, seeing no one was willing to take the ball from her. 'Not the exploring part, obviously, you sort of have to be on your own to do that, but the communication! I've seen him hold the attention of a lot of small children and adults with wine in their hands. Not the most receptive audience, I'm sure you'll agree. But he held them in the palm of his hand! If you'll forgive the cliché,' she added, feeling she'd gone way over the top.

'And the writing's excellent,' put in the agent. 'We've all agreed that. We just needed—'

'A bit of extra zing,' said a young woman in a tight white shirt showing a lot of cleavage. 'Which Sian seems to have produced!'

Sian smiled broadly at her, deciding that if this woman ever needed a kidney she'd volunteer.

'Um,' one of the other men, with curly hair and no tie, said, 'so would you like to show us what you've got?'

Sian produced her sketchbook. 'Of course I haven't got much here. Gus and I' – her glance was accompanied by a blush she hoped no one would notice – 'haven't had much chance to work together just recently, but I love him – I mean, the project, the concept of Gus as the new adventurer.'

She hunted for a handkerchief so she wouldn't have to watch them looking at her drawings.

'Yes,' said Gus, looking at her now. 'Sometimes you have to take a risk with someone, and not always take the safe option, even if that seems the best idea at first glance.'

'Absolutely,' said Sian, holding Gus's eye and ignoring the rest of the room, 'it may seem scary but it's less of a risk in the long run. The boring option is more dangerous.'

Someone, Sian thought it might have been Gus's agent, cleared his throat. Another man, who hadn't spoken before and wore a suit, sat forward.

'Well, it seems to me we've got a very committed author, a fantastic project and an illustrator who is unusually tied in with the whole premise.' He pulled Sian's sketchbook towards him and flicked through the pages. 'Oh, I like this!'

It was one of Rory, running, his arms flung back, a stick in one hand.

'Oh,' said Gus after a minute, having looked at it. 'That's Rory.'

He and Sian looked intently at each other. Sian swallowed, hoping she wasn't going to sneeze or cry or show emotion in some other noisy, messy way.

'Is this your son, Gus? Are you and Sian . . . ?' said a woman who hadn't spoken before. She was wearing an enviable little suit the colour of ripe tomatoes and had curly black hair and perfect make-up. 'Interesting.'

Gus's agent frowned. 'I didn't know you had a partner, Gus.'

'Currently it's a business relationship,' said Sian, breaking Gus's gaze.

'But that may change?' the woman in the red suit persisted.

'Obviously they don't want to talk about their private life in a meeting like this,' said Gus's agent.

'But it would add something . . .' said the woman, a little plaintively.

Sian was slightly bewildered by the turn the conversation had taken. It seemed a little unorthodox to be discussing an author's love life or lack of it in a meeting but if it helped to clinch the deal did it matter? The whole meeting had taken a bizarre turn the moment she'd entered the room. Looking around at everyone's faces, including Gus's, she realised her entrance seemed to have cast a spell on them all – a good spell too. There were smiles all round.

A man in the braces cleared his throat. 'Well, couple or not, I think I can confidently say we'll be able to make you some sort of offer very soon. We'll have to do the numbers, see what publicity we'd be able to drum up – supermarket deals, things like that – but I'm very excited about this. Really, very excited.' He beamed at everyone and then stood up to indicate the meeting was over.

*

Gus's agent kissed Sian on both cheeks. 'Well, you brought the rabbit out of the hat at the perfect moment! Things had gone a bit flat after everyone's initial enthusiasm. You can tell when the energy has gone out of a meeting.'

Gus said, 'Sian, this is Rollo Cunningham, my agent. The best there is, so he tells me. Rollo, this is Sian my . . . well, she's my . . .'

'Illustrator will do for now,' said Sian with a smile.

'But we go back a long way,' said Gus.

Sian looked at her feet. She'd done her best to show Gus that she loved him by going to the meeting and putting aside all her inhibitions to help his project, but whilst he'd run with what she'd been trying to say, she still didn't really know how he felt about her. Fiona may have just thought Gus loved her because she wanted it to be true. She needed to hear it from him.

Gus looked at Sian. 'We need to talk.'

'We absolutely do,' said Rollo. 'We need to thrash out the details and make sure we're all on the same page. Now I know a nice little place just round the corner. It's early but that means it'll be quiet.'

'I should go back to my parents—' Sian began.

'Unless they're in dire need of their next dose of medication I insist you come to lunch!' said Rollo. 'You're going to be a vital part of this project. Particularly now the publishers seem to have fallen in love with you.'

'Do you mind?' asked Gus. He seemed anxious that she should be happy with the plan.

'No, it's fine.' She wanted to reassure him now. 'My parents are both in good form,' she said to Rollo. 'I'd be very happy to come to lunch with you.'

Sian followed them down the road. They couldn't walk three abreast and she felt it was far more important that

Gus and Rollo should be able to talk than it was for her to have her arm held.

They turned into a narrow door, Gus waiting for her so she could go ahead of him. It was dark and cave-like, but as her eyes got used to the gloom she saw there weren't a great many tables but they were spread with white table-cloths and sparkling glasses. Rollo was talking to the maître d', obviously an old friend, who ushered them to a table.

'Old-fashioned English food here,' he said. 'Brilliant for nursery puddings with custard.'

'Perfect place to take Richard then,' said Gus, looking meaningfully at Sian.

'It would be.' Sian allowed Rollo to pull out a chair. She felt Richard deserved a bit more explanation than she could reasonably give here. A pang of guilt attacked her yet again; she'd made him so miserable. She still couldn't quite believe that Gus actually loved her back and hadn't just created the flat so Rory wouldn't be homeless or have to live on a sink estate.

'And excellent chips!' Rollo went on. 'Whatever else we have, we must have chips. And fizz.' He looked round and a waiter immediately came forward. 'We need to celebrate!'

A bottle of champagne was produced and poured.

'Here's to the book?' said Rollo, raising his glass at them both.

'To the book,' said Sian. 'It's going to be fantastic. And here's to them giving Gus loads of money for it.' She looked across at Rollo who smiled and raised his glass again.

'Yes, and to Sian,' said Gus, 'who saved the day.'

'I didn't! I just barged in – and, well, made a fool of myself.'

Rollo and Gus were shaking their heads. 'They had gone a bit quiet,' said Rollo. 'We needed an extra element. Lovely illustrations by you, as well as your presence for publicity purposes.'

'You wouldn't want me for that. Gus is the star!'

'A star sometimes needs a satellite,' said Rollo, 'and you are a very lovely one, if I may say so.'

'Hear, hear,' said Gus.

Fortunately for Sian's nerves, the waiter returned to pour more champagne and to bring them menus.

The meal seemed to last for ever. Sian kept looking at Gus, who kept looking at her. She felt his foot on hers and wasn't sure if it was there on purpose or if it had just landed there by mistake. Either way, she didn't move her foot and just enjoyed the contact, hoping it was a sign they could make things right between them.

'So,' said Rollo, when he'd eaten his 'Dead Baby with Extra Jam and Custard', 'What are you two going to do this afternoon? Any plans?' When neither of them replied he went on: 'Rather bizarre turn in the conversation towards the end of the meeting, I thought.' He paused and then turned to Gus. 'So, are you two together then?'

They looked at each other but Sian couldn't read Gus's expression. Was that horror and panic at the very thought they might be seen as a couple? Or something else? Her heart, which had been going up and down like a lift in a hotel all through the meal, went down to the basement and lodged there.

'Er, well . . .' Gus started.

'Heavens. I haven't put my foot in it, have I?' blustered Rollo. 'Are you sure neither of you want a stickie? I know it's lunchtime but I think a liqueur is as good a way to celebrate as any. We've got a great book deal to wrangle! Or a brandy?' He trailed off.

'No, really, I'll fall over if I have any more to drink,' said Sian. She'd had two glasses of champagne and her share of a bottle of red. She just wanted to leave now.

'So, tell us, what's the next stage with the book?' asked Gus, getting back to the matter in hand.

'The publishers do the number crunching, make us an offer which we refuse—'

'However big it is?' Sian asked, glad to have something to say.

'Yup. Never accept a first offer. They're lucky I didn't put it out to auction.'

'I thought they were the only ones interested?'

'Well, yes, but there were a few I didn't pitch to. We still could go down that route if they don't come up with something acceptable.'

'How long will we have to wait?' asked Sian.

Rollo shrugged. 'Dunno. They could be quite quick or they could keep us waiting for days. I'm hoping for a quick response though, while their blood is up, so to speak.'

'It's all so nerve-racking,' said Sian.

'Yes,' agreed Gus, 'and odd. I feel a bit like a slave being sold to the highest bidder.'

Rollo nodded. 'Quite normal. No need to worry. I'll see we get a good screw out of them.' He paused. 'Now, are you sure there's nothing else you want? In which case, let's have the bill.'

Rollo paid the bill with a flourish and a lot of badinage with the staff. 'Right,' he said, 'can I give you a lift anywhere in my cab?'

Sian stuttered something and Gus said, 'We're fine, thank you.' He went on to thank Rollo for all he had done and Sian added hers too. At last they waved him goodbye.

'He's obviously a great agent, brilliant at his job,' Sian began.

'But we need to talk privately,' Gus finished for her.

Sian's heart did a loop the loop and ended in the middle, at neutral. This sounded like good news but could also be bad.

'Yes. Shall we find a café or something?'

Gus shook his head. 'I need some fresh air, somewhere green. I don't think well in London.'

Sian smiled. 'Fortunately, being a Londoner, I know a place we can go. Follow me.'

It didn't take Sian long to get them to a little secret garden, hidden behind old buildings and new tower blocks, attainable only along an alley in between an ancient half-timbered pub and a firm of solicitors that looked as if it dated from the same period.

'Oh wow!' said Gus. 'Who'd have thought this was here?' He looked at the trees, tall and old, and the flowerbeds; there was a bit of grass, benches and a bird-bath consisting of a draped maiden holding a basin in her arms.

'I had a job just by here once. I used to come here with my sandwiches,' said Sian. 'I'm not sure that it didn't used to be a graveyard or something.'

'It's an oasis.'

'Yes. Shall we sit down?' She indicated a bench near where some pigeons were looking for crumbs. 'To talk?' It was time.

Gus looked apologetic. 'Do you mind if we walk? I'm better when I'm walking.'

Sian smiled, falling in next to him, wondering what he meant by being 'better'. But she was horribly nervous.

Gus might be about to thank her for all she'd done for the book, or tell her that he was going to marry Melissa, despite what Fiona had said.

Gus took hold of her hand and pulled it through his

342

arm in the old-fashioned way, keeping her close to him. She felt a tiny flutter of hope. 'I want to say thank you for coming,' he said.

'It was the least I could do. I said I'd help and then . . . I took it back. That was wrong. I had to put it right.'

'Does Richard mind you coming?'

'No. No, he doesn't know.'

'You came without telling him?'

'Yes.' Gus had stopped, released her arm and was looking at her sternly. 'Gus, Richard and I aren't together, we never really were.'

'You're not?' He looked confused. 'But you slept with him!'

'I didn't! I slept with you! I just let you think that I had because I was angry and hurt and I thought you were with Melissa.'

'Lissa? Good God, whatever gave you that idea?'

It seemed very slender evidence now but at the time it had seemed definitive. She let them walk on in silence for a bit while she considered what to say. 'I saw you together, after you hadn't been in touch, you weren't available when I called you . . .' Although Fiona was sure that he and Melissa weren't together, until she heard it from Gus, she couldn't be certain.

'She just introduced me to someone with land to rent and money to invest. She's a great girl and all that but – no. I can't believe you thought we were together all this time and you didn't say anything. You should have done.'

'Fiona said that, but at the time, well, I was terribly hurt. And you didn't take my calls. I turned to Richard.'

Gus didn't appear to think her reason was valid. 'Oh yes, Richard, aka Mr Darcy.'

This was unfair; she had to stick up for him. 'He's a good man and I feel terrible about it.'

'Why? He's got a big house and a fast car, why are you worried?'

'Because I broke his heart. When I told him—' She stopped.

'What did you tell him?' he asked quietly. He'd taken back her arm and was holding on to it as if she might escape.

No woman wants to be the first to use the word 'love' in a relationship. 'I said I couldn't be with him. Not when – Well, I finished it.'

He looked at her intently. 'What are you saying?'

'I think you know.' She met his gaze but she couldn't say it.

'Are you saying, or rather refusing to say, what I want to say?'

This was stalemate. Neither of them seemed to want to be the first to say it, but until she'd heard those all-important words she couldn't be absolutely sure he did love her. Her own feelings were too battered for her to take the chance. 'Then why don't you go first?' she said gently.

He swallowed and took a breath, bracing himself. 'I've never thought of myself as a coward before but this is the scariest thing I've ever done. I love you, Sian. When I came home and saw you I fell in love with you all over again, long before I knew about Rory.'

Sian didn't speak for a while. She couldn't think of any words and thought she might cry. He'd said it. He'd finally said he loved her. The last tiny piece of her that had been clinging on to doubt let go.

'Oh, Sian! Darling, please! I've told you how I feel. Please don't keep me in suspense.'

She hadn't meant to torture him. She just had to be sure. 'I'm glad. When Fiona showed me the flat – don't be angry, she was desperate – I thought you might have done it so Rory wouldn't be homeless.'

'Of course I didn't want him to be homeless but it was you I had in mind. It was you I wanted to save, not Rory, because Rory had you.'

'That's lovely,' she said quietly.

'Well, you're a good mother.' The corner of his mouth twitched. 'I know why Rory likes dragons! He lives with one!'

Sian took a breath and turned in indignation towards Gus. 'I am not a dragon!'

Gus took her face in his hands and kissed her for a very long time. Sometime during the kiss she became glad she had taken a breath; it was coming in useful.

Sian became aware of someone entering the garden and broke away. Gus moved back too. 'So, we can face our uncertain future together?'

'Oh yes. I'd rather have an uncertain future with you than a life of luxury and security with Richard. And I do want you to know that it was only ever for Rory that I wanted it. It was never for myself.'

'Really? I thought he lived in a mansion.'

Sian nodded. 'It's a big house but the kitchen isn't all that wonderful.'

Gus frowned, obviously confused. 'Are you telling me—'

'I mean,' went on Sian, determined to pay him back for calling her a dragon, 'if you're spending that much on a house the kitchen should be more than "OK".'

Gus was looking a bit worried now. 'The kitchen in the flat is minute. Is this going to be a problem?'

Sian was enjoying having the upper hand – she knew it wouldn't be for long. 'As you should know, size is not important. His kitchen had the wrong sort of marble

345

worktop. It reminded me of chopped-up meat – like those very coarse terrines you get in France.'

Gus struggled to take this in. 'Are you telling me you turned Richard down because the marble in his kitchen, in a mansion, with swimming pool and stabling, wasn't to your taste?'

'How do you know about the swimming pool?'

'Don't you remember, Rory told me at tea that day. Now, come on, tell me, which was it: the kitchen, the pool or the stabling . . .' he teased.

'I told you. The marble. And I wasn't too sure about the fireplace in the sitting room either.'

'And that's why you rejected him?'

She looked up at him, wide-eyed and innocent. 'What other reason could there be?'

'You're a minx! But you're definitely better off with me, marble or no marble. I'm glad you made the right choice.'

'But no, Gus, I didn't.' Sian became serious. 'You don't get it. I didn't make a choice between you and Richard. It's more that I just chose not to be with Richard. I couldn't choose you, you see. I didn't think I was being offered a choice.'

'What choice?' He looked confused.

'Well, Richard was offering me security and the love of a good man, but you . . .' She stopped for a moment. It was important that he understood. 'I didn't think you were offering me anything.'

'You didn't know I loved you?'

'No! How was I supposed to know? You never said it, not even at times when – they tell me – most men are willing to tell the woman they're with that they love them. I mean when they've just had amazing sex. I thought that for you it was, well, just great sex.' She looked at her feet, hoping he wouldn't think that great sex was enough, even though sometimes she thought possibly it was herself.

'Oh, God, I'm such a fool for not letting you know, for making you feel I didn't love you. I thought if I used the L word it would frighten you. It frightened me!'

'I thought it was commitment that frightened you.' Even now she felt vulnerable expressing her own deepest fear, that he was a wanderer, emotionally as well as geographically.

'No. I've never wanted to commit to an employer, or a career that I haven't created for myself, but after I met you . . . I knew that once I'd found my soul-mate, I wouldn't want another.'

She sighed and, as the park was now empty again, he took her back into his arms.

'I do love you, you know?'

There, she'd said it too. They both knew how they felt about each other and it was wonderful.

Later, after they'd sat on a bench and talked and kissed and kissed and talked some more, Gus said, 'So what are your plans?'

She looked at her watch. 'Oh my God, my train! I must dash.'

'We'll get you a taxi. I'll come with you to the train.'

'To think I nearly forgot! What sort of mother am I?'

'You know Mum's looking after Rory, you don't need to worry about that.'

'And you don't need to come to the station with me. What have you got to do now?'

'Just pick some things up from my friend's flat where I stayed last night. Could you get a later train?'

'I'd have to pay a huge amount extra.'

They left the park and hurried along, him holding on

to her, easing her way through the crowd until they got to a street corner where they could hail a taxi.

She turned to him. 'You don't have to come with me, I'll be fine.'

'I don't want to spend a moment apart from you if I can help it. I'll come.'

'Gus, do be sensible!'

Just then someone from behind jostled her a little and she stepped off the kerb awkwardly. The next second pain seared through her ankle and she landed on the ground and there was the screech of brakes.

'Oh my God!' said a woman.

Chapter Twenty-Five

Fiona and Rory were making biscuits, but Fiona's mind was not on it. While Rory was merrily choosing which cutter to use next and calculating if he could fit a dinosaur in that bit of rolled-out dough, his grandmother was desperately trying to imagine what was going on in London. Had Sian got to the meeting in time? Had she managed to do any good when she got there? And how had Angus responded? He'd been so furious with her, maybe he'd said she had nothing to do with him? It would have been awful if Sian had had to retreat, red-faced, carrying her portfolio away in disgrace.

The phone rang. She wanted to run to it in case it was news but she had to make sure Rory was all right first.

'OK, darling, I'm just going to get that. Don't fall off the chair or anything. Hello?'

When she came off the phone ten minutes later she was a little fraught. When it rang again she picked it up immediately. It was James.

'Hello, my love, you sound a bit stressed.'

'I am! Of course there's no real reason for me to worry but I've just had Penny, Sian's mother, on the phone. Sian's sprained her ankle quite badly which means they can't come back until tomorrow. Angus is with her but I still don't know how the meeting went.'

'Oh, that's very unfortunate, but presumably Rory's all right? He's not lost and at large in London?'

In spite of herself, Fiona chuckled. 'Of course not, Rory's with me and although he's a darling and very easy, I'm finding it slightly hard to concentrate on him when I'm so preoccupied with my own son.'

'Would you like me to come over? I could help entertain Rory, cook you some supper?'

Fiona was torn. She wanted to accept, rapidly and gratefully, but should she? Would she be somehow falling down on her duty to Rory if she let James come? Was it like the babysitter smuggling her boyfriend into the house against orders? Then she pulled herself up short. Of course it wasn't like that. There was nothing that she and James might do that could possibly harm Rory. 'Yes please!' she said.

Knowing he was on his way was extremely cheering. It wasn't that she and Rory couldn't have had a perfectly happy time together – if only she could stop worrying – but just having James around would make it all more fun, somehow.

First she had to tell Rory that his mother wasn't coming home until tomorrow.

'You were a long time,' said Rory, looking up from where he was pressing boiled sweets into biscuit mixture in order to make a coloured glass panel in them. Fiona decided it wasn't the moment to wonder if tea pots *did* have glass panels.

'I was, I'm sorry. First of all Penny, your granny, phoned and I'm afraid there's been a change of plan.'

Rory paused, sweet in hand.

'Mummy's hurt her ankle. She's all right, though, there's nothing to worry about,' she said quickly as she saw a flicker cross his face. Reassured that he believed her she went on. 'She's staying in London tonight with her parents, your grandparents. Which means, darling boy, you can stay with me another night! Won't that be fun?' She hoped she didn't sound like a doctor telling a child an injection wouldn't hurt, knowing full well that it would.

'OK. Where's Gus?' Rory added as if his father's whereabouts was much more important than his mother's ankle.

'He's staying there too.' In spite of herself Fiona found herself wondering where he would sleep. Presumably not with Sian but she couldn't help hoping. 'He'll bring her home tomorrow morning.'

'Oh.'

His face didn't fall, exactly, thought Fiona, but he wasn't thrilled. Resigned, more. 'My friend James is coming over, though, to keep us company. I think you've met him.'

'I think so,' said Rory, wrinkling his forehead but seemingly encouraged by the news. 'Will we have the biscuits later?'

'After tea, yes. Now, what would you like?'

'Pasta?'

'Oh yes, lovely pasta. Hey, I tell you what I've got, alphabet pasta! We could have it in some clear chicken soup? Would you like that?'

'I don't like soup.'

'What, no sort of soup at all?'

'I like tomato soup. Tinned.'

'I haven't got any of that but I have got spaghetti. Would you like some with tomato sauce? Ketchup . . . ?'

Fiona was halfway through cooking the menu they'd finally agreed on, which had required compromises on both sides, when James arrived. He'd brought a bottle of wine for Fiona and a book for Rory.

'Hi, Rory,' he said. 'I'm James. I gather you had a birthday recently so I've brought you a present.' He handed over the brown paper bag. 'And I thought later you might give me a game of chess. I brought a set with me. Can you play?'

Fiona opened her mouth to say he was far too young and then shut it again. She poured James a glass of wine from the bottle she already had open.

Rory withdrew the book. It was *The Jolly Postman*. 'We had this at playgroup in London but they wouldn't let us read it ourselves in case we lost the letters.'

'Oh, I'm sure you wouldn't lose the letters,' said Fiona, feeling it was rather a big ask for them not to.

'I hope it's not too young for you, Rory, but it was all I could find in the shop at short notice.' James was apologetic.

'It's not too young at all, and very kind of you to bring anything. Isn't it, Rory?'

Much to her relief, Rory came up trumps. 'Yes. Thank you very much,' he said, and Fiona hugged him.

'So,' James went on. 'How about a game of chess before supper? Have we time?'

'Oh, yes. I'll call when it's ready.'

They went into the conservatory to play.

'Right,' said James, 'the back row are all the posh and powerful pieces. The little chaps in front are called pawns but they are much more useful than they seem to be.'

Admiring his patience, knowing she'd never be able to teach anyone to play chess, even if her mind wasn't mostly in London, Fiona watched him explain what each piece could do. He was so good with Rory. Then she went to clear up, glad of an opportunity to worry in private.

Fiona considered as she finished cooking and made a salad: was it reasonable to ring Penny and ask her about the publisher? No, not really. Angus could have rung her direct and told her, but he had never been a very good communicator and if he wasn't worried he never understood why anyone else might be.

And was Angus staying with Penny and her husband? And what had Sian's father's reaction been to Angus? Presumably he'd be grateful that Angus had brought his injured daughter back to them but he might have been harbouring a grudge against the father of Sian's illegitimate son for years. That would be ghastly for everyone. Particularly for Angus who had shown himself to be completely responsible with regard to Rory. Exemplary, even. But how would Sian's family respond to him?

And then there was the publishing meeting. Had Sian rushed to the rescue to good effect or did the publishers just think their potential new author was allied with a madwoman and drop him like a hot coal? So many questions she needed answers to. But now it was time to get James and Rory to the table. And find out who won at chess.

'He shows a real aptitude,' said James. 'A little reckless with his pawns but you'd expect that from a beginner. You did jolly well, Rory! You know how every piece moves now, don't you?'

'I like the horses – knights – best,' said Rory.

'I like them best too,' agreed Fiona. 'But mostly because they look like horses.'

'Can you play chess, Fona?' asked Rory.

'Well, I know the moves but I'm not very good.'

'We can play sometime,' said Rory, having identified an opponent he might possibly beat.

Rory was asleep, the kitchen was cleared and the second bottle of wine was opened.

'I should go,' said James.

Fiona didn't want him to go. 'Do you have to open the shop early tomorrow?'

'No. In fact, Mrs Pie-Woman is opening up tomorrow and has offered to stay all day. She was terribly keen. It seemed the least I could do, so I said yes.'

He looked down at her and she looked away, biting her lip to stop her smile of pleasure. She didn't want him to see how much she wanted him to stay.

'Rory's a very good sleeper,' said Fiona, hoping that James would pick up the clues without her having to spell it out.

'You mean he's not likely to want to come into your bed in the night?'

'No. He's got my mobile by his bed and if he wants me, he's going to ring me up. We practised last night. He rang me several times and I answered him in my bedroom on the house phone.'

'And you have got another perfectly good spare room?'

Fiona gave up trying to hide what she wanted. 'I have, but the bed's not made up. My bed, on the other hand, has clean sheets on it and a very much more comfortable mattress.'

He took her into his arms. 'It comes to something when a beautiful woman suggests to a man that he should sleep with her because she has a very comfortable mattress.'

She giggled up at him. 'Well, we're getting older, these things are important.'

'Not as important as other "things",' he said, taking her by the hand and leading her up the stairs.

Sian moved and was woken by a pain in her ankle. She opened her eyes to find herself in her bed at home. Just for a second she was confused. Then she remembered falling over. She lay back, trying to put her memories in order.

She knew Angus had used her phone to call her mother,

and there'd been a lot of discussion about whether or not she should be taken home or directly to A and E. She'd wanted to tell him that her parents lived next door to a retired GP who might well help but she couldn't seem to get his attention without it hurting.

Finally he'd slipped her phone back in her bag. 'Apparently your parents live next door to a retired GP,' he informed her.

'I knew that,' Sian said, wincing. 'I was trying to tell you.'

'Anyway, she's in and there'll be a welcoming committee for you when you get home.'

Angus managed to find a cab almost instantly. He was brilliantly calm and reassuring, and Sian started to realise that having a boyfriend who was used to surviving in any sort of terrain – including a busy city – could have its advantages. The cab managed to drop them off right outside the front door and Angus insisted on carrying Sian into the house, although she felt she could have limped in. Her father paid the taxi; her mother guided Gus.

'Well,' said her father, glowering in the doorway as Gus passed with Sian in his arms. 'This is a fine state of affairs. What happened to you?'

Sian realised he was somehow blaming Gus. 'I just missed my footing as I stepped off the pavement,' she explained quickly. She'd hated being surrounded by anxious faces.

'Louise is on her way round,' said Penny, clearly trying to defuse the tension by fussing around her daughter. 'Let's get you on to the sofa and she can take a look. We're all ready to take you to Casualty if that's what Louise thinks is needed.'

'I'm sure it's not that serious. It's just very painful.' Sian bit her lip to stop herself crying out as she tested her foot on the ground.

'Better not give you any painkillers until we know you don't need an operation,' said Gus. 'I know it seems hard. I'm sorry, Sian.' He picked her up again and Sian's parents guided him into the sitting room and Gus laid her on the sofa. 'Have you got any ice?' He addressed Penny who rushed off and came back with a bag of French beans.

'Sorry, I couldn't find any peas,' Penny said, handing the bag and a tea towel to Gus who pressed it gently to Sian's swollen ankle. Sian looked up at them all staring down at her leg, and suddenly felt horribly awkward. Luckily, she was saved from further embarrassment by Dr Louise's arrival.

'Here's the victim,' said Sian's father, ushering a slim, grey-haired woman to Sian's side. 'See what you think. I think she should go to hospital, but she doesn't want to.'

'Can't say I blame her,' Louise said with a reassuring smile. 'Hospitals are best avoided, in my opinion. Now, let's have a look.' Gently, she probed Sian's ankle. 'Ouch. That must be painful, but your young man has done the right thing getting ice on it.' Sian winced, more at the term 'young man' and the effect it had on her father than in pain this time. 'We need to get some sort of bandage for a bit of support,' Louise continued, unaware she'd made everyone stiffen, for different reasons. 'A tubular one would be best.' She looked enquiringly at Sian's parents.

'There's a chemist on the corner,' said Penny.

'I'll go,' said Gus, clearly keen to be able to do something rather than look on helplessly. 'Is there anything else we need?'

'Paracetamol is OK for the pain. Don't take ibuprofen for a couple of days though. You don't want to reduce the swelling really, it's the body doing its healing thing. Can we have a few more cushions, get the ankle right up?'

'We have paracetamol, but better get some more,' said

Penny, smiling at Gus to try and counterbalance her husband's scowl. 'So that and a bandage. What about some Deep Heat or something?'

Emily shook her head. 'You don't want to encourage blood to the area. Massage or heat of any kind will delay healing.'

'Can I have a drink of water?' asked Sian, feeling a bit pathetic.

'Of course!' Everyone scurried about, trying to make her comfortable.

'Don't sleep with the ice on it and if it's not a lot better in forty-eight hours, see your GP or local A and E department.'

When Louise had been profusely thanked and had gone home and Gus had returned from the chemist with bandages and paracetemol for the invalid, Sian's parents and Gus stood over the sofa looking at her.

'Well, Gus,' her father said gruffly, 'no need for you to hang around. We can look after our daughter now.'

Sian felt this was a stab worse than a sprained ankle.

'I'd prefer to stay if you don't mind. I feel partly responsible for her accident,' said Gus, admirably calm, Sian thought.

'But you didn't feel responsible for getting her pregnant?' said her father.

Sian and Penny had gasped in unison. 'Don't be ridiculous, Stuart. Gus didn't know anything about Sian being pregnant. Now let's everyone have a drink. Maybe you shouldn't, Sian? You've taken painkillers, but I certainly need something. Stuart, can you sort that out while I put sheets on beds? Gus? You will stay, won't you? I need to clear some stuff out of the spare room, but there's still a bed . . .'

Sian had watched her father give Gus a drink, produce

crisps, and they both sat down, watching each other with that wary look dogs have when they can't decide whether or not they'd win if they started a fight. Sian didn't know what had got into her father. He could be a little old-fashioned and fathers were often very protective of their daughters but he wasn't usually quite so confrontational.

'So, you're an explorer, I gather?' said Sian's father, forcing himself to be polite.

'Yes, which is why I was totally impossible to contact.' Gus smiled in Sian's direction. 'We've already had the row about "why she didn't tell me". I completely understand how you must feel about it though.'

Sian's father looked into his glass. 'Hmm, well, I suppose if she didn't tell you, I can't blame you for not knowing.'

'And Gus is brilliant with Rory, Dad. You should see them together,' Sian said from the sofa, willing her father to leave Gus alone. None of this was his fault. She'd been as much to blame as he had.

Her father took a big sip of his drink. 'Well, if Rory approves, there's not much I can say, is there?'

'I want to reassure you,' said Gus, 'I'm determined to be the very best father to our son that it's possible to be.'

Sian suddenly wished she had a drink. She needed something to wash down the lump in her throat. She thought she spotted her father looking a bit teary too, although she wasn't sure if he'd quite forgiven Gus yet.

Thankfully her mother returned, insisting that Sian be carried up to bed and left, to rest, alone. She'd bring her some supper on a tray later. Gus dutifully carried Sian upstairs with Penny leading the way and Stuart muttering 'be carefuls' behind. Once Sian was safely in bed, Penny shooed the men out of the room. Sian suddenly panicked. Her son! 'What about Rory? I must ring Fiona.'

'It's all right, darling, I've rung Fiona, and they're having a lovely time,' Penny said, patting Sian's hand. As she tucked the duvet round the rest of her daughter, leaving her injured ankle safely on top, she whispered that she'd keep the peace downstairs.

Now, the morning after, Sian heard a knock on her old bedroom door and Gus came in holding a mug of tea. He put it on the little table beside her and went to open the curtains.

'How's the invalid? Sleep well?'

Sian struggled to sit up and took the mug Gus handed to her. 'I feel exhausted! What a day we had. How are you? How did you sleep?'

'Fine.' He paused. 'We went to bed quite late. Your dad and I got talking.'

This was a relief. However much she loved her father, Sian would have found it difficult and very annoying if he and Gus hadn't got on.

'Yes,' Gus continued. 'We got through quite a lot of whisky. He does pour big measures, your dad.'

'But he's forgiven you for making me pregnant?' Sian asked anxiously. She couldn't bear her father to hold a grudge. She loved them both dearly and she wanted them to get on – more than get on – but her father could be so stubborn sometimes. He might refuse to see the good in Gus.

'Think so. From what he said, I don't think he ever really blamed me. He just needed to hear both sides, hear it from me, properly. And be sure I wasn't going to leave you in the lurch again – not that I did it deliberately last time, but . . . Anyway, it's natural to be suspicious of your only daughter's partner.' Carefully he sat down on the end of the bed. 'I can't imagine how I'd be if our daughter was being pestered by someone I thought was a bit off.'

'"Our daughter",' Sian repeated. 'Do you think there will be one?' She smiled.

'Well, I'd like that,' he said, taking her hand and gently stroking it. 'On the other hand, another boy would be good too. I'd love to be involved with a child right from the beginning.' He grinned. After a slight pause he said, 'Your mum is so lovely. She's a brilliant granny.'

'And so's Fiona!'

'I rang Mum, by the way. Rory's fine. They do get on very well.'

'Yes. We're very lucky.' She sipped her tea. 'My parents though, they're going to want me to stay but I want to get back as soon as possible. Will you back me up?'

He gave her a long, lingering look that made Sian's stomach flutter and her breath quicken. 'Well, I do have a lot of very good reasons to want you in your own home.' Then he leant forward and kissed her, and as if acting independently his hands cupped her breasts.

Fortunately he pulled away after some minutes. Sian felt she had neither the physical or moral strength to stop what was going to end up as much more than a kiss.

'You're absolutely right. It's essential you get home absolutely as soon as possible.' He was slightly breathless too. 'But only if your ankle is up to it.' He stood up. 'Get out of bed. See if you can put it on the floor.'

With him helping her, she eased herself out of bed and very carefully tested her foot. 'It's not up to any weight-bearing but I'm sure I could get home, if you came on the train with me.' She looked at him. 'Do you have anything else to do in London? Sorry, I didn't think to ask.'

'I've got to pick up my stuff from my friend's flat.' He looked at the clock on the bedside table. 'I reckon we could make the eleven o'clock train if I go now.'

Although not happy about it, Sian's parents accepted

that she was well enough to go home with Gus's support. 'You won't do anything silly, will you? Gus can perfectly well pick Rory up from school without you,' said Penny.

'And he's not the complete shower I always assumed he was,' said her father, his twinkling expression showing he knew his language was a bit ridiculous.

'Let's call a cab,' said Sian, 'so it's here when Gus gets back. Or nearly.'

'I could run you to the station,' said her father.

'No,' said her mother. 'A cab is quicker. They know the rat runs. Leave it to the professionals.'

Chapter Twenty-Six

Gus insisted on them going first class. 'You're injured,' he said, 'you need a comfy seat. And I can afford it! I'm about to be a successful author!'

All Sian's instincts went against this extravagance but once she was seated in her comfortable seat, facing the right direction with a table in front of her, she decided that sometimes instincts were wrong.

'This is bliss, actually,' she said.

'You deserve bliss,' said Gus. He was sitting next to her to give her maximum leg room, prepared to fight anyone who might want to sit opposite. 'Don't argue,' he added as she opened her mouth to do just that.

'I really think you should go back to bed. You've had a shock. Bed is the best place,' said Gus when they got home. He helped her out of the cab they'd picked up from the station, unlocked the door and half carried her through.

'Don't be ridiculous! I've sprained my ankle, not had major surgery.'

'No, trust me,' Gus said firmly. 'I'm an expert on these things. I'm going to put you to bed and then bring us both some lunch.'

'Oh, so you're coming to bed too, are you?' said Sian, suddenly much more enthusiastic about the suggestion.

'Of course. You're far too delicate to be left alone.' He grinned. 'But as we'll be having a perfectly innocent lunch up there, I'd better get your order. What would you like in your sandwiches?'

'I think it'll be a choice of cheese or cheese. Possibly a tomato if we're lucky.'

'My absolute favourite,' said Gus. 'Now, let's get you upstairs.'

He picked her up and staggered up the twisty staircase.

'So, what would your ideal house be like, then?' Gus asked a while later. 'You seem to be rather hung up on details, like marble and fireplaces.'

They were tucked up in bed together eating rather inelegant sandwiches and Sian's head was resting comfortably on Gus's shoulder. Sex, Sian decided, was even better when she knew Gus wasn't going to abandon her shortly afterwards, even if a sprained ankle had made things a bit awkward some of the time. Sian wriggled closer to him. 'Honestly, if you're with the right person I don't think it matters where you live, although I'd prefer there not to be earwigs likely to fall on me.'

He laughed and kissed her hair. 'But seriously, you'll need space to paint furniture?'

'Ideally, yes. And you'll need an office, if you're going to write and run a business.'

'It might take a while before we can find the perfect place.'

'Of course, but perfection is worth waiting for. Why do you think I've hardly looked at a man for nearly six years?' She smiled up at him.

'That's very flattering.'

'Yes, I shouldn't have said that really. It'll make you too pleased with yourself.'

'I am quite pleased with myself but I still feel foolish for not telling you I loved you. We would have been together for longer.'

'Lots of men can't ever say it.' She kissed his cheek, glad that he hadn't pointed out she – independent, modern young woman that she was – hadn't said it either. Kissing her back took a long time.

At about two o'clock, Gus helped Sian into the shower, insisting she couldn't possibly manage without him getting in too. They were just about out of it again when the argument about picking up Rory began. Sian desperately wanted to be there waiting for him when he came out of school. He'd only just started, she should have been there yesterday; she longed to see him.

Gus's argument that she could hardly walk and he could easily pick up Rory and bring him straight home wasn't working.

Then they both realised there was no food in the house and it was agreed that they would take the car to school and then all go to Fiona's. She would want to know how they had got on at the publishers anyway.

Rory was very excited to see them both, particularly as his mother had an interesting bandage and had to hold on to Gus in order to walk. His eyes kept darting between his parents as he skipped along next to them. He'd obviously picked up on the fact that things between his parents were different today.

'Annabelle says,' he began, 'that mummies and daddies live together most of the time. Will you and Gus live together most of the time, Mummy?'

'Well, darling—' Sian started gently.

'That's the plan, mate,' said Gus, cutting to the chase. 'How do you feel about it?'

'That's cool,' said Rory, nodding thoughtfully. 'Everyone liked the shelter you built.' He stopped to put his school bag back on his shoulder. 'Do I have to call you Dad?'

Sian and Gus looked at each other. 'It's up to you, mate,' said Gus.

'Do you have to call me Rory?' he asked.

'I do!' Gus was indignant.

'You call me mate!'

Gus laughed. 'Well, I expect I'll call you both.'

Rory seemed disappointed. It seemed there were down-sides to Gus turning from friend to Dad. 'I like it when you call me mate.'

'And I like it when you call me Gus. Maybe we'll do both? That OK with you, Mum – Sian?'

'I'd prefer it if you don't call me Mum too often, Gus, but if you slip up from time to time I'll survive.' She grinned at both her boys. She couldn't help it. She was so happy. She'd never thought she'd be this happy.

'Cool!' Rory ran ahead to the school gate, his mind undoubtedly on the traffic-light biscuits he knew awaited him at Fona's house.

'Well, he doesn't seem too traumatised,' said Gus as he helped Sian limp along.

'No. I wonder how it will be for him? Very different, really. I mean, he's used to my dad but having a man there all the time could be tricky.' She paused. 'One of the reasons I didn't even think about men before was I couldn't cope with the thought of a stepfather for Rory.'

'You thought about Richard,' Gus reminded her.

She nodded. 'I tried to think about him. I mean, I did think. He seemed like a good solution to a problem, but in the end . . .'

'I know the end. And I'm quite happy to be it.' He kissed the top of her head. 'Can we go a bit faster? Rory's waiting.'

Sian was relieved they could both dismiss Richard so easily, even if she still felt a pang when she thought about

365

their last meeting. But Richard would be far better off with a woman who really loved him. She held on to Gus a little tighter.

When his parents had caught up with him, Rory had another question. 'If James is still there, can we play chess again?'

'James? Mum's friend? Was he there last night?' asked Gus, frowning as he helped them both into the car.

'Yes. He's nice. He bought me a book with little letters in it and taught me to play chess. I told Miss Evans I could play chess and she said I was the only boy in Reception who could!'

'I'm sure,' said Sian, feeling proud of her son but wondering exactly how much chess he played and how much he crashed the pieces into each other.

Gus was scowling and it occurred to Sian that he was not too pleased at the idea of Fiona having a friend who stayed the night. She felt a little guilty. She realised she'd been so wrapped up in the dramas going on in her own life that she hadn't given much thought to Fiona's love life – or otherwise. Had something been blossoming quietly while she'd been living a melodrama? The more she thought about it the more she thought how lovely it would be if it had. She really liked James. And Fiona deserved someone really nice.

'Maybe he didn't stay the night,' she said diplomatically. 'After all, Rory would have gone to bed before he would have gone home.'

'Oh, he did stay,' said Rory, who had inconveniently good hearing. 'He was there at breakfast.'

'Right,' said Gus, and pointed the car for home.

Although the back door was unlocked and there were two cars in the drive, the house seemed to be empty. Sian physically prevented Gus from going upstairs to look for his mother by needing his arm to get Rory a snack. She knew Fiona wouldn't mind and it would help distract Gus.

'Oh, I'll do it,' said Gus. 'Rory, Sian, sit down and I'll see what I can find.'

'There are biscuits,' said Rory. 'In that tin.' He pointed to the cupboard beside the one Gus was now peering into.

'Maybe you should have something a little healthier?' suggested Sian. 'Biscuits afterwards?' As she wasn't in her house and couldn't walk, she didn't have her usual authority.

'Yes, mate,' said Gus, looking into the fridge. 'How about I make you a monster sandwich? Three layers? One of my special BLTs?'

Rory frowned, probably wanting to ask what a BLT was but not wanting to reveal his ignorance. Sian helped him out. 'Is there bacon, lettuce and tomato in the fridge, Gus?'

'Have you ever known there to be less than an entire supermarket in my mother's fridge?' he said.

'In which case, can I have one too?'

The bacon was beginning to sizzle and Sian was cutting bread for toast when they heard Fiona's laugh followed by a male voice. A second later she appeared in the kitchen looking decidedly rumpled with her cardigan buttons done up wrong. Behind her came James who was dressed in trousers and a shirt that was unbuttoned rather far down.

'Oh hi!' said Sian quickly, noticing that in spite of her untidiness, Fiona was looking amazing, as if she'd just had a facial or something. 'We're raiding the fridge, I'm afraid. Gus is making me and Rory BLTs.'

'We came down – we were coming for tea,' said Fiona, sounding apologetic and caught out. 'But I'm so glad to see you. I can't wait to hear how you got on with the publishers yesterday. And Sian! Your poor ankle! Is it very painful?'

Possibly unnerved by the sight of her son wielding a fish slice in a faintly threatening manner, Fiona seemed slightly breathless.

Feeling amused but helpless, Sian did her best to make it look as if there was nothing on earth wrong or strange about Fiona appearing in her kitchen in the middle of the afternoon looking as if she'd just got out of bed. It was her kitchen, after all. 'It's fine if I don't put weight on it. I don't think it's serious,' Sian said. It was dawning on her that if Fiona hadn't realised they were there, then her bedroom probably looked just as rumpled as Fiona herself did. And going on how Gus had reacted to the news that James had stayed the night, it was likely he'd be far from pleased to walk past his mother's room to find the bed unmade.

'So what were you two doing when we arrived? The house was deserted,' asked Gus, sounding suspicious.

Sian's instincts seemed to be spot on.

'We were upstairs . . .' Fiona started vaguely.

'I was helping your mother sort out something in her bedroom,' said James calmly, but not very helpfully, and with no hint of a guilty conscience.

Sian gulped, frantically trying to think of a way to rescue her friend without seeming completely mad. 'Oh yes!' she said quickly. 'That dodgy hinge on your wardrobe! I remember you telling me about it. You couldn't do it yourself without a ladder or a tall man.'

'You should have asked me, Mum. I'd have done it,' said Gus, frowning at the bacon.

'I expect she did, Gus,' said Sian. 'But you probably forgot.'

Fiona's eyes sparkled with laughter as she hid her smile

behind her hand. 'That's right! Men, eh? What are they good for?'

'Excuse me,' said James, appearing hurt, 'I did fix the dodgy, um, thing . . .'

'Hinge,' Sian provided.

'I really don't remember you asking me, but you could have asked again.' Gus now had the bread knife and as he hunted round for a bread board, looked a little dangerous.

'James has done it now,' said Fiona, 'so no need for you to worry. Now do tell me, how did you get on in London? I've been on tenterhooks. If James hadn't come round—' She stopped suddenly.

'To fix the hinge and help you look after Rory,' Sian put in, beginning to feel like a prompt in the wings at a play put on by the local am dram troupe.

'Oh come on! Rory's not that hard to look after!' said Gus, slapping bread into the toaster.

'No I'm not,' said Rory, and all the adults looked at him as if they'd forgotten he was there.

'Of course not, darling,' said Sian. 'But it's nice to have company, isn't it?'

'Is it too early for a glass of wine?' said Fiona, to no one in particular.

Sian wanted to giggle. It was so wonderfully ironic that Gus was being very much the same with James as her father had been with him: the nearest to hostile he could be without being rude. And with just as little reason.

'Far too early for wine, Mum.' Gus pointed to the table. 'Why don't you sit down. I'm going to make tea. You too, James,' he added grudgingly.

They pulled out chairs and sat down although Sian could tell by the way she was fidgeting that Fiona had just made exactly the same leap Sian had a couple of minutes earlier; she'd realised that there was plenty of evidence in her bedroom that they'd been doing something more exciting than fixing a hinge, and was desperate to get out of the room. She kept giving the door furtive, longing glances.

'So, Rory,' said Sian, still trying to think of ways to help Fiona. 'Did you miss me?'

'No,' said Rory, in an 'as if' kind of way.

'We played chess,' said James. 'It was fun, wasn't it, Rory?'

'Yes. I like the knights best,' he said to Sian.

'So do I, because they look like horses,' said Sian.

'That's what Fona said,' said Rory.

'Oh, Fona – Fiona,' Sian interrupted, having a brainwave, 'you couldn't be a love and lend me a cardigan, could you? I'm a bit chilly.'

'You can't be cold,' said Gus, 'it's really warm.'

'Yes, but for some reason I feel chilly,' said Sian, wishing she'd had a better idea. 'It's to do with being injured.'

'I'll get you a sweater,' said Gus, heading towards the door.

'No!' said Sian. 'You're cooking. I'll be fine.'

'Well, make up your mind!' said Gus, hovering. 'I can easily run upstairs.'

'Or I could get you a scarf,' suggested Fiona, standing up to block Gus's route to the door, probably annoyed with herself for not reacting to the prompt earlier. 'If you don't need a sweater . . .'

'Oh, don't rush off, Mum, we've got some news!'

'Brilliant! Can I guess what it is?' asked Fiona.

'Well, let's get this sandwich made first,' said Gus.

'I could get Sian a scarf while we're waiting,' Fiona tried. She was looking rather desperate now.

'I'm sure Sian will be fine once she's had a cup of tea. It's just on its way.'

'So tell us, what's this news?' asked Fiona, apparently giving up trying to find excuses to leave the room.

'Sian was brilliant at the publishers,' said Gus, putting down a plate in front of Rory. 'She swooped in and saved the day.'

'Like Superman?' asked Rory, looking slightly daunted by the size of his sandwich.

'Very like,' said Gus, 'only of course she had her tights on over her knickers, not the other way around.'

'How do you know?' asked Fiona. It seemed she wanted to get her own back on her son.

'Presumably it was all hidden under her cape,' said James, for Rory's benefit.

'I wasn't wearing my cape as I went in my everyday persona as Sian, mother and illustrator. And I didn't do much really.' Sian stole a bit of lettuce that had fallen on to Rory's plate.

'You totally saved the day,' said Gus. He kissed the top of her head. 'My agent, Rollo, said so.'

Sian blushed, embarrassed by his public display of affection, although she wasn't sure why.

'Gus, you kissed Mummy,' said Rory.

'Yeah, mate,' said Gus. 'She's my girlfriend now. And we're going to live together. We discussed it.'

'Did you?' said Fiona, clapping her hands. 'How lovely! I knew you were right for each other. This is wonderful news.'

'But you're my dad?' went on Rory, unaffected by Fiona's enthusiasm.

'The two things are not mutually exclusive,' said Gus. 'Which means I can be both your dad and your mum's boyfriend.'

'You are clever, darling,' Fiona said, patting her son's hand. 'Who says men can't multi-task?'

371

Gus looked at Sian. 'When you've eaten your sandwich, we could go up and look at where we might all live together – until we get a house, anyway.'

Sian intercepted a stricken glance between Fiona and James and realised she had to try once more to save her.

'It's so kind of you to let Gus alter your house so we can live here,' she said quickly. 'I can't wait to see it. Is all the decorating done and everything?' She didn't want to remind Gus that she'd seen it already even though he knew. She also wanted to save Fiona from huge embarrassment. The cardigan tack had failed, she had to think of something else.

'Not quite,' said Gus. 'Just a couple of walls not painted yet.'

'Oh!' said Sian, having had a lightbulb moment. 'I'd love to choose some colours. Fiona, do you remember you said you had a paint chart for Farrow and Ball?'

She glared at her friend, willing her to pick up that this was her chance to get out of the room.

'You don't need to worry about that now!' said Gus. 'Come on, let's go.'

'No!' squeaked Sian. 'I mean, I'd love to have the paint chart with me. I can't just run down and get it.'

'The paint chart?' said Fiona, aware that Sian was trying to help but not immediately understanding how.

'Yes. You said it was in your bedroom, in your bedside table. Do you remember? We were having a chat about bedtime reading and you said it was cookery books and paint charts. You said you had a Farrow and Ball one.'

There was the risk that the man of her dreams and the father of her child would think she'd gone completely mad but she was doing her best for her friend.

'Bedside table!' Fiona jumped her feet, her reactions possibly sharpened by guilt. 'Oh yes! I'll go and look!'

And she ran from the room before anyone could think of any reason why she shouldn't go.

'And, Gus, is the second batch of bacon burning? I think I can smell it,' Sian said.

'Oh.' Gus returned to his frying pan.

Sian and James regarded each other as Rory manfully bit into his sandwich, spilling bits of tomato and mayonnaise as he did so.

Very soon afterwards Fiona came back in. Her hair was brushed and lipstick reapplied. 'Sorry, Sian, I couldn't find the colour chart, but I brought you a scarf and a cardigan in case you really were cold.'

Sian put on the cardigan and decided she was glad to have it. 'I've just realised. I'll never get up all those stairs with my bad ankle.' She sighed, feeling wistful.

'What's the problem? I'll carry you up!' said Gus and then looked at the pan full of bacon.

'Let me take over there,' said James.

In that second, Gus decided to accept James as part of his mother's life. He seemed to realise he was being ridiculous and that his mother had a right to see whomever she liked. 'Thanks,' he said, handing James the spatula. 'I want to take my girl and my son up to the attic.'

Sian protested, laughing, as he swept her up, carried her out of the room and started up the stairs. 'Rory, you go ahead,' he said to his son.

'You'll put your back out,' Sian said, giggling helplessly.

'I'll take the chance.'

Rory ran ahead. 'Is this my room?' he said, running back from the ship's cabin room with the round window. 'Can it be?'

'Course it's your room,' said Gus. 'No girl would want to sleep in there.'

In and out of the rooms he ran, delighting in the way

373

the space had made a double bedroom for his parents, a sitting room and a place to make bedtime hot chocolate.

Sian was equally delighted as Gus carried her around. She'd forgotten or not noticed so many details. When Fiona had shown it to her she'd been rushed and distraught.

'Actually, I think I'm going to have to put you down,' said Gus.

'Oh, OK.' She tried not to wince as he dumped her on the double bed.

'What are you doing?' Rory was indignant at seeing his mother lying on the bed, his father panting slightly next to her.

'Having a rest. Your mum's no feather.'

'Cheek!'

Rory ran off, bored with his parents and probably remembering the traffic-light biscuits.

A little while later he came up again. 'You've got to come down now. Fona and James have opened some champagne.' He frowned. 'I said you were having a rest and they laughed!'

'You two don't look as if you need champagne,' said Fiona as Gus and Sian found them in the conservatory. 'But we've opened the bottle so you have to have some.'

'James is like a grandfather,' stated Rory, who was drinking something from a champagne flute that Sian assumed was elderflower. 'We discussed it,' he added importantly.

'I'm honoured,' said James.

Gus stood there silently, possibly working out the permutations of this, until Fiona interrupted his thoughts. 'Actually, darling,' she said to him, 'you'd better look at your phone. It rang.' She handed it to Gus.

'You didn't answer it, Mum?' He took the phone and pressed buttons.

'Of course not.' She sat down and accepted a glass from James, who then handed one to Sian. 'That would be like opening your exam results.'

'Maybe you'd better take it outside?' said Sian. 'I can't bear this sort of suspense.'

'It's probably just his phone company offering him an upgrade,' said James with a twinkle. 'No need to worry.'

Only Rory was unaffected. Having finished his drink he ran out into the garden and turned himself into an aeroplane. The others sat and sipped nervously.

'We should have waited to see if we should have had a toast,' said Fiona, 'but I'm afraid I've started mine already.'

'Me too,' said Sian.

'There's another bottle,' said James.

'And that's why I love you!' said Fiona. And then she blushed.

They could see Gus pacing outside on the terrace and Rory racing down to the shelter, his arms outstretched. Fiona started picked dead bits off the geraniums and Sian waggled her toes, testing to see if her ankle was improving. James put the chess pieces in their proper places.

Then Gus walked back in. He seemed subdued.

'What? What's the matter?' said Sian.

'That was Rollo.'

'Yes? We'd kind of assumed it was,' said Fiona.

Gus looked pale, as if he was in shock.

'Darling, please tell us! If it's bad news we can cope,' said Fiona, taking his arm.

'And we don't need a house any more,' said Sian, trying to reassure him.

'Would you like a brandy?' suggested James.

Gus began to smile. 'No, it's good news. It's an amazing

deal. Enough money to set up the business and maybe even put a deposit on a house!'

'That much?' said Sian. 'Surely not.'

'Two-book deal and' – this seemed to be the most exciting part – 'they're talking about a television programme. One of the people at the meeting was from a TV company apparently. That's why they can offer so much.'

Fiona went to him and hugged him. 'Darling! This is wonderful.'

Sian, slower because of her injured ankle, got there next, and put her arms round him.

'I think I'll fetch that other bottle of fizz,' said James to no one in particular.